Ghosts of El Grullo

Ghosts of
El Grullo

Patricia Santana

UNIVERSITY OF NEW MEXICO PRESS

ALBUQUERQUE

13 12 11 10 09 08   1 2 3 4 5 6

Library of Congress Cataloging-in-Publication Data

Santana, Patricia.
Ghosts of El Grullo / Patricia Santana.
p. cm.
ISBN 978-0-8263-4409-0 (alk. paper)
1. Mexican American families—Fiction.
2. Women college students—Fiction.
3. San Diego (Calif.)—Fiction.
4. Domestic fiction. I. Title.
PS3619.A57G48 2008
813'.6—dc22

2007040980

Designed and typeset by Mina Yamashita
Text composed in Sabon LT Std, a typeface designed by Jan Tschichold.
Display font is ITC Eras Std, designed by Albert Boton and Albert Hollenstein in 1976.
Printed by Thomson-Shore, Inc. on 55# Natures Natural.

In memory of

my mother and father

❈ ❈ ❈

Part One

Y ella bajó y bajó en columpio,

meciéndose en la profundidad,

con sus pies bamboleando

en el «no encuentro dónde poner los pies».

And she went down and down in the swing,

rocking in the depth,

with her feet wobbling

in the I-don't-know-where-to-set-my-feet.

—From *Pedro Páramo* by Juan Rulfo

One

I could tell, even then, she wasn't sure I knew how to drive or where I was going. She clutched the car door handle, but didn't say anything, certain in the way only a mother can be certain that *llueva o truene*, come hell or high water, I'd get there.

Fair enough. I'd just gotten my driver's license, and I was known in my family for being a daydreamer. Or maybe she'd noticed this was my third time slowly cruising down Oak Place, our green Rambler with three on the tree cruising in first, the car's motor straining and begging, but I was distracted by the beautiful homes that surrounded me—too distracted to notice it was time to shift into second gear.

I couldn't help it. I wanted to linger in front of each of these mansions—elegant, genteel, untouchable homes—choosing my favorite, pretending I was making my way up the circular driveway, underneath the marble columns of my Mediterranean-style getaway. Same as when I was younger and our father sometimes took us on Sunday drives up the coast to La Jolla and Del Mar, driving slowly past the gardens that he kept manicured and trimmed during the week. You know the ones, ritzy neighborhoods with tree-lined streets and stately homes, front lawns the size of soccer fields. Those Sunday drives past my father's clients' houses made me feel the way Dorothy must have felt when her house landed in Munchkin land and suddenly her world was in color and beautiful and fairytale-like beyond imagination. That was how we brothers and sisters felt when we landed in the Technicolor side of town. And while Papá was busy explaining to Mamá something about the ultramodern sprinkler system he put in this yard, or the diseased Brazilian pepper tree he cured in that yard, my brothers and sisters and I, our eyes bugging out, would point and say, "Hey, look at that one!" and we'd all turn to look at a Tudor-style home, then, "that one's mine," as we passed a smaller French Provincial chateau of red brick. My favorite was the Victorian two-story, although the Craftsman with its cozy porch took my heart away as well.

So how did I know the architectural style of these mansions? My Saturday morning house cleaning job at Mrs. Kastlunger's provided a stack of *Architectural Digest* and *Better Homes and Gardens*, and the moment Mrs. Kastlunger drove out the long graveled driveway of her home to Jessie's Beauty Shop, I'd set the broom against the wall or the dust cloth on the table and make myself comfortable on the couch, a delicate, wafer-thin cookie in one hand and a stack of magazines on my lap. It got to where I could measure in magazines the amount of time it took Mrs. Kastlunger to get her hair permed and styled and return home: two and a half magazines—unless I paged through them a little quicker, in which case I could get through three magazines per Saturday. Words like "Craftsman," "Victorian," and "Queen Anne chair" were not lost on me. My cleaning job lasted most of junior high and then part of high school before I passed it on to my younger sister Monica. Time enough to dream of the day I would have my own Frank Lloyd Wright–inspired home.

Here we were on Oak Place again, and maybe it was a subconscious thing, but this is where I wanted to be. This is where I hoped the tea party would be.

A quick glance at the engraved invitation tucked partially under my thigh told me otherwise: 1450 Oak *Drive*, not Place. Making an immediate U-turn in the middle of the street, I was relieved—okay, grateful—that she kept her eyes on the road, straight ahead, pretending that she hadn't noticed that yes, indeed, I didn't know where I was going.

I remembered seeing something that said Oak Drive at the other end of the busy intersection. Sure enough, when we got to La Jolla Boulevard, I had to make a left turn. Dammit. There were three cars ahead of me, a line behind me. Embarrassed, I slowly stuck my arm out to signal a left turn.

"What are you doing?" my mother said. "Get your hand back in. Some driver can come by and just rip it off."

"The signal doesn't work," I said, annoyed at her for my lack of direction sense. "This is what you're supposed to do when you're turning."

"Ah, I see," she said, and was soon rolling down her window and making jerking, pointing gestures to let the drivers behind us know we were coming through.

I shook my head, embarrassed. Daughters of the American Revolution—ahuwa!—ready or not, here we come.

The thing was this: Mrs. Billings, the girls' vice principal, had called me in the previous week to say she had nominated me for the Daughters of the American Revolution Scholarship, and that I had won.

"Daughters of the American Revolution?" I asked. "What's that?"

She smiled, our pragmatic, no-nonsense VP, unashamed of her favoritism. "It's five hundred dollars, my dear. That's what it is."

Hence, the tea party in La Jolla to honor the award-winning daughters and their mothers.

La Jolla was on the other side of town—way other side. Looking at the mansions, each more magnificent than the last, made me ache, made me want to go home and put a delicate Irish lace tablecloth over our green Formica dining table, made me want to scrub the orange vinyl love seat until it shone.

We arrived—1450 Oak Drive—and I couldn't have asked for a nicer place to park the Rambler. American Colonial, I supposed, judging from the columns, a little bit of brick on the front facade, the brass eagle-shaped plaque over the front door. Of course American Colonial, *pendeja*, I said to myself: a fitting home for a Daughters of the American Revolution tea party!

Eight other cars were parked ahead of me on the long circular driveway, so Mamá and I had a bit of a trek to the front door. A colorful cluster of roses on our right and an expansive lawn on our left led us to the front door. I was sporting a forest green polyester suit my mother had made for Ana María and which I'd now inherited, while Mamá was wearing her usual going-out-to-fancy-places beige brocade suit she made four years ago for my sister Carolina's wedding. It was the only nice suit she had, but since Mamá didn't go out to fancy places that often, it looked practically new and would do just fine for the few special events she did attend.

What I didn't get was, why me? I had nothing to do with the

American Revolution, nor did my family. Believe me, my ancestors were nowhere near Boston and the East Coast in the dawn's early light. Now if they were offering an Emiliano Zapata scholarship, say, or an honorary membership to the Padre Hidalgo Society Club, yes, then I could understand. But me, a daughter of the American Revolution?

"You're smiling to yourself again," Mamá said in her usual soft-spoken Spanish. "Just remember, 'he who smiles alone smiles with the devil.'"

"Tea parties, tea parties," I said, carelessly tossing my hair back. "All these tea parties we attend. 'Tis a bore, Mamá, 'tis a bore."

We had now reached the front door, and my mother gave me her look. I knew that look. It was a look that said she was not amused by my sarcasm. It was a look that said, I love you even though you are being ungrateful and sarcastic in the face of free money—five hundred dollars to go toward your college education.

I rang the doorbell.

The white-haired lady who greeted us at the door looked ancient, looked as if she had been sitting right next to Betsy Ross, urging her to finish the flag. I glanced at Mamá, who gave me another one of her looks, shaking her head no. I bit my lip to keep from laughing disrespectfully.

The lady seemed pleased—*surprised-pleased*—to see us. I could tell because when I shook her hand and said my name, now turning to introduce my mother, the American revolutionary granny looked just that: surprised-pleased. My name on the list of scholarship recipients—Yolanda Sahagún—must have conjured in her mind a dark-haired, dark-skinned Mexican from south San Diego, a Chicana kid who just might make it out of the barrio.

I avoided looking at my mother as I was thinking this. I knew that she knew what I was thinking, and she'd disapprove of these alienating thoughts. But thinking these mean things about Granny made me feel feisty, made me feel ready for this tea party.

We entered what looked like a vestibule or the receiving parlor. A formidable spiral staircase stood before us, a plush red carpet draped over the steps of the stairs, looking like a grand dame's evening gown, and protected by an intricately designed balustrade. The staircase looked familiar—*Better Homes and Gardens? Architectural Digest?* The hostess was explaining that just one more mother and daughter pair was expected before the program was to begin.

Then it came to me: Of course, how could I have forgotten this staircase, this lovely mansion? And so right then I was expecting Elly May to come bounding down, taking two steps at a time, and give me a welcoming, insider kind of hug. We'd saunter off to the pool in back and talk about the good ol' days before they were the Beverly Hillbillies, back when they were just hillbillies.

Granny—not real Granny from the TV program, but Betsy Ross's cohort—led us to the living room. I glanced back at the stairs one last time, a tad hopeful that Jethro would appear and, like he does to all the womenfolk he's fond of, gracefully pick me up and fling me over his shoulder, carrying me out to the expansive front lawn where we'd romp about, thereby rescuing me from what promised to be a boring tea party with a bunch of old biddies from Plymouth Rock.

We entered the formal living room where a group of twenty or so women stood: award-winning daughters and their mothers and the distinguished members of the San Diego chapter of the Daughters of the American Revolution. We were introduced all around—Mrs. Sahaygun and her lovely daughter Yolanda. My mother nodded politely, smiled, extended her hand, and I followed suit—nodded politely, smiled, extended my hand. Most of the girls looked like spitting images of their mothers—not only the physical features of nose, cheeks, face shape, eyes, but hairstyles and posture and clothing, a certain tilt of the head. There, for instance, was a pair standing near the huge fireplace with heart-shaped faces and protruding, strong jaws, their red hair in identical shoulder-length bobs, both wearing smart, tailored pantsuits (something you'd find on the elegant racks at The Broadway and not fresh off the presser plate of your mother's old Singer sewing machine), pantsuits cut close to their figures, tasteful bellbottoms and big buttons on the jackets—Mom was in a burgundy color, Daughter was in a light, complementary mauve. Both of them were smiling identical smiles at something one of the other mothers was saying. I was struck by the similarities of these mother and daughter pairs, a resemblance that made me suddenly self-conscious.

We were led over to them, the burgundy and mauve mother and daughter, and as we stood in front of the fireplace with its large brick mantelpiece, I made a quick, casual assessment of our image in the antique oval mirror above the mantel: My mother, with her kind, moon-shaped face, was smiling at something the burgundy mother was saying while I stood next to them, quietly assessing the situation. My hair was down to my shoulders, brown like my mother's, but not curly anymore, thanks to the jumbo pink rollers I'd put on this morning for the straight hair look, the look deceiving and untrue as it hid my naturally curly hair, as naturally curly as my mother's.

Once we were assembled, about twenty of us, we were asked to remain standing for the Pledge of Allegiance. A joke, an icebreaker kind of joke, and I was about to laugh along with everyone else when I glanced at my mother and noticed she had her hand over her heart and was at attention. She wasn't laughing. Like the rest of the women in this formal room, my mother was respectfully gazing at the flagpole in a discreet corner of the room, next to the bay window. Then in unison, everyone began to recite the Pledge of Allegiance. My mother's mouth was moving, but I doubted that she knew the Pledge of Allegiance. I inched closer to her in an effort to hear what she was whispering. "Dios te salve, María, llena eres de gracias . . . Bendita eres entre todas las mujeres . . ." Of course, the Hail Mary. Then it was done with, and we were asked to sit down. I smiled at my mother, tried to catch her eye, let her know that I was in on her secret of pretending she spoke English—the Hail Mary, of all things!—but when she finally did look at me, her head slightly tilted up, she had a superior smile, as if to say, What's your problem?

Refreshing cucumber sandwiches and dainty pastries were served on ornate silver platters, along with the good old tea. Not the *té de manzanilla* or *hierba buena* that we had around the house for constipation and *pedos*, but real black tea leaves scooped from decorative tin boxes. I was sure this was English tea, and I thought there must be something ironic about this. We revolted against them in order to enjoy their tea two hundred years later in affluent homes in the land of the free and the brave. I wasn't sure this was ironic, but I wanted it to be.

Next on the program was a record album that played a narrative of the story of the Revolution. There was some John Philip Sousa music in the background, a few cannonballs exploding, while a very somber-sounding man narrated the highlights of the American Revolution. The recording lasted a dreadful twenty minutes or so, and throughout this interminable time, I wondered how much of this Mamá could understand, or whether she had discreetly and gracefully adapted to the language barrier situation by filling in the blank spaces with prayers in Spanish. In that moment it occurred to me that I didn't really know how much of the English language my mother understood in the first place. I'd never heard her speak more than a thickly accented "nice to meet you," nor had I ever seen her listen to English without one of her nine eager translator-children in attendance. Yet here she was, in this elegant home, looking every bit the demure and stately lady in her beige brocade suit, her hands clasped on her lap, her posture attentive and regal, celebrating the American Revolution: Mamá.

The hostess turned the album over, more John Philip Sousa music and cannonballs but without the narrator. It was perfect background music for what I suspected would be forthcoming: a rambling speech about ideals and being good citizens. I reached over for another cucumber sandwich and then settled in for the lengthy discourse, perhaps a puritanical jeremiad thrown in for good measure, the kind of speech that let you comfortably daydream.

What really got me, though, was that my mother didn't seem overwhelmed by the luxury around her. Unlike me, she was not gawking at this and that: the baby grand piano, the thick, ornately woven rugs that graced the honey-colored wooden floors, the splendid fireplace, the African sculptures perched on the mantel, the beveled oval mirror over the fireplace. I was trying to drink it all in, memorize each object so I could describe everything to my sisters when I got home, and so when I had my own mansion, I would have decorating ideas already in place.

I glanced at my mother, wondering if she had noticed the sumptuous drapes, but Mamá was attentively listening to the DAR president who was, in that moment, formally introducing herself and the members of DAR, now that the cannonball recording was over. The leader made a great and proud point of mentioning that in order to be a member of DAR, you must have some affiliation by way of heritage with the American Revolution. Then the hostess asked each mother and daughter to introduce herself and perhaps mention something remarkable about her own family history. They started with the pair at the other end, working their way to us.

It dawned on me why Mamá was not visibly impressed with the affluence about her. Peel back time, getting past the dumpy houses and shacks Mamá had lived in throughout her married years; erase, for a moment, the image of lopsided wooden fences and piles of junk—wood remnants and broken machines—in the backyard that Papá dreamed of someday fixing; ignore the raggedy screen door, constantly torn up by kids barging in and out; pretend you didn't see the broken La-Z-Boy, the cracked glass coffee table—orphaned furniture now adopted by the Sahagún family. Peel back time and you would see a young Dolores Ramos, the señorita of the house, sitting on the edge of the fountain in the courtyard of her parents' colonial mansion in the small town of El Grullo, Jalisco, Mexico.

My mother was not one to tell stories of her growing up. She was private and quiet about her upbringing; she was private and quiet about everything having to do with her life. What little I knew of my mother's life before marriage had been gleaned through tidbits of overheard conversations between my *tías*—her sisters—and my older sisters; what little I knew of her young life was what I'd concocted as I walked through the long, columned corridors during summer visits to my grandparents' home, the house where my mother grew up.

Didn't everyone have some degree of fascination with houses? I refused to believe I was the only one who felt this way. Somewhere in our childhood, or even as adults, we had been moved by at least one house, one home that entered our being, made us react to it in uncommon ways, a house that sheltered our spirit—my mother's home in El Grullo was that home to me.

I was startled out of my thoughts by my mother's voice.

" . . . Dolores Ramos de Sahagún. I was born in 1917 in the middle of the Revolución Mexicana. I was born a few hours after Mamá supplicated to the soldiers not to hang Papá, who was a small landowner."

At first I thought I was hearing things, seeing things. Surely that couldn't be my mother who was talking in English, soft and halting, just above a whisper, but precise in her choice of words. I looked around the room, half expecting to hear the words come out of someone else's mother whose name also happened to be Dolores Sahagún. But no, it was *my* Dolores, all right.

I was in a discreet state of shock.

I glanced around the room to see if the other women understood her, and I saw that not only did they understand what she was saying, but they were spellbound, bending forward to listen to her soft voice. One mother had her teacup raised halfway up to her lips, but seemed not to notice that she had paused midway up, entranced like all the guests. My mother, in the meantime, took her time, looked quietly, respectfully at her listeners. "We were driven from our home," she said as an explanation. Her hands were folded on her lap, her posture regal and confident as if she were used to telling stories to a large audience, as if this were just another evening of storytelling with mothers and daughters.

"We sought refuge in Autlán, a larger town nearby. Our home in El Grullo was violated—made into a barracks for soldiers. It was a time of confusion, of insecurity. A time of, of—*como se dice 'lealtades*,'" and she looked to me for the English word.

"Loyalties," I barely managed to say, stumbling over the word, stunned and overtaken by what she was saying and how she was saying it.

"Yes." She nodded to me her thank you, then looked back at the silent, engrossed audience of mothers and daughters before her. "Yes, loyalties uncertain."

I didn't correct her word order. Her accent and her incorrect English syntax sounded like poetry. Sounded as if she had been practicing and waiting for just the right moment to tell her story.

Then she stopped, smiling shyly, looking down at the porcelain teacup and saucer on her lap, self-conscious before the enthralled group.

"Oh, please, Mrs. Sahagún," the president said. "Don't stop now. Tell us more."

The woman with the teacup came to, quietly, deliberately setting the cup on its saucer, never having taken a sip, nor even remembering that she hadn't taken a sip of her English tea. My mother's words—yes, *my* mother—had her pleasantly discombobulated.

"My English is not very well," Mamá said, looking at me for confirmation, for me to say, Yes, my mother doesn't speak English, what do you want to ask her, same as I did when the Jehovah's Witnesses came knocking at our door, Mamá too polite to just send them off with a slam of the door, or when a life insurance agent came calling and inquiring about our life insurance needs. There was always a son or daughter nearby to say she didn't speak English, what do you want? The hallelujahs, as we called them, or the pesky salesmen politely but quickly turning away, knowing that making a sales pitch here with children translators and all, well, it would just be too much work. Yet there was my mother, speaking in a precise, gentle English, a language I had never heard her speak before, artfully sharing her story with these mothers and daughters.

"Please tell us more, Mrs. Sahagún," the DAR president repeated, touching her shoulder as encouragement.

Yes, Mamá, I said to myself, please tell me more.

My mother nodded. "*Gracias.*" And she proceeded: "The soldiers lived in our beautiful home for a year, and then the revolución was over. Who wins? *¿Quién sabe?*—who knows, yes?"

The women nodded reassuringly, as if they themselves had been contemplating this very question for some time now.

"We returned to our house—it was violated; we were *simbólicamente* violated. There were many tortures and hangings there in our home while the soldiers lived there, hangings from the ceiba tree in the corral. Many brutal murders."

"How did you know this?" one mother asked in a whisper. "Was blood splattered all over the house when your family returned?" This mother and all the other mothers and daughters and I, too, were caught in Mamá's narrative web, imagining vivid scenes of our own to complement her story.

"Blood?" Mamá considered this a moment. "Possibly there was blood present, but I was only a year old when we returned to the house, and Mamá never mentioned this to me. We know of the brutal hangings from the tree because the *ánimas*—what you call 'ghosts'—cannot rest. They live in the house, walk the corridors at all hours of the day and night. They are without rest. *Atormentados*—yes, tormented. They want to tell us their story," she said, leaning back against the couch. "But we cannot hear them."

The resounding dongs of a grandfather clock could be heard from the hallway—one, two, three, four—letting us know that time had, indeed, continued onward.

That was it. Her hands folded on her lap as they had throughout her extraordinary discourse, her posture upright as if she had been holding court, gracious, gentle queen that she was. She looked at each mother-daughter guest and smiled, flattered by their attention.

And we sensed, sadly, that with this last intriguing statement—"They want to tell us their story, but we cannot hear them"—she had come to the end of her story.

Silence. Nobody dared to speak. We held our breaths. Stunned, caught unawares and transported to another time, another revolution.

Well! So my mother *would* tell her story—given the right moment.

After a few minutes of silence, as we fully digested this tale—who could top such a story?—the spell was broken. Or was it broken, I wondered, as all the mothers and daughters now stood, shook hands, bidding each other farewell. Because I sensed a grogginess had descended upon us, as if we had been in a temporary hypnotic trance, a deep sleep, as if we should have shaken our heads in an effort to come to, to regain consciousness of our present reality. There was a line forming in front of my mother, for it seemed each and every listener wanted to shake her hand.

Mamá was a diminutive woman, her short curly hair practical, dressed in the unassuming beige brocade suit—a dress with a matching jacket—a suit both modest and dignified, like my mother, who smiled kindly at each guest, thanked them with a nod. It occurred to me, made me smile even, that for then, for those moments of leave-taking and gracious thank-yous, Mamá was truly the mistress of this elegant La Jolla home. The true daughter of the revolution.

Then the award-winning daughters and their mothers took their leave of me—princess-daughter of the reception that I had become!—shaking my hand before slowly making their way to the foyer and out the door.

Mamá was nodding and listening attentively to something the president of the DAR was saying to her. They were in an intimate huddle, both women standing near the open secretary desk, a quill pen set near the many tiny compartments that housed neat stacks of letters, a small porcelain box perhaps filled with paper clips, a long rectangular embroidered box most probably holding pencils. It was as if the president were relaying confidential information for my mother's ears only. As I watched my mother respond politely and gracefully, nodding now and then to whatever the hostess was saying, I wondered about her. The two women seemed, in this brief time, to have become close friends, to have established a comfort and ease in their interaction that made me wonder if there was something beyond words that bound them. And once again I imagined young Dolores Ramos, dressed in the finest of fabrics, hair neatly braided and wrapped around her head by her favorite servant Sarita. I thought about these two women before me—the one who lived in affluence in La Jolla now, the other one who lived in affluence in El Grullo long ago.

We were the last to leave, of course, and I sensed the hostess had skillfully choreographed this order of leave-taking. I sensed she did not want to let go of my mother, seemed dazzled by her graceful and attentive composure. So there you had it: Dolores Ramos de Sahagún was an enchanting enigma even to others.

"Mrs. Sahagún," the hostess was saying, "it has truly been a pleasure to have met you and your lovely daughter." I could tell she really meant it. "Perhaps we can get together . . ."

"Thank you," my mother said gently, "thank you very much for your hospitality," not allowing the hostess to finish her invitation to my mother for another tea party or luncheon or whatever. In a gracious and regal way, my mother was letting her know that a social relationship with this La Jolla woman was obviously out of the question, so no need to offer invitations that would never be accepted.

The hostess now turned to me, perhaps disappointed, regretful, and said, "My dear, what a charming and beautiful mother you have." Resigned.

I smiled my thank-you.

I knew what she was talking about, the kind of beauty Mamá had. And it made me ache with pride and love and envy. I wanted her beauty to envelop me. Like the beautiful homes that now surrounded us, the formidable mansion my mother grew up in, I wanted her beauty to shelter me and permeate my own being, instruct me and tell me how to be a woman. I wanted to be the daughter of my mother.

We headed south down Interstate 5, both of us quiet and pensive. I had a hundred questions for my mother, but when I glanced at her I could tell she was deep in thought and, besides, I was in the driver's seat and should be paying attention to the road. That was not the time to ask her about her impressions of the tea party, to ask about her life. Because that was one of the hundred things I was wondering. We'd just been to a beautiful part of town, where affluence reigned, and now we were headed to, well, we were headed home—a neighborhood in direct contrast to the one we were leaving. Didn't this conjure memories for her of a time when she was also part of the affluent society? Didn't this make her sad, regretful? Plucked from her lovely mansion and doting parents—for what? To live the rest of her life in poor, rambling shacks with a wild Don Quixote dreamer of a husband? (It was no secret to us kids; we knew from very young that our father planned and dreamed and schemed while our mother quietly counted and saved the *centavitos* he brought home from his odd, in-the-meantime jobs, something to tide them over until his business took off.)

And this stuff about the Mexican Revolution—why didn't I know this already?

"Mamá," I finally said, feeling shy and awkward—my mother some-times had that effect on me. "What did you think of the tea party?"

"The tea party, yes," she said. "I think it was very nice of those women to honor you in that way. It makes me feel proud of you, proud that others honor you."

"But they're the Daughters of the American Revolution, Mamá," I said, now laughing. "We have nothing to—"

"Watch out for that blue car that's zigzagging up ahead," she said.

I smoothly switched lanes to put some distance between the blue car and me, proud of my rookie driving.

Then, "Yes, you do, *mi'ja*," she said. "You have everything to do with the American Revolution, and watch that you keep your distance from the car in front of you."

I wanted to laugh and say, Thanks for the advice, Mrs. Expert Driver, to my mother who had never in her life driven a car, but I didn't. Instead I asked her what she meant by that, that I had everything to do with the American Revolution.

She smiled. God, she was so beautiful it hurt me, angered me, con-founded me.

She shook her head. "For now, Yoli, just keep your eyes and thoughts on the road," she said and turned to look out her side window.

I got off at the Palm Avenue exit, turned left on Hollister, now driving parallel to the train tracks that carried cargo north and on to the central valley, freight trains rumbling through Palm City, loading and unload-ing what? Machinery? Food? Industrial products? I thought about this a moment, realizing I didn't know what they carried, and then I took another left onto my familiar Conifer Street, driving down the length of the Not-A-Through-Street, parking the Rambler in front of our house.

As we walked up the steps to the front porch, I could hear the phone ringing, followed by my little sister Luz's high voice. "Sahagún resi-dence," she said with a fake, clipped British accent, "downstairs maid speaking."

We were home.

Two

"A guy called you this morning and Papá answered the phone," Luz reported all in one hurried breath.

I set my DAR citizenship certificate on the coffee table, placing it strategically on top of the sliver of cracked glass. Mamá was already in the kitchen, so she didn't hear Luz say this.

"What, pray tell, are you talking about?" I asked. I was still feeling giddy from the afternoon tea party, so Luz's statement didn't fully register.

"Yeah, pray is what you better start doing, all right," she said, shaking her head with bleak foreboding. "Some guy called you a couple of hours ago and Papá answered it, and next thing you know, he's shouting at the guy, 'Yolanda Sahagún, did you say?'" Luz raised her voice to a hysterical level. A perfect impersonation of our father. "'No, my daughter is not here and don't you be calling her anymore. Leave her alone. You guys just want one thing and you're not going to get it from my daughters.' I was standing nearby, hoping to get to the phone first," she added as an apology. "But as soon as he slammed the phone down, he turned to me and says, 'These guys calling you girls up are just a bunch of *changos*—the whole lot of them." Luz said this in perfect, righteous Spanish—exactly like our father.

Dammit!

"What the hell is wrong with that man?" I said, ready to scream. Suddenly delightful tea parties with delicate porcelain cups, Queen Anne chairs and Chippendale writing desks were fading away into a distant, fuzzy memory.

"He's out back," Luz said. "Told me to tell you he wants to talk to you *inmediatamente* when you got home. So start pray telling," Luz added for good measure.

"Ha, ha, you're so funny," I said, sticking my tongue out at her as I walked out the front door headed to the backyard.

I took my time, pausing to smell a Mr. Lincoln rose or stopping to watch the honeybee that was poking around in the star jasmine. Yes, I took one leisurely step after another, pretending that I was mistress and guide strolling along with a few select members of DAR, instructing them on the flora of the manicured English-style gardens of the Sahagún Estate.

In a romantic world of euphemisms, the words to describe my home would be "cottage" or "bungalow," at once conjuring something small and quaint, cozy and warm, filled with love, family, and good food; a friendly wooden porch large enough to seat two or four people; a guy come courting a girl; the couple now stealing a kiss on the porch swing while the younger sister watched on the other side of the porch, shooting I'm-going-to-tell-my-father-on-you looks; a quilted afghan of different shades of pink squares draped over the white wicker rocking chair; the mesmerizing sound of the nearby ocean's waves crashing on the beach like dramatic overtures of music; the refreshing, healing smell of salty air.

In a world of realism, the words to describe my home were: "There was an old woman who lived in a shoe. She had so many children she didn't know what to do." Replace "old woman" with "kind mother." My mother could never grow to be an "old woman." No, my mother would always be my mother, neither young nor old, neither rich nor poor. Your mother was your mother, your lifesaver, your lighthouse, your buoy, your anchor—the litany of nautical metaphors most certainly increasing as you yourself became a woman, then a mother.

Replace "cottage" with "shoe" and "seaside" with "freewayside" and you pretty much got the picture.

There was no bitterness in my description, please understand this. I was a realist and a romantic at one and the same time. Both cottage and shoe lived happily in my mind, very rarely arguing with each other for dominance. It was my reality, after all, the shoe and the cottage, and if at times I heard the rushing "waves" of cars speeding by, or actually tasted the salty ocean air—and not exhaust fumes—hovering like silent fog above Interstate 5, then let it be so.

I could offer an objective reality of sorts: there was a magnificent garden that came with this shoe-cottage house. Not "magnificent" by my standards alone, but continually proclaimed as such by our neighbors—even the old German couple up the street whom I'd never seen smile, their stern faces at once somber and rigid, when they took their daily evening walk down our Conifer Street, arms folded behind their backs, creating the feel not so much of a stroll down Conifer Street as of an inspection. Yes, even the German couple called our garden "magnificent," stopping every evening in front of our house to survey the latest blooms, directing polite and heavily German-accented questions to my mother who, for example, might be digging trenches for her November sweet pea planting, asking her what kind of fertilizer or food she used in her soil. Some kind of question like that. Were this elderly couple French, I would say they called our garden *magnifique*, but they were not French, and chances were if they were French we neighborhood kids would not have made so much fun of them as we did this rigid German couple with their puckered-into-wrinkles lips. Our "German spies." I'm not sure why we nicknamed them that, or who started it, but it stuck and suited us Conifer Street children just fine. Every street must have a mandatory German spy for the sake of neighborhood intrigue, or so I must have assumed from very young. Besides, I didn't know what the German word for "magnificent" was, or if such a word existed in German.

The mood and magnificence of our garden changed with the season: In winter it could be described as quiet but intense, pink and yellow snapdragons taking their place next to marigolds, cyclamen, and azaleas, colorful winter flowers appropriate for San Diego; in the spring, the lively party began, a rambunctious spray of sweet peas taking charge of the lopsided, peeling picket fence with a sentry of calla lilies posted at each end of the fence; and by summer, the earthly celebration was in full swing, the roses and dahlias, begonias and impatiens and vincas, along with the regal amaryllis and gladioli and the attendant petunias, periwinkle blue and pink hydrangea all settling comfortably into a harmonious pose.

And that was only the front yard.

I don't mean to sound the trumpet in describing our shoe-cottage garden, but in moments when the wicker rocking chair image slowly faded to the image of the kind woman who lived in a shoe with all those kids and a few lopsided aluminum patio chairs on the porch, I reached for anything of beauty I might have and claimed it with the proud step of a peacock suddenly spreading its train in splendid regalia.

I headed to the backyard. Yes, yes, I knew: my oldest sister Carolina would have called this passive-aggressive behavior. Me? I called it wanting to hold on, at least for a few moments, to the magic of this afternoon's tea party before erratic, moody, unreasonable, incomprehensible reality—in the form of my father—set in.

It was true that the backyard could easily be seen as a junkyard of leftover, recycled wooden planks and discarded toilets, rolls of chicken wire and rusty machine parts, three bicycles each with two flat tires, a doughnut shop of rubber tubes and car tires, broken tools and orphaned furniture someday about to be mended or repaired, polished and greased—a packrat's delight, a fix-it man's treasure trove, my father's future projects. But there was the catch, the beauty of our incongruous yard: we had, amid this junk pile, an orchard of fruit trees to rival any farmer's orchard in the San Joaquin Valley. For what we were lacking in house space—three minuscule bedrooms for eleven people, sometimes twelve or thirteen when our aunts came up from Mexico for lengthy visits to help my mother with all of us kids—we made up in property, plenty of yard, and land for growing things.

We had the usual citrus trees—oranges, lemons, ruby grapefruit— and two avocado ones, a guava and prune tree as well. But it was the quince, fig, and pomegranate trees that reigned over the rest—their autumn fruits our favorites. Each tree was encircled in its little mound of dirt, the mound acting as a dyke, so that when it was watered nothing was wasted. The fruit trees stood in no apparent order but were close enough to each other to provide a canopy of shade in the warmer months of the year and a spooky phantom of rustling leaves during the autumn Santa Ana desert winds.

He was over by the back fence, a box of tools on the ground at his side, fiddling with the hinges or the door spring. Wearing the same pin-striped suit he had owned for at least fifty years, he looked incongruous— ridiculous, really—this Mr. Handyman Comandante. It could be worse, I thought to myself; he could've been wearing his frayed old *charro* suit.

He was holding the metal hinge as he tried different size nails in the holes, determined to get this right so the neighborhood dogs couldn't come poking in from the alley and our dog Flicka couldn't get out at the first sign of heat. He was in deep concentration, not looking up as I approached. Thin and small and slightly bent from thirty-odd years of stooping, tending rich people's gardens, Lorenzo Sahagún looked like one of the tree branches he often trimmed—a tree branch with some sharp thorns.

"Make yourself useful," he said. "Hand me the hammer." He didn't even pause to look at me, studying, as he was, the proper placement of the hinges on the fence.

I bent down to get the hammer and hand it to him.

"We're going to put new hinges and a tighter spring on this door. The problem is," he said as he hammered each nail into the hinge holes, "that when people come in from the back, they *push* instead of *pull*." He shook his head, disgusted, then handed me back the hammer. "But I've solved that problem. No, don't put it down. I'm going to need it in a moment."

"You wanted to talk to me inmediatamente?" I said as if I were a fed-up soldier once more, twice more, three times more being ordered to report to the fickle, domineering commander in chief.

He looked up at me quickly and stopped what he was doing.

"In case you haven't noticed," he said, now looking at me square in the face, "I'm teaching you how to mend a fence so that when you get married you can teach your husband how to do this. Give me the hammer."

"When I get married?" I started laughing, now realizing that my lingering stroll in the yard had served to fill me with pent-up, volcanic-style anger. "How am I ever going to get married if you keep hanging up on the guys who are trying to call me?"

He looked up from whatever he was doing. "No me rezongues, señorita," he warned.

"I'm not talking back," I said. "I'm simply commenting on the irony of your 'husband' remark."

"See?" He said. "That's the problem with you modern-day kids." He began hammering, but I wasn't sure he was doing this right. Shouldn't he have been using a screw instead of a nail? "You young people spend your time just thinking of comebacks for your parents—*rezongar* is all you *chamacos* know how to do."

"Ay, Papá . . ."

"Don't 'ay, Papá' me," he said. "Don't be disrespectful, Yolanda," he warned, now giving me his full attention. "That's why I have you kids help with these things that need to be fixed around the house. So that you learn how to fix things with your hands, not just with your head. Instead of wasting precious time thinking of the best disrespectful comment to throw back at your father, make yourself useful and hand me that measuring tape."

"Who called me?" I said, making an enormous effort to sound controlled and calm.

"I don't know who called you," he said. "What does it matter? I don't want these changos calling you girls. It's disrespectful . . ."

"How do you know they're changos? Were you a monkey, too, in your good old days?"

My father's face turned red, and I knew I was pushing him, knew he was about to explode, but I didn't give a shit. Let him rant and rave all he wanted. This was so déjà vu it wasn't even funny. Anytime any of us girls wanted to have a boyfriend, we had to go through this arguing crap with him, as if it were part of the Sahagún daughters' rite of passage. Let him shout and accuse me of talking back. Just a few more months and I would be out of here, going to live at the dorms—get off this ridiculous family planet. Besides, I knew I was one of the few in the family who could get away with this kind of back talk.

"Are you listening to me?" he said, shouting as though I were on the other side of the house, in the front yard maybe and not standing right next to him. "Just because you're going to a fancy university doesn't make you the king of Rome, just remember that. And you're very fortunate, señorita, that your sister is lending you the Rambler for your commute."

Then I remembered, in that moment, as he was blah, blah, blabbing, that he didn't know I was planning on living in the dorms. For that matter, neither did my mother.

"I won't need the stupid ol' Rambler. I'm going to be living at the dorms," I said in a heated rush before I thought to count to ten to get ahold of myself before I blurted out something I was later going to regret.

At first he didn't say anything, as if he were letting this fully register in his brain lest he misunderstand my words. He studied my face carefully, then back to his hinge, took the hammer's head and plucked out the nail he'd just hammered in. He did this with a dramatic yank. Then he set the hinge, crooked nail, and hammer on the ground.

Oh, shit.

"I think I didn't hear you right," he began. "Would you please repeat everything you just said?" I could tell he was making an enormous effort to sound controlled and calm.

This wasn't at all how I'd planned to tell them. This wasn't the strategy I'd devised all week long. Too late now, Yoli.

"I'm planning on living at the dorms," I began. "I have enough financial aid to cover that expense. I can get a lot more studying done . . ."

"Don't even think of it, Yolanda," he said. "What a disgrace! Don't even think of it, do you hear?"

"But Papá . . ."

"No, Yolanda," he said, shaking his head as if he were ridding himself of evil spirits. "Don't add insult to injury with your protests."

"Why don't you at least listen to me? Maybe there are some good reasons . . ."

"Good reasons for abandoning your family?" he said, his voice rising.

"I'm not abandoning my family, for Pete's sake," I said.

"Good reasons for leaving your home, your mother, father, sisters? You, a single woman?"

"I get good grades in school. I win scholarships and awards and honors. What? Don't you trust me? What do I have to do to make you trust that I'm mature and sensible and can take care of myself in this big world? Why is it my brothers can go and live on their own when they're not married, but we can't?"

"Don't toy with me, Yolanda," he said.

"*Pero* Papá . . ."

"Don't 'pero Papá,' me," he said. "You want to know what you can do to win my trust and confidence in you? Is that it? Then fine, I'll tell you," he said with the smug expression of someone who has an ace up his sleeve. "You can start by not talking back to me."

"No, Papá," I said, and though I felt weary with the effort this was taking, the wave of fury was washing over me and now there was no stopping me. "The problem is just that, that we kids *don't* talk back to you enough, don't question your old-fashioned rules. We live in the United States of America, Papá . . ."

He stepped forward suddenly, as if he had a mind to lunge at me or slap me. "Don't you ever talk that way to me, do you hear me? Shame on you, Yolanda Sahagún. Qué falta de respeto. I'm ashamed of you! Is this how I taught you to speak to your elders, to your father? Then I apologize to you for not doing a better job of teaching you to be respectful."

He brushed off his suit jacket as if it were covered with dust or something, though it was perfectly clean—just old and frayed and ridiculous, like him. "Where's your mother? Does she know this is how you talk, Ms. Highly Educated, Soon-To-Be-In-The-University daughter? Shame on you, Yolanda. I've had enough of your foolishness."

"Here," he said, now handing me the hammer, a nail, and a wooden sign. "Hammer this on the alley side of the fence." And before I could even open my mouth and continue our discussion—I hadn't finished!—*el comandante* in his ridiculous pin-striped suit was marching off through the orchard in the direction of the house.

Well, fine and dandy, Mr. Lorenzo Sahagún, I said to myself, seething. We'll just see about that!

I opened the gate, positioned the sign, ready to hammer it. That was when I took a good look at it. In meticulously printed handwriting the word "POOL" was painted in red.

And as angry as I was at him, I didn't have the heart to correct the misspelling.

The hell with it, I thought, as I hammered away. Let people think we have a pool in our backyard.

"Does your mother know you talk this way?" Why did he always have to end his little scoldings with this? "Where is your mother," he'd say, as if it were all up to her—up to her to do what? Be referee? Be taken to task for not disciplining her charges? After all, Papá was the comandante—the commander in chief—but Mamá was the sergeant or lieutenant or whatever the second in command was. Yes, we were her charges. So was his "where's your mother," or his "does your mother know you're talking like this" a message to us that he was giving her the ultimate responsibility and blame for our disrespect? Was he saying that any hint of rebelliousness in his children was Mamá's doing?

I went in search of my mother, desperately hoping to get to her before my father did. I needed to let her know of my dorm plans. Me and my big mouth—dammit, Yolanda! What was it about my father that brought out in me the stupid anger, got the better of me? Why couldn't I learn to be calm in the face of an argument with him?

Where was she? I needed to talk with her inmediatamente!

In the garden or seated at her old Singer sewing machine, that was how I saw my mother. That was where she was mostly whenever I called out to her—"Mamá, can I go over to Lydia's . . ." "There's a basketball game at school. Can I go . . . ?" I could say that my mother was in the kitchen a whole lot of the time, too. Of course I could say that, what with eleven or more mouths to feed, but my need to think of the cottage and not the shoe directed me to the garden or her sewing machine, the rat-tat-tat-tat of the machine's humming as my mother expertly slipped a fuchsia-colored palazzo pant through the machine's needle plate, then the click of the presser foot lifter, then the scissor snip of thread indicating she was done sewing that portion of the garment. My wardrobe was either sewn by my mother or handed down from my sisters, whose wardrobe was sewn by our mother. Take your pick, Yolanda. My mother's sewing machine vied for first place with the garden because it, like the garden, was a constant in my life, the black ornate curlicue iron with the similarly ornate gold letters printed on the arm—SINGER CO—an important fixture in my life, its humming the most familiar music of my childhood.

Then I spotted her, over in the garage standing in front of the wringer washer. She was rinsing a load of clothes one by one, wringing each garment by hand before expertly sliding it through the wringer. I stepped up to catch it on the other side. The pair of pants came out on my side unnaturally flat and stiff like they'd been dead for a couple hundred years, pants ready to be clothespinned on the line to dry.

"He hung up on a guy that called me," I began.

She didn't say anything to this, just glanced at me a moment before redirecting her attention to the washer, selecting the next piece of clothing to go through the wringer. I supposed she felt this information wasn't worthy of a comment: he did this all the time; no daughter was immune to his telephone screenings. But I also sensed in her silence that she was waiting for me to tell her the real reason I was here, helping with the wash.

So I started over. "Mamá, I want to live in the dormitories at the university."

At first she didn't say anything. She turned off the rolling wringer pins, dried her hands on her apron, and gave me her full attention.

"I know," she said. "Ms. Tagore called."

Ms. Tagore was my English teacher, my favorite in the whole world. And for some reason—maybe the reassuring sound in my mother's voice—I suddenly felt relieved and unburdened.

I remembered once as a little girl, a frightening storm had come to San Diego one night, a downpour of rain as I had never before remembered, and I tossed and turned, unable to sleep. My father was working a graveyard shift at the Hotel San Diego, and so I was naturally the one sleeping with my mother. "Naturally" because little sisters Luz and Monica could comfortably double up with Ana María and Carolina on the bunk beds, and because it was well known in the family that I was the nervous sleeper, the one who remained awake in bed the longest, far into the night when everyone else was in a deep sleep. So when my father got the graveyard shift—11 p.m. to 6 a.m.—it went almost without saying that I would be my mother's roommate. I slept with my mother in their bed during that time, cocooning my small, nervous body against hers, surrounded by the comforting, familiar smells of Pond's cold cream, or camphor oil, or the spicy medicine smell of an aching-joints ointment, sensing that I was still a caterpillar in its initial growth and needed to be protected by my monarch mother butterfly. But the rain poured down with great gusto, and all I could think of was our dog Flicka outside, most probably drenched and shivering and frightened by the loud rain. She was an outdoor dog, our loyal brown mutt Flicka, lying in wait every day just outside the front door, waiting for one of her eleven masters or mistresses to come out and take a walk down the canyon or to a friend's house or just to Brown's Market. In truth, our Flicka was never alone for very long. But this rain! My tossing and turning awakened my mother, who had been lying on her side, her back to me. She turned slightly toward me and asked, amid the noisy rattle of metal rain gutters and rain tapping against the window, what was wrong, why couldn't I sleep? I told her about Flicka out there in the cold, my worry that our dog would be drenched and afraid. At first my mother didn't say anything, as if she were considering my words, thinking this through. Then, with a gentle sweep, she pulled the blankets off herself and over me. I heard her feet and shoes shuffling on the floor until each foot found and slipped into its corresponding slipper. She stood up and gently patted the bedspread at the foot of the bed until she felt her blue chenille robe. A few swishes and I knew she had it on, tied securely with the attached belt. I made out her shadowy figure as she walked to the closet, the metallic jingle of clothes hangers being scooted on the rack until she found the umbrella. Then she walked out of the room, out of the house through the back door, into the rain in the middle of the night to check on our dog. I knew that in a few minutes, she would return and turn on the night-light set on the table next to her side of the bed. Since the bed was pushed against the wall, I didn't have a night table or lamp, just the cubby denlike safety of a wall on one side and my mother's warm body on the other.

I loved our dog Flicka—we all did. She was loyal to each of her masters and mistresses, but it was I who had chosen the name Flicka after the story of the horse, *My Friend Flicka*, back when I went through an intense stage of being in love with horses, and "Flicka"—the Swedish word for girl—seemed the perfect name for our dog. My brothers and sisters came up with names like Chico, Cookie, Flaca—even Fido, for goodness' sake—but I held tight for Flicka, somehow even convincing my oldest sister to read the story. She did, and then it was two votes for the name of Flicka versus one vote each for all the other names. (Later, when Carolina went through her Chicanismo stage in college, she questioned why we ever thought of giving our dog a Swedish name when there were so many beautiful Mexican names.)

It seemed to me that my mother had been outside for a long while—too long. And again I became restless, this time my restlessness tinged with guilt that I should have practically forced my mother outside into the storm. It wasn't as if Flicka were some wimpy, helpless creature, after all. And then I saw a flash of light—someone's flashlight, maybe?—followed, a few moments later, by a clap of thunder that made my heart leap to my throat, my God, and my mother outside! My first reaction was to hide deeper under my blankets, but the thought that it was I who had driven my mother out into the rain, into the thunder and lightning because of my silly worrying over our dog, made me instead scoot over to my mother's side of the bed, which was still warm with the imprint of her body, get up out of bed, and tap the bedside table until I found the light switch. What if the lightning had struck her? I thought. What if she was sprawled on the ground this very moment, dead—and all because of me!

The door to the backyard had a window and I peered through it, my hands cupping my eyes like blinders, my face pressed against the glass. The rain was coming down in torrents—there was water everywhere, so much so that I could have been on a boat in the middle of the sea, peering out the ship's window looking for our captain as the boat tossed and swayed dangerously, all of us soon to be drowned. But where was our captain? And then another flash of lightning, and I saw her coming toward the house now, the pale blue of her chenille robe, one hand on the yellow umbrella, the other holding something that I couldn't make out. Slowly and carefully she made her way, stepping around the bigger puddles, until she was here, where I waited for her with the door wide open, wanting her to hurry in, to be safe and warm so that she could protect and warm me.

Flicka was fine, my mother reported, as she set two figs on the kitchen table. The soft black oval-shaped fruit was wet and muddy, having fallen from the tree with the force of the wind. My mother had made her a makeshift doghouse with a few planks of board, a kind of lean-to under the trees. Now go to sleep Yolanda, she said impatiently—or perhaps patiently after all, considering the mission accomplished. "You have school tomorrow." Then she marched me back to her room. I noticed the hem of her blue chenille robe was muddy wet, and I imagined her having bent down in the mud, under the fig tree, making our dog a dry lean-to, arranging the planks of wood—these remnants finally good for something!—as she built a shelter for Flicka. And then just as she was about to leave and come in out of the rain, I was sure she had paused and reached down, her robe folding and brushing against the wet dirt, to pet our friend Flicka. To reassure both dog and daughter that everything was going to be okay.

Three

Shopping for school supplies. Now that I would be going to *la universidad*, my mother insisted on the requisite visit to Fedmart. My younger sisters, seventeen-year-old Monica and twelve-year-old Luz, along with my best friend Lydia, piled into the Rambler with my mom and me. My older sister Ana María opted to stay home. It was a hot August day, and I wasn't too thrilled about this family shopping outing to Fedmart, certain that UCSD's bookstore had everything I needed.

"Yes, I'm sure it does," Mamá said, "and for double the price." And she shut the passenger door securely as I started the car.

The thing was this: my mom was miraculously frugal with money. And if at times this was exasperating—why can't I buy that dress at The Broadway? Why do all my dresses have to be sewn? Debbie bought this cute floral skirt *on sale*—most of the time I was grateful for her wizardry with money. It didn't take a lot of brains to figure out that if it wasn't for my mother, we probably wouldn't have had much to eat growing up in a home with nine children, my father being the foolishly generous one with money. But more about them later.

Luz and Monica were in the backseat talking, trying to decide what kind of lunchbox they wanted this year, and here I was about to embark on a new adventure—college life at the University of California at San Diego. Listening to them decide over a Barbie-decorated lunch pail, or Mickey and Minnie Mouse, or something with horses (for Monica, of course) made me long for such wonderfully simple pleasures and dilemmas.

Don't get me wrong. It wasn't that I was afraid of what awaited me, this new journey, so to speak, it was just that I had a feeling it would be a much longer distance from home than the twenty-five miles north of Palm City it took to get to the university in La Jolla.

I know, I know. Lydia had already scolded me for getting all *simbólica* about going to college. "It's just college, Yoli," pragmatic Lydia said. "Don't add more weight to it." Then she said with what she thought was a clever afterthought, "You want weight? Wait 'til you buy all the required textbooks for your classes. Then you can get weighty with symbolism." My forever friend Lydia.

I was driving on Main Street making my way to Palomar Street where most of our shopping was done. There was a cluster of our popular stores—Fedmart, White Front, Pic 'n Save, Yardage World, Kresge's, Big Bear Market—modest stores between gas stations; car supply shops; a Polynesian restaurant with tiki décor; a Mexican restaurant with enough hanging donkey piñatas to get the customers braying in unison after a few margaritas; and of course, the ever-popular Otay Farms fresh produce stand. These were our stomping grounds, where we shopped. Steadfast, practical stores for the working poor. Again, no great feat to figure out we were part of the working poor. How did you think I got so many grants for college? Yes, okay, I graduated with honors from high school, won some scholarships for tuition at the school of my choice, but it was the grant money that would allow me *to live in the dorms*. Yes, you heard right: I would be living in the student dorms.

The guy who called me the other day, the one my father hung up on? Turned out he was the president of the Las Americas Club and had called to inform me that I had won a thousand-dollar scholarship. I couldn't wait to tell this to my father. And when I did, his short answer was, "Good, congratulations."

No apologies, no recognizing that perhaps he needed to be less erratic, not jump to jealous conclusions when answering the phone and hearing a guy's voice on the other end asking to talk with one of his daughters. Heck, how about, "I apologize, Yoli. From now on I won't answer the phone, and yes, feel free to let all potential suitors clog the lines"? Okay, okay, I knew I was asking for miracles, but this little tidbit of the real picture—the "chango" who called to say I'd won a scholarship—gave me a definite advantage over my father, and one that I needed as I nervously awaited Ms. Tagore and Mrs. Billings's knock at our door.

My mother was in on the visit and its intent; Papá, on the other hand, had no idea what this was all about. "A visit this evening from Yolanda's teacher and vice principal," is what I heard her say to him.

I was standing, hidden, near the kitchen door, listening in. "Why?" she said to his question. "¿Quién sabe? Perhaps to announce another scholarship." She said this casually as she served him his *café con leche*. "Maybe they think telling us in person is a more effective way of communicating the good news than by means of the telephone."

How I loved this mother of mine!

Ms. Tagore was my honors English teacher and the most sophisticated, classy person I had ever had the honor of knowing. Ms. Tagore happened to be quite beautiful, is what I was saying. She was born in India of an Indian father and an American mother, her exotic beauty combined with elegance (tailored woolen suits in the winter, cool white linen in the spring). My mentor and favorite teacher wore her straight black hair down to her waist, and the length of her miniskirts was tasteful enough to be professionally above criticism from her (most certainly!) envious women colleagues, and yet stylish enough to make us high school girls yearn to be her someday. Her beauty alone would have been cause to have every guy at my school in love with her. But that wasn't all: she raced her Porsche on weekends.

And Mrs. Billings? Well, she was our stern, no-nonsense girls' vice principal, grandmotherly looking with her short silver hair and below-the-knee skirts, dark suits worn all year long. And while most of the tough girls at my school couldn't stand her, Mrs. Billings was known to have a soft heart for high-achieving students like me. So with these two formidable advocates in place—a strategic balance of glamour and schoolmarm rigidity—I braced myself with crossed fingers as they knocked at the door.

This was going to be a tough sell. I knew they knew that. My oldest sister Carolina had studied psychology at San Diego State, but she had lived at home and by the time she graduated she was already married and living in her own house with Tom. And then when Ana María went to Kelsey-Jenney Business College, she took the city bus into downtown San Diego every day for nine months of schooling.

The two women sat on the brown couch while my parents sat across from them on the orange vinyl love seat. Alone in the green velvet armchair, I kept my mouth firmly shut lest I open it and screw up the whole plan. My job was to serve the coffee and cookies, which I thought I could manage to do with some amount of grace. The thing was, this was an important moment in my life as my destiny became the topic of discussion: to live or not to live in the dorms; to get or not to get my father to loosen the reins on me—and through it all, having my favorite teacher in the whole world coming to my shoe-cottage house, wearing a gorgeous red dress, drinking coffee from one of three unchipped cups that we owned, and speaking lovely, elegant words on my behalf. Yes, an important moment in my life.

"Living in the dorms would give her convenient access to the library for studying," Mrs. Billings offered. "Keep her focused."

"UCSD, as you know, is a world-renowned university," Ms. Tagore added. "We know that you would want your daughter to have the best learning environment possible."

They spoke slowly in English, making sure my father (because they knew he was the one they needed to convince) could understand them.

In the meantime, my father could not, understandably, keep his eyes off Ms. Tagore. "Ah, I see, I see," he nodded in agreement at everything she said, his head bobbing up and down, up and down, like one of the silly string puppets we bought every summer at the San Juan de Los Lagos market in Guadalajara. Poor man, I was thinking with great satisfaction, he's a goner.

"More coffee?" I whispered to Mrs. Billings.

The sound of my voice seemed to shake him out of his trance long enough to remind him why we were there in the living room having coffee in the first place.

"But these dormitories," he said, clearing his throat, watching as I poured my vice principal more coffee. "They are for girls only, yes?"

"The building houses young men and women—in separate wings, of course." Ms. Tagore had a great smile. "There is a resident assistant who keeps an eye on everyone."

"Mr. Sahagún," the stern, no-nonsense Mrs. Billings added, "I want to congratulate you and Mrs. Sahagún on raising such a mature, responsible daughter. She is a daughter who quite clearly knows right from wrong. And did you know there is a popular Newman Center on campus for Catholic students with activities such as Mass, spiritual retreats, catechism-style weekly meetings?"

In all of this, my mother was quiet, deferring to my advocates and not wanting my father to suspect that she was in on this.

Then he turned to look at her.

"Well, Dolores," he said. "Our daughter has proven herself to be a mature, responsible student, all right. Why, look at her grades! And as these two very intelligent ladies have just mentioned, she will be able to study better with the library nearby. The Newman Center is a very good thing too. Yes, yes, I absolutely agree with these women. *Por cierto que* I've felt this way all along, but Dolores, I want you to feel comfortable with this, too."

We all turned to look at my mother who sat quietly with her hands folded on her lap. "Well, Lorenzo, if you are sure . . ."

"Yes, yes," he said, nodding his head, smiling at the beautiful Ms. Tagore. "Of course, yes. I think it is the best thing for our Yoli."

"Well then," she said with just the right amount of hesitation, "it is fine with me."

And as my father reached for the coffeepot to refill Ms. Tagore's cup—when in my life have I ever seen my father serving a woman coffee?!—my mother glanced at me and winked.

❀ ❀ ❀

"This is what I have on my list," Lydia called out to me from her spot in the backseat.

Lydia and I had our list of school supplies for our first year in college. She was going to go to San Diego State, which was across town from my university, and had opted to stay home and commute, forfeiting any college culture experiences in the dorms. Instead, she got a new navy blue Ford Pinto. I was pretty pissed at her for not applying to UCSD like I had. "*Pa'que?*" She said. She wanted to be an elementary school teacher, and State had a solid teachers' program. "But you, Yoli," she said in that tone she got when she thought she had some insider information or extra sensory perception, "you need to go to UCSD." At which moment I had only a few seconds to decide whether I wanted to get sucked into her philosophical ruminations by asking her why, or just ignore her all-knowing tone of voice. Lately I'd been opting to swallow my pride and ask. After all, this was not the time in my life to squelch my intellectual curiosity—even if it was just to hear Lydia's reasons for why I should go to UCSD and not to State.

"So why should I go to UCSD and not to State?" I asked her.

She didn't answer right off. She jotted down one more thing on her list of school supplies. Then she looked up at me as if she were seriously considering my question, all the while looking thoughtfully at my eyes, my nose, my cheeks, my ears—as if the answer lay hidden somewhere on my face.

"I don't know, really," she finally said. "But there's something about you being near the ocean and Torrey pine trees that just seems so you. And besides," she added, "you don't know what you want to be when you grow up, so you might as well be near the ocean and those endangered trees while you're trying to figure it out."

For once—don't ask me why—Lydia made perfect sense to me.

We arrived at Fedmart, and before I could even say "lickety-split," Luz and Monica had taken off in the direction of children's clothing, toys, and lunch pails. Mamá, Lydia, and I headed to the school supplies section.

A package of 8 1/2 by 11–inch college-ruled notebook paper—check.

A pack of number two pencils—check.

A big, fat eraser—check.

Spiral notebooks, one for each class—check.

Ballpoint pens and highlight markers—check.

Three-ring binder—check.

Inexpensive, uncomplicated calculator—check.

Small stapler and staples—check.

Paper clips—check.

Lots of packs of spearmint gum—check.

And this.

My mother waved me over as she reached for something in the shelves and pulled it out. It was some sort of briefcase satchel thing and, as I walked over to her, I noticed it was made of faux leather, like the stuff the Rambler was upholstered in. It had straps and heavy-looking buckles for securely closing it, two big pockets for extra stuff, and a longer shoulder strap. It was the size of five lunchboxes put together. And even without books, empty as it was at the moment, it easily weighed a ton. It looked like something 007 would never carry; it looked like something Agent Smart most certainly would.

"I don't need that," I said right off, so there was no question about it, not even pausing to consider this contraption.

My mother didn't seem to hear me. "I had one just like this when I went to school," she said. "Sturdy and practical. Very comfortable on the shoulder. It should do just fine."

"No, I won't need that," I tried again. "Backpacks are what students wear nowadays . . ."

"You mean those things I see young people carry, making them look like *viejitos* hunched over with a bag of rocks slung over the shoulder? Do you want to have a crooked, *jorobada* back for the rest of your life?" she asked.

"Hey, that's really neat, Yoli," Lydia said, now standing next to me and examining the bag. She had a funny grin on her face, which I didn't appreciate. I hated it when she took my mom's side.

"¡Qué suerte!" my mother said, having just looked at the price tag. "It's on sale."

Yes, my point exactly. It was on sale. Dirt cheap. *Please* take the stupid thing, Fedmart was silently begging us.

I was about to protest, really put my foot down on the matter, when I stopped myself long enough to hear my mother saying something about the satchel she had in *la secundaria*, the satchel that she had set on a bench on her way home from school. Just for a few minutes while she and her cousin Chayito enjoyed a *raspado* in the *jardín*.

"It was then that he must have done it," she said.

"Done what?" Lydia and I asked at the same time.

"I must have been looking the other way. Maybe I got up and walked away from the bench for a few seconds. Chayito must have been in on it."

"Done what?" I asked, wanting her to get to the meat of the story. These little reminiscings were so rare for my mother, but when they did come I wanted them all in one big gulp.

"He put a love letter in one of the pockets of my school satchel," she said in her soft Spanish. "I didn't see it. He was clever about it, but later that evening when I was doing my homework, looking for my favorite pen, I spotted the ivory-colored envelope. A love letter. *Una declaración* . . ."

"Who?" Lydia asked the question that was burning in my mind.

"Yolanda's father," my mother said, now turning to examine the other bags, perhaps shy and self-conscious about what she had just divulged.

So how could I *not* buy the damn contraption, for Pete's sake?

Four

Weekend orientation at UCSD. My mother and father were driving me to the campus, our first time, and just as we hit La Jolla we were enveloped in a thick shroud of fog. No kidding. It was so thick and sudden that all you saw were brake lights in front of you like evil, red-eyed monsters appearing out of nowhere in a gray spooky fog, watching your every move. Just like that. There we were driving along Interstate 5 on a bright and cheery September morning, listening to my father's *norteña* cowboy and mariachi music on Radio Ranchito, and for once I actually didn't mind listening to this accordion-filled, dorky polka music. (After all, it was a part of hearth and home and everything else I saw trailing farther and farther behind me.) But no sooner had we entered the La Jolla area and the fog curled around us as if we had just stepped into a scary Twilight Zone. I was trying hard to ignore the symbolism in all of this, concentrating as I was on the gray quiet around us, but it was difficult not to wonder if this fog was some kind of sign. My father immediately turned off the Radio Ranchito music, and then there was a nervous silence in the car. Both of them were sitting up very straight and tense, intently studying the road ahead of them, looking for the lane lines. The dull red lights of the car ahead seemed to be our best guide. My father was hunched forward as if the car were about to take off into orbit and he wanted to be sure he had a good grip on the steering wheel so he wouldn't get ejected into the outer limits. My mother, sitting next to him, was alert and still, as if she were holding her breath. She was wearing her favorite light blue jacquard dress, and her black patent leather handbag was propped in standing position on her lap, her hands folded over the handle strap, as if on a moment's notice she could leap out of the car with purse securely in hand. She looked straight ahead, her eyes fixed on the gray gloom that surrounded us.

They were both small-boned people and, judging from their body frames, seemed to be a perfect fit. And were you to look at their faces, the same thought would cross your mind: that Dolores Ramos with her fair skin, curly brown hair, and green eyes, and Lorenzo Sahagún with his fair skin, curly brown hair, and blue eyes might be brother and sister. Or a husband and wife who had, over time, rubbed off on each other.

What was that saying? Caras ven, corazones no conocen—or something like that: you could see the face but not the heart. I would add: you could see their similar faces, yes, but not their dramatically distinct personalities. That was to say, *you* wouldn't see it, but we who lived with our parents did.

That was as far as I wanted to delve into the mystery of my parents, for there were more pressing things to think about, namely that I was on my way to my college's weekend orientation to meet staff and administrators, like the provost of my college (what the heck is a provost?), to check out the dorms I would be living in during the school year and also during this weekend, and take a general tour of the campus. To get a feel for the lay of the land, if you will. And yes, I'll admit it, I was nervous as all hell.

Of course I was nervous. I'd just left the secure, bright, and sunny confines of Palm City, my familiar and gentle barrio in south San Diego, and was now heading north to what I thought might be another world, and—once I saw the thick fog enveloping us—I was certain it would be another world. A part of me wanted to scream and order my father to make a U-turn—¡rapidito! ¡Ahora mismo!—temporarily adopting my father's hysterical ranting tone, and admit that I'd taken this university foolishness a little too far, so let's just giddyup on back home now. Another part of me, though, the sensible, intelligent one, said with a firm and solemn voice, in bold and italics: *Yolanda Sahagún, this was your choice. Nobody forced you. Nobody tied you up and gagged you and made you sign on the acceptance letter's dotted line; it will be a wonderful experience, Yoli, and many people—teachers, friends, family, why, even strangers—are very proud of you, so cut the crap already.*

My God, and this was only orientation weekend.

I took a deep breath, leaned my head against the backseat, and closed my eyes. Long deep breaths, trying to remember what it felt like the time I came to La Jolla for the DAR tea party, or better yet, what it felt like upon leaving La Jolla and heading home. Deep breath, Yoli, deep breath. Then it came to me, what my mother had said in the car that time, about me having everything to do with the American Revolution. What did she mean by that? I leaned forward, put my hand on the back of her seat and was about to ask her, but I instinctively stopped myself, sensing that my mother's words, enigmatic and cryptic, were revolutionary in and of themselves, words perhaps too radical for my father's ears. This was not the moment to ask her.

We got off at La Jolla Village Drive and headed west, cautiously driving down the busy boulevard, our Rambler looking like a patrol car cruising the streets, suspicious and alert to trouble at any and every corner.

Then it seemed we had arrived, a big building suddenly looming before our befogged eyes, next to a row of dumpsters by the parking lot. There was a man tossing garbage in one of them and I rolled down my window and asked him if this was UCSD. He smiled, shook his head. No, this was the VA hospital. We needed to go that way, he said, pointing northwest.

Of course, the VA hospital!

The three of us were all surprised that we hadn't recognized the VA hospital, what with my brother Chuy being interned there every so often when he refused to take his meds or when the medication couldn't subdue him enough to act "normal"—whatever the hell that might mean— what with the fact that we'd been coming here often. Too often. How could we have forgotten the showdown just last year between my father and the doctors?

Chuy was diagnosed with manic depression and mild schizophrenia. When the VA doctors told this to my mother, father, Carolina, and me, there on the fourth floor of the psychological ward when we came to discuss Chuy's case and to pick him up because he was going to be released from the hospital, they also asked if there was a history of schizophrenia in the family—any other brother, sister, uncle, aunt acting in the same way—not in touch with reality, violent?

My father exploded. "Qué esquizofrenia y qué nada," he said. "That's an insult to our family. Come on, Dolores. Let's get Chuy's things and let's go. Where is he? I want to see that son of mine. You people have a lot of nerve. He serves this country, comes back mentally damaged, and you want to put the blame on his lineage? *Pues bien*, fine, say what you want to say, just remember, he wasn't like this before he went to Vietnam."

"Mr. Sahagún," one of the three psychiatrists in attendance said, "we're just trying to explore all possibilities . . ."

"No, you're not," he said, his voice rising, his face red. "You're trying to put the blame . . ."

"Lorenzo, *por favor*," my mother said.

"Stay out of this, Dolores," he snapped at her.

"Papá," began my oldest sister and psychology major Carolina, "it's important to ask these kinds of questions . . ."

"*Tú tambien*, disrespectful daughter," he shouted at Carolina. "Nobody asked your opinion! And you, too," he said, pointing to me as if he expected I'd be the next to protest. The odd thing was that I had no intention of contradicting my father. For some reason, I was on my father's side, feeling as indignant as he.

Then turning to the doctor, he said in his heavily accented English, "Just give us whatever medicines he has to take and let's be done with this little game."

Nobody said a word. They all stared silently at Papá.

Then a knock at the doctor's door and the nurse ushered Chuy in, my most wonderful brother in a family of wonderful brothers.

He shuffled slowly toward us, groggy and lethargic, slightly disoriented. He was wearing a pair of jeans and a rumpled T-shirt, some flip-flop sandals. His hair was disheveled, like he'd just been awakened after three months asleep on the ward.

Blinking, refocusing, he suddenly grinned at us, as if he'd just figured out who we were. "Time to go back to Kansas," he said.

My father shook his head, tense and quiet, waving his thank-you to the man as we shifted into reverse and headed out. My mother didn't say a word, was sitting stiff and alert and looking out the windshield like a copilot following strict orders to keep watch. Any other wife would have been for sure sighing exaggeratedly, exasperated with her husband's driving, a snide remark here and there about his bad sense of direction. But not my mother.

First there was a general meeting in one of the lecture halls on Muir Campus, a meeting meant to reassure parents that their children would be in good hands, and that these students had chosen one of the best universities in the nation to attend, blah, blah, blah. I tried to concentrate on what the guy was saying, but mainly I was getting ready for the moment we'd be touring the dorms, how my parents were going to react when they realized that it was pretty much a coed situation—guys on the same floor as women, just in another wing of the building.

This occasion was rare: having both my mother and father in attendance for school-related stuff. In elementary school, it was usually my mother and an older brother (our chauffeur, since Mamá didn't know how to drive) who went to the open houses, and even though my mother always paid the voluntary PTA membership dues, she never went to a PTA meeting—what with her limited English and all.

Papá's role in our formal schooling was even smaller. But no, that wasn't true, I thought, as I suddenly remembered the times my father did his own kind of teaching—what I called the Lorenzo Sahagún Schooling for His Nine Children: With the latest *El Mexicano* newspaper in hand, he rounded up his nine children, calling out to all of us in the girls' room, then walking out the back door, through the patio, to the boys' room. Calling us all into the living room, lining us up—oldest to youngest—to read aloud a paragraph or two from the newspaper. I remembered one particular evening, the day before Imperial Beach's Sun 'n' Sea Festival, my head in pink jumbo rollers. I was standing in line, two from the end—like the Von Trapp family—for my turn. It was sticky warm that evening and I had amazing menstrual cramps, so I wasn't in the mood for Papá's Spanish language lessons; I wasn't in the mood to tolerate his shouts and obvious impatience with our mispronunciations. "Qué!?

Cómo?! Repite eso," he would say. When it was my turn, I looked at him with all the righteousness I could muster—how old was I? Twelve? Thirteen?—and in Spanish (we only spoke Spanish to our parents) I said, "I refuse to read from this stupid newspaper. You can't force me to. This is so stupid." I could hear immediate silence in the room—whoever was talking now stopping in midsentence, and whoever was walking now stopping in midstep—all for sure holding their breaths in anticipation of horrendous fireworks.

At first he didn't saying anything. Papá's blue eyes looked at me curiously, as if wondering if he had misunderstood me. Then he said, uncharacteristically calm, "First of all the word is *'periódico'* with an 'i' before the stressed 'o'—not 'peródico,' *¿entiendes?*"

I made no sign, no nodding. Not a word. Just kept staring at him with all the courageous defiance I could find.

"Second of all," he continued, "I don't want you to go out into the world speaking Spanish like a *pocha* and having people laugh at you."

What could I say to this? Suddenly I had the worst headache in the world. "No, I can't do this," I said, "I can't, do you hear me?!" Then a flood of tears, crying hysterically, making Amparo Rivelles's sobs seem lame compared to mine. "This is so stupid—and, and besides . . . I have a headache."

"Well, it's no wonder!" he said, laughing. "With those things on your head."

I ran out of the living room in a huff, straight to the girls' room, a trail of giggles from my sisters behind me.

The Lorenzo Sahagún Schooling for His Nine Children. Funny that I should have remembered it as I embarked on a new kind of schooling of my own.

We made our way to the dorms. Our guide—an upperclassman—led us into the twelve-story building, showing us the common areas: living room suite, kitchenette, bathrooms. Then we were there, my room for the weekend. I quickly glanced around to see if my roommate had settled in yet with her belongings. Oh, said the guide, as if my glancing around had reminded her, my roommate couldn't make it after all for the orientation.

I would have the room to myself that night. Then our guide shook hands with my parents, wished me good luck, and then exited, leaving me alone with Mom and Dad.

My mother and father were sitting on the edge of the bed watching as I inspected the small room, the dark wooden closet, the gray metal bookcases, and desk. As I turned to look at them, I noticed my mother discreetly slipped her rose petal rosary under my pillow. She knew that I wouldn't sleep soundly and peacefully—if I slept at all. Nervous sleeper that I was even with a houseful of people around me, how could I sleep alone, never in my life having done so? How could I not be scared?

There was a momentary awkward silence in the room as we three looked at each other, one of those well-here-we-are kinds of silences.

"This reminds me of the time your tíos Abelardo and Ernesto and I came to the States for the first time, during the Cristero Wars."

My mother and I quickly looked at my father, grateful that he had broken the ice.

"When things got bad in Jalisco, my mother arranged for us to go in a train up to Nogales, then on to Arizona and over to Los Angeles. Talk about new adventures." My father was smiling, looking out the window at the dorm building just across from us, but not really seeing it. No doubt he was now back in the strawberry fields in Los Angeles, 1929, waiting for the civil unrest in his home state to simmer down, writing letters to his mother and sisters—"and my many novias," he added, glancing at my mom, and then giving me a wink. "I had wanted to be a charro, to tell you the truth, a fancy, professional cowboy. I wanted to travel the world with my beautiful horses. Instead, my mother sent me and my brothers to the United States, out of harm's way . . ."

I hadn't known this, that my father had been a farm worker in the late '20s here in the States when he was barely twenty years old himself. Not much older than I am now. His journey had been a whole lot longer than mine. That was comforting to know.

My mother listened quietly, attentively, my father being the storyteller,

liking the limelight. Her hands were demurely folded on her lap, the patent leather black purse perched next to her on the small bed. Papá was
the storyteller of the family and she was the listener. She was the one
who handed us the pencil or the microphone; she was the one who set
the stage on which our stories came alive. The behind-the-scenes person, both discreet director and enthusiastic audience in our lives, this
was Mamá.

And then we were in the parking lot and I was hugging them good-
bye for the weekend. Ana María would be by tomorrow afternoon to
pick me up, they said. I was fighting back the tears, giving them a reassuring, dopey fake smile. Papá hugged me first and then hopped into the car,
starting the ignition. Mamá was slower, more deliberate in her embrace.
She wrapped her petite but strong arms around me, and as we hugged,
she whispered something, then let me go, a big grin on her face—proud
and happy and sad and worried and a whole lot of other mother emo-
tions I couldn't yet fathom.

"What did you say?" I asked.

"My daughter of the American Revolution," she said.

❋ ❋ ❋

The sound of cannonballs in the distance, marching, and laughter.
"Periódico, periódico," the man shouted in sync with the marching.
It was foggy and I couldn't get a clear picture of who was talking—at
times it sounded like my father, at times it sounded like my Vietnam veteran brother Chuy. The marching—strong, heavy, and synchronized—
became louder and louder as if a battalion of a million soldiers was
approaching. I was in a jungle, lying on muddy ground drenched from
storm after unrelenting storm. My ear was being forced against the
ground by someone or something, thrust down against the sticky mud.
But even as I struggled to make out who was holding me down, there
was no one there. Someone or something, yes, just forcefully pressing
my ear to the ground, ordering me to listen, to listen, to listen. Then my
own sounds: first a whimper, then throaty, full-blown sobbing. I awoke
with a start, out of breath. I felt sweaty and cold. I reached under the

pillow for the rose petal rosary, clutched it in my hand, rubbing the scented maroon-colored beads.

Then I started to cry. Alone in this dark room on the tenth floor of Tioga Hall, before daybreak, before the sunlight came streaming in and comforted me and reassured me that it was just a bad, silly dream, I would admit it once and for all and then be done with it: I was scared of ghosts; I was scared of dreams.

I wanted to go home.

Five

September 1973. At that very moment I was looking down from my window on the tenth floor of Tioga Hall with a perfect view of the Pacific Ocean. I had a double room, which I shared with a roommate, and each of us had a single bed, desk, bookshelf, and closet. That was the first time in my life I had ever had a bedroom that I wasn't sharing with four other people. Yippee! I thought as I looked around at the walls decorated with posters of forests and mountain scenes and wise words from Thoreau and Kahlil Gibran. A poster of Santana's *Abraxas* album cover—powerful, beautiful, mystical, psychedelic colors; some sort of angel-devil in fluorescent reds and blues with magnificent wings, this angel-devil straddling a bongo as it made its way to black magic woman herself, who was lounging, like a queen on her throne, on a chair draped with sensuous, silky, and velvet-rich fabrics, naked with voluptuous big breasts, a white dove perched in front of her crotch, a picture that beckoned the audience to enter its world of symbolism and mystery and sensuality—was taped to my door. I loved to stare at that poster as I lay on my bed across from it, to understand what it was trying to say to me. I wondered if the black magic woman song was about a woman who was black and magical, or if she was a woman—whatever her color—practicing black magic. Wonderful. Enigmatic. I loved the song and artwork for this very reason, because it said something different to me every time I listened to it and studied it. But because of the sexual nature of the painting, I kept it taped to the inside of my door, so for the few times Mamá and Papá had come by, I opened the door and kept it open while they were visiting. When I ushered them out of my room, I closed the door behind me, and black magic woman once again had dominion of my sanctuary.

So there you had it: for once in my life I didn't have to fight with my four sisters about what I could or couldn't put on the walls of our bedroom.

The ocean just yonder—La Jolla's Black's Beach—was within walking distance, and my roommate was organizing a beach party for next Thursday night, her party an attempt to counteract the apparently dreary social life that existed on this campus.

I looked out the window, scanning the parking lot below for my sister Ana María's car, asking myself once again: I finally had the decent spot of space I'd always wanted for myself, that I dreamed of and begged God to give me, so, *tonta*, why were you feeling excited and packed and ready to go home?

On my bed sat a small duffel bag with my clothes for the weekend and the Fedmart satchel that Mamá had bought me. She didn't just buy it for me; no, she *insisted* I get it, clear in her mind that this was what I would need to carry notebooks and pencils to my classes. I didn't have the heart to tell her I would never use it. (Maybe these briefcase contraptions were used in Mexico, I thought, and maybe romantic suitors slipped love letters into their pockets, but not here.) She bought it and I accepted it, taking it with me to the dorms, bringing it home on weekends filled with a notebook, pencils, and pens. How could I explain to Mamá that the satchel was dorky? I didn't. I accepted it, and as soon as I was on campus, I headed for the bookstore to buy myself a regular backpack like all the students'.

Last weekend I watched as she sat at her Singer sewing machine, making me a tennis outfit for the tennis class I was taking. It was a little one-piece number, white with navy blue trim around the collar and armpits. Had a matching kerchief-styled cap. I protested when she bought the Simplicity pattern, told her she didn't have to go to all that trouble. She insisted, seemed excited. Mamá had never played tennis, had probably never been near a tennis court, but she knew just what I needed to be a winner. I didn't have the heart to tell her I was second to the worst in my class. I didn't have the heart to tell her I would probably never wear that outfit. How would it look? There she was, Yolanda something-or-other, doofus tennis player, walking onto the court with the rest of her class, paired off with another doofus who could barely hold her racket. Oops, now there she went, running after balls, hitting them over the fence, tripping over her own two feet. Boink, now one ball zonking her on the forehead. Ah, but what an outfit—dressed like the pros!

Mamá began and finished the outfit that same weekend. On Sunday evening, just before Ana María was to drive me back to the dorms, she handed it to me. "Try it on," she said.

Halfheartedly, I tried it on. Mamá smiled, pleased. "It fits perfectly."

What I couldn't see, not until years later, was her own wish to be a tennis player, to run across the courts in a cute little tennis dress, athletic, strong, and carefree. What I didn't yet understand was that I was her legacy; I would do for her what she could not do.

I took the tennis dress outfit with me to the dorms, folding it and then carefully placing it at the bottom of the drawer, not to be used until my swing was stronger, more confident, and I could skillfully hit the ball over the net.

❀ ❀ ❀

Ana María was honking the horn of the Rambler, parked illegally just below me. I waved to her from ten floors up, not sure she could see me. But she knew I'd be coming down in no time flat—as I did every week-end; she knew I missed her and the crowded chaotic bedroom we five sisters shared at one point in our lives.

"Don't even ask, okay?" Ana María warned, looking angry as we pulled out of the university's drive, making our way onto Interstate 5 south. "Just be glad you don't have to be at home during the week and put up with his crap. There are some clothes on the clothesline. If you bring them in, I'll do the dishes after dinner."

And that's all she offered me all the way home.

Now that Carolina was married and no longer living at home, twenty-one-year-old Ana María had taken it upon herself to act the part of oldest sister of the house. She had attended Kelsey-Jenney Business College and now worked full-time as the head secretary at Southwest Junior High. Like Carolina, Ana María wore a mantle of motherliness mixed with melodramatic foreboding and authoritarianism. I listened to her, took her seriously, because I knew that in some odd, unnatural way, she was wise beyond her age.

So the first thing I did when we got home was bring down the clothes, tossing the wooden clothespins into a little basket, folding each garment. Little Luz and Monica missed me enough during the week—tired of crabby Ana María—that on weekends they stayed near me like devoted groupies to their college dorm sister.

"He's on the warpath again," Monica said. She was wearing her usual jeans and a T-shirt and the scruffy, brown cowboy boots Mamá bought her at the veterans' thrift store some time ago. Monica wore them any chance she could because, she claimed, they made her look like a true horsewoman. Even now at seventeen, her love of horses had not diminished, promising to be a lifelong passion—or perhaps (the more cynical me thought) a kind of survival escapism from her familial reality. So she gave me the full weekly home front report, filling in where Ana María remained silent, dramatically cryptic.

"Last night he got home at three in the morning and woke Ana María up to dial some long-distance phone calls for him." She stood with legs apart in a V, arms akimbo in some sort of cowgirl stance. "So Ana María says we should be glad he has a second night job at the Hotel San Diego and we don't have to see much of him."

I brought down the last garment, carefully folding the colorful floral blouse in a neat square before setting it on top of the pile of folded laundry. "And Mamá?" I asked.

"Ladies," twelve-year-old Luz called out to us in her best hoity-toity rendition of a British butler's voice, "dinner is served."

Nopalitos—tangy cactus from our backyard—combined with scrambled eggs, tomatoes, onion, and refried beans. For dessert, a compote of *membrillos*—the quince fruit cut into wedges and cooked in sugar and water—another favorite.

We four sisters and Mamá sat at the table eating, Ana María abnormally quiet as she wore her mask of stoicism and impossible patience. She looked a lot like Amparo Rivelles in the *telenovela La Cruz de Marisa Cruces*, with her thick eyelashes, the long-suffering pained expression on her face. But I dared not say this to her because she was liable to take it to heart and play Amparo Rivelles's role to the hilt. And besides, I knew something was up.

Mamá, on the other hand, seemed light and free and happy—even humming as she joined us at the table. I was stuck in the middle between Mamá's cheerfulness and Ana María's martyrdom. Luz and Monica looked from one to the other of us sisters. They too knew something was up.

But I finally opted for celebration, and gave my mother and sisters the weekly report on college life, keeping it cheery and funny. This week something interesting actually had happened: I was in a deep sleep at five o'clock in the morning when the loud fire alarm went off, practically scaring the poo-poo (my mother's present so I didn't say "shit" or "caca") out of me. We all tumbled out of beds, headed for the stairs—ten flights of stairs for me, thank you very much. Once all the residents of the dorm were standing out in the quad in the light fog, some in pajamas or boxers, students wrapped in blankets, one girl with her teddy bear held close to her chest, wondering who the wise guys were, the RAs shouting instructions for us to be patient while the building was checked, right then the streaker ran through the quad past the hundreds of students shivering in the cold, damp morning. And we all started laughing and cheering and whistling, applauding his brave grand entrance and exit as he rushed by.

"You're kidding? Completely naked?" Luz asked as she poured herself some milk in a glass.

"Yup," I said. "*Con todo y pirinola* just dangling there for the world to see."

They all started laughing. "Ay, Yolanda, por favor," my mother admonished me with the greatest grin I'd ever seen.

Even Ana María forgot her sad lot in life long enough to chuckle with us. "Boy, I wish I could've seen that," she said.

"Hee-haw," said Monica. "Giddyup."

"*Ya muchachas,*" my mother said, "that's enough." But she still had her delighted grin.

Not until the dishes were cleared from the table and Mamá, Luz, and Monica had left the kitchen, knowing it was Ana María's turn to wash, did she finally speak up.

"You're so lucky not to be here during the week and put up with this anymore. He comes home three, four in the morning—never at midnight when work is over. Slamming doors, talking—no, *shouting*—into the phone for the long-distance operator. Twice that week he woke me up and said he wanted me to be his secretary, tell the operator, who couldn't understand his English, that he wants to make a person-to-person call—at three in the morning," Ana María said, her lips pressed into a grimace—her attempt to not cry.

"And Mamá?" I asked.

"Yeah, Mamá protests, pleads with him to not wake us up. 'Lorenzo, por favor,' she begged him, 'look at the hour. How can you wake her at this hour? She needs her rest, she works. Who are you calling at this hour? Why don't you get some sleep, call later in the day . . .' Same old stuff."

"And what does he say to this?" I asked out of habit, although I already knew.

"He ignores her, as usual," Ana María said. "He has no time for a woman who cannot speak English to the operator, who cannot tell the operator that Lorenzo Sahagún—*el señor* Lorenzo Sahagún, he reminds me—wants to make a person-to-person call to Mexico City. Three o'clock in the damn morning, and I have to be at work at eight."

"Who is he calling at that time?"

"I don't know," Ana María said impatiently. "Some *licenciado* something-or-other. It doesn't matter. When he does get connected to the person, all I hear is my father explaining that no, it can't wait until later, he has a great plan for a partnership investment—crap like that. The phone call lasts less than fifteen seconds. They hang up on him and he's left sitting there with the phone in his hand, jotting down notes like some madman, like he didn't even notice that they hung up on him." Then Ana looked me straight in the face. She looked weary and fed up. Disgusted. "Just be eternally grateful you don't have to put up with his crap anymore. Just be grateful for that."

But I wasn't grateful. I felt deeply guilty, as I knew Ana María hoped I would feel. I felt as if I'd abandoned my three sisters and Mamá to Papá's anger and erratic behavior. I had left them alone, week in and week out, to stand in the middle of Papá's incomprehensible, private warpath. If he were drunk, we could blame it on that. But no, Papá was not a drinker. There was something else going on that we couldn't quite figure out. We were confused because we didn't understand Papá's war—or maybe, yes, scared because we *did* understand these phantoms waging a battle in his mind, and because we were terrified of becoming the casualties—or terrified of becoming like him.

And again I could hear the voice of the doctor at the VA hospital: "Mr. Sahagún, is there a history of schizophrenia in the family—any other brother, sister, uncle, aunt . . ."

"But Mamá seemed almost happy," I said, trying to find a nugget of good in all of this shit.

"Yeah, I'm glad about that. She's happy because he has two jobs and so he's not around that much. She'll take any little scrap of the good part of it and make the most of it, thank goodness for that."

Ana María finally let loose, like a pent-up volcano. She was sobbing, her arms resting against the sink, the dish scrubber still in her hand, and I hugged her and let her cry it out, wishing I could take all of them—Mamá, Luz, Monica, and Ana—back with me to paradise in my La Jolla dorm. It was as if Ana were begging me to stay home: "Help me, Yoli. I'm being squashed and drowned by a crazy man," while my mother was begging me to stay away. "Study, learn, and understand, Yoli." Is that what she wanted? But what kind of daughter of the revolution was I if I abandoned them? What was my revolution? And all of this—this seemingly unstoppable chaos—reminded me of the *Titanic*, of the brave people left to die. Mamá, Ana María, Luz, and Monica would stay behind because there was room on the lifeboat for just one person. As if my mother had chosen me, frantically pushing me toward the lifeboat and away from the sinking ship.

Pheasants, breeding pheasants for their tasty, dark meat. Their beautiful feathers would bring in extra cash, too. That was my father's reasoning the time he decided to raise pheasants in our backyard. I was nine and had the job of keeping my little sisters away from the backyard as my father built a large pen in which to house and let the pheasants roam. Then he went off to some farm in the back hills, as the newspaper ad instructed, to purchase his pheasants.

The pheasants made a horrible mess of poop, which my father ordered us to clean up. He even kept a weekly schedule on the refrigerator so we wouldn't forget whose day it was to pick up the pheasant poop. He wanted us to learn, he explained amid our protests, what owning a business entailed. On the kitchen table every evening during the time of the pheasants, Papá kept a notepad with numbers and figures, dollar signs scribbled here and there, and he worked on these papers deep into the night, every night. His estimation of profit, expenses. The eggs, the meat, the feathers, he must've been thinking. What a gold mine! But within a day or two of purchasing the birds, either the hens or the cocks or both—we weren't sure which—were making incredibly ugly sounds early in the morning. There was cackling, crowing, screaming, whistling—sounds that would surely drive the whole neighborhood crazy. You see, my father knew nothing about pheasants and their mating rituals; he only knew that these birds could turn a profit, so he tolerated the sounds.

I got out the *P* encyclopedia and read up on pheasants, thinking that in some small way I might help my father in his business. I was especially intrigued with the information on golden pheasants, which the encyclopedia noted adapted well to captivity and were a favorite in zoos. What we had were ring-necked pheasants, and even at the age of nine, I felt the injustice in the fact that the male pheasants had brightly colored feathers while the females had duller feathers. "It's a mating, survival thing," Carolina explained to me once as she and I sat on patio chairs near the pen observing the pheasants. Carolina was fifteen at the time but already showing signs of being a behavioral scientist. "See? The cock is the aggressor, the one who has to win his lady, so he has to be handsome. If she's going to pay any attention to him and consider mating with the dandy rooster he had better have a nice set of feathers on him."

I looked at her and then started to giggle. Carolina could be pretty funny even in the most serious of ways.

"No, I'm not kidding," she continued. "It's pretty much the same in most of the animal kingdom, I think."

One of the pheasants, pecking at the ground in search of seeds, stood near us. It was a dull female.

"If that's the case," I said, now tossing the handful of seeds to the poor uninteresting female, even though I'd been saving them for one of the pretty feathered cocks, "why do human females get all dolled up? Why do ladies put on makeup and lipstick, like they're trying to put on pretty feathers?"

The hen was gratefully pecking away at the seeds and had soon consumed all of them.

Carolina stared at me a moment, seemingly at a loss for words.

"You know, Yoli, you're just nine years old and although that's a pretty interesting question, I think it's best just to keep your eyes on the poop since it's your turn to clean up today. And just remember, before you ask any more of your questions, I'm only fifteen years old. I don't know it all—yet."

And little by little, as the weeks passed and you could count the months—two, three, four—I noticed there were fewer papers and notes with jottings and dollar amounts scattered on the kitchen table. I had gotten used to seeing my father sitting at the kitchen table after the dinner dishes were cleared and washed, his briefcase opened, displaying an assortment of pens and pencils, notepads, a calculator. When I couldn't fall asleep easily (as was so often the case) it was reassuring to see the kitchen light still on late into the night, to hear a cough or the movement of the chair as my father pulled up closer to the table, attended to business in the kitchen.

But it seemed there wasn't a market for pheasants. Nobody was in a hurry to buy tasty pheasant meat, nor pheasant eggs—even the feathers didn't do well, my father finally donating a bag full of the brilliant green, golden, and red cock feathers to a Boy Scout who came by to ask for them for a project his troop was making. And then one morning, very early, the pheasant screeching must have woke my father up once again, and this time he marched outside, tired from lack of sleep, annoyed as hell, and grabbed the noisy cock, twisting its neck in one clean break. And then another and another.

What I remember the most of that final day of the time of the pheasants is the stony, emotionless look on my father's face as he sat on the ground surrounded by twenty broken-necked pheasants. That look in his eyes as he sat motionless, staring straight ahead of him, in a temporary stupor while my mother scrambled to collect and place the lovely feathered birds with their dangling broken necks in a trash bag. The hellish sounds had not only disturbed my father's sleep, you see, but mine, too. And now I stood at the back door window, staring not so much at the horror of the feathered carcasses scattered over the whole backyard, nor at my mother who worked quickly and expeditiously before we children awoke and saw our father's massacre, but at my father. The horror of recognizing the look in his ocean blue eyes that spoke of unfathomable depths of despair and defeat, the fear I felt as a nine-year-old favorite daughter seeing that in her *papi*.

Six

Anthropology, general literature, biology, and college composition—I took my classes seriously; I took notes with the flair of a diligent A student. My part-time work study job at the Central Library kept me busy between classes. Afterward, I rushed off to my room and, checking the time on my watch, quickly turned on the little TV my brother Armando bought me as a high school graduation gift. I settled down on my bed to watch another installment of *Corazón Salvaje*, the classic Mexican soap opera based on the novel of the same name. Juan del Diablo was incorrigible, and although I knew he would ultimately win over Monica the nun (I had read the novel a few years back), I was fascinated by his courtship technique.

Don't get me wrong. I studied diligently every evening, way into the night. I was up to date on all my assigned readings, term papers, and chapter notes. I made the dean's list in the winter quarter, and I was confident I'd make the list again this spring quarter—a perfect finale to my first year in college. This was the only luxury I allowed myself: thirty minutes with the tormented lovers, Juan del Diablo and Monica. I was not one to sit around all afternoon watching soaps, but this particular one had begun in early summer, and because I had already read the three-volume novel, it was too tempting not to snuggle up on the couch next to Mamá and Ana María and watch Juan del Diablo win over the beautiful, mesmerizing religious novice, played by the ever-popular blue-eyed Angélica María. Who would win her for his bride—Juan del Diablo or God?

It was how he got her that was so interesting. Ha! Wasn't that true of all relationships? Take, for example, my present sweetheart, Ernesto. Handsome, kind, gentle, and patient—very, very patient. I cannot stress enough how patient he was with me, understanding we young Catholic women had demons and angels warring in our minds, the battlefield heavy with the conflicting smoldering smoke of guilt and lust.

I can't help it. I don't want to. I want to be loved. I want to be held—oh, ever so tightly! I want him to kiss my cheeks, my forehead—and I want him to feel the warmth of my lips, the moistness, the desire that is making me dizzy. Yes, I feel dizzy. I feel blind. I see but I cannot focus my eyes on any one object—oh, I don't want to! I like it like this. I can only feel—only feel—and that is all I want. My head is groggy—my whole mind is! And I love every minute of it. I feel I'm being carried away by things that should not carry me away; I feel I'm thinking things that I should not think. I feel I like these things—oh, I feel! It's not sensible; it's not simple. No. It's very complicated and confusing—and I don't care. It makes me feel different from what I usually am. It's a wonderful feeling. I'm out of my own control; I'm out of my own senses—I'm out of my head and I love it. I can see my head rolling farther and farther away from me. I smile groggily, for I can no longer see it. It has vanished and I don't care. I don't want to see it. My eyes are droopy. Hold me! Hold me, for I want to feel, not see! I, who am blind with yearnings.

No, this wasn't an entry in my diary. I had written these words last year on a hot April day, dry and silent and lethargic. Ms. Tagore had turned off the lights and asked us to close our eyes for a few minutes, then open them and begin writing whatever thoughts came into our minds, an exercise in stream of consciousness. At the time, all I could think of were the mysteries of sexual yearnings and passion. I said to myself, go for it, Yoli, just do it, and lo and behold these sensual, horny musings are what rushed out of my subconscious.

I don't know why, but when I wrote this little piece that last year in high school, I felt the courage, I felt bold—yes, that's the word—bold enough to start proclaiming some of my hidden, diarylike feelings to the public, or at least to an appreciative audience (in this case, my lovely, sophisticated English teacher, Ms. Tagore). I was upping the ante, no longer the young and fragile adolescent who began each year's diary with an all-in-caps warning: SO HELP ME, IF ANY ONE OF MY SISTERS IS READING THIS, AND I FIND OUT—AND BELIEVE YOU ME, I WILL FIND OUT—I WILL KILL MYSELF AND YOU WILL

LIVE WITH THAT FOR THE REST OF YOUR MISERABLE LIFE,
FOREVER AND EVER, AMEN!!

This "Yearnings" piece—I was sure my sister Carolina, our resident
Ms. Freudiana, would agree—was a kind of subconscious civil liberties
proclamation, my way, perhaps, of joining the ranks of the women's
movement and the sexual revolution. Still, I never showed the piece to
my family (I might be bold, but I wasn't stupid), fearing that were my
parents or brothers—maybe even my sisters—to read this piece I would
spend the rest of my life condemned to pray the rosary five times a day,
with an extra ten Our Fathers and twenty Hail Marys and fifty Acts of
Contrition thrown in for good measure. In other words, another Scarlet
Letter story, except that my letter Y (for "Yearning Yoli") would be
made of sarape fabric, a brightly colored pattern of stripes in turquoise
blues, forest greens, sunflower yellows, and rosa mexicana. Pinned to
my bosom, the bright, striped letter would be flapping coquettishly, teas-
ingly in the breeze, in defiance of my lifelong penitence. Yes, my lovely
sarape fabric Y would be an improvement on poor Hester Prynne's
boring scarlet letter.

That was last year. Now that I was in college, living in the dorms,
much as I liked the kissing and groping and touching, my boyfriend was
a bore, and I'd just broken up with him.

"He's about as perfect a man as you will ever find," Lydia said to me
that weekend. We were sitting on the front porch of my house, our legs
propped over the porch railing, absentmindedly looking out at the freeway across the Kastlungers' field. We were trying to shake our lethargy
long enough to walk over to Brown's Market for a couple of bottles of
cold soda. "Black Magic Woman" was playing on the radio.

Lydia had been my best friend since junior high. Somehow, amid
the arguing and stomping off in opposite directions in a huff that often
happened between best friends, we'd been able to weather many storms
in our friendship. I figured Lydia was my Jiminy Cricket conscience.

"You better not let him get away, or you'll really prove you're a
pendeja." She was wearing her usual frayed denim overalls, which she
always wore with pretty feminine blouses—a delicate floral with long

sleeves, or a white starched blouse with a lace collar, or soft sheer pastels—to balance, she once explained, the rough Farmer John look of the overalls. She insisted her choice of clothing made an arresting, schizophrenic fashion statement—guaranteed to *descontrolar*, to confound the most discriminate fashion stylist, certain to intrigue the guys. I loved her anyway, this dear friend of mine.

We finally managed to get our weary, lazy bodies up and out onto Conifer Street, headed the two blocks to our neighborhood market. It was so hot that both of us had decided nothing would do but to have our hair up in goofy pigtails—no matter whom we might run into.

I didn't say anything. Instead, I wondered dreamily if I had what it took to be a black magic woman.

"He treats you like a queen and puts up with your moods. I know of at least five other women who would like to steal him away from you, but they know he's crazy in love with you, tonta."

"Maybe that's the problem," I said, now looking closely at Lydia. "Maybe he's too crazy in love with me."

She shook her head, warned me that I'd be asking for it. What did I want, some macho man who would beat me up now and then? Or maybe I wanted the kind of guy who played games with me, screwing with my mind?

"I don't know what I want," I said.

"Well, then you *are* a pendeja," she said.

We walked into Brown's Market, said hi to Mrs. Brown, silently regretful that one of her cute sons wasn't working the cash register. Why was it they always seemed to be working when one of us younger sisters was hysterically ordered by my two older sisters to make an emergency run to Brown's for Kotex? We got a bottle each from the cooler and placed them on the counter as we dug in our pockets for money. The family's fine, thank you, we said to Mrs. Brown as she returned us the change. Then we walked back out into the heat.

"It's just that he's so nice," I explained to her. "And patient. He's not exciting anymore. I mean the whole relationship with him isn't exciting. I have him now; he's in love with me, y qué? There's gotta be more to it than just the chase, and yet when I come to the end of the chase, it's so boring."

"Yoli, open your eyes, man. He's got a beautiful physique; he's handsome and strong and very macho looking without all the shit that comes with it. *Híjole*, Yoli, what more can you ask for?"

"Juan del Diablo," I said.

"What?" she said. "Who?"

"Juan del Diablo. I want him to be Juan del Diablo and me his black magic woman."

✿ ✿ ✿

My roommate and I were getting ready for the party at Black's Beach. She was quite the social butterfly, it seemed, used to organizing these things up in the Bay Area where she was from. Like Lydia, her best friend opted out of coming to UCSD, so she and I, initial strangers to each other, were assigned to be roommates. She was a nice enough girl with long brown hair that she wore in a homey, Mother Nature kind of braid. I was relieved to see her taping posters with Thoreau and Emerson quotes. She loved my *Abraxas* poster. After that, I figured we'd do just fine as roommates, although she wasted no time in taking off to make friends on campus and was rarely around the dorms. She was always inviting me to join her new group of friends, but I'd been hesitant, preferring, when I wasn't in class or working at the circulation desk, to spend the time studying on the seventh floor—the Library of Congress *P*s of language and literature. Had this party been planned on a weekend, I certainly wouldn't have been going, my weekends being my time to scoot back home as quickly as I could. My roommate planned this party on a Thursday to make sure I would come.

Within a few minutes, we were walking across the street from campus with bags in tow. The beach was not far, but we had a bit of a trek down a steep path. Our straw bags were packed and bulging with towels, flashlights, and chips and sodas, and I was looking forward to this party because I hadn't yet been out to the famous Black's Beach.

It was twilight, just enough light to get us to the beach. As soon as we turned right onto the residential street I could practically hear myself gasp. The houses were stunning. Magnificent. Huge estates, one after another. I slowed down to gawk at each one, take it all in: the expansive lawns, circular driveways, four- and five-car garages, walls draped with thick bougainvillea vines, gardens so immaculate and orderly and colorful it made me feel I was on a Hollywood movie set. Once more Dorothy was opening the door of her black and white world and stepping into the colorful land of the Munchkins.

"Hurry," my roommate said.

I looked at her a moment, blinked a few times, trying to get my bearings, remember where I was.

She, of course, wouldn't be impressed with all of this, having come from the wealthy suburb of Hillsborough where mansions were plentiful.

I picked up my pace to catch up with her. She was already ducking under the closed bar that extended like an arm the length of the path, the city's way of informing the public that the path and the beach were closed for the night. I followed suit, ducking under the pole as we made our way down the steep incline to the beach.

It felt spooky, I'd admit that. The more audible the sounds of the waves crashing, the more it felt as if there were some invisible force beckoning us to follow the sound, leading us down the canyon into the dark grooves and ridges and caves of this formidable, secluded beach I'd been hearing so much about lately. Like maybe I was entering a haunted forest.

When my roommate mentioned to me, back at the beginning of the school quarter, that Black's Beach was a legal nudist beach—that meant you could walk around the beach, secluded as it was because of the cliffs, naked—I tried not to show my shock. I should've known this, shouldn't I have? I was the native San Diegan; she wasn't. But somehow this bit of San Diego info had never made it to my cozy confines in Palm City. And now, as we were making our way to the beach, I was praying that nobody was going to get naked, or if they did, I was hoping it would be too dark to see anything.

The neat thing about this beach, she was telling me, was that it was so secluded you had privacy for a whole lot of stuff.

I was about to ask her what she meant by that—sex? Suicide?—when our conversation was interrupted.

Hey, we're over here, someone called out to us.

And soon we were setting up camp, extending our towels on the soft sand, handing each other bottles of soda or beer. I accepted a soda and then plopped myself down on the towel, the initial introductions over with. There were about ten people in the group and I was relieved to notice they were all clothed.

I opened a bag of chips and passed it around to the group.

"Hey, we have brownies, people," someone said. "Oooh-wee, let's have us some fun already."

Someone's portable radio was on and—no kidding—Elton John was that very moment singing his new song "Goodbye Yellow Brick Road." (And Lydia wondered why I constantly found symbolism in my life. It was everywhere, tonta, I told her. Around the corner, in your closet, on the train tracks, amid the sweet peas, at the beach, under the freeway, on the radio.)

It was dark now and someone had finally gotten the fire ring started, the planks of wood tossed in for a bonfire. We were all sitting around in a circle. Good-looking surfer-type guys with blond hair, and pretty, perfect-looking girls with straight hair down to their butts, wearing skimpy cut-off shorts and halter tops or baby doll blouses in colorful paisley patterns. I was the only one in jeans and a little sweater top (for the cool evening breeze), and feeling—compared to these people—dorky.

One guy was talking about his spring break plans. His parents were forcing him to go on a family ski trip to the Swiss Alps, and he was bummed because he'd rather go to San Felipe like most everyone else. But then it seemed the others had similar complaints: the family's week-end cabin in Aspen; a father-son hiking trip on the Incan trail in Peru; a New York trip because her mother can't be away for too long from "Bloomies" and her much-adored Bergdorf Goodman.

I was quiet in all of this conversation, stunned by what they were saying so nonchalantly, and I was also trying to figure out whether the mother was having an affair and why this girl wasn't disgusted or something. Was Bloomies the restaurant where her mother met up with this Goodman guy? Why wasn't this daughter outraged?

"The good thing about it is," she added, "it's a nice little shopping spree for me, too."

Ah, so her mother bribed her with shopping sprees.

Now someone directed the question to me: what was I doing during spring break?

"I'll be staying in Palm City," I said.

Oh, wow, someone said in the darkness, wasn't that in Palm Springs? Palm Springs was really cool during spring break.

Someone piped in, saying he'd never heard of Palm City, and before I could open my mouth and explain, another girl interrupted and corrected him: No, she believed it was on the island of Kauai. Quite a paradise.

And I felt my face grow warm thinking of the effort it would take to try to explain Palm City. What should I say to these people? Should I tell them my spring break was going to be spent in a barrio of mainly poor Mexicans with a few immigrant Germans, Poles, and Swiss sprinkled about? Should I tell them I lived in a modest—no, I wouldn't say ramshackle—house with a bedroom I'd shared my whole life with four other sisters? Should I mention that we only had one bathroom for the eleven of us? They would never in a million years understand.

So instead I said, "It's kind of an off-the-beaten-path resort on the Pacific Ocean. Only a few families have vacation homes there, and we all fly there during vacations, you know, spring break, summer, winter."

My roommate winked at me and smiled approvingly. (After all, don't forget, she did have sensitive, egalitarian Thoreau quotes on her walls.)

"Yes," I said, smiling and feeling emboldened by her approval, "Palm City's my little bit of paradise."

Then before I could even get the words "Oh shit!" out, a little handmade cigarette in white rolled paper—a joint—was being passed around. I froze, absolutely terrified and panicky. This was my first time at a pot party—is that what this was?—and if I thought my high school

"Yearnings" essay would earn me a condemnatory letter *Y* pinned to my bosom, you could imagine what I thought being at a pot party would get me: yes, a lifetime sentence at Alcatraz with ne'er a gentle little birdfriend anywhere near my prison window.

As I was trying to untangle my folded legs to get up, the joint was passed to me. I stared at it until the guy next to me reached for it and showed me how to take a deep drag and hold my breath a few moments. Then he passed it back to me and I tried it, did exactly what he said, though my hands were trembling as I took my virgin toke. The smoke burned my throat, and immediately I felt parched and dry. I coughed and sputtered, reached for my bottle of soda for relief. A few people chuckled, but nobody was paying too much attention to me as each eagerly waited to take a turn for an expert drag of the joint.

But already I could feel a buzz in my brain, like when I drank two cups of black coffee to pull an all-nighter for the paper due the next day—only this buzz felt different, like an out-of-body experience, as if I were some ghost hovering over this campfire, watching these college kids, feeling detached from this group. And this terrified me and made me sad at the same time, and I was thinking that maybe Elton John was right, and I should have just stayed on the farm, forgot all this highfalutin university stuff because this was not my world and never would be my world, just go back to my plough, and when they passed me the joint again, I took it, looked at it a moment, and then passed it on because I was thinking that my future lay beyond the yellow brick road, and then I felt like crying and laughing and I didn't know why.

It didn't take me long to gather my few things, stuff them in my basket, and excuse myself from my roommate. Terrible case of cramps, just started, no Kotex or tampon with me. Gotta go, but this sure was fun. (I hated to do this, use my pretend-you're-on-your-period excuse, but it did come in handy now and then to get me out of uncomfortable situations.)

My roommate seemed a little worried, bless her. She wondered if I'd be okay going back up the path in the dark alone. I showed her the flashlight we both packed. I'll be all right, I reassured her, waving her concerns away. Extra-strength Midol is what I need, I whispered confidentially, as if I were in a commercial.

I made my way back up the hill as everyone waved bye-bye and blew silly, drunken kisses in the air. Lots of nonsensical giggles. For a moment, as I looked at the blackness awaiting me, I was tempted to make an about-face and stay at the party and risk being locked up in a penitentiary.

I had the flashlight on, lighting my way up the dark path. The crashing waves sounded like they were coming after me, and I was afraid if I looked back I might turn to salt or something, that the evil that hid in the shrubs, in the darkness, in the cliffs, would envelop me and claim me for its own. And wouldn't you know it, I mumbled the guardian angel prayer, " . . . Ever this day be at my side to light and guard, to rule and guide. Amen," about twenty times before I made it to the top. I was panting and out of breath and trembling because of the what? Steep incline? Snakes on the road? An angry attack dog? What if I had taken one more drag of the joint, what if it had taken me over the edge? "Mr. Sahagún, is there anyone else in your family . . . ?" What if the pot made me crazy like my father? Like my brother? What if I was genetically predisposed? Then what?

Now that I was at the top amid the mansions, I felt a little safer, relieved, though I was gasping for air. Had I run up the hill? I didn't remember. There was a sprinkling of lights in the yards and long driveways, which helped guide me to the main road and over to the campus. To keep me calm and unafraid, I studied each mansion, trying to decide which one I liked best, which one I would choose to live in. The houses were a way back or hidden by walls and well-placed shrubs, and it was hard to get a good look at each house in the dark, but then I spotted one house brightly lighted inside and its curtains not yet drawn.

I stopped to look at it from my spot on the street, wishing I had binoculars so that I could get a good view of the furnishings inside. I felt like I was looking at a live and in color beautiful houses magazine; I felt like a gentle, harmless Peeping Tom who only wondered how other people lived in luxury, who wanted to understand what made a family functional, what kind of things constituted the right ingredients for a happy home. And as I stood there watching the house, I saw a woman come into the room and sit down on a cushiony-looking winged armchair—Queen Anne, perhaps?—next to the huge bay window with its French panes. I shifted my position a little, edging closer to the driveway for a better view of the scene inside. This was the window square glimpse I got: She was alone in the living room or den, a book on her lap, her hands folded on top of it. She was staring across at the fireplace. From what I could see, the woman looked pretty, in her thirties maybe. She was wearing a long-sleeved shirt and slacks, a smart sweater vest. Her hair was a golden blonde, straight and simple, down to her shoulders, feminine and snappy at the same time. Maybe she was the wife of a professor or a research scientist; perhaps she was the president of an important women's charity organization. She seemed to be absentmindedly staring at nothing in particular in front of her. What did it feel like to live in a house like that? To have that kind of luxury? Was she happy? Lonely? Angry? Annoyed with the maid who forgot to buy her favorite brand of yogurt? Was she thinking that she needed to hire a new gardener? Was her daughter improving in her piano lessons? Was her son skillful enough to make the advanced hockey team? Would it be takeout for tomorrow's dinner again? Why had her husband been coming home late from work all this week? Were they a normal family?

Then she started crying, just like that. I was sure that's what she was doing. She had her hands covering her face, and her whole body was moving as if she were sobbing convulsively. I felt like I was watching a silent movie and I had to fill in the blanks with dialogue and sound. I felt immensely terrified for her and for me; I felt like I should run up the driveway and knock on the door and hold her, let her cry it out on my shoulder. "Oh, please, ma'am, it can't be that bad," I wanted to tell her, patting her back reassuringly. "Look at this beautiful house you have. How can you be so unhappy in such a beautiful home?" But then I told myself, that's stupid, Yoli, maybe some tragic thing happened in her life—a car accident, a death in the family. Maybe her husband was erratic and moody; maybe he terrified her and the kids all the time. Maybe she had some good reason to cry—after all, even wealthy people had sadness, too, didn't they? Couldn't they also have insane members in their families? And what if you did run up to her front door in an effort to console her, and she looked at you as if you were some kind of Peeping Tom criminal? What if just as you said, "Please, ma'am, don't cry. I understand exactly how you're feeling," she were to slam the door in your face and call the police on you? Don't be stupid, Yoli, you can't enter this stranger's life just like that and think you'll make everything okay. What did you know of her tears?

And for no good reason that I could think of, I felt afraid for my family and me.

Seven

Okay, I'll confess: I tried the Catholic students' Newman Center only once at the beginning of the school year, for Mass and a little social afterward. But I might as well have been back at the pot party discussing spring break plans. It was the same kind of people, really. They were some nice, quiet ones. Then there were the others, the students who had taken years of Latin de rigueur in junior high and high school and were discussing, at the ice cream social that evening, the merits of this dead language in Mass. There were those who applauded the English version of Mass, but the more vocal yearned for the days of Latin Mass, an intrinsically important and lovely—their words, not mine—reminder of Catholicism's roots. One guy, the most vehement pro-Latin one, every now and then sprinkled his discussion with some *ominus pluribus* gobbledy-gook. Show off twerp that he was. And the priest was nice enough—young, peppy, lively—and didn't look anything like our white-haired Father Stadler at St. Charles Church. No, this priest was young and alert and just as ominus pluribus intelligent as the next guy, though he argued in favor of Mass being in a language that the people could understand. Ten points for him.

I don't mean to be disrespectful, but I just didn't fit. It was not the kind of Catholicism I was used to—we were definitely speaking different languages. Yes, I knew the rosary upside-down in Spanish and English (sorry, twerp, not in Latin), but still, the discussion felt too intellectual and distant and clinical. And the priest? Well, he was trying hard to be everybody's buddy or brother—and being used to the likes of our patriarchal Father Stadler, it just didn't feel Catholic enough to me.

Or maybe that was just an excuse. Maybe I was rejecting the Newman Center because I was getting ready for something else, preparing myself for a grander, more global view of the world. Whatever the case might be, it didn't take long for me to find something on campus akin to home.

❈ ❈ ❈

"I'm a Chicana," I announced to my mother and father one weekend near the end of my first year in college.

"You're a what?" my father said, pausing in his chewing.

We were in the kitchen. I was heating some tortillas while Mamá served him a glass of milk. He was sitting at the kitchen table and immediately set his rolled-up, half-eaten tortilla on the table to give me his undivided attention.

"*You* are Mexicans," I said pointing to one then the other with my authoritarian, know-it-all finger, "but I'm a Chicana."

"What do you mean you're a Chicana?" my father said. "No, Yolanda, you are *not* a Chicana; you're a Mexican, the daughter of Mexican parents. I've heard about those *disque* 'Chicanos'—a bunch of rabble-rouser *politiquillos*. People who don't know what they are, so they make up some word that sounds like 'chicanery'—*una chicanada*. Do you have any idea what that word means?" I could tell my father was trying to be reasonable, though his face was already turning red as he picked up his tortilla and then put it back down and then picked it up again, his rolled tortilla getting colder by the second. "A 'chicanada' is a trick, a deception . . ."

"Maybe to you," I said, "but to me the word 'Chicano' comes from the Meshica Indians, from the word 'Meshicanos,' or 'Mexicans' . . ."

"Ah, so you're saying that you, with your blue eyes and white skin, are part of the Meshica tribe," he said, now chuckling. "*Vaya*, a little *indita* in our family."

My mother said nothing. She looked at me with that look that I'd come to recognize, the look that said, *no le des cuerda*—don't wind him up. Leave it alone, Yoli.

I ignored her look.

"You have something against our Indian blood?" I said to my father, now turning from the stove to face him full on. "Are you ashamed of our Indian heritage? Are you one of those Mexicans who say they only have 'Spanish' blood because they don't want to be associated with their Indian heritage? Is that it, Señor Blue Eyes, eh? Ashamed of your mestizo heritage, are you?"

"What the devil are you talking . . ."

And before he could finish, I stormed out of the kitchen in a righteous rage.

❀ ❀ ❀

"Boy, Yoli, are you an idiot or something?" Carolina said to me on the phone later that evening.

"You know, Carolina, I called you because I thought you'd understand. If I recall correctly," I said to her, "there was a time when you were quite the righteous Chicana yourself."

"Yes, and as I recall," my oldest sister said, "you were quite the cynic about my revolutionary politics, not unlike—what did you call him?— Señor Blue Eyes." And she started laughing, and couldn't stop, and I could hear her husband Tom in the background asking her what was so funny, but Carolina, our Righteous-Chicana-Turned-Miss-Psychologist, couldn't stop laughing long enough to explain her vindicated joy.

When she finally did calm down, she tried to be serious in her advice to me, though I could hear the smile behind her words: "Yoli, don't be a tonta. The last people you want to be talking revolutionary politics with are our parents," she said. "No, Yoli, keep your politics on campus."

❀ ❀ ❀

There was a world beyond my home that continually had my eyes bugging out and mouth agape in disbelief. A world of zany intellectuals that I yearned to be a part of. There was, for example, the young professor who, just as he began his fifty-minute lecture, had the habit of jumping on the desk in the big lecture hall of two hundred plus students, now squatting on the table, puffing on one cigarette after another as he discussed the theme of Death—with a capital D—as seen in the books he selected for the course: *Death in Venice*, *The Death of Ivan Ilych*, talking about this "fucked up character" or that "absofuckinglutely wonderful protagonist." I felt breathless and excited every time I walked out of the class, and I remembered the times I used to cuss as a teenager, Lydia and I thinking we were hot stuff and so radical to be using words like "*cabrona*" and "pendeja" and "*pinche*." But here was this brilliant professor giving the word "fuck" a whole new intellectual dimension. And that was only my general literature class. Who knew that the word "*chingar*" had so many meanings? Ay, *madresita*, what was a simple, humble Chicanita to think of all of this? Leave it to the world of the Mexican protagonist—or is he an antagonist?—Artemio Cruz to have introduced me to the multiple meanings of a single word. ¡Qué chingón!

El Movimiento Estudiantil de los Chicanos de Aztlán. Yes, you heard right: also known as MEChA, I was a new recruit of this student group. I was hungry for enlightenment, for knowledge and for a view of the world beyond the sheltered perimeters of my Palm City. I wanted to see the world with new eyes, but I wanted to see it with people who came from a place like mine. And without MEChA, I sensed I would be too lonely and alienated to see the light.

I was at the entrance to the Safeway Market in La Jolla, a stack of flyers in my hand, passing them out to customers as they walked in, politely asking them to boycott grapes and head lettuce. I felt incredibly self-conscious and timid about this. Most of the customers grumbled something, looked the other way. One man shook his head and called us, my partner and me, "a bunch of communists who don't know their ass from a hole in the ground." And as humiliating as this comment was (yikes, he was talking about me!), I couldn't help but appreciate the imagery of his insult.

As a Mother's Day gift, I bought tickets to a play on campus, something called A Doll's House.

Carla, the president of MEChA, told me she'd seen it last weekend and felt that every woman should see it. When I asked her what it was about, she said it was a cautionary tale for women. Progressive and revolutionary. A clear and accurate depiction of the subjugation of women.

Huh?

So I tried again. "Do you think my mother would like it?" I asked.

"Like it? I don't know if anybody really *likes* a cautionary tale, but I think every mother, wife, and sister should see it . . ." she said with the cryptic air of one who is wise beyond her age.

Now that I knew my mother spoke and understood more English than I had thought (remember the tea party?), I didn't feel hesitant about asking her to go. Nevertheless ("nevertheless" being my latest favorite word I employed in all my class essays), I invited her in a nonchalant, no-big-deal way in case she didn't really want to go. So, in passing, all I said was that there was this play on campus, maybe she'd like to go, but if not, that's okay, we could do something else . . . And before I could finish the sentence she was saying, "Sí, qué linda idea." Gee, not only did she say yes, but she actually thought it a lovely idea. How little I knew my mother!

I bought two tickets for the weekend before Mother's Day, my sisters opting out. Then I got hold of a copy of the play—apparently it was required reading in some literature classes, considered a classic, and so easily available at most bookstores. I read it the night before so that I could tell her the plot as we drove to UCSD. But after reading it, when I closed the book and turned out the light, I was feeling kind of weird, like maybe this wasn't such a good idea, this play for my mother. An uncomfortable feeling swept over me and made me feel nervous and wary, and I wasn't sure why.

She wore the beige brocade dress and matching jacket and a pair of beige pumps. The familiar patent leather handbag was hanging from her arm, ready to be taken out for the evening.

And I was flattered by her choice of attire.

So for fun and to get into the spirit of this theater outing with Mamá, I decided to wear the forest green polyester pantsuit I had worn to the DAR event.

As we headed off onto the freeway, I sensed my mother had grown more confident of my driving because she wasn't clutching the door handle or anything like that, although she was purposely quiet the whole way up to UCSD—her way of letting me know that I needed to concentrate on my driving and not get distracted with chatter.

Once there, we quickly found our seats, great seats, just three rows from the stage. The audience, I noticed, was made up of mainly fellow college students, but that was okay. My mother didn't seem to notice as she sat quietly, hands folded on her purse over her lap, waiting with happy anticipation—I could tell from her smile as she stared at the black velvet curtain—for the lights to dim and the action to begin.

Then there was that scene at the end of the play when Nora was talking to her patronizing, selfish husband, pretty much telling him off, realizing what a twerp he was, realizing he was not the man she had thought. It was a powerful scene. Her epiphany: realizing he has been treating her like a doll in a dollhouse. I glanced over at my mother to see how she was reacting, wondering what she was thinking. My mother looked, simply put, totally spellbound, leaning forward, her eyes fixed on the scene before her, as if she were memorizing every single word of Nora's proclamation, memorizing it so that when the opportunity arose, say, when Papá was on the warpath, she could recite the very same words to my father. Or maybe that was what I was hoping she'd do.

That brought up a whole bunch of other questions: Was my father like Torvald? Had he treated my mother like some featherbrained dimwit? A furry little animal? His little squirrel? Or was this just another instance of me insisting that the fictional characters mirror real personages in my life? Was this just another way of me finding symbolism and messages in my life?

No matter. Mamá seemed to have really enjoyed the play.

When it was over, we all stood up to applaud with a well-earned standing ovation. Mamá was beaming with excitement, or determination, or with something.

On the way home, I asked Mamá what she thought of the play, about Nora leaving her children and husband like that, knowing, even as I asked it, that since my mother was a devout Mexican Catholic woman, which was like having a triple dose of religion: one, Catholic; two, Mexican; and three, woman, she would no doubt disapprove of Nora's actions.

She didn't say anything at first, as if she were considering the question, and this in itself surprised me. Was she trying to find just the right words—words that weren't incriminating or too revealing, but still honest? I mean, what did I expect her to say, good Catholic mother that she was? Yet with nine children, poverty, and an erratic, tempestuous husband, what was the only possible answer?

We were nearing downtown with its cluster of bright lights. The historic El Cortez Hotel where I had my senior prom stood apart from the other buildings. And then we passed the lights, the big city, heading south past the San Diego–Coronado Bay Bridge, which always instilled in me awe or pride or something. Maybe even some unexplainable nostalgia of days past.

"We live in different worlds, Yoli," my mother finally said.

I glanced at her, at her profile, the round face, but I couldn't read her.

And as if she sensed it, that I couldn't read her, she explained: "Me. Nora. You, too, Yoli," she said, now turning to look at me. "I'm so proud of you, going to college, learning things I never learned, meeting interesting and intelligent people. You are a part of another world, *mi'ja*," she said, smiling, gesturing with a nod ahead at the road. "You are going to go places I never went. I can see that already. All I ask," and here she looked earnestly at me, as if she wanted to be sure I memorized this request, "is that you not forget where you come from and that you respect your childhood home. You never know when you might want to return, looking for a familiar, loving face."

That's all she said, and I had the good sense to leave it alone. To take what she offered and not get greedy or pushy, lest she regret having told me this much.

Just as we pulled up to the front of our house, I remembered the comment she had made about my having everything to do with the American Revolution. Ask her. Do it, Yoli, now, before she gets out of the car. Hurry, she's reaching for the door handle.

But I didn't ask her. I felt timid and self-conscious. It would come out, one petal at a time, I said to myself. Maybe tomorrow or the next day. A month from now. Then I'd ask her for more. In the meantime, I could think about it and formulate my own ideas, look for a worthy cause. Yes, plan my own mission as a revolutionary Chicana daughter.

Not until we had walked inside the house did I realize that she never answered my question about Nora's decision.

"*Buenas noches*, Yoli," she said, kissing my forehead before walking into the bedroom for the night.

And not until later, restless in bed, turning this way and that, did it occur to me that yes, maybe my mother had answered my question.

Eight

When I drove up to Chuy's trailer park space in Imperial Beach, I noticed that both he and my brother Octavio—the confirmed bachelor of the family—were on the patio discussing something. Octavio lived in the same trailer park, just a few doors from Chuy, and in that unassuming, selfless way that brothers and sisters have when they are unconditionally loyal and devoted to each other, he kept an eye on Chuy, making sure he was taking his meds, makings sure he was eating well.

I was here to drop off a Tupperware full of *chiles rellenos* and rice that my mother had sent them, and also to remind them that they needed to come by on Saturday evening, while my mother was shopping with Carolina, to deliver her surprise Mother's Day gift. As I drove into the parking space, I noticed they were both holding caulking guns.

I got out of the car, hugged each one, handed Chuy the care package.

"What are you guys doing?" I asked.

"It's for his windows," Octavio explained as Chuy walked up the steps into his trailer to put the Tupperware away. "It's for the ghosts. They come every night and Chuy's had it with them, wants them to leave him alone. We're caulking the windows shut so they can't get in." Then he checked his gun and moved back over to one of the windows to continue where he'd left off.

"The war's not over, Yoli," Chuy said, walking back out with a new tube of caulking. "It just takes another form."

I watched as he carefully, steadily applied a thick white line of caulking to the exterior of his front window.

I nodded. After all, who was I to question his ghosts and his war?

❖ ❖ ❖

The plan was to have Carolina drive our mother to the shopping center Saturday evening the day before Mother's Day, keep her away from the house long enough for Octavio, Chuy, and my father to assemble the beautiful pink quarry stone fountain in the backyard. As it turned out, Octavio couldn't stay long. He had to go in to work that night after all. He dropped Chuy off at the house, and my father said it was no problem; he and Chuy could put the fountain up together, with the help of Ana and me.

In many ways, the assembling of the fountain turned out to be like assembling a puzzle. At least that was what it seemed like to me as I observed the pile of multishaped stones, each stone having a specific spot on the fountain. Since the fountain did not come with instructions, it was up to us to figure out where the stones went. Papá instructed us to make piles of similarly shaped stones, and once that was done we'd build the fountain, making sure every stone was in its proper place before cementing it. Ana and I immediately got to work lugging the heavy bricklike stones to make piles. Chuy, in the meantime, remained planted in the same spot, watching our father, hesitating, considering, as if he wasn't sure this was a good idea.

"Get going, get going," Papá ordered Chuy. "We haven't got all night." And it occurred to me that Papá was always like this with Chuy, impatient and dismissive of Chuy's mood. He refused to believe there was something wrong with him.

Papá went to the garage for a bucket in which to put the cement mixture. Soon Ana and I had set the base, a neat circle of pink stone. When I glanced over at what Chuy was doing, I noticed he had seated himself next to a pile of the stones and was slowly and methodically applying a white line of caulking to the edges of each stone, like when you outline the object in a coloring book before filling it in.

"Chuy," I said in a whisper, quickly getting up, glancing over at our father who was in the garage preparing the cement.

Just then the phone rang inside.

"Can you get that, Yoli?" Ana said, laden as she was with four heavy bricks.

I hesitated, still looking at Chuy, but the insistent ringing phone finally won.

I ran in to pick it up.

It was somebody for Monica, one of her girlfriends wanting to know if Monica could go to Farrell's Ice Cream Parlor with her tomorrow. She knew it was Mother's Day and all, but maybe she could go for a little while. I explained to her that after breakfast we girls were taking my mother to Balboa Park, so she probably wouldn't be able make it, but I'd tell her that she . . .

"Yoli! Yoli!" I heard Ana screaming.

I dropped the phone and ran out.

They were staring at each other, Chuy and my father, in a standoff posture, my father crouched, ready to pounce on Chuy while Chuy stood at attention, looking beyond, standing very still, as if he were listening for the sound of enemy footsteps. My father had a shovel in his hand and now raised it like a spear, threatening to attack Chuy with it. Chuy had the caulking gun in his hand.

"Put that shovel down, Papá," Ana was shouting and crying at the same time.

"What the devil do you think you're doing?" my father shouted at Chuy. "Are you stupid or something? You don't use caulking for this."

"No, I'm not stupid, Papá," Chuy said calmly, too calmly. And I knew that voice, knew when it had gone into automatic pilot like some robot voice that temporarily belonged to someone else. A kind of defense mechanism. "You're the stupid one," he said in a monotone, controlled, artificial voice.

My father raised the shovel, about to hit Chuy with it, but Ana and I grabbed hold of my father's arms, screaming, "Stop it! Stop it, Papá."

He let the shovel drop, but he was heaving with an anger and rage of no return. "You want us to believe you're crazy, is that it?" He shouted at Chuy who hadn't moved, who seemed to not even be aware of my father's presence a few feet away from him. "You're not crazy; you're just trying to fool us into thinking you're crazy. Isn't that it, you sneaky son."

"Stop it, stop it," Ana María and I begged, both of us crying, in our own way just as hysterical as our father.

"I'm not sneaky and I'm not your son," he said quietly, like he was reciting something. "The moon is my father, not you."

"How dare you say that to me," he screamed, now bending down to get the shovel. "You can fool everyone else, but you can't fool me with your little act . . ."

"Chuy, go, please go," I said.

And just as I was moving toward him, getting ready to take him by the arm and coax him out of harm's way, he took a clean, strong punch at our father, just like that, and my Papá immediately went down, his skinny frame not able to withstand the strength of such a blow.

Then I was pulling Chuy away. "Go Chuy, hurry, before he gets up. Go over to El Chango's house." El Chango was his best friend who lived just across the tracks on Harris Street. "Go over there. I'll call Octavio."

Chuy let me lead him away from the piles of stone in the backyard. He seemed to be in shock, confused by what had just happened.

Once he was safely out of the yard, making his way down Conifer Street, one slow, careful step at a time, as if he were walking in some thick jungle, part of the reconnaissance, careful not to step on a land mine or a venomous serpent, this jungle full of a hundred dangers, I ran to the phone, which was still dangling in the air they way I'd left it a few minutes ago. And as I dialed El Chango's number, my fingers shaking so much it was hard to dial, to turn the rotary, I wondered how much Sahagún melodrama I could take.

El Chango answered, thank God!

"He's walking down the street to your house," I said, crying, not even identifying myself. "Please take care of him until Octavio can . . ." My sobs made my words unintelligible, I was sure. Calm down, Yoli, how can he understand you?

"I'll pick him up," he said and hung up.

Relief and sadness washed over me.

Then I walked back out to the yard.

Ana María had him sitting on the ground against the back gate. And in all of this shit, for some reason I remembered the sign that was tacked to the alley side of the gate—"POOL" instead of "PULL"—and the rage rose in me to such an extent that I had the urge to yank the stupid sign off the gate and hit him over the head with it. I wanted to scream and cry and shout to the world that I'd had enough of this fucking drama.

Now I was standing in front of him.

"Shame on you! Shame on you, Papá," I shouted with a rage I never knew I had. "How can you provoke him like that? God forgive you for your actions, Lorenzo Sahagún, because I won't. Are you sick, too, is that it? What kind of father are you? God have mercy on you, Lorenzo Sahagún." I said it all in one rush, as if time were running out and I had to say it now as he was slowly getting up, as he held onto the gate for support. Now is when I needed to plough into him, hurt him in some way as he'd hurt my favorite brother.

"He's right, you know," I said because now I couldn't stop myself. "You're not our father. The man in the moon is our father. Shame on you, Lorenzo Sahagún!"

Ana María quickly looked at me, startled, and like me, was expecting our father to slap me or something. But he didn't. He stared at me like some wild, confused animal, blood dribbling from the corner of his mouth. As he leaned against the gate for support, I could tell he was hurting real bad, either his face from the slug or his body from the fall, or both. He looked at me, then at Ana María, and without a word to either of us, made his way unsteadily through the fruit trees. A slow shuffle, like he was in pain, like he was a ninety-year-old viejito in less than a moment's time. A broken, brittle tree limb that had fallen to the ground.

Ana was still staring at me. "Yoli, why'd you say that?" She looked at me as if she was wondering who I really was. "Man, that was pretty harsh. You sound just like Papá and Chuy, only madder. He's our father, you know."

"What are you talking about, Ana?" I said, now directing my anger at her. "Every weekend I come home and all you do is complain about him—'oh he does this, oh he does that; you should be grateful you don't have to put up with his crap during the week.' Well, maybe it's time we stop taking his crap, okay?"

"You're right, Yoli," she said, sitting down on the base of the fountain. "I know you're right, but you also know that I would never have gotten away with that, with what you just said. You know that, don't you?"

I didn't say anything.

Then I started to cry and soon Ana was crying too, and then we wrapped our consoling arms around each other. And there we were, two sisters sitting on the unfinished garden fountain, hugging each other for dear life.

But my talk with my father wasn't over. Yes, Ana was right: she never would've gotten away with what I just said. For sure my father would have slapped her or taken her car keys away. But me, he just stared at me, dumbfounded and at a lost for words. I was his match.

He was in the bathroom washing his face, pressing a wet towel to his cheek. I stood at the doorway watching him, a frozen bag of peas in my hand.

"Here," I said, handing him the cold bag, "put this on your cheek. It'll help the swelling."

"Leave me alone," he said. "I've had enough of your speeches, you disrespectful daughter."

"Tomorrow's Mother's Day," I said, "and we kids want it to be the best ever. My mother doesn't need to have one more thing to worry about with Chuy. She doesn't need to know what just happened."

"Don't tell me what I can and can't tell your mother," he said. "Who do you think you are?"

"I'm Yolanda Sahagún, daughter of Dolores and Lorenzo Sahagún," I said in a shaky but determined voice as if I were trying to convince myself more than my father. "I'm nineteen years old and old enough to move out of the house forever, never to speak another word to my father, to see my mother only when he is not around."

"Are you threatening me? Is that it?" He stared at me, the wild look in his eyes returning.

I was sure he was going to slap me, but I didn't move. In truth I was terrified as I stood there watching him press the frozen bag of peas against his swollen cheek.

"Leave me alone, *chamaca ingrata*," he said with an impatient wave of his hand. I detected a weariness in his words, a wish to be done with the whole fiasco.

Satisfied, I walked out of the bathroom, leaving him alone.

Nine

Mother's Day. We sisters along with our sisters-in-law Sonia and Marisa were busy in the kitchen preparing breakfast: waffles; *chilaquiles* with plenty of *salsa casera* mixed in; orange juice and milk; cut-up melon and strawberries; and warmed flour and corn tortillas. Armando, Tom, and Tony were outside in the back setting up tables and chairs for the Mother's Day breakfast. They arrived early that morning to assemble the fountain. Even though it wasn't cemented together, at least Mamá would have an idea of what it was going to look like once it was completed. Not one of us—Ana, Papá, Chuy, or I—said a thing as to why we hadn't gotten very far in the setup. "Too many distractions," was all Ana offered when Octavio asked.

My mother and father had been instructed to wait in the living room, read the paper, listen to music—whatever—until they were called to the back for a delicious Mother's Day breakfast. Carolina was directing traffic in the kitchen, having set up a system similar to an assembly line. Now and then she called out from the back screen door to our brothers and her husband, telling them where she wanted them to place the tables. No, not in the sun. Closer to that tree, yes, that was it. She nodded, now blowing a kiss to her honeycito-husband Tom.

And then it was time to eat breakfast and Luz and Monica led my mother by the hand to the backyard.

"¡Qué lindo!" she managed to say, her voice weak with emotion.

We'd transformed the backyard into a festive arena with tablecloths in a blue and white gingham pattern, each table decorated with fat, voluptuous periwinkle blue hydrangeas in white porcelain vases, plump hydrangeas from our very own garden. And in the middle of the patio, the tables surrounding this centerpiece like a wagon train circle, a handsome fountain stood tall and elegant with a jumbo red bow at its pinnacle.

"I hope this is the fountain of youth," she said, smiling as she walked around it, inspecting it, admiring it. Mamá was wearing her pale green dress with yellow and blue primroses, the bodice lined with bright yellow buttons. She looked like a young, carefree girl with curly brown hair—nothing like a fifty-seven-year-old mother. It was a dress I'd seen her wear only a few times over the years, but each time she wore it, she looked younger and more beautiful.

"This is a perfect fountain for our garden," she proclaimed.

How did we ever get it here without her knowing it, she wondered. Who put it together, and when?

We all smiled, pleased with ourselves, although when I glanced at Ana her smile was forced, more of a grimace. She was trying very hard to conceal her hurt or anger or whatever. Chuy stared at the fountain, as if he were trying to figure out what it was. Papá, I noticed, stood in the back, apart from us. Silent. Was he sad? Repentant? Regretful, at least? I couldn't read him.

"Come, let's eat," said Carolina, clapping her hands.

It was a natural division, not at all planned: the guys were sitting at one table, the women at another, the four grandchildren at their own smaller table.

"Ay, Dolores," I said in the most exaggerated macaw-sounding voice I could muster as I imitated the snooty Doña Antonia. "*Carita de luna.*" Which made everyone at our table start laughing.

I wanted the moment to last for more than its due; I wanted to sit there with my sisters and mother morning after morning basking in the warm May sun, imitating (as I was that very minute) my mother's fellow Guadalupana who thought she was God's gift to the church club; I wanted to discreetly pantomime, lest she be lurking in the bushes in her yard next to ours, Socorrito's busybody shuffle in her furry blue mules. Forever. I wanted each of us to thoughtfully answer the questions, If you could be anything in life, what would it be? If you could live anywhere in the world, where would you live? Or this one: If you could marry anyone in the world, who would it be?

I looked at my mother who was looking over at Monica who was telling us she wanted to be a horse trainer and raise thoroughbred horses for racing. On second thought, I thought as I looked over to where our father was talking with my brothers at the other table, maybe I wouldn't ask that last question. What's done was done, after all. But that would be the thing, wouldn't it? To know whom my mother would have wanted to marry, other than our father. Or maybe this was the question I needed to ask as I'd gone from one boyfriend to another: Why did my mother choose my father?

After everyone had had his fill of breakfast, Carolina clapped her hands and called for *atención*. She announced to my mother that each of us had a little something to say to her on this Mother's Day. Then one by one Carolina directed each brother and sister to come up before the group and share something that honored our mother.

We began with the oldest.

Armando remembered the time when he was fifteen years old and Mamá was pregnant with Luz. They were walking to the market and she said she needed to stop a moment, rest on a bench. Armando in his teenage impatience had mumbled something about her looking like some tired old cow. Any other mother would've spanked him on the spot. Instead, Mamá had simply smiled tiredly and said, "Moo."

"You all think I'm some kind of Latin lover," Octavio said, now that it was his turn. He sounded a little defensive for some reason. "But did you know that Wanda was the one who broke up with me just out of high school? Did you know that? And there I was, sitting in my Pontiac on the driveway listening to music on the radio, all sad and confused. Mamá came out of the house, asked if she could join me. So there we were, brokenhearted me and Mamá, just sitting in the car listening to the music. No questions, no advice. Just listening to the music."

Wow, this was news to me, that Octavio should have had his heart broken! I could tell from the expressions on my brothers' and sisters' faces that they were surprised too.

Tony recalled that it was Mamá who bought him the James Brown album he had been wanting for his sixteenth birthday.

"The best oatmeal raisin cookies in the world," Chuy said quietly, more a whisper. His eyes looked distant, as if he were momentarily back out there in the swamps and jungle and humidity. We nodded in understanding: the batches of homemade oatmeal cookies our mother sent him when he was in Vietnam.

Here was another good one, said our resident psychologist and behavioral specialist Carolina: When Mamá applauded Carolina's stand in bringing Tom over to meet the family for the first time. At this, we all turned to look at my father, who was trying to ignore us, pretending to be busy cutting another piece of cake.

And now it seemed that our impromptu tributes were taking on a competitive spin. We all wanted to claim Mamá for our own.

Ana María said she loved watching the Mexican telenovelas every weekday at four o'clock with Mama, now giving married Carolina a kind of ha-ha-look-what-you're-missing-out-on look.

I refused to be outdone. "Thank you for believing I'm a daughter of the American Revolution," I said in the most dramatically cryptic voice I could muster.

Huh? My brothers and sisters look at me.

I just smiled at them.

"Yes, well, you might be the Daughter of the American Revolution," piped in Monica, "but you don't have the most beautiful cowboy boots this side of the Rio Grande given to you by our mother."

"Yeah, Monica," Ana said, "it's getting a little ridiculous, don't you think? You practically sleep in those clunkers."

Monica stuck her tongue out at her.

Hey, hey, Carolina clapped her hands, reminding us that this was about Mamá, so cut it out.

Our mother was silent in all of this, as if she was overwhelmed with the outpouring of tributes.

And then it was little Luz's turn.

She paused. For a twelve-year-old, she was a confident girl, our old soul. Sometimes pretending to be the English downstairs maid with a perfect Cockney accent, and other times, as if nothing else would do, impersonating a lofty English butler, her British accent and rigid composure being her specialty. But for the moment she seemed to stumble over her words, desperately trying to find the right ones. She started by thanking our mother for taking her to Woolworth's for ice cream after the visits to the downtown orthopedic shoe store. Her eyes filled with tears. How Luz took to heart her role as the youngest! Then she said what we were all thinking, "Thank you for being our *mami*."

It felt like we'd just finished reciting the rosary, a litany of "*ruega por nosotros*" (pray for us) punctuating each tribute to our mother. Each tribute a rosary bead.

Mamá stood in our midst, a big grin, at once both shy and proud. Her face was a little flushed from so many compliments, and it occurred to me that maybe she wasn't used to so many flattering pronouncements all at once. I made a note of this, reminding myself that we kids needed to show our gratitude to her more often.

She bowed slightly, her eyes looking, I don't know, maybe sad and knowing. "Gracias, mis changuitos," she said.

Yes, I thought proudly, we were her little monkeys, weren't we?

Enough of this, someone said. It's getting too mushy. There's so much *maíz*, I'm getting a stomachache. Get it? Maíz. Corn. Corny.

Ha, ha, you're so funny I forgot to laugh.

Later, I would realize that we should've had our father say something nice too. Or why hadn't he thought to jump in with an anecdote? After all, he loved to talk, to tell stories of the past. Why hadn't any of us thought to ask him? Or could it be that in that moment of heartfelt memories, in that moment of claiming her, Mamá belonged to us children and only us?

Afterward, when Armando and Sonia, Tony and Marisa, and Carolina and Tom went off to see their mothers-in-law and Papá left for work at the Hotel San Diego, we four remaining sisters and Mamá piled into the green Rambler, making our way to Balboa Park for a mother-daughter picnic.

We parked near the Organ Pavilion, hopping out of the car and gathering our bag with sodas and old bedspreads from the trunk. We made our way toward the lily pond.

I'd been to this beloved park and important tourist destination just a few times in my life: the first time was when I won a blue ribbon in the sixth grade science fair for my rock collection, the prize being a trip to the science exhibit in Balboa Park; and the two times my drama class had fieldtrips to Old Globe Theatre productions. You probably wouldn't find this in any tour book describing our famous park, but for me Balboa Park was all about the trees and the seductive vegetation. Nowhere in the guides to San Diego would it say that Balboa Park instilled in Miss Yolanda Sahagún an intense primal horniness that she couldn't explain. Trees, trees, trees abounded—tall ones, skinny ones, fat ones, round ones. (About now Carolina, the duchess of Freudian interpretation, would nod and say, Aha! I knew it all along: you're obsessed with trunks, with the woody axes of trees, with the shafts of columns. All of it phallic, she would say. A clear case of penis envy.) And while I leave Carolina to figure out my psychological profile, I will continue to confess—it is a confession of sorts, isn't it?—that when I thought of Balboa Park I thought of my junior high boyfriend Francisco Valdivia and my intense adolescent desire to engage in some heavy sexual romping.

Francisco and I walking hand in hand, lagging behind the drama class as we made our way through the Alcazar Garden toward the Old Globe, I used to long to sneak off with him into one of the canyons thick with vegetation. That's right, just break away discreetly from the group ahead of us, plunge into a thicket of tangly vines and soft peat moss, our own bodies in a tousle of passion and great making out, breathlessly groping breasts and penis like you can never imagine. And somewhere in the distance, a few junior high school voices would ask, "Where are Francisco and Yoli?"

But for now, as I walked with my mom and sisters toward the lily pond, the most racy and inappropriate thought about Balboa Park that I would allow myself was this: Who would think—meandering through this thicket of vegetation, as if it were some kind of Tarzan and Jane jungle, a wooden walking bridge here and there overlooking the canyons, the canyons thick with Australian and South American conifer trees, southern Magnolia, California pepper, Melaleuca, and names appropriately poetic like sapphire dragon tree, Brazilian butterfly tree, lemon-scented gum tree, parrot's beak coral tree (those trees again!)—that San

Diego was a semiarid area. Because when I thought of Balboa Park, yes, okay, maybe it was all about those penis trees.

"Hurry up," Monica called out to me as she in her clunky cowboy boots and the rest of the women crossed the street way ahead of me toward the lily pond and the botanical building.

The pamphlet I grabbed at the info station said it was one of the world's largest lath structures, built in 1915 with more than 2,100 permanent tropical plants along with seasonal floral and plant displays, a carnivorous plant bog, and "touch and smell" garden. What the pamphlet didn't say was that this Garden of Eden was a perfect romping place for—well, you know where I was headed with that one.

In good-natured, competitive form, we sisters scattered under the filigreed wooden lath structure in search of the strangest flower. Just as soon as we spotted one, we called the rest of the group over. "Oh, look at this weird one. Wow, it's the best."

"No, come over here . . ."

In all the hubbub of finding the most exotic flower, we hadn't noticed that our mother had stopped looking and was sitting on the brick ledge of one of the flower exhibits. She was looking beyond everything, just gazing ahead of her at nothing or everything. That is, Luz, Monica, and I hadn't noticed her sitting there, but Ana María had. Looking solemn and maybe even scared, Ana was standing at her side as if she were guarding our mother.

We called out to them, waving them over to check out the evil-looking, spidery orchid we'd just spotted, but Ana María shook her head, looking serious and annoyed. No, they weren't leaving their spot.

I went over to them. "What's the matter?" I said, now noticing that Mamá's face looked pale and drawn.

"Nothing," our mother said before Ana could open her mouth. In her soft Spanish she explained that she just felt a little dizzy for a moment. "The smells of this garden . . . so beautiful," she said slowly, as if she were trying to catch her breath, take gulps of air to help her. "I think I'm having an allergic reaction to this lovely Garden of Eden," she said, now smiling.

I stared at her, dumbfounded. Did Mamá realize the import of her words, of what she'd just said? Or was this just some casual, off-the-cuff, harmless remark not meant to be imbued with double meanings?

"I'm fine now," she said, gathering her purse and getting up. "But I think I need some air."

I called out to Monica and Luz and we all headed out of the garden toward the lily pond and the lawn area.

We spread our old blankets—twin bedspreads in a design of bulging maroon and purple roses on their thorny stems—on the grass. And while we sisters rummaged in the bag for our sodas, Mamá took off her sweater, which had hung loosely, like a cape, on her shoulders. I glanced at her as she set her sweater on top of her legs, covering the hem of her dress. She was rearranging her slip under her dress, it seemed, moving her legs a bit to get a better grasp. Then I did a double take as I observed her discreetly set her garter belt and nylons next to her on the grass. I was so shocked all I could do was stare. Then she rubbed the soles of her feet on the grass. The sweater was covering her bent knees and legs so all you saw were her naked feet.

"Yes," she said, smiling more to herself than to us, as if she were alone, in another world or another time, "this makes it all worth it."

I noticed I wasn't the only one to have witnessed this act of, of what? Rebellion? Brazenness? All four of us were staring at Mamá. Had she stripped completely naked we could not have been more shocked. She, meanwhile, was impervious to our stares, impervious even to our presence. We were there but we were not there for her. I glanced at the pair of nylons rolled up in doughnut shapes with their attendant garters. With her knees still slightly bent she gently fell back on the blanket, looking up at the sky. The sweater modestly covered her legs, yes, I knew this, and yet there was something in her actions, something in the way she was lying on the grass that made me see her with new eyes. She was looking up at the blue sky, one hand resting on her forehead, shading her eyes from the bright sun. She continued to rub the back of her feet against the grass. And for those moments, on that Mother's Day in 1974 in Balboa Park in San Diego, California, United States of America, planet Earth, she was not my mother anymore, but rather a young woman, sensual and mysterious. She was Dolores Ramos again.

Luz and Monica claimed they were getting hungry, and Monica conveniently remembered going on a fifth grade fieldtrip to the Museum of Man and watching a lady there make tortillas for the customers for twenty-five cents.

"Can we go?" They asked our mother.

And before either Ana or I could protest, sure that we had just better head on home, Mamá nodded and said, "Of course. *Una tortillita* is just what we need."

Luz and Monica were up ahead with Mamá, while Ana and I walked slowly behind, purposely putting some distance between us and them so we could talk privately.

"She's been like this a lot lately," Ana said. "Absentminded, in her own world. I came home from work during lunch the other day because I forgot the keys to the Xerox room, and there she was sitting on the front porch with the plant clippers on her lap, looking straight ahead at the canyon across the street, her gaze fixed on something, you know. I got out of the car, walked up to her, and asked her if she was okay, and she looked startled to see me even though she must've seen me driving up to the front of the house right in the direction of her gaze."

"What'd she say?" I asked. The marine layer was coming inland, a chill in the air. Soon it would be overcast and gray.

Before Ana answered, she slowed down, purposely creating more distance between us and Mamá and the girls. Then she said, "She looked at me all surprised. 'Oh, when did you get here?' she asked me. And she looked out of breath and tired. Like she looked right now in the botanical garden."

"What do you think's wrong with her?" I asked.

"It's our father," Ana said without missing a beat, as if she had been waiting for just the right moment to have this conversation and make these observations. "He's making all of us sick," Ana said, her voice quivering. "This is just too much already."

"Maybe we should discuss this with our brothers and Carolina . . ."

"Oh, don't get me started on Carolina," Ana said, her whisper now more of a hiss. "Ms. Psychologist says that she read an article the other day that talks about this thing called seasonal affective disorder—something about lack of light in the winter, getting depressed. You know what I told her?" Ana said, now stopping and looking at me full in the face. "That crap was all fine and dandy, so why don't you let him live with you and Tom during spring, summer, winter, and fall, and we'll take him the other seasons."

I couldn't help smiling a little.

"It's not funny, Yoli," she said. "His moodiness is going to drive us to the loony bin. Look at the shit he pulled on Chuy yesterday. Wanting to attack him with a shovel, for God's sake."

Once at the Museum of Man we spotted the Mexican lady, all decked out in an elaborately embroidered Oaxacan *huilpil*, her braided hair crowning the top of her head, in an exhibit booth with her metate and masa, making little balls out of real cornmeal mixture, then patting them to pancake flatness before setting them on the *comal* to heat. As we approached her, she smiled at my mother who in turn smiled back and said, "Buenas tardes."

A look of recognition, of camaraderie, perhaps?

For a moment—a jealous moment—I felt like there was a barrier between us sisters and my mother and this woman, as if the metate and the masa and the whole tedious process of making tortillas the ancient way connected the two women in ways that we modern-day, Americanized daughters would never understand.

A squirt of butter from a plastic condiment container, a sprinkle of salt, and we were all happy. Well, maybe not all of us. Even with a freshly made tortilla, Ana was out of sorts. Quiet and tense.

We walked about, less interested in the museum exhibits surrounding us and more in taking little bites of our tortillas so they would last longer. Then we came upon an exhibit titled "Footsteps through Time: 4 Million Years of Human Evolution" and we stopped to check it out. There was this lifelike, seriously hairy model of an early man standing in a cave exhibit. The woman next to him was almost as hairy but with round, lifelike breasts, which I glanced at before directing my complete attention back to the man. I was staring at his penis, which I assumed was lifelike, though I wasn't sure since I'd never really had a good, long look at one, when Ana María suddenly said, "That's Papá," pointing to the very Cro-Magnon I was looking at. "Yes, our father's just like this damn caveman here. 'Hey, woman, where's my food?' the big oaf says."

We looked at her, startled, not sure if she was joking or not. There was a sharpness to her voice that I wasn't used to hearing in her. And when she saw that she had our undivided attention, she continued. "Yes, siree, there's our caveman father making his demands on the women gatherers of the cave. Demands, demands, good old Neanderthal that our father is . . ."

Then she started crying.

A few museum visitors looked our way as we sisters and Mamá stood before the lifelike Cro-Magnon man and woman, staring at this hairy, ape-looking couple, not sure what to say.

"But you see," she said, now turning to look at our mother square in the face, "we're not cave people anymore. You can leave him, divorce him . . ."

"Ana María, he's your father," our mother said sharply. "Don't talk that way about your father."

"Yes, he's our father, but he's going to drive us as crazy as him!"

Luz and Monica look startled, as if they'd just been shaken out of sweet dreams and sleep. They looked from Mamá to Ana María and back.

"How can you stand it?" she continued. "How can you stand his mood swings? Why do we have to put up with this crap? Leave him, leave him," she said, and there was a rising tide of hysteria in her voice, an anger and bitterness and frustration of no return. And although we were in the building seemingly safe from the foliage and brambles, safe from the invasive roots of hundred-year-old trees, sidewalks and streets away from the dark, deep canyons, I knew that the venomous serpent lay hidden nearby, biding its time before it sprung forward and attacked.

Mamá must have also sensed Ana's rising hysteria, because she was hugging Ana María, letting her cry against her chest, softly shushing her, consoling her.

"He's your father, Ana," she said in a low voice so only we sisters could hear. "Be patient with him. He loves you all very much, he just doesn't know how . . ."

"No!" she said, pulling away. "Stop making excuses for him. I hate it when you do that. I just hate it! And I hate him, too."

"Ana," our mother said, now taking on a firm, authoritarian voice. "That's enough."

"If you loved us," she said sobbing, no longer caring who in the whole museum could hear, "if you loved us you wouldn't make us put up with him."

And here Ana looked at me, as if to say, Help me out, Yoli. Say something.

And for probably the first time in my whole life, I didn't know what to say. And maybe I was speechless because I was stunned by my own hesitancy to jump right in and second what Ana was saying. Should I say, "Yeah, leave him, Mamá"? Or should I say, "Well, Ana, he is our father, you know, and in his own way he—" Oh, but that sounded so lame. For how long were we to make excuses for our moody father? And this worried me, my hesitancy.

Just then one of the museum curators walked over to us, concerned and alarmed, wondering if everything was okay.

"Is everything okay?" I said, now waking up, the lightbulb in my head sparking alive. "How can everything be okay," I said, motioning with my head toward the beastly Cro-Magnon, "when you've got this ugly-looking brute of a guy looking at us, expecting us to cook and wash laundry and clean the cave and take care of the hundreds of kids he's impregnated us with?"

The poor old lady was taken aback, speechless. Ana María stopped crying, wiped her wet eyes, listening to me. They were all staring at me.

"See that big club in the brute's hand?" I continued. "Why doesn't the cave woman have it instead? She's the one that needs to bonk him on the head with it anytime he starts demanding things of her. 'Hey, woman, where's my supper?' Bonk! 'Make sure those kids of ours behave, woman.' Bonk! Bonk! And with that shriveled-up old turd of a penis, who wants him anyway?"

My three sisters burst out laughing—even my mother couldn't help smiling. And there we were in the middle of the musty museum laughing uncontrollably, our attempt to cast out the anger, the hurt, the confusion. Exorcise the demons.

Somehow we got through four million years of human evolution without being permanently depressed.

Ten

The end of summer, 1974. Soon I would be heading back to the dorms for my sophomore year. My sisters were visiting our aunts in El Grullo for a couple of weeks, but since I had a full-time summer office job at North Island Naval Base, I stayed put. My father had a nighttime job, so only my mother and I were home on that summer evening. Miracle of miracles: I had my mother all to myself.

Months and years later, I would play this summer evening over and over in my mind, trying to decipher hidden messages. I might be in a profound sleep, and then suddenly I'd be awake, out of breath. I would look around me at the darkness, see shadowy outlines of the dresser, a desk, clothing strewn over the chair. Mamá's story of Joseph the Prophet would flash through my mind. Did I just have a nightmare? I would ask myself each time in those first lucid moments of waking. Then I would do all I could to quiet my heart and listen. "They want to tell us their stories but we can't hear them." Wasn't that what she had said of the El Grullo ghosts? I would wonder what she meant to tell me—if she *had* meant to tell me something. Sleep would leave me, and now it was only Joseph the Prophet and I who were awake, waiting for dawn. Waiting to understand.

The summer evening was warm and gentle, and my mother and I were sitting in the living room reading, the front door open, a breeze filtering in through the screen door. The evening caressed us, invited us to look up for a moment from whatever we were doing and take notice. I did this. I sensed this was an important evening. I knew it even as I was living it. In the distance, I could hear someone watering a yard, the sound of talking, a dog barking. The whooshing waves of the cars on the freeway. I was curled up on the green velvet armchair reading *The Awakening*, a novel that years later in graduate school and beyond I would come back to over and over as if for consolation from an understanding, old friend—"Her face was captivating by reason of a certain frankness of expression and a contradictory subtle play of features. Her manner was engaging." I looked up from my book a moment, stole a glance at my mother, who was sitting across from me on the couch, reading passages from her thick Bible. And I fancied, in my youthful zeal to relate to tragic literary heroines, that the author was describing both my mother and me.

Later, much later, I would try to remember what prompted Mamá to set down her Bible and begin telling me the story of Joseph the Prophet. Had I mentioned to her a nightmare I'd had? Had she just then been reading those passages in Genesis? Perhaps she'd had a bad dream the night before? My mother had never been the storyteller of the family—she'd left that to my father. Aside from the glimpse into her life she offered at the Daughters of the American Revolution tea party over a year ago, she seemed to prefer to be a listener, not a talker.

"Wouldn't it be nice," she said to me, now setting her chunky red Bible on the sofa next to her, "if we could interpret our dreams?"

And then she told me the story of Joseph the Prophet.

Was it the details of Joseph's brothers and their deception and envy that entwined me? Was it the whispering sound of her words? Or was it simply the fact that my mother and I were sharing an evening alone together and she was telling me a story? No matter. I felt the drama of her words and the wonder of Joseph's journey and his ability to interpret dreams. I felt the magic of the moment.

It was twilight now, the light in the room changing, growing more shadows, a stillness out on the street as people started to make their way indoors to dinner preparations, summer school homework, to a favorite TV program. We could hear the metallic banging on an old grill, a neighbor trying to get the pilot light on, and the urgent whistle call as Benji beckoned his dog Chamuco home.

"I wish I could interpret my dreams," I said when she finished telling me the story of Joseph. "I have such strange, vivid dreams. Sometimes I think I lead a double life—this life here and the one in my dreams." I laughed, self-conscious.

My mother smiled. "Joseph's ability to interpret dreams," she said, "is what saves his life." Her green eyes were greener than I'd ever remembered, her cheeks flushed a feverish bright pink. No doubt this uncharacteristic storytelling had left her exhausted. "You're fortunate to remember your dreams, Yoli," she said. "Listen to them."

And then she said no more, turning instead to look out the screen door from her place on the brown couch. Directing her attention to another task at hand. Turning to face, perhaps, what only she knew, in that moment, was eminent.

This was my evening with Mamá.

When she finished telling me the story—an hour later? Twenty years later?—it was time to go to bed. We made our way to our bedrooms, she to hers and Papá's, and I to the one I shared with Luz, Monica, and Ana María. But for now, for the weeks that they were away, I had the girls' room to myself.

I couldn't sleep. I tossed and turned, feeling afraid to dream, afraid that Joseph the Prophet might appear unannounced and, like some phantom, decide to interpret my dreams for me because mine were the vivid, weird kind that were his specialty. And if he did appear—just the thought made me scoot farther under the sheet—well, if he did decide to drop by and interpret my dreams, he would do nothing less than scare the hell out of me.

I heard Mamá coming down the hallway toward my room.

"Yoli," she said softly. "Estás bien? Are you afraid?" She didn't say it in a mocking way, the way my sisters were apt to do, knowing that I was a nervous, light sleeper. She said it in a motherly, concerned way, as if she were asking me if I had a stomachache. She knew me well.

"Yes," I whispered back. "I am." Then, "Mamá, can I sleep with you?"

I had the wall on my left and my mother to the right, she, as always, guarding me against bad dreams and nighttime phantoms. I felt protected and safe, my sleep sound and dreamless as I cocooned my nineteen-year-old self next to my mother.

Eleven

"When you see her, just act normal," Ana María was telling me as we drove south on Interstate 5, having picked me up at the dorms, now headed home for the weekend. "Don't get all *llorona* or anything like that. You know she's proud. The last thing Mamá needs is to be comforting *us*."

I couldn't breathe. I rolled down the window, leaning my head against the car door, wanting the wind to refresh me, to sweep my cares away.

Gallbladder cancer, a few months to live, and I was supposed to "act normal" toward my dying mother.

"Are they sure?" I asked. "I mean, maybe they got it mixed up. What about radiation, chemotherapy? Ana, there must be something." I wasn't sure what, though. "Does she know? Did the doctor tell her?"

"Yes," Ana said. "He told us both at the same time. About three months to live." Her voice sounded shaky and heavy. "There's nothing we can do."

We were now passing National City, and I lifted my head to glance at the familiar red and gold billboard in Gothic-style print: Psychic Palm Reader, Next Exit.

❖ ❖ ❖

Another snapshot of Mamá: It was September—the last September she would be with us, although we didn't know this yet; final judgment of her cancer came later, in October. That is, we children didn't know it yet, but given the turn of events of this scene, now I understand that Mamá must have known all along this would be her last September alive.

We were preparing a surprise party for Monica, who was turning eighteen. We sisters and mother were carefree, knowing that Papá had a graveyard shift job as a bellboy at the Hotel San Diego, so he wouldn't be there to make a scene, to throw the strange young men out the door, embarrassing us with his theatrics and bullish, fierce, unwarranted anger. We had begged Mamá not to tell Papá about this party—this one time, please don't tell him. We were afraid he would not go to work that night, and that he would instead insist on staying home and chaperoning, that he would ruin everything with his temper. All it took was one little thing—a kiss on the cheek from a guy-friend; a flirtatious wink; a guy and girl holding hands—to set Papá off. So Mamá reluctantly granted us that wish for Monica's birthday party: not to tell Papá about it.

Luz was filling large bowls with tortilla and potato chips, smaller soup bowls with guacamole, ranch, and bean dip; Mamá was deep-frying miniature, flutelike taquitos; and Lydia was setting the sodas on the food table outside while Ana María cut chunks of watermelon for the fruit platter. My older brothers and their wives and kids were on their way with more goodies. Walking up to all of us in the backyard, Carolina, with her husband Tom, was carrying the full-sheet birthday cake she herself had decorated with a western scene replete with brown mountains, a green saguaro cactus, a yellow hot sun, and topped off with a plastic cowgirl in leather chaps and cowboy hat standing next to her plastic golden palomino. Future psychologist Carolina was a firm believer in encouraging her patients—oops, I mean her *sisters*—in their dreams and passions. I had to admit, though it bugged me to think Carolina and I could ever be on the same wavelength, I had followed suit: my gift to Monica was an old edition of *Black Beauty* with colorful, finely drawn illustrations that I found in a musty bookstore on Adams Avenue.

Two days before the party a freakish tropical storm had blown into San Diego—first the wind, dramatic and uncharacteristically warm, followed by fat drops of rain for about thirty minutes. Then it was gone. I saw this as a good omen. Cleansing. Cathartic. I swept the leaves from the sidewalk, from the backyard where we had set up a table with the record player and stacks of albums and 45s, my hair in pink jumbo rollers for the straight hair look. Christmas lights dangled from the guava and quince trees—same as whenever we had a party.

By seven o'clock most of our friends had arrived, obediently punctual since this was a surprise party. Then, half an hour later, Monica was casually escorted to the backyard, having gone to the Chula Vista Shopping Center with two in-the-know girlfriends. Surprise! She laughed, giggled, embarrassed, self-conscious. She was smiling hugely and receiving birthday hugs from her friends, none of us knowing that in less than two months she would again be hugging these friends, all of us brothers and sisters hugging each other for dear life in unfathomable and immense grief.

I was the appointed picture-taker.

The party was good. We sisters and girlfriends were experts in choreographing perfect dancing music, in knowing which songs were the ice-breakers, fast dances followed by the intense "Daddy's Home" and "Angel Baby" slow dances, the oldies of our brothers' generation, guaranteed to make our young hearts swoon with romance and tickle with lust.

By ten o'clock we had all settled into wonderful dancing patterns. Fortunately, Monica was quite a social butterfly and had heaps of friends, so there were plenty of guys to dance with. So that was what we were doing: eating, laughing, bear hugging to "Samba Pa Ti," Mamá and our next-door neighbor Socorrito sitting on metal chairs borrowed from St. Charles Catholic Church off to the side in a vigilant corner of the patio, the two women chatting with old Don Epifranio, his cane every so often flirtatiously tapping Socorrito's knee. Love had no age boundaries, I thought as I adjusted my camera to zoom in and, from across the patio, discreetly took a picture of the three of them.

He came in from nowhere, it seemed to me. Like a wave that rose unexpectedly, higher and higher, and you stood there in frozen horror, realizing—too late—that it was the Big One, the tidal wave you'd only seen in documentaries, watching as it engulfed you, swallowed you, promising to take your breath and life away in one dramatic, intentional, slow-moving, monstrous swoop. Papá was upon Monica, who was dancing a slow bear hug dance with her favorite sweetheart, Héctor. He seemed to rip them apart violently, fiercely, and Mamá and Socorrito and Don Epifranio, most of the guests at the party, hadn't seen it yet, what was happening. I stared in horror as he pushed Héctor away from his daughter, now clutching Monica's upper arm, drawing her near him as if he were protecting her. From what? Dragons? Evil men? Future heartbreaks?

"No!" I screamed, dropping the camera, the clatter of pieces shattering. I ran to them. By then everyone was aware of some kind of disturbance, and so they abruptly stopped in midsentence, in mid–dance step, looking to the middle of the dance floor where the shouts were coming from. Everyone was instinctively still, except for Papá who was heaving and breathing hard, his face red and angry and sweaty.

Monica was crying hysterically, "Why, why are you doing this?" while Héctor stared at my father, stunned and groggy, as if he'd been roughly awakened in the midst of dreaming lovely swoon-filled, romantic things. As if he, Monica's sweetheart, were facing an evil dragon.

I was now in front of my father, shouting and crying, "Leave us alone! Just leave us the hell alone!" knowing, as I said this, that this was a déjà vu moment, that it seemed the Sahagúns had too many of these kinds of melodramatic scenes. And as I was sobbing and shouting, I was thinking that I'd had enough of all this fucking drama. My brothers Armando, Octavio, and Tony quickly came forward, while Chuy remained seated, as if the violent confusion had only served to click him into automatic pilot. He sat still and unemotional, watching the turntable, listening to "Daddy's Home," the irony of the timing of the song and what was now happening maybe not lost on him. So he kept his eye on the turntable, as if he'd been ordered by his commander to do so—his duty while waiting for the inevitable ambush. But the rest of us brothers and sisters, cousins and uncles and aunts, our classmates and best friends, our sweethearts—all of us—stared at this angry, heaving, incomprehensible creature that was our father. He stood slightly crouched, with his dukes up, ready to slug anyone else who dared defy him.

My oldest brother Armando spoke first, slowly. "Papá," he began, his voice sounding tired. This was nothing new to him. He was the Patron Saint of Patience. The eldest of nine children, Armando had learned to handle our father, to calm him down somewhat. "Papá, why don't you come and have something to eat and drink. There's some . . ."

"*Cállate*," he screamed at Armando, shrugging off Armando's hand from his arm. "Ay tú, so calm and mature. Who do you think I am, eh? I am your father, do you understand? I am your father, el señor Lorenzo Sahagún. Don't you dare talk to me as if I were a child. Chamaco ingrato, you are my son and I brought you into this world. How dare you talk to me in this way." Then, turning to look at all of us, "How dare you have a party in my house without my permission? Disrespectful, wretched children! Get out, all of you—now!"

"Pero Papá," Armando began again.

"Didn't you hear me?" He said. "All of you, all of you, get the hell out of my home."

And then she was there, standing next to Papá, our mother who normally protested with "Lorenzo, por favor . . ." followed by a resigned, hopeless backing off.

But now she was standing tall, as tall as her petite stature would allow, next to him, in her favorite light blue jacquard dress, and she said, "This is enough, Lorenzo." And Mamá's voice was strong, clear, and sure of itself—like I'd never in my life heard before.

"What, what did you just say?" He was shouting at her, even though she was only inches away. "How dare you allow these parties, this obscene dancing. What kind of mother are you to allow your kids to run wild—"

"This is enough, Lorenzo," she said again. She stood firm, her green eyes staring intently into his blue eyes, her arms crossed resolutely as if she were a general and had just given the final command. "It must stop now, this moment, and if it doesn't, then I will call the police and have you removed. I will have you locked up until you learn to stop your rampages." She didn't say what we were all thinking, what Papá himself must've been thinking: We will have you interned in a hospital like your son Chuy.

It seemed that Papá was in shock and could only stare at this new woman whom he thought was his loyal, obedient wife. Dolores Ramos de Sahagún—the old Dolores that he married thirty-four years ago—was nowhere in sight. He searched her face.

She understood his confusion, and this seemed to give her more courage and strength. "You have a choice, Lorenzo Sahagún," she said with what sounded like gentle compassion, a kind of pity in her voice that I had not heard before. "You can join us in celebrating Monica's birthday, or you can go inside and pack your bags and leave immediately. The choice is yours, Lorenzo, and we will stand here until you have made your choice."

Papá stared at all of us now—at Monica, whose face was red and puffy from crying, at his other sons and daughters, at Socorrito, at Don Epifranio, who was leaning on his cane, at all the guests who, in silence, stared back at him.

Then without warning, he turned to Monica and her sweetheart, and his eyes were teary. "*Perdónenme, hijos,*" he said, now asking for our forgiveness.

And to our mother—his Dolores Ramos de Sahagún whom he married thirty-four years ago, plucking her from a comfortable, privileged family life—he said, "The Jarabe Tapatío, Dolores. Will you dance the Jarabe Tapatío with me?"

❂ ❂ ❂

The irony was not lost on me. Fountain of Youth, the Eternal Fountain, Immortality. What I knew was that Mamá was dying. I watched her as she sat on the edge of the fountain trimming the dried blooms of a geranium in its pot. Where not too long ago you would have found my mother on her knees in the flower beds pulling weeds or trimming, pruning, digging tidy trenches for her sweet peas, now she tired easily and had taken to sitting on the edge of the fountain to do what gardening she could from there. I watched her, though she didn't know she was being watched, as she picked out the dried geranium blooms and twigs and tossed them into a brown grocery bag she had set next to her on the ground. She was pale and drawn, her round face—her carita de luna— now caved in, already looking skeletal. Her face was a pale yellow as the cancer spread to her liver. She was thin, deathly thin. Not unlike the pictures of Holocaust victims on liberation day.

And it occurred to me as I stood there at the back door window watching her, that I had been doing this my whole life: standing at the doorway watching my mother. She was deeply intent on her chore—clipping or pulling out the dried geranium twigs—as if there were no more important job to be done. The fountain's soft splashing did nothing to soothe me. Instead, I wanted to run outside, grab her by the shoulders, and scream at her, "Mujer, fight for your life, goddamit." Radiation. Chemotherapy. *Curanderos*—all of it, do it all. Just don't fucking give up.

Suddenly she looked up, as if someone had called out to her.

She spotted me at the door, smiled, and shook her head no, as if my thoughts had quickly rushed off to meet her. Or maybe she knew that all my life I'd been standing there watching her.

"No, Yoli," she seemed to be saying, "leave it alone already. What's done is done."

❈ ❈ ❈

I was sitting on a chair next to Mamá's bed, where she was resting. She looked weary and sallow, distracted and worn down by her physical pain. On her nightstand sat the thin prayer book *Quince Minutos Con Dios* and the rose petal rosary, and I was wondering if the fifteen-minutes-with-God booklet included a firm talking to with this entity. If my mother only had fifteen minutes with God to plead her case, could she please argue to be allowed to live another thirty years, at least?

Ana María told me that when they got back from the doctor's, after he told her she had three months to live, just like that, three fucking months to live, she walked into the house, headed straight for her bedroom, got out her rosary and her little book, and crawled into bed, silent and stoic. Given that death decree, what could anyone possibly say to God in fifteen minutes? Why would anyone want to?

Ana María, Monica, Luz, and I took turns sitting with Mamá. We chatted with her, or simply sat quietly watching over her as she napped. We refused to leave her alone, though she feebly protested, knew we had better things to do. "Don't worry, I'll be fine," she told us. But we stayed put. This vigil with Mamá perhaps had more to do with comforting ourselves than with comforting our mother. As much as I wanted to hold on to the fresh smell of my mother's cold cream, the perfumy scent of lipstick and face powder, even the familiar camphor oil in the green miniature-size bottle, I was surrounded and overcome by the smells of medicine and death—acidic, sour, and tinny. The curtains were drawn, though it was midafternoon, the room shrouded in premature shadows.

"Your classes," she suddenly spoke. "How are you doing?"

French, contemporary Latin American literature, political science, and chemistry.

I told her about my favorite, the lit class, the new writers I was being introduced to. One of them, the one who most intrigued me, I told her, was Juan Rulfo.

"Your countryman," I said. "From Jalisco too."

"Is that so?" she said weakly, now turning her gaze away from the closed curtain, shifting her head slowly, carefully toward me as if her pillow were full of thorns. "Tell me more about this *paisano* of mine," she said.

So I told her about her famous literary compatriot, about his collection of short stories that dealt with religion, politics, poverty, despair, and the horrible human condition. I told her about his views on naturalism, how man was but a victim of his circumstances, of natural forces. I avoided telling her about his novel, because already I'd said too much: all the characters were dead—phantoms—when they told their stories.

"He's so fatalistic," I said. "It's disturbing."

"Why disturbing?" she asked, her voice tired and faraway.

I looked at Mamá. "He gives us no hope."

She closed her eyes and slept.

❊ ❊ ❊

My mother died in the season of the pomegranate, the fig, and the quince. She died three months ahead of the doctor's schedule, before she could make our favorite membrillo compote. She died in the middle of the autumn season when students were finishing up midterms and papers written with MLA specifications; already browsing through the winter schedule, hoping there were still late-morning classes left as opposed to early-morning classes; wondering if they were going to pass chemistry or had to take it over. Mamá died in the season of the pomegranate, that leathery-skinned fruit, its membrane encasing orderly rows of ruby kernels looking like children tucked snugly next to each other, perhaps for protection. She died in the season of the womanly fig, with its dark, thin peel and its milky stem like a mother's breast, the inside pink and fleshy, the passage to lovemaking and childbearing. Mamá died in the season of the quince, this misunderstood fruit she understood well, cooking the hard, tart apple-looking membrillo into our favorite sweet, syrupy compote. Our mother died in my season of melancholy and introspection, that season of dried palm fronds and pepper tree branches randomly scattered on the streets after the Santa Ana desert winds had announced their presence, the backcountry fires filling the sky with smoke and flakes of ashes. And I hated her for dying at that time of year, at that time of her life and mine. I hated her with the same intensity and passion that I loved her. Mamá, who was strong and fierce and unyielding in her religious convictions and family loyalty—her loyalty to us, her nine children; her loyalty to her explosive, unpredictable husband. For this I hated her and I loved her. And because Mamá had left me with questions that would haunt me and tease me and torment me into winter and spring and summer, only to return autumn after autumn with deeper melancholy and anguish. My every season would be shaded with questions about this woman who left us, after all, in the season of the pomegranate, the fig, and the quince. And I would argue with her all the rest of my life, asking her, why autumn, why when the pomegranates are ripe and the membrillo ready to cook? Why in my season of melancholy introspection when I need you the most? And were she to have died in spring, or summer, or winter, I would've asked her the same question: Why spring? Why summer? Why winter? Why die at all at that time of your life and mine? How could you die right when I was getting to know you? How could you die before you met my children? And because this was a one-sided argument, Mamá would remain quiet, or else she'd simply look at the road ahead of us and say to me, "Watch out for that blue car that's zigzagging up ahead."

Part Two

Me acordé de lo que me había dicho mi madre:

«Allá me oirás mejor. Estaré más cerca de ti.

Encontrarás más cercana la voz

de mis recuerdos que la de mi muerte,

si es que alguna vez la muerte ha tenido alguna voz.»

I remembered what my mother had told me:

"You'll hear me better over there.

I'll be nearer to you. You'll find the voice

of my memory closer than the one of my death—

if death has ever had a voice."

—From *Pedro Páramo* by Juan Rulfo

Twelve

Even then, as the bus wound its way out of Guadalajara, west toward the Pacific coast, towards El Grullo, I wondered if I knew where I was going and whether clutching the door handle—of a car, of a house, of a past—might lead me llueva o truene, come hell or high water, to where I needed to be.

I looked out the window and saw the city behind us, the factories, stores, the traffic thinning as we headed out to small towns and verdant subtropical terrain. Soon we left the city altogether, making our way through the fertile Jalisco land—Rulfo country, I thought—toward rural towns and villages. I was on my way to visit my mother's sisters, to ask them the millions of questions I had never asked my mother. It occurred to me that my mother probably would have revealed very little about her life anyway. What I knew of my mother was like looking at movie previews, teasers. I was traveling to her hometown as I had done nearly every summer of my life, but this time I was looking for the complete, unabridged story of Mamá.

When she died, I dropped my French, poli sci, and chemistry classes. The only class I didn't drop was the contemporary Latin American lit class. I couldn't. I needed to hold on to Juan Rulfo, have him near me. He had become my friend and my guide as I followed him into haunting terrain, into a fragmented, oxymoronic world. In truth, he was my connection to Mamá and the world she came from.

The bus ride was circuitous, uphill, now downhill—much as my journey into Mamá's history, I suspected, would be. Like Juan Rulfo's stories, there would be ironies and contradictions, frustration and horror. Or had I been too influenced by Jalisco's famous son?

Tía Rebeca was the storyteller of Mamá's family. It was Rebeca I would—what was the word my mother once used? Ah, yes—*supplicate* to tell me everything she knew about Mamá. The three-hour ride to

El Grullo wound and curved up mountains and down valleys, and I was suddenly very tired. The weight of the funeral and the sudden emptiness of our home after the loss of our family's pillar, followed by indecision and then the decision to take a winter quarter's leave of absence from the university, added to planning this trip to El Grullo to see my mother's sisters—all of this suddenly weighed heavily on me. I closed my tired eyes, letting my mind drift, taking me back to the El Grullo summer when I was eleven years old and I was beginning my adolescent descent into hating my mother with the kind of fury that only a daughter who furiously loves her mother can have.

Mexico. Jalisco. El Grullo. Avenida Netzahualcoyotl. We went there every summer that I could remember to visit my grandparents. And when they died, we continued to visit my mother's sisters, Tía Rebeca and Tía Celeste—the comatriarchs of the Ramos home. All the way from San Diego we traveled—my mother and father and brothers and sisters and I—not only a long distance, so far from home, from my native Conifer Street, but far from our way of doing things. To visit El Grullo was to go back in time thirty, forty—maybe a hundred—years, to cobblestoned streets, the open-air market, the plaza. Rows of hibiscus shrubs and rosebushes lined the town square where an intricately designed wrought-iron *quiosco* stood with decorative scrolls on its pillars. The tall cathedral across the street, the single most prominent structure of this town, of probably any Mexican town, rang its bells—the hollow, urgent resounding dong, dong, dong—for morning and evening Mass.

My great-grandfather was one of the founders of this town, and his son, my grandfather Ramón, had built this enormous square house at the turn of the century, just before the revolution. Designed in the colonial tradition with a courtyard in the middle and corridors connecting each side of the square, this was one of the oldest mansions in El Grullo. The two massive front doors, heraldry carved into their panels, with heavy wrought-iron knockers, were kept open during the day. Large mango trees and thick bougainvillea vines stood opposite each other, guarding the entrance into the courtyard where ferns spilled wildly out of clay planters surrounding the fountain. The few tourists who happened along this way always stopped in front of the opened doors, peeking in, requesting permission to snap a photo of the garden, of the large columns lining the corridors, or the high ceiling with its thick wooden beams. Only the bedrooms, kitchen, living and dining areas, and bathroom were enclosed, their doors leading out to the corridors and the courtyard. Huge spiders, poisonous scorpions, and anguished phantoms had dominion here. It was a formidable house; it was a frightening house.

I opened my eyes a moment as the bus made a long, complicated curve around the mountain. Raising my legs and extending them out to the empty chair next to me, I rested my head against the window.

The summer of my eleventh year, when I began to seriously hate Mamá, coincided with my obsessive interest in eavesdropping on Tía Rebeca's stories. This middle sister with the brilliant, lively green eyes and short, curly auburn hair could easily have been mistaken for an Irish woman from Dublin. Her white, pearly skin seemed unnatural, unearthly, and so when she told stories, I listened. My aunt Rebeca customarily sat in the main corridor across from the front doors most evenings, cross-stitching one of her intricately patterned tablecloths, now and then lifting her head at the sound of footsteps past the front doors on the street's sidewalk. "Adiós," came the greeting from the street as a passerby walked past, glancing into the open front doors. "Adiós," was Tía Rebeca's response, the "adiós" sounding almost flirtatious, mocking, or singsongy—like a long ellipsis at the end of a sentence, an "adioooos" drawn out and played with, sounding more like a word of three or four syllables, a word filled with multiple meanings. Godspeed to you. I commend you to God. Or simply a word that acknowledges our presence in and our departure from this world. To God I commend you, I might say to my mother. Adiós, Mamá. To God, Mamá. But always an "adiós"—whether you were just passing by or whether you were one of the people now stopping and chatting while on the way to the market, to Tortillería La Unica, to the *mandamás* for household supplies. And these were the people—young, old, men, and women—who provided her with the material for her stories. It was as if, sitting there listening to a wife's woes or an old man's litany of aches and pains, Tía Rebeca were also cross-stitching their tales into her beautiful cloth.

That story of the summer when I was eleven caused an ugly argument between my mother and Tía Rebeca. A young bride being possessed by the devil was such nonsense, she said, disgusted, to Tía Rebeca. And didn't Rebeca know that I was listening in, as usual? What a story to tell. Lies and provincial superstition, heresy is what it was. Tía Rebeca had defended herself, of course. Don Tomás, owner of one of the largest watermelon plantations in the state of Jalisco, had related the story to her. Not only was the infamous cemetery where the exorcism had been performed next to his land, but he himself had witnessed the exorcism, and certainly Don Tomás was no liar.

Yes, Tía Rebeca admitted, she knew I was listening in. "Let this serve as a lesson for her," she had said.

I had not heard the end of the argument—did the bride truly have the evil eye cast upon her, the doings of an envious ex-girlfriend of the groom, or was it just another story told to pass the time away on a tropical humid evening in an old mansion? And what was the lesson I was to learn from this story, I wondered at the age of eleven. But that night I had a sleepless, feverish night. Flying devils in blazing red capes swooped down to snatch a young woman in a beautiful lace wedding dress who sat under a black scraggly tree. I heard wails and screams and saw a lit candle with rusty nails stuck into it like a grotesque porcupine. I uttered a jumble of incoherent noises. And then I must have screamed. That long delirious night when I was eleven, Mamá stayed at my side, placing a cool, damp towel on my forehead, caressing and brushing away my hair from my sweaty forehead. The next morning I felt as humiliated as a soldier must feel when he is sick and it is his enemy who nurses and comforts him. I was now indebted to my mother.

The stories continued throughout that summer, and I eavesdropped, furtively listening in with the kind of attentiveness only a daughter who wants to hate her mother can have; like an obsessed detective, I sought to find fault with my mother at every turn, and I was certain Tía Rebeca's stories held evidence that would justify my hating Mamá. Didn't all daughters go through this with their mothers? Hate them one month, love them the next?

We were now entering the town of Unión de Tula, so I knew we were nearing my destination. I looked out the window as we passed the Presidencia Municipal, neat, easy to read street names on the corners of commercial buildings: Durango, Yucatán, Veracruz—names of Mexican states. We made our way past the cathedral to the western outskirts, headed for El Grullo. I closed my eyes. This had been a weary three-hour bus ride, and I would be happy and relieved to arrive home. Home, did I say?

We had come to the bridge that marked a fork in our destination: either we drove over it, passing through the towns of Autlán and La Huerta, toward the Pacific coast, or we continued onward into the valley toward El Grullo. I felt my heart beat faster, knowing that in about twenty minutes we would be entering El Grullo. It was like this every time, this excitement to be arriving in El Grullo, and I wondered what it was about my grandparents' home and their town that kept my sisters and me wanting to come back. Even I, with my fitful nights of sleep, my nervousness, the teasing from my sisters about my fear of ghosts and scorpions, even I wanted to come back every summer. If my home in Palm City teetered between "shoe" and "cottage," there was no ambiguity about what my grandparents' home was. It was a respected old mansion in the heart of El Grullo, a house that reflected the history of Mexico, the rise of small landowners and the middle class. A house that allowed me to be wooed by genteel, old-fashioned, respectable young men. A home that allowed me to be a Ramos princess for the summer with an army of suitors at her beck and call. Martín Macías. José Luis Zepeda. Jorge Martínez. Handsome young men who were introduced to my sisters and me by our plentiful cousins. Birthday parties, community fiestas, weddings, baptisms. The distinguished Ramos family members were much-sought-after guests at these celebrations. And if the festivities were taking place in summer—as it seemed so many of these glorious events did—then it would be such an honor, Doña Rebeca, if your nieces and nephews could attend. And of course the older generation, the generation that went to school with my mother, the pillars of this community, were always excited to see Dolores Ramos.

The bus made the customary stop at the bridge. A woman about the age of my mother got on, deliberately and carefully, laden as she was with bags. She picked the empty seat next to me, smiling at me as she settled her bags underneath her seat.

I was in no mood to chitchat with anyone, so I quickly closed my eyes, leaning my head against the window, and feigned sleep.

I once asked Ana María why Papi wasn't coming with us—again—on this summer vacation to El Grullo. I was twelve years old and we were getting ready for our annual trip to our grandparents' home.

"Don't you know, stupid," she said as she applied the red coral lipstick to her thin lips, "she needs to get away from him—at least for a little bit. And he's probably happy to get rid of us for the summer, too, so he can go off with his *putas*." And she smacked her lips, the bright orange color now evenly applied on her mouth. I never asked her how she knew this, where she got her information. She was a wise and knowing fourteen-year-old, the leader of her group of friends, and I was lucky she was telling me that much.

But after she told me this, I listened in as much as possible on adult conversations—on my mother's conversations. I observed her closely as she did the packing, as she selected the items we needed for our two-month summer stay in Mexico. She was efficient—cool summer dresses for the girls, lightweight pants for the boys. And she seemed so happy, smiling to herself as she neatly folded her favorite yellow summer smock—an ugly rag of a thing with grotesque sunflowers, the black centers looking like huge one-eyed monsters—and placed it tenderly, it seemed to me, in the blue vinyl suitcase. It was then I knew I hated her, hated her happiness, hated her for wanting this separation from my father. It was *her* fault they were having problems, *her* fault he sought other women—even if they were putas; it was her fault, not my father's, not my papi, who bought me a miniature toy horse and a Barbie doll every birthday, who used to pick me up and twirl me around and around, he was that strong.

After Ana María told me this, I didn't ask him why he wasn't coming with us this summer, why he hadn't come last summer. I knew he would say that it was because he had a lot of work and the boss couldn't give him time off. Not wanting to compromise him by forcing him to think of some gentle excuse to cover up my mother's cruelty and rejection, I didn't ask him anymore, this wonderful, handsome papi of mine.

"¿Estás bien?" the lady sitting next to me asked, tapping me on the arm.

I opened my eyes and saw her extending a Kleenex to me.

Self-consciously, I took the tissue and dabbed at my wet eyes, then blew my nose.

"My name is Abundia Páramo," she said, smiling.

"Mucho gusto," I said. "My name . . ."

"No," she stopped me, "don't tell me. I know who you are. I knew it the moment I got on the bus and laid eyes on you. ¡Qué cosa!" She said. "You are Dolores all over again."

"Dolores?" I asked. "You knew my mother?"

"Of course I knew your mother, *que en paz descanse, pobrecita.* Everyone knew your mother. Why, you could say Dolores Ramos was our very own El Grullo princess. Sí, sí," she nodded, looking out the window, remembering. "For a while there, she and I were rivals for Lorenzo, your father, you know. But in the end she won him. See? You could have been my daughter. Vaya, ¡qué cosas! Did I say 'won him'? I'm not sure that was a winning or losing—no offense to your father or you, *niña,* but the truth is the truth; facts are facts."

I wanted to ask her more, but I was afraid that if I interrupted to ask her, she would suddenly realize what she was saying and to whom and would stop talking, so I said nothing. Simply listened.

But it was as if she had read my thoughts, and she suddenly became quiet. She reached into one of her straw bags and pulled out a ball of yarn and knitting needles with a small yellow square of already knitted work.

"See? The beginnings of a child's sweater. I have grandchildren. ¿Ya ves? I married, after all. Not your father, no dear God, not Lorenzo. I married a fine man. Granted—I will grant you that," she said as she positioned her needles to resume her knitting project, "my husband was not as handsome as Lorenzo. Madre Santísima, who could resist those blue eyes, his wavy light brown hair. I don't blame your mother one bit for being caught under his spell. He was a handsome, flirtatious devil— pardon my talking that way about your father. Still alive, qué no?"

I nodded.

"As the saying goes, 'hierba mala nunca muere,'" she said. "Pardon my talk, but you must know that is what all of El Grullo must be think- ing these days: bad weeds never die. The difference between everyone else in El Grullo and me is that I'm the only one willing to be honest and out in the open with it." She paused and looked me over carefully—my face, shoulders, body—sizing me up. "What are you, seventeen, eighteen?"

"I'm nineteen," I said.

"Nineteen," she said, pausing a moment to consider something. "Yes," she finally said. "That is as good an age as any to tell you what's what."

The bus was now entering El Grullo, and I felt relieved and anxious at the same time.

Abundia Páramo was silent, her knitting needles clicking, clicking. She looked up now and then, out the window. Probably her way of tell- ing me that her chatter was over. When the bus finally rolled into the depot, she was ready to leave, her two bags retrieved from under her seat now on her lap. As we got up and moved to the front of the bus and out, I asked her if I could help carry something for her.

She smiled and thanked me. "No, niña," she said. "You'll have enough to carry in your own life."

A child pushed past me to get to her family, and I moved aside to let her, watching as she skipped over to her siblings. When I turned around to say good-bye to Abundia Páramo, she was nowhere to be found, had simply disappeared.

❖ ❖ ❖

Yes, she was everyone's princess, Tía Rebeca said with a good amount of pride. My two tías and I were sitting in the main corridor, with a view of the opened front doors and the street beyond. It occurred to me that my aunts and I were sitting in the familiar position of the three Ramos sisters of summers past, as if I had taken the place of my mother. It gave joy to neighbors, friends, and merchants to please la señorita Dolores, she continued. She was kind and humble and gracious.

My tías were generous in their stories of Mamá and what she was like growing up: a daydreamer, quiet and respectful. Whenever the merchants and peddlers came to town with their sumptuous array of fabrics, Dolores always had first pick. And even though the two younger sisters stood in her shadow, they were never envious or jealous of Dolores. You couldn't help but love this gentle, compassionate princess.

My tías told me all the things proud sisters might say of their recently deceased favorite sister. They made no mention of the years of her courtship to Papá or her marriage. Their memories were not like mine, memories of shouting, some crying, doors slamming. The constant melodrama of the Sahagún family in Palm City—enough drama to vie for a prime-time soap opera spot on television. A tiny, three-bedroom shoe of a house teeming with nine children and eleven complex personalities.

When I prodded a bit further, "What about Mamá's marriage, was she happy as a married woman? Did she love my father? Did he love her?" my Tía Celeste, the former nun and the youngest of the three, with her soft features, light brown eyes, and long, curly eyelashes patted me on the arm, asked if I would like to drink some hot chocolate before going to bed. Both sisters stood and headed for the kitchen as if they'd just remembered they had something about to boil over on the stove.

It occurred to me that they would not say anything bad about my parents' marriage, about Dolores's husband. He was still alive, and—after all—he was still my father.

While my aunts were in the kitchen preparing a bedtime snack for me, I wandered about, walking the corridors of this big square house. I peeked into the formal living room, the grand piano in one corner looking tired and warped, having sat in this room in the humid subtropics for close to eighty years. Directly across from the piano were French Provincial–style sofas and chairs, the velvet upholstery now a faded, muted blue, hinting of a time, in its prime, when such furniture was considered elegant and rich, a reflection of one's socioeconomic status—anything that had to do with the French style of life was considered elegant and rich. Aristocratic and privileged. I tried to imagine what it must have been like to grow up in a small town founded by your family—a family that was respected and revered. What must it have been like to be la señorita Dolores, and—the big question for me—what must it have been like for Dolores to marry and slowly but surely descend into unexpected poverty? She must have loved him—why else would she have sacrificed such comfort and privilege?

I was in the library, which smelled of wood and musty books. The massive shelves from floor to high ceiling housed hundreds of heavy, leather-bound books. Mamá, like her two sisters after her, was an avid reader. Well, at least I had inherited that from her. At least that much.

This is what happens, then, with the death of your mother, that moment you realize you were her daughter and didn't know her very well, and she is no longer alive for you to get to know. You are compelled to know her story, to put the bits of anecdotes together, to walk the corridors of her childhood house, peruse the library with its yellowed, musty books and find something of your mother in every nook and cranny of her home. You absentmindedly tap on the piano keys, wondering how many times she did this too, and whether she tapped the same rhythm as you. Poof! Your mother is gone, and you are left with a father you love and you hate, with siblings you adore who get on with the daily chores of life, but who have your mother present in ways that you cannot surmise. You each have a bit of her—but what, what is that bit? When you look at your reflection in the mirror and see the same round face, pudgy *chata* nose, the same curly brown hair, you wonder what part of her you really are.

My tías called out to me from the kitchen, and I called back, "Allá voy." Coming, now taking a shortcut through the courtyard to get to the opposite end of the house.

As we had our hot chocolate and *pan dulce*, I asked my aunts about my old summer beaus, what had become of them, those immaculately mannered El Grullo young men who had the honor of escorting us sisters for walks around the jardín in the town square every summer when we visited during our teenage years. Most of those boys were the sons of similarly privileged families. Those teenage summer visits to El Grullo made me feel like royalty, like I truly belonged to a privileged class, made me forget—at least for the summer—that I was from a poor barrio in *el norte*.

It was late now, and the rich hot chocolate and sweet bread made me tired and ready for sleep. Tía Rebeca led me to Mamá's bedroom—that is, the bedroom that was hers until she married Papá at the age of twenty-three. With a push at the massive, slightly warped wooden doors, my tía and I entered Dolores's bedroom.

"Buenas noches, niña," Tía Rebeca said, kissing me on the forehead and hugging me good-night. She softly closed the thick door behind her.

What struck me about Mamá's bedroom—a bedroom I was familiar with because of summer after summer vacations here during my childhood and teenage years—was that the furniture was simple, nondescript, no frills. No French Provincial. Just a small, unadorned dresser and mirror, a brass bed, and a chest of drawers. This señorita—the eldest daughter of the Ramos family—could have had the most elegant, ornate furniture brought in from Guadalajara or Mexico City. Instead, when she was a young woman, she chose whatever the local furniture store had to offer. Was it the same with her beaus? Did she purposefully choose the simplest man, the one less adorned, less laden with money than the others? Why had she chosen Lorenzo Sahagún?

I changed into my nightgown, got ready for bed, grateful that a bathroom had been added adjoining the bedroom, so I didn't have to walk back outside into the open-air corridors, across the courtyard to the one bathroom at the opposite end of the house as I used to. Turning off the bedside lamp, the room now completely dark, I quickly scooted deep into the cool sheets, the bed massive and sturdy. But I couldn't sleep. Perhaps the caffeine in the chocolate, the sugar of the sweet bread? No, I knew better. No need to find excuses, for this was standard procedure for me. My sisters used to tease me, say I should take a hefty supply of sleeping pills with me when I went to El Grullo. Each summer we visited, in those rare moments when they took pity on me and my insomnia, they tried to talk some sense into me: Have you ever even seen a ghost? Heard anything weird? Smelled the strong perfume or the cigar smell? No to all their questions, but still I was afraid of the ghost stories I had heard— surreptitiously overheard because my mother forbade me from listening to them; she knew I was much too impressionable. So after I promised to make their beds daily during our summer stays there, Carolina and Ana María filled me in on the stories. Either that or else I would hide in the shadows of the long corridors in a quiet, dark corner, and listen to my aunts and mother talk.

I slid back up, turned on the small lamp next to my bed, and propped the pillow against the brass headboard to support my back. I wrapped my arms around my bent knees close to my chest. This too was standard procedure when I couldn't sleep. Then, and when I was young, I thought that with the light on and my waiting for them, surely the phantoms would not dare present themselves. And so I thought about the other summer, the summer I turned twelve and my hatred for my mother had grown threefold.

That summer—hotter and more humid and more impossible than most summers here in subtropical El Grullo—Tía Rebeca's stories had taken on another tone, a mysterious tone, both beautiful and ugly. Confusing.

"This woman was a saint, to be sure," Tía Rebeca was saying. "A simple, honest woman. That's all."

Mamá and Tía Celeste remained silent. With arms folded in identical positions across their chests, neither one encouraged the third sister to continue.

I lay still in the hammock, just beyond the well-lit circle of three women.

"The story is a simple one, I promise—no magic, no supernatural events," Tía Rebeca said. "Normal daily circumstances, this I assure you."

Still neither sister responded. It was as if they were in a trance, hypnotized by the lethargic warmth of the night, silently looking out past the lit section of the corridor, down the dark hallway that led to the open front door.

Occasionally I heard footsteps nearing the house, and then passing the front door. "Buenas noches," sounded softly, floating through the dark halls like a ghost toward the women sitting under the chandelier.

"Buenas noches," the three sisters called back in unison.

"I tell you, she really was a saint," Tía Rebeca said, folding her arms in like fashion. She was not to be outdone by her sisters.

This was a little game they played. Tía Rebeca knew that her sisters were playing hard to get, that they pretended not to be interested in her stories. But she also knew she was the best storyteller in all of El Grullo—perhaps in all of Mexico.

"And she was ugly," Tía Rebeca said.

Mamá and Tía Celeste turned from gazing down the dark corridor and now looked directly at Rebeca.

"Yes, indeed, she was very ugly, poor thing."

I watched as a confused moth circled the chandelier. Its wings fluttered, making a quick tap-tap-tapping sound against the prisms.

"How can she be ugly and a saint at the same time?" I called out from my dark place on the hammock, realizing—too late!—that I shouldn't have let on that I was within hearing distance.

"She was a saint, no question of that. But she was no beauty queen." Tía Rebeca shaded her eyes from the light above, peering into the dark corner from which the question had come. "Shouldn't you be in bed?" she asked me.

"Yes, she should," Mamá said, getting up from her chair and looking into the shadows for me. "Go to bed now, Yolanda." Her use of the word "Yolanda" and not my usual nickname "Yoli" was her way of showing her firmness. There was absolutely no pleading or whining or arguing with her when she issued forth such decrees followed by "Yolanda," detestable mother that she was.

I got up from the hammock where I had lain, wrapped in the rope netting like a cocoon, hoping to be unnoticed by the women. As I walked slowly away from them, from their cozy circle of light, the long corridors grew darker. I was ashamed to tell them that I, already twelve years old, was afraid of those dark halls where no one had ever bothered to install lights.

When I reached the bedroom that was mine for the summer, my stomach suddenly felt sick. I had not gone to pee. The one bathroom was at the opposite end of another dark walk through the corridors.

Why did all the creepy crawlers of El Grullo scramble out at night along those halls? Why was *I* the only one to encounter them? I walked carefully, quietly. Perhaps I would not disturb a tiny scorpion (the tropical yellow ones were the worst), or a hairy-legged spider the size of my whole hand ("good" spiders, I was told, because they ate scorpions, so I was not to kill them). Perhaps these little enemies of mine—pernicious enemies I battled every summer, my heart in my throat—would not challenge me that night.

But worse than these intrusive pests were the ghosts. I knew all about these phantoms that walked the dark halls, those shadows that moaned and wailed in the night out in the corral under the ancient ceiba tree. For often I stood outside the kitchen door early in the morning before any of my brothers and sisters awakened, listening as each woman whispered her ghost incident. Above the noise of sizzling *huevos con chorizo* in the frying pan, I could hear the sisters, huddled together in a conspiratorial circle of three, hurriedly sharing what they'd just experienced—the noises, the presence, the smells—before any of us children awakened and entered the kitchen.

Tía Rebeca's voice became more audible as I neared the bathroom. How could the saint be ugly? My copy of *The Children's Book of Saints* had drawings of golden, angelic young women far too beautiful and perfect for their earthly surroundings. Tía Rebeca must be teasing. Surely a saint could not be ugly.

At last I reached the bathroom. A cricket jumped out of my way—or I jumped out of its way. I could not really tell, as my heart was beating madly. I quickly sat on the toilet and closed my eyes, hoping not to discover any living creature crawling along the bathroom wall facing me.

I couldn't pee. I was too nervous. No matter, I thought to myself, trying to feign courage, an artificial nonchalance; I would sit here until it came out, for I would not tolerate another degrading sit on the chamber pot in the middle of the night.

"Her husband was no beauty either," I heard Tía Rebeca saying. Had she just begun to tell the story? Or was that the end?

"He was an ogre in the ugliest sense of the word. He beat her, he mocked her, he threw her out of the house even. And what did this young bride do? She waited. Like a stupid dog, she waited for him to calm down. She would sit on the front steps until his rage had passed. It could be pouring rain, freezing outside, snowing . . ."

"It doesn't snow in El Grullo, Rebeca," Mamá reminded her.

"Just the same," she said, "he was a devil of a man . . ."

And so Tía Rebeca's story began: Mean, domineering husband who demanded his food be on the table just as soon as he walked into the home from work or the bars. His saintly, ugly wife always had it ready, was at his beck and call. Then one afternoon my Tía Rebeca paid that saintly wife a visit, excited to tell her about Florita and her new, fantastic husband. She mentions to this saintly wife that Florita—ugly, pimply-faced Florita—had a marriage made in heaven. The saintly, ugly wife was absorbed in the details of Florita's heaven-made marriage. But in Tía Rebeca's excitement to tell this saint about the perfect marriage, she had accidentally left the back door open and the chickens had scrambled in, pecking at this, poking at that. The poor woman of the house listened, mesmerized by Tía Rebeca's details: it was known that on Sundays, Florita's husband himself insisted on making breakfast for her—*huevos rancheros*, tortillas, *un cafecito*, pan dulce. This poor young wife listened, enraptured, every now and then looking out the window with a dreadful realization that her husband would soon be home and the food would not be ready. And the silly chickens, like silly Tía Rebeca, continued clucking away in the kitchen.

Then the young wife saw him first. He was lumbering up the dirt path to the house. And Tía Rebeca saw the young wife's face turn pale. By then the chickens had hopped onto the kitchen table. Quickly giving the poor woman a kiss on the cheek, Tía Rebeca practically flew out the back door. The beast of a man was stomping up the front steps when the young wife discovered that one of the chickens had pooped on the kitchen table. No time to clean it, she grabbed a cup and set it, inverted, on top of the poop. Of course, the ogre demanded his dinner. Poor thing, how she trembled! She could not look him straight in the eye. She only shook her head, staring fearfully at the cup.

"No dinner!?" the brute roared. "I'm hungry, you lazy bitch. Give me anything, you hear, anything."

"No, don't nod your heads," Tía Rebeca said. "I know what you are thinking: 'Yes, this is why she was a saint. A martyr. A kind woman—even if she is ugly—to have to put up with a brute like that!' But I tell you, this is not what made her a saint. So simple? If obedience and suffering were what made a saint, there would be no end to sanctifying the women of El Grullo. Even Dolores here—why, you would be a saint, if that were the case . . ."

I could not see the three women, their faces and expressions, or how my mother reacted to this last comment. But I could hear a silence that wanted to communicate something sad on that muggy summer night of my twelfth year, a silence full of hints, implications, and truths gliding through the air, down the corridor toward me like an invisible phantom messenger.

"But here's the miracle that made her a saint," Tía Rebeca said, continuing her story. "The young woman looked him squarely in the face. 'Ah,' she must have thought, 'now I understand what I have been living, chained to this life of subservience and humiliation with a man who does not deserve me, with no escape from this drudgery, nowhere to run for at least a little bit of respite.' Who knows, perhaps her guardian angel nudged her, whispered some words of encouragement. Well, one never knows for sure what does it, eh? Guardian angels. Or maybe just being fed up and tired of it. Anyway, this skinny but smart woman had a look of triumph as she slowly picked up the cup. 'There,' she said to her husband, pointing to the chicken poop, 'There is your dinner.'"

❖ ❖ ❖

I turned off the light, scooted back down, rearranged my pillow, telling myself that I was being ridiculous about all of this. Just go to sleep, Yoli, I told myself, taking a few deep breaths. Deeply in, in, in, then slowly, slowly out. After a few minutes of that I could tell it wasn't going to work. I was still nervous. Those memories were feeding my mind, and the mattress was lumpy, the room too warm. Stifling. I sat up in bed and waited. The room was black, and I couldn't make out much in that deep darkness. The crow of an energetic rooster could be heard in the distance. A donkey braying. Some firecrackers going off, sounding like gunshots, or gunshots going off, sounding like firecrackers. And there I was, 1974, sleeping in Mamá's bedroom. That is, the bedroom that was hers growing up, the bedroom that she left in 1940 at the age of twenty-three when she married Papá. Terrified lest my wishes come true, I waited and watched in the darkness for the phantom to appear before me. I waited to listen to its story, for I was certain it had the answers to my questions, this phantom and others that had been walking the long, hollow halls of that home since the Mexican Revolution, since Mamá was born. I imagined they cavorted with Mamá, a tiny infant in her lavishly decorated crib. Did she gurgle with pleasure as these shadows hovered over her, or was she terrified, letting out a piercing infant shriek that brought Abuelita and the maid Sarita rushing over to the crib?

Tía Rebeca's story of the saint was over, and while the women closed the front doors, the kitchen door, and the door leading out to the corral, I was able to sneak back to the other end of the corridor, a little breathless and trembly from I don't know what. Under my blankets I waited, knowing that Mamá would come in to check on my sleeping sisters and me.

They were mumbling, saying something to each other, my mother and two aunts.

"It's my life . . . leave me alone about it . . ." Mamá was speaking, her voice low and angry.

Some more talking, words I could not distinguish.

" . . . for this you cry, woman?" I heard Tía Rebeca say.

Cry? Was my mother crying? Was that what she meant?

I covered my ears with my hands and tightly closed my eyes. "Don't listen, don't listen," I whispered over and over to myself.

When my mother entered the room, I lay motionless, feigning sleep. I could hear her going to each bed, making sure each daughter was lightly covered with a sheet. Then I heard her nearing my bed. She bent down to kiss my forehead, but I stirred suddenly, moving my face away from hers, sighing as if in deep slumber. No woman so ugly in my eyes could be a saint. She left the room, confident that we were all resting soundly.

I couldn't sleep that oppressive, humid night when I was twelve. If only we could be gone from this house, I thought as I tried to find a comfortable sleeping position. Just go home, was what I wanted, and never come back to this wretched place full of taunting whispers and half-told secrets.

Then I heard the noise, a swishing sound along the floor, the long cape brushing the tiles as the phantom walked through the dark corridors. I had heard that sound many nights when I couldn't fall asleep quickly. The rhythmic swish-swish-swish of the cape nearing my bedroom, wanting to steal me away in the night, I was sure. And I would pray with such urgency and fear—five, ten Hail Marys—my head deep under the covers, until the sound had ceased. But that time, mature and brave twelve-year-old that I thought myself to be, I did not hide. I knew I would have to confront the demon sometime soon—better now, to get it over with once and for all. I peered out from under the sheet and saw her. She was standing in the doorway staring at me, and the moonlight coming in through the opened window lit her as if she were a heavenly vision. We stared at each other for a moment, my heart thumping wildly. I had been found out.

"Sleep now," she said. "And tomorrow you can think about my story. Buenas noches, niña," Tía Rebeca said, and she was gone.

The light of the moon did not disappear when she left, as I thought it might in some ghostly, haunting way. As I lay there in bed without moving, staring at the spot where she had stood, I noticed a spider walking across the moonlit area. It was an enormous spider, almost the size of my hand, the "good" kind that eats venomous scorpions and so was not to be killed. I got out of bed, picked up one of my shoes and, holding it tightly in my sweaty hand, aimed high. The spider continued its walk across the doorway. Sensing me, perhaps knowing it was in danger, the ugly thing began to scurry toward the shadows, a safe hiding place. I slammed the shoe down, slammed it again and again, until this wicked, pernicious enemy of mine was mutilated. But there were too many in that big old house, and even as I killed that one spider, I knew I would never come close to killing them all. With the edge of my shoe I scraped and scooted its smashed remains away from the moonlit doorway and into the darkness.

❁ ❁ ❁

Was it so for all young daughters, or just the *consentidas*, the favorites, that we were quicker to forgive our father his imperfections than we were to forgive our mother hers? I looked around me at the floor, my heart beating wildly, my hands clammy and cold, expecting to see a monstrous, evil spider skittering toward me. I listened for the swish of the phantom's cape, this phantom coming to steal me away, but all I saw was darkness and a nineteen-year-old daughter sitting up in bed, waiting for her mother to tell her story.

Thirteen

Lydia and I were sitting at the kitchen table, early January. It was cold outside so I was making us some Mexican hot chocolate, putting an extra triangular wedge for each of us into the hot milk. Then I took the wooden *molinillo*, tapped it softly against the hard chocolate, coaxing the chocolate to melt quickly at the bottom of the tall, slender clay pot on the stove. Once the hot milk had melted the tablet, I rubbed the handle of the molinillo against my palms in quick, back-and-forth swipes. My mother had a way of doing this that made the chocolate milk foam nicely. I took a peek inside. No foam, but it had melted pretty well, just a few grains of chocolate at the bottom. I poured the hot liquid into a coffee mug for each of us. My mother always made us our *chocolatito* on Sunday evenings before settling down to watch the *Lawrence Welk Show* followed by *Bonanza*. I stared at the red and yellow striped hexagonal box of chocolate as Lydia and I talked.

She'd helped me moved my stuff out of the dorms, now that I would be living back at home, commuting to UCSD. No question about it, I would need to help Ana María with the household and with our little sisters Luz and Monica. Help fend off el señor Lorenzo Sahagún's erratic wrath.

"Yoli, what's wrong?" Lydia asked. "You've been so quiet."

I stared at the foamless hot chocolate.

Was it because of my mother? She asked. Was I going through some sort of depression? What happened in El Grullo?

I set the box of chocolate on its side, rolling it bumpily back and forth in short sweeps, something I'd always done when I was young, wanting to hear the kind of rhythm a hexagonal-shaped box had.

I didn't say anything. The only sound was the rhythmic bump-bump of the box on the table.

I had learned something new, but not from my aunts who were too respectful to lead me into darkness. What for? they must have reasoned.

Why stir up the past? What's done was done. But I did retrieve a lost trinket, given to me in the way of info from Abundia Páramo. It seemed my parents' marriage, thirty-odd years later, was still talked about as if it were legendary. That much I gathered from Abundia's chatter. But only that much. So, for now, most of my mother's history lay quietly hidden within the halls and rooms and corral of her childhood home in El Grullo, and in the walls and rooms and garden of her adult home in Palm City, leading me to conjure in my mind, from my own memories, the rest of the stories. The need to know and understand her life seemed suddenly, desperately connected to my need to know and understand, little by little, my own. That is to say, to know my mother was to know myself. Yet even as I tried to recount in a linear, chronological way the turn of events in my life, I knew that my whole life would unfold before me in this way: a going forward and backward. Like the tide during full moons and new moons, the rhythms of my life would reflect my own longing, my own journey.

"Yoli? Are you listening to me?"

I looked at Lydia as if her voice were coming from far away and I was trying to recognize it.

"What happened in El Grullo? Did something happen?"

"You want some more?" I asked Lydia. "I'm sure I can make it frothy this time."

I got up from the table, carrying the box of chocolate tablets in my hand, and walked toward the stove.

Lydia got up, put her hand on my arm, stopping me. "No, Yoli," she said, "that's enough for now." And then she hugged me and let me cry, knowing in her intuitive best friend sort of way that my trip to El Grullo this December was more of a rosary than the exorcism I was hoping for.

✿ ✿ ✿

I was looking for the black satchel case my mother bought me at Fedmart for my first year in college, the satchel that I took with me to the dorms but never used. Now where was it? I knew I had put it away somewhere

here in the closet, next to my shoes. Then I spotted it, way in the back, and reached for it. It was empty except for a few pencils, stray sheets of paper, and it was in perfect condition since I'd never used it. Then I walked into my parents' bedroom, a room where now only my father slept. It looked exactly the same—as if my mother were still alive. Her clothes were in the closet and her toiletries still sat on the dresser. For a moment I surveyed the room, took stock of my surroundings. I stood perfectly still in an effort to listen for ghosts, for my mother to appear before me the way Hamlet's father appeared before him. But no, nothing. Not a sound, not a sign. Only a parents' bedroom shrouded with questions and incomplete answers. I went directly to the dresser and quickly, stealthily, opened the top drawer and took the two items I was looking for. Just as I was about to close the drawer, I noticed a pamphlet way in the back as if it were meant to stay hidden. A thin booklet, yellow with age and use. It was in Spanish. I don't know why I bothered, but I paused to read the title. It was instructions on the rhythm method, how to avoid getting pregnant the Catholic way. I quickly closed the booklet, felt sick to my stomach, as if I'd just been punched. A lot of good this Catholic way of not having too many children did my mother. When did she get this booklet? After which child was born? The third? The fourth? The sixth? And I felt a combination of sadness and deception. Betrayal. Had it worked, had she gone by the book, maybe I, being number seven, wouldn't have been here now. Surely she would have tried to stop getting pregnant after six children! How did she feel about having so many kids? And I couldn't stop myself: a wave of self-pity washed over me as I realized I would probably never know; I would never get the chance to ask her now or later—when I myself would be pregnant. This wave of self-pity commingled with the fury and sadness of realizing that I knew my mother very little.

I took the booklet and put it in the satchel along with the other items. Then I was out of the bedroom, crossing the living room, slamming the front door behind me.

The Imperial Beach pier was just a few minutes from our house. I parked nearby and got out of the car, satchel in hand. It was twilight now, dim lights in the bars and shops nearby, but because it was winter, the pier was quiet, just a few fishermen casting their poles or rummaging in their tackle boxes. I walked the length of the pier, quickly and deliberately, as if I were on a mission, as if I were a secret agent and my satchel held highly confidential information. What could I do with the satchel anyway, now that my mother was dead? Yes, yes, I knew the answer: I could fill it with stories of my mother, both real and imagined; I could fill it with photos of my mother, or with her favorite trinkets—the gold *pensamientos* earrings, the compact powder case with a filigreed design, her favorite perfume— and then pass the satchel down to my children and their children. I could, in my effort to keep my mother alive, share with my children memories of her, recount with much affection and fun, for example, how I came to possess this dorky-looking satchel from Fedmart.

I came to the end of the pier, my mission about to be completed. The ocean was calm that evening, and I was far enough out that the sound of the waves crashing at the shoreline was muted and distant. It was only me and the placid ocean and the horizon. As I stood there staring at nothing and everything, I suddenly remembered that song—what was it? Something about Billie Joe MacAllister jumping off the Tallahatchie Bridge. There was a part in the song where the mother mentions that that nice young preacher saw her daughter and Billie Joe throwing something off the Tallahatchie Bridge. I never figured that part out: what had the girl and Billie Joe MacAllister thrown off the bridge?

I took one last look at the items in the bag: the little booklet on the rhythm method, the prayer pamphlet my mother read in her last days titled *Quince Minutos Con Dios*, and her favorite rose petal rosary. Then I buckled the satchel shut and in one strong, vicious swoop, tossed it over the pier into the ocean. I'd had it with this religion. What good did fifteen minutes with God do my mother? What good did a lifetime of saintliness do her? Here, God, keep your rose petal rosaries and your fifteen minutes—cram them up your ass, if you will. I had no use for God, or for his smug cohorts and silly prayers. "Happy are those who have suffered on Earth, for theirs is the Kingdom of God." "Happy are those who are called to His supper . . ." "Lord, I am not worthy that you should come unto me, only say the word and my soul shall be healed." "For thine is the kingdom, the power and the glory . . ." "Puerta del cielo—ruega por nosotros. Torre de marfil—ten piedad de nosotros . . ." Stop it! I had no use for these incantations that were nothing more than the wailings and laments of witches and phantoms. Go away! I no longer wanted them in my life, for they neither comforted me nor made me feel devoutly penitent; these phrases and chants were just haunting vestiges of my upbringing.

I watched as the satchel wobbled uncertainly on the surface of the water like a helpless bit of raft, or a remnant of car upholstery. Drifting farther and farther out to sea, perhaps poked and prodded by a dolphin, maybe rescued by a fisherman. Drifting toward another deserted island, this brand-new-looking satchel that was never used. An insignificant bag bought at Fedmart.

Fourteen

He stood at the kitchen counter making something, and was so focused on whatever it was he was doing that he didn't hear me come in. I watched him from the doorway, his back to me. He was small and sprightly, and I would like to say that his bark was greater than his bite, but this wasn't so. Yet now it didn't matter, because without Mamá alive to be blamed for our misbehavior—those brief moments of rezongando, talking back, a quickly quelled spurt of rebellion from this or that child—our father had very little leverage. It didn't matter anymore. He could rant and rave all he wanted, for there was no one who would patiently listen to his rants and raves anymore, no one to heat his tortillas and cold dinner when he came home late, no one—at least not me—who cared whether his bark or his bite was greater. Mamá had been dead three months now, and whenever I looked at my father, the thought—cruel and angry and honest—came to mind: why couldn't it have been him instead of her?

The moment our mother died, *he*—this man, this Mr. Lorenzo Sahagún—became both dictator and prisoner, trapped in his own ridiculous, unforgettable actions with no one to rescue him from himself. Sitting next to the telephone, the morning after her death, paging through a small, tattered telephone book he kept in his shirt pocket at all times, my father called out to whichever daughter happened to be walking past the living room at just the moment he found the desired phone number.

"Monica," he had said, "dial me this number and say that el señor Lorenzo Sahagún wants to talk with . . ." and next thing you knew, one of us daughters became his *secretaria*, dialing a long string of numbers to towns and cities in Mexico. As soon as the desired person answered at the other end, our father—el señor Lorenzo Sahagún—would take the phone and brush his daughter-turned-secretary aside so he could talk in peace.

Talk in peace? Is that what I just said?

"Don Vicente," he shouted into the phone, loud enough for the neighbors to hear, loud enough for Socorrito next door to stop in her tracks and think, Aha! Lorenzo is up to some more of his *tonterías*, foolishness that promises to be interesting and worth relating to the rest of the neighbors. She would go quickly to her bedroom and stand just behind the curtains at the window from which she could view the goings-on next door. With her own morbid optimism, Socorrito must have been thinking, Well, at least Dolores doesn't have to put up with him anymore. That's one good thing about her dying. No more putting up with Lorenzo.

"Lorenzo Sahagún here." A pause. Don Vincente replying with greetings. "Dolores? That is why I am calling you. Dolores has just passed away—yes, yes, cancer. She died last night . . . she went quickly, didn't suffer . . ."

Didn't suffer?

I had been standing in the hallway, listening to his voice, which sounded excited, full of pomp and importance. El señor Lorenzo Sahagún knew that for at least a little while he would be the center of attention, lavished with sympathy and compassion.

The urge to rip the phone from his hand and slap his face overcame me. Someone was knocking at the door, brothers and sisters, aunts and uncles were already here; there was much crying, some crying soft and private, and other crying loud and communal. People whispered their consolation to each other, the quiet reverence broken every so often by my father's booming voice on the phone, announcing once again that his wife was dead, yes, yes, cancer . . . terrible, I know . . . The funeral is tomorrow at ten in the morning—as if he were announcing a grand celebration and everyone was welcome to the party. People turned to look, to listen to what all the excited, almost happy shouting into the phone was about, while my father stood there oblivious to us all, stood apart from the respectful, genuine grieving that was taking place out on Conifer Street, on the porch, at the front door, in the kitchen, out in the backyard, sobs and moans and hugs of sadness. Yes, yes, she died last night, well actually early this morning, died of cancer, you didn't know? Yes, well, thank God she went quickly, Dolores did, didn't have to suffer . . .

And I stood there in the hallway staring at him, transfixed by his behavior, wanting to kill him with my own two hands.

"This is how he mourns," Carolina said quietly, standing next to me, her arm around my shoulder as we both watched Lorenzo from a distance. It was as if we were watching some nonsensical circus performance and trying to understand its purpose. "It is his way of dealing with his grief," she said.

I shook my head, still staring at my father who was probably on his ninth phone call, Luz having taken over to dial his calls, relieving Monica who was confused by all the commotion going on around her, confused and awkward like all of us. After all, this was our first up-close death. So now baby sister Luz, with her eyes red from all her crying, was obediently dialing the number Lorenzo called out with his dash of self-importance. What, was he fingerless, this foolish man? Why couldn't he dial himself? And I felt swept away by the tremendous urge to hit him, to rip the phone jack out of the wall, my wish to hurt him as he had hurt Mamá and me and everyone he ever loved.

"No, Carolina," I finally said. "No, this is how he deals with his guilt."

❀ ❀ ❀

He reached for the can of Carnation condensed milk. Rice pudding again.

Just a few days before my mother died, my father had this brilliant idea of cooking his specialty for her. He set about the kitchen, placing his ingredients on the counter—the rice, the sticks of cinnamon, milk, raisins—claiming she was losing too much weight, certain that what Dolores needed was his famous *arroz con leche*. My sisters and I didn't say anything. We let him pretend that his rice would bring her back to health. Didn't he know that for the last two days she was at the stage where she couldn't swallow anything but liquids? My God, was this man so unaware—so self-absorbed—as not to realize that his wife was dying?

Papá turned and saw me standing there watching him.

"Would you like some?" he offered. "I put in extra raisins at Luz's request."

"Sure," I said. I walked over to the refrigerator, reached for the carton of milk, now pouring myself a glass. Otherwise, Papá's rice pudding was just too sweet.

"I have some news for you," he said, looking over his shoulder as he served me some rice pudding. "I've already told your sisters."

He'd been offered the position of manager at the Del Sol senior citizen apartments in San Ysidro, he told me, and it meant that he would have a small one-bedroom apartment to live in. It was only about seven miles from the house.

"Qué bueno, Papá," I said, congratulating him. "I think that will be good for you."

He seemed relieved that I was congratulating him, sincere in my congratulations. After all, he was as relieved as I was: He probably wanted to get the hell away from here just as much as I wanted him to be gone.

He walked over to the table with the plate of rice pudding. I tried not to look startled as he placed it in front of me. There was a mountain of raisins on the top—too many raisins to make this rice pudding edible—the pudding looking like it had been infested with a hundred dark bugs.

Fifteen

Since the time our brothers left the house—married to wives or to bachelorhood—our shoe-cottage had become a female house, *la casa de las damitas*. Yes, Papá flitted in between jobs, in time for breakfast and dinner, in time to bark orders or snore on the green velvet armchair, but still there was a feeling I had—as if I'd awakened from a dream and sensed something was different: the sudden smell of star jasmine permeating the evening; perhaps the rearrangement of a table; sheer living room drapes no longer tied back with a sash—that in this seemingly patriarchal family, the order of command had subtly changed and that our home belonged to us women—and maybe it always had.

But once again, something had changed. There was a stillness in our home that was never there before. The nervous energy, the emotional electrical currents inherent in a large family with contrasting, complex personalities—yes, the poltergeist of our childhood—that permeated the house throughout my life were no longer. The ghosts seemed to have quieted or had simply left. Or were biding their time. A kind of silence in this house—a house now inhabited by only us sisters—that was deafening. Impossible.

Every so often I had to remind myself of where I was in time—month, season, school year. For with my mother's death, time seemed to have become squiggly, wormy lines running parallel one moment, intersecting at another. Sometimes feeling as if it were yesterday, sometimes sensing it was tomorrow, but most of the time reminding myself that I was somewhere in the present—whatever that might be. Every so often, then, to keep focused on the here and now, I took inventory of the present status of things: I lived at 2215 Conifer Street—the same home all my life—with one room for five sisters, another one for our parents, and a partially attached, private entrance room for my four brothers. And after years of living scrunched up in this shoe-cottage, few of us were left. My brothers and oldest sister Carolina were on their own:

Carolina was married to Tom, she now working on her master's in psychology; Armando was married to Sonia; Tony was married to Marisa; and Octavio lived on his own in a trailer park nearby, swearing to be a bachelor forever. And then there was Chuy, our Vietnam veteran brother, who, when he was not interned at the VA hospital, when he was out of the hospital, regularly taking his medication, stabilized and normal—whatever that meant—lived a couple of trailers away from Octavio in Imperial Beach about four miles from our house. So now it was only us in the casita: twenty-two-year-old Ana María who threatened every so often to elope with ever-patient Roger when we sisters got on her nerves; eighteen-year-old Monica, two years younger than I, who was in her senior year in high school and kept herself busy with homework during the week and horseback riding lessons on weekends; our baby sister Luz, thirteen and active as a junior high cheerleader and Associated Student Body secretary—immersed enough in school activities so that perhaps she didn't feel the loneliness; and I, in my second year of college. The house now seemed too big, and even though we girls could take over our brothers' room, spread out, the luxury of only *two* sisters sharing a room and not five, we four remaining sisters preferred to stay inhabiting the girls' room as we had done all our lives. And now that our mother was no longer there, the urge to huddle in a sisterly cocoon seemed imperative.

It was my turn to do the dishes, and as I dried the last fork and set it in the drawer, I looked around me at the familiar green Formica kitchen table and matching chairs, the bowl of artificial grapes, apples, and bananas in its center. The house seemed to be missing something, as if it were only partially furnished, naked and hollow. Or was it just that I wished my mother were with us now, relishing not having our father living with us? But it was more than that: there was in me a feeling of anticipation—as if all of us sisters were waiting for something; waiting to make a decision about marrying or not marrying Roger; waiting for the next cheerleading competition; waiting for love to sweep us away. Waiting. Waiting. As if our mother's death had pushed us to another level of reality.

I took the winter quarter of classes off because at the time I filled out the leave of absence form university studies seemed irrelevant to my life. But I knew it would be only for a quarter. Something about spring got me going again, energetic and full of projects. I knew I would be ready to join my normal university student life once spring kicked in. In the meantime, I worked at the JCPenney department store. Yes, our father checked in with us every day, had dinner with us on weekends; older brothers and sisters checked in as well, but in reality, this was a house headed by damitas, young ladies trying to make a path for themselves.

Lydia was envious of our semi-independence, but she was also trying very hard to cheer us up. "At least now you don't have your father breathing down your back every minute, putting restrictions on you, asking you a thousand controlling, domineering questions. '¿A dónde vas?' '¿Cuándo regresas?' 'No regreses tarde,' 'Vete con cuidado.' Jesus Christ, I can't breathe at my house."

Monica spent all her time in what used to be our brothers' room. She didn't let anyone in. When we called to her to help bring in the laundry or to remind her that it was her turn to do the dishes, she came out of the room onto the patio, closing the door quickly behind her. She quietly, obediently headed for the sink, washed and dried the dishes, then returned to the outside room. Luz, on the other hand, sat in the living room for long periods of time on the phone. Brushed me away when I told her to come eat. I'm not hungry; leave me alone.

We were in the kitchen spreading butter on our tortillas—freshly made, warm flour tortillas Socorrito had just sent over wrapped in a dishtowel—and then sprinkling them with salt. The butter melted deliciously, surrendering itself to the warm tortilla as soon as it made contact. That's how I described it to Lydia.

"Jesus, Yoli," she said, now folding her flour tortilla in half and biting into it. "Do you have to equate everything with love and passion?" She pretended to be exasperated with me, though I could tell she was pleased. I hadn't been very funny in a long time.

"*Pobre tortilla*," she said, now addressing the one she was holding, "you haven't a chance, do you? All you want is to be appreciated as a delicious *tortilla de harina* with a little melted butter on you and some sprinkles of salt, but here you have Doña Shakespeariana finding signs of love and passion in every nook and cranny." She shook her head. "Ay, por Dios," she said, sad and resigned. "What's a tortilla to do?" and she took a big, last bite of it.

❀ ❀ ❀

Finding signs of love and passion. I'd just finished my shift at JCPenney. It was brisk out, Presidents' Weekend sales in February, and as I was buttoning my navy blue pea coat I stopped in my tracks, spotting a collection of classics on sale in the bookstore's display window. Twenty hardbound, olive green books with gold lettering for the sale price of $49.99. I couldn't resist. I went in for a closer look. *Jane Eyre*, *Anna Karenina*, *Wuthering Heights*, *Treasure Island*, a collection of Henrik Ibsen's plays.

As I was paging through the small volume of *Alice's Adventures in Wonderland*, with its colorful illustrations, a guy's voice behind me said quietly, "I bet you anything Lewis Carroll was high when he wrote that book."

I turned to look at the smiling face of a guy with light brown eyes and curly brown hair. Cute. Good looking. He was about five feet four to my five feet. Perfect size for me, I immediately thought, though I didn't know why.

"What makes you say that?" I asked.

"It's too wild and good not to have been inspired by drugs," he said.

"Does everything wild and good have to be inspired by drugs?"

"No," he laughed. What a great smile he had. "But it usually is. You can never tell about these mathematicians, though, what goes on in their minds. I think you have to be on drugs to find logic in the ultimately illogical nature of humans."

"I think you're starting to sound like Mr. Carroll himself." I smiled, feeling suddenly dopey, like maybe I was on drugs.

"So does that mean you'll let me invite you for some hot chocolate over at Kresge's?" he asked.

I was blushing deeply.

"I can't promise you the spectacular kind of wonderland characters Carroll can," he added, "but Kresge's does have some funky customers now and then," and we both laughed.

But he was wrong: he did offer me a spectacular wonderland, one that I'd never experienced before. Thank you, Lewis Carroll, for having brought Johnny Mendoza my way.

He happened to be in town visiting his family for this three-day weekend, though he was on his way back up the next day to Berkeley where he was finishing his last year in history, now applying to law schools throughout California. And me? he asked.

"Literature?" he said, smiling and nodding. "Are you going to buy the set, then?" he asked.

"Hmmm . . . don't know," I said. "It is a pretty set, though. I love books, love to collect grand ones, love to read them . . ."

"Love to be taken away into a wonderland?" he suggested.

"Yes," I laughed. Did I look fat in this jacket, I wondered. Why was my face warm and flushed?

That was the thing, then, the sign: I felt self-conscious and out of breath, blushing like some awkward adolescent. I felt the magic of the moment like I'd never felt before with any other guy. Yes, I'd go ahead and say it: I felt like Alice about to tumble down into the mysterious tunnel.

A few months later, in that first summer without my mother, I would thank her for this spring gift of my falling in love, this valentine. Perhaps it was her way of saying to me, Let me distract you for a minute, Yoli; you are concentrating too much on your anger over my death, on your anger toward your father. Ya basta, Yolanda.

His parents were from the state of Jalisco, just like mine. He was born and raised in south San Diego, just like me. Could it have been a better match? Our communication consisted of letters, both of us waiting excitedly for spring break when he could come down to visit. In the meantime, I concentrated on my classes of my second year of college. Spring arrived with a burst of color and fragrance and drama I'd never before noticed. The sweet peas climbing and covering the fence enclosing our yard had invaded the premises with rambunctious gusto. It was as if the fence itself, draped in delicate, translucent violet, red, pink, and white blossoms, were preparing itself for a feast. So fitting, so appropriate. I was, after all, falling in love.

And then spring break was upon us and I was getting ready for our date: dinner and *The Godfather: Part II* in Mission Valley. Understand that the only face-to-face contact we had had was at the bookstore at the Chula Vista Shopping Center in February two months ago; understand that he left shortly thereafter for Berkeley; understand that our only communication up to that moment in the spring of 1975 had been through funny, witty letters—our thoughts, our humor in sync, Hermann Hesse in his life those days, D. H. Lawrence in mine. Understand that at the tender and yielding age of twenty, I was in love.

Lydia and my little sisters Monica and Luz celebrated my emotional state of mind. Ana María didn't. Preferring to ignore my outrageously good humor the past couple of months, Ana removed herself to the living room, paging through a stack of *Brides* magazines. She was getting married to Roger in June. Still, she was somewhat patient with me and my attendant ladies, for she could surely hear Shelley Fabares in our bedroom belting out a dreamy, lovesick "Johnny Angel" for the fourth time that evening, and she hadn't yet shouted at us to change the damn record. She was patient with me, Ana María was.

Monica lay on her side on the bottom bunk, her head propped on her bent arm; Lydia and Luz sat on the top bunk, dangling their legs to the rhythm of "Johnny Angel." They watched me put on my makeup, first a thin line of eyeliner and then the mascara. And that was it, no eye shadow or anything. I was reading in a magazine, I explained to my audience of three, that when it came to makeup, less was more.

"More what?" Lydia asked. "More pimples on your face for him to see?"

Monica and Luz giggled.

"How about more farts for him to smell," Monica offered, happy to join in the fun. She and my brother Tony had a perverse fascination with pedo jokes.

"No," Luz offered, "how about more crusty *lagañas* for him to wipe from your eyes."

"Now that's romantic!" Lydia said as the three of them doubled over with laughter.

Wonderful to hear laughter in this house where laughter had been absent too long, though I worried about Luz, who was thinner than I'd ever seen her. She looked like a twig of a person. And I'd heard her crying when she thought we weren't home from school or work yet, heard her crying in the backyard, by the pomegranate tree as if she were our old dog Flicka wailing for her dead mistress.

But now she smiled at her lagañas joke.

"Very funny, you three stooges." And I smiled at their silliness. "No," I said. "More kisses."

It was windy when he came to pick me up, now opening the passenger's door to his yellow VW van to let me in. I wore black slacks and a yellow blouse with a black satiny collar. My brown hair was down to my shoulders and Ana María—yes, Ana María!—had lent me her favorite musk perfume. He was wearing a colorful Hawaiian-print shirt and jeans.

As we drove to Mission Valley, our conversation was easy and fun. It was as if I had known Johnny Mendoza my whole life. But I wasn't surprised. After all, his family was from the same region my family was from, and so we were connected by common heritage. And I felt a thrilling, breathless anticipation in the air made more dramatic and auspicious by the uncommonly windy conditions of the evening.

"Hey you," he said, smiling and glancing at me as we weaved our way onto the Interstate 8 ramp. "A penny for your thoughts."

"A penny?" I said, drunk-happy. "No," I shook my head, smiling. "My thoughts are worth much more than that." And we smiled at each other like two goofy, in-love zombies.

Sitting at a small candlelit table, I was quite simply in a state of euphoria.

He asked me what book I was reading, referring to my little plan of reading every one of the collection of classics I bought back in February.

"*Twenty Thousand Leagues Under the Sea*," I said, trying to ignore Lydia's voice in my head whispering, "Tell him *Moby Dick*, tonta, and then stare enticingly down at his crotch."

Johnny served me more tea, pouring slowing and carefully. He had strong, manly hands, small but thick—hands that I wanted to hold and kiss forever. My thoughts made me flush.

Then he asked me if I'd ever taken speed.

His question caught me off guard, then I remembered that our very first conversation at the bookstore was about this very subject matter: whether Lewis Carroll was high when he wrote his famous book.

"Speed?" I asked. "Well, let me see . . . there was this one time when I had to pull an all-nighter. Fifteen-page paper due the next morning and I hadn't even begun. I drank coffee, black tea—a lot of it—but nothing was working, so my roommate offered me a No-Doz tablet. That's speed, isn't it?"

He looked at me as if he were studying me, as if what I'd just said didn't make any sense to him and he was politely trying to figure out what I meant.

No, he finally said. No-Doz tablets were concentrated caffeine, that's all.

"Oh," I said, feeling stupid, embarrassed. I obviously didn't know anything about drugs, and where two minutes ago I would have thought that was a good sign of my character, now I was feeling dorky and lame. Like some uncool person.

What about him?

"Yeah, sometimes," he said. "Like when I have to pull all-nighters for finals," he quickly added.

The cashew chicken and Mongolian beef and steamed rice arrived, and we were busy serving ourselves helpings from each plate, both of us quiet and pensive.

"Where do you get it?" I finally asked.

"You know what a dealer is, right?" he asked just before taking a forkful of rice and eating it.

I paused a moment before answering, feeling afraid that this might be a trick question. I already had one minus point for my No-Doz answer.

I knew that the Las Vegas casino people who dealt the cards were called dealers, and that's all I came up with. So I ventured that as my answer, thinking maybe this was leading to his wanting to invite me to Las Vegas for a weekend.

"Yeah, that's a dealer," he said, sitting back on his chair, sighing softly, "but I'm talking about people who deal drugs."

"Oh, you mean a drug pusher," I said, now feeling cool, back on track, relieved that even with twenty years of living in a world where words like "Holy Days of Obligation," "Lent," "Hail Marys," and "Our Fathers" dominated my life, I knew what a pusher was. And in that moment as I was looking at my Johnny Angel from across the small square table, I felt proud of the fact that I not only knew the word "pusher," but I'd actually even known a few back when I was in high school.

"Why do you ask?" I said, feeling a little giddy. And even though I knew the comparison was obvious, a cliché, I couldn't help thinking of the symbolism, the image that first brought us together and how I was feeling in that moment: I felt as dizzy as Alice must have felt in her descent down the rabbit hole.

"I deal sometimes," he explained. "That's what's going to get me through law school."

"Oh yeah," I nodded, matter-of-factly, as if my sweetheart had just told me that he'd taken on a second part-time job at Sav-On Drug Store, working at the pharmaceutical counter to help finance his expensive law school education.

Gorgeous, sexy Al Pacino—Godfather Number Two—was absolutely right in getting the family into the drug business. And when his brother Fredo proved disloyal to the family, Michael Corleone was absolutely right in having him killed off. He's outta here; no more wimpy screw-ups from the likes of him. Like Al Pacino, I was thinking there in the dark Cinema 21 Theater as Johnny held my hand the last half of this deliciously long movie, Johnny could do no wrong. I was sitting next to the man I was planning on marrying, and my incorrigible padrino

Michael Corleone, with his calculated ruthlessness as the new godfather, could do nothing to deter me from my romantic thoughts and long-term plans. I was—had I mentioned this already?—deeply in love.

Spring break was over and my Johnny Angel was back at Berkeley, while I returned to classes at UCSD, with kisses and promises to write every day, reminding each other that summer was just around the corner. I was patient, as love would have me be, as Lydia would have me be, Lydia who was a little worried about my emotional state of mind. "This is too quick," she warned. And I couldn't help thinking that maybe she was saying this, warning me, because she felt loyal to my ex-boyfriend. She might really be thinking that it was unfair to fall in love so quickly, my ex's parting footsteps still within hearing distance. I loved Lydia even if she was too motherly and sensible.

There was an uncommonly strong storm for this time of year. I looked out the window, down below to the eucalyptus grove surrounding the Central Library. It was hailing, the ping-tapping sound of little pellets of ice against the window. Johnny hadn't answered my last letter, and it'd been four days already. My phone calls to his apartment in Berkeley went unanswered. I was on the seventh floor, language and literature, books sprawled on the table, unopened. The library was an ultramodern, spaceship-looking library, and I was hoping that any minute we would blast off and in a matter of seconds land in Berkeley, and I would be in the safe embrace of my Johnny Angel. The geometric mushroom library, as I affectionately called it every time I made my way to its entrance, was surrounded by floor-to-ceiling windows—enough windows to see outside in any given direction; enough windows to hope that I would catch a glimpse of my Knight in Shining Armor galloping in through the eucalyptus woods to rescue me from D. H. Lawrence's dreary world of coal miners.

I kept calling at odd hours, like when I first got up, before I went to bed, lunchtime, between classes, study breaks at the library where there was a public phone in the far corner, near the quiet reference section, until finally Lydia said, "Enough, Yoli."

But it was not enough, and I finally got the courage to call his parents' house, thinking that something must be wrong. His mother's voice was kind and soft, like my mother's. And it occurred to me that my own mother must have had plenty of phone calls like these, phone calls from desperate young women wanting to know where Armando or Octavio or Tony or Chuy were. My mother, like all mothers—being all-knowing—instinctively understood that her son had moved on, had abruptly, disrespectfully dropped this girlfriend and had not had the decency to let her know; my compassionate mother would feel badly for the desperate young woman, wanting to console her, reassure her that Octavio's been so busy with work and all, certainly he'll call as soon as he can . . . Now I explained to this mother that I hadn't been able to get ahold of Johnny and was worried that perhaps something was wrong and he couldn't get ahold of me. His mother was kind and polite, said she'd heard from him yesterday and that he told her he was busy with papers and midterms, spending most of his time in the library. Their conversation was just a few minutes long, she said with empathy. I thanked her. Yes, I said, I've been so busy, staying late at the library myself. He must've tried calling while I was away (I knowing full well that I had purposely been staying home every evening so as not to miss his phone call). Nothing. But I didn't want to say good-bye to her, though it was time to do so. And for a moment she was my mother, her kind voice, the tacit understanding between us that it seemed to be a woman's lot to wait and wait. I wanted desperately to meet her, to hold her, to have her really be my mother. To ask her if perhaps she knew my mother as they grew up in Jalisco, maybe crossed paths at the Cathedral of Our Lady of Guadalupe in Guadalajara, or while trinket shopping in the large San Juan de Los Lagos market, or on an afternoon's bus ride to San Pedro de Tlaquepaque.

I said good-bye, hung up, going back to my book, opening the chunky *Norton Anthology of English Literature* to page 1,697, the required reading of D. H. Lawrence's "Odour of Chrysanthemums." Thank God it was a miserable, gloomy, wet spring day, because like the wife in "Odour of Chrysanthemums" who waited for her coal miner husband to return from work, I was waiting—waiting for Johnny Mendoza to call or write or something. Knowing, with every day that passed without a letter or a phone call, that he had moved on. Like the wife in the short story I was reading, who was now dressing her husband's corpse, preparing it for the funeral, I winced with my own kind of fear and dread. Thank God it was a miserable, gloomy day: my heart was breaking.

What was this gift of falling-in-love feelings that my mother had given me? How could this short-lived euphoria be a gift if it had such a sorrowful, abrupt ending? If my mother wanted to stir feelings in me beyond the feelings of anger, couldn't she have been more gentle? And why did I attribute this incident of falling in love to my mother? But there you had it: she had stirred life back into me, reminded me that I could have love feelings even in the midst of my grieving; that I could watch a movie as if I were part of the drama; that I could go to dinner with a charming young man and still blush and smile and laugh. A reminder that I had life left in me yet—no matter what the past and the future held.

Sixteen

Lydia and I drove to the Chula Vista Shopping Center for the early summer sale at JCPenney, with 20 to 40 percent off on most items. I needed a new bathing suit, some shorts. Lydia wanted to buy herself a fun, floppy straw hat and some sandals.

Lydia referred to her figure as "pleasingly plump," frustrated by her efforts to lose weight and unable to. She had resigned herself to being Hardy to my Laurel.

"They have these new swimsuits that are like tummy tuckers—makes you look slender," I told her.

"Forget it, Yoli," she said. "I'm not going to wear girdles to the beach. My Bermuda shorts are about as risqué as I'm going to get."

We were at the corner of Broadway and H Street when we both spotted the yellow VW van making its way to the parking lot of Big Boy Restaurant. Johnny was driving, and there was a girl—short hair, pretty—in the seat next to him.

I didn't say anything, pretended I didn't see them. After all, how sad could a person allow herself to get?

I got through spring quarter, made the dean's list again, happy to know that we had higher than normal levels of rain that season. Happy to know that the heavens were crying with me. And cry I did. Almost every night, I cried myself to sleep, puffy eyes the next day and the next. Kaput, just like that, no letter, no explanation. Lydia didn't agree about there not being any explanation: there were signs, she said. Things were a little too perfect. And remember in his last letter, she reminded me, he mentioned something about "laying the cards on the table," wanting me to feel free to date others if I wanted.

"Yoli," Lydia said to me that spring of 1975, that spring of my flash-flood heartbreak, "that was a big hint. He must've known you were falling for him fast. Man, Yoli, you're an open book. You wear your heart—what's the expression?—you wear your heart . . . um . . ."

"On your sleeve," I said. "Thanks for the consoling words, Lydia."

Lydia tried to snap me out of it, but I would not be dissuaded: Johnny Mendoza was my Mr. Right, the man of my dreams, and for some unknown reason he had slipped away. No explanation. No closure. No nothing.

"And what about the dealer stuff, Yoli?" Lydia had tried to reason with me. "Man, thank God he dumped you. He probably would've got you into all that stuff. Thank God *and* him that he hurt you like this. It could've been worse. You could've been a drug addict by now."

We came to the parking lot, and she turned off the ignition. I started to open the door to get out. "Wait," she said. "That was Johnny in the yellow van, wasn't it? I could tell by the look on your face. Don't pretend you didn't see them." I was miserable once again. Thoughts of slimming bathing suits and fantastic discounts at JCPenney were out the window, and in their place, clouding my vision, were a yellow van and a good-looking guy and girl in it.

"Do you want to go over there?" she asked. "We can do it. You have a right, you know. Kick the cabrón in the ass."

At first I didn't say anything. Lydia had all along thought the end of our short-lived love affair was for the best, yet here she was, being the loyal friend at my side, sharing in my hurt and outrage. A question of pride, perhaps. I thought about what she'd just said. It was an interesting suggestion, a proactive kind of plan. Then I started to laugh, first softly, a giggle, then we were both laughing out loud, doubled over, laughing hysterically until it hurt our sides, tears streaming down our faces. Laughing, laughing while a few people walked past, heading for the shopping center, curiously looking over to where two girls were sitting in a car in the parking lot, laughing their heads off, the curious passersby not knowing that we two lovely, bright women were contemplating kicking a cabrón in the ass.

❀ ❀ ❀

The thing that did it to me, devastated and traumatized me for life, I was sure, was another image of a man and woman very obviously *together*.

The shock was not seeing Johnny with a pretty girl, but seeing my sixty-five-year-old recently widowed father with a pretty girl. And girl she was—somewhere in her early twenties.

Lydia wanted to buy some fabric for a new pantsuit she was making herself, so we drove over to San Ysidro Boulevard where three fabric stores were within walking distance of each other. We were cruising on the boulevard, looking for a parking spot, when I saw him coming out of a real estate office that had a huge sign taking up much of its window: Se Habla Español. Papá and the young woman were leaving the office, walking down the three steps, his arm around this girl-woman. He was saying something to her and she smiled back, looking at him. Maybe giggling. I wasn't sure. I was focusing on her person: she was a *morenita*, dark-skinned with scraggly black hair that came to her shoulders. She wore a see-through beige chiffon-looking blouse, too tight for her big breasts, which were being held up, stiff and at attention, by a black lacy bra. The black skirt was just above her knees, the fabric thin enough to reveal that she was not wearing a proper slip, for I could see the shadowy outline of her legs under the skirt. Her high heels were pointy, outmoded stilettos in black patent leather. She looked like what some of the Mexican American kids of my high school disparagingly referred to as "Tijuaneros," those humble, poor students who were fresh from Mexico now arrived in el norte, immediately placed in English as a second language classes, tacitly considered second-class citizens by those of us who were born on this side of the border. Tijuaneros, we called them, though most were probably not from Tijuana, but from farther inland. And yet these soft-spoken recent immigrant students survived, flourished, created their own cliques, unaware of or indifferent to the status we savvy, smart-mouthed, English-speaking students had assigned them. She looked like that, then, my father's girlfriend: trying to look all prettied-up and *catrina*, but really just a poor, raggedy girl from some rancho.

"Finally," Lydia said, finding a parking space and easily driving into it.

"You okay?" she asked, now turning off the ignition and opening the door. "You look like you've just seen a ghost."

"Yeah," I said. "Must've been something I ate."

"Yeah, well stay away from those hot dogs at Kresge's. Shit, stay away from all hot dogs," she said. "Those weenies, they're bound to get you into trouble in some way or another." She laughed, slamming her car door shut as we made our way to the first yardage shop.

❀ ❀ ❀

I was four years old the time I begged Papá to let me go to work with him again, like he'd taken me the week before. Just for a little while, I tried negotiating with him, telling him that Armando said he could pick me up on his way home in about an hour. Please, please, por favor, Papi, just a little while. I want a milkshake like only you know how to prepare. But Papá shook his head, firmly saying no, not this time. Too much work to do, no time to make you a milkshake. *La semana que viene, mi'ja*, promising to take me to his restaurant job next week and make me a delicious milkshake, there in the quiet kitchen, after the restaurant was closed, and only Papá and I there with his janitorial supplies on a cart with wheels: mop, broom, Lysol, sponges, a bucket. He would take a break to fix me the most delicious, frothy milkshake I had ever tasted in my whole life. He was promising me that for next week, not this time.

Then Mamá came into the living room, having overheard my pleading. "Yes, Lorenzo," she said, "take her." And she stared at my father long and hard, not taking her eyes off him even as he got up and tried to leave the room. Her stare, the way she stood and just looked at him seeming to block his way, made him pause and hesitate, fidget with his car keys, get them out of his pocket, put them back in, disoriented by her stare, her suggestion.

He took me then, after all, and while I had the important job of wiping gooey stuff and crumbs from the restaurant tables, Papá swept and mopped the hallway and then the men's and women's restrooms. We had been there for about an hour when there was a knock at the back door of the restaurant, near the kitchen. Papá quickly looked up, seemingly startled. "Yoli, stay out here. Wipe the chairs for crumbs, too," he said, now heading for the kitchen, to the sound of more persistent knocking.

"Just stay out here; don't come into the kitchen yet. I'll call you when your milkshake is ready." And then he hurried behind the flapping double doors that led to the kitchen.

Even at the age of four, I had a natural curiosity for people. I wondered what kind of person had sat at this table with a few catsup spots near the edge of the table, someone messy, I was sure, someone who had probably ordered a hamburger and fries. Another table had a sandy pile of sugar with five empty sugar packs crumpled next to the mound. Had a desperate mother simply grabbed a handful of the packets and given them to her little kid, something to keep the little boy from whining and crying, something to keep him from disturbing all the customers? Is that why there was this mound of sugar?

I could hear some whispered talking in the back, over in the kitchen. I thought it must be time for Papá to make my milkshake, suddenly afraid that he might've already made it, and I hadn't been able to watch him do it, the way he scooped an extra big helping of ice cream and dropped it into the tall metal container, then the milk, the plump red strawberries, even a raw egg for extra frothiness, then mixed it with the milkshake mixer. I hope he hasn't already made it, I thought as I walked to the kitchen, opening just one of the double door flaps, making my way in.

The woman was standing, her back against the big metal refrigerator door, while Papá stood pressed against her, her blouse unbuttoned. Papá was touching her black lacy bra. His face was smothered there between the two mountains, and her eyes were closed, her lips slightly parted as she moaned softly. Was she in pain, I wondered? Was he checking her chest for breathing? And I wondered if I should ask Papá if he needed help with her, call the ambulance the way we did whenever we heard the crash of cars on the freeway, saw people being pulled out of crumpled cars onto gurneys there on Interstate 5. Did this woman need help? Was Papá holding this fainting lady up so she wouldn't fall? She had her hands in his hair, and though I meant to call out to them, ask if I could help, something held me back. I looked around the kitchen, spotting the milkshake mixer untouched and clean on the counter. Good, he hadn't yet made my milkshake. And I quietly walked out of the kitchen, instinctively knowing that I must be quiet, that they should not know that I was there. Sensing there was a secret about this, but not understanding why or what it meant. Years later as a teenager, my own sexuality awaking along with my intense ambivalence toward my parents—alternating between loving my mother and hating my father, or hating my father and loving my mother—I would remember this moment and see it for what it was.

So I made my way back to the front of the restaurant noiselessly, picked up the damp terry cloth I had set on one of tables, slowly, deliberately pushing the mound of sugar to the edge of the table, the sugary sprinkles falling to the floor as if a glass snow globe had just shattered, and all the white sparkling "snow" inside was falling to the just-mopped floor like a sudden disastrous snowstorm.

✿ ✿ ✿

Lydia settled for a forest green polyester fabric since dark colors would make her look thinner. I was relieved that it didn't take all afternoon for her to find the one she wanted; I wanted to get home as soon as possible.

Once home, I burst into the house, calling out to my sisters and not waiting to catch my breath. Ana María, Luz, and Monica were in the living room watching TV, and I quickly proceeded to tell them what I'd just witnessed. Our mother hadn't even been dead a year, and already this man was on the prowl, I said. They were shocked. Shameless womanizer is what he was, Ana María said as she walked over to the TV and turned it off. Luz began to cry, said we had no right to talk that way about our father. He is our father, you know. Monica looked at each of us, and she looked exhausted, looked like a cowgirl who had just been in the corral trying to train a wild horse, rein in the horse, but had been defeated. Now she walked out of the living room, past the kitchen, out the back door to her new lodgings in what once was the guys' bedroom in the back.

Believe us, Ana María reassured Luz who looked at us with anger in her eyes, forever loyal to our father, we had reasons to feel this way about el señor Lorenzo Sahagún. Then and there, Ana María and I decided this called for a family conference of all our brothers and sisters.

❖ ❖ ❖

On Sunday evening they arrived, our older brothers and sister. Carolina came with her Tom, but Armando and Tony did not come with their wives, and Octavio was here alone. The only sibling not present was Chuy, who we had decided didn't need any more problems in his life.

We brothers and sisters all gathered together in the kitchen. Armando and Tony leaned against the counter, impatient to know what this emergency *conferencia* was all about, while Octavio looked in the refrigerator for something to eat. How I longed for the days when we were little, those days when the conversations with my brothers and sisters were about go-cart making, or last year's Sun 'n' Sea Festival in Imperial Beach, or the upcoming neighborhood hide-n-seek game on a full moon night. I longed for the times when we nine siblings celebrated Christmas or Thanksgiving without a greater care in the world than whether our father was going to embarrass us with another horrendous rendition of "El Corrido del Caballo Blanco," we children suppressing giggles, or whether he would make us read the *El Mexicano* Tijuana newspaper out loud in front of company, each of us in line to read a paragraph, one at a time, interrupting our recitation every few words to correct our pronunciation with his typical impatient loud voice—"What? Say that word again"—until one of us, usually Luz or Monica or I, would run out of the room sobbing, thereby making our father wave his hand in exasperation and proclaim the Spanish lessons over. Even praying the rosary together in the cramped living room for an interminable fifteen minutes, even that I longed for.

And for a moment—just a moment—a feeling of being disloyal to my father crossed my mind.

"I saw our father with a woman—a very, very young woman," I proclaimed, though not with the same vehemence and anger that I originally had had.

They all turned to look at me.

Carolina was the only one who seemed shocked. "What did you say?" she asked.

"So?" Armando said. "What's wrong with that?"

What's wrong with that? We three older sisters were talking at once, by turns angry and frustrated that our brothers just didn't get it. Our mother not even dead a year and already he was making a damn fool out of himself. And she was easily forty years younger than he was—*forty*!—I repeated.

"There's nothing wrong with that," Octavio said. "He's entitled to some loving, Yoli, he really is."

"Yeah," Tony said, "I don't see what the big deal is. If Papá wants to have a young girlfriend, that's his business."

"Oh it is, is it?" Ana María said. "Come on, guys, don't you get it?"

"Get what?" they asked. "All he wants is some loving. He's probably really lonely."

I shook my head, frustrated—no, angry—with these brothers who naturally seemed to defend the male of the species no matter how foolish and preposterous the situation. And for a moment I wondered about this loyalty to our father from my brothers—from Luz, even. Was it just a genetic predisposition? Why were some of us more loyal than others?

"Maybe that's all *he* wants, but I can name a few enticing things *she* wants," I said, and the three of us older sisters nodded vehemently while Luz and Monica quietly listened, somehow knowing that they were getting more information than they ever had, and maybe a little nervous and confused about what all that information meant.

Then we listed what she was after: marriage, a green card, his house, and then poof!—just like that—dump him. How could a sixty-five-year-old man keep up with a twenty-something-year-old woman? It was perverse, ridiculous, and so obviously a trap.

"Hey, you don't know that for sure," Octavio, Mister Romeo himself, said.

"Oh, come on, Octavio," I said, "what else could she want?"

"Papá's not bad looking for a sixty-five-year-old," reasoned Armando. "He's in better shape than a lot of guys my age. He's not fat . . ."

"No," Ana María said, "he's not fat, all right. He's a skinny little man who has delusions of grandeur. And being with this hot little señorita is just one more delusion. She's going to screw him in more ways than one," Ana warned.

"Leave him alone," Armando said, now straightening himself where he had been leaning on the kitchen counter listening to us, though I sensed a tone of sadness or compassion in his voice. "He's entitled to some loving . . ."

"And she a marriage license, a green card, his house, et cetera, et cetera. And what was he doing coming out of a real estate office anyway?" Carolina piped in. Tom just listened, kept a respectful silence.

"What makes you think Papá's thinking of getting married?" Armando said.

"Good point," said our resident psychologist Carolina. "Maybe we should have this conferencia with him."

"Hey, wait a minute. He's a grown man, old enough to make decisions for himself," said good ol' loyal Octavio.

"Well he *should* be old enough, but he isn't. He's acting like a child. Maybe we should give him a little of his own medicine, get on his case about his dating habits, the way he's always given us a hard time," Ana María said.

"What are you talking about, 'hard time'?" Octavio asked.

"Of course you wouldn't remember," Ana María said. "You guys never had to go through the crap we girls went through just to get permission to let a guy phone us." Then she got up from her chair. "Just forget it, *hermanos*, forget we called you over for this discussion. In your eyes, Papá can do no wrong, so just forget we ever bothered you with our silly, inconsequential concerns."

"No, hold on," our oldest brother Armando, fatherly and sensible, said. "I think you do have a point. Maybe we need to talk with Papá about his life. You know, see how he's doing and feeling."

"Yes, good idea!" We sisters agreed, feeling happy that we'd come to some sort of meeting of the minds. "When should we have this little conferencia with Papá?" We wanted to know. The sooner the better.

"Just be easy on him, okay?" Armando said. "Remember, he's probably going through crap himself. You don't know."

Going through crap himself? These men, I thought to myself, annoyed and pissed off, always sticking up for each other. What is it that we didn't know about Papá? I could tell you everything that there was to know about him—all of it leading to his ridiculous, patriarchal machismo. Papá was born and raised on a ranch in the state of Jalisco, although his family also had a house in the town of El Grullo, where the eleven brothers and sisters lived during schooltime. Their holidays and summers were spent on the ranch, which I'd never been to. Our visits to Mexico were dominated by the Ramoses, Mamá's family. By the time I was a young girl, Papá's parents and most of his siblings had moved to the big city of Guadalajara, and since there were so many aunts and uncles and cousins, it seemed more convenient to stay put in my grandparents' home in El Grullo. Mamá had only two single sisters still living in the large house, so there was plenty of room for all of us kids when we swooped down on them like the monarch butterflies wintering in Michoacán—only we were butterflies summering in El Grullo. It was a natural home base away from home. And besides, Papá never came on these summer trips with us anyway.

But no, that wasn't true. The truth was that he came on every one of them except for the summers when I was eleven and twelve, those summers when I set out—successfully—to hate Mamá. But Papá was with us all the other summers, especially with us that summer of 1968 when I was thirteen years old, and I had cultivated a fine hatred of everything having to do with my parents' Mexico. I tried to think back to why I hated Mexico so. Freud would probably say it had to do with my relationship with my parents. Fair. Then he'd go on to say I had penis envy. Not fair. Wouldn't you be envious that your brothers were not obligated to endure torturous summer trips to Mexico while all the women of the family had to? Then Freud would look at me sternly and say, Your ambivalent feelings toward Mexico have everything to do with your subconscious love-hate for your father. Wait a minute, I'd protest. It's Mamá I couldn't stand when I was eleven and twelve years old, not Papá.

Papá, in fact, could do no wrong in those days. Freud would be patient with me, let me protest and disagree with him even though he was, after all, the renowned Sigmund Freud. He'd politely clear his throat. My cue to shut up and listen to the good doctor. Mexico equals Papá, he would say. We'll add your mother to the mix, if you like. Think Electra complex. Just think about it, he'd quickly add, as I began to protest against his insinuation that I have—or had had as a young girl—unconscious, sexual feelings for my father. He again cleared his throat. Session was over.

Seventeen

The saguaros—those giant cacti with tentaclelike, fat, upturned branches—stood guard along the two-lane desert highway. The grooves and ridges that ran along their trunks and branches contracted and expanded during the rainy and dry seasons, or so I had been told in science class. To contract and expand like some quiet, slow-heaving monster. I couldn't help feeling that in some threatening way these huge cacti were watching me, keeping their eyes out for me were I to suddenly leap out of this stifling station wagon and run and run, faster and faster, paying no heed to my father's shouts, my mother's desperate pleas, my sisters' screams of fear for me. Faster and faster I would run in the hot desert sun, north on the highway, back to my San Diego, to my friends and to safety. This scenario was often on my mind, its terrifying drama guaranteed to cause my parents a nervous breakdown there on the spot, or at least some wonderful deep parental guilt for the rest of their lives. They would find me dehydrated, limp, clothes torn to shreds, dead at the foot of a giant saguaro in the middle of their broiling hot Mexican desert.

This is what I thought at the age of thirteen in 1968 as I stared out the car window at the dusty stretch of sand, the scattered rocks and clumsy boulders on the arid hills, our baby blue Chevy station wagon making its way south through Mexico's Sonora desert, to El Grullo.

"We'll soon be coming to Parque Nacional Gran Desierto del Pinacate," announced my sister Carolina, who had a map of Mexico in one hand and *Fodor's Guide to Mexico* in the other. She acted as if this were her maiden trip there. It was irritating to be a reluctant witness to Carolina's transformation. Now that she was in college, she was a changed woman, a "socially and politically conscious Chicana"—her words—and one of her missions in life as a transformed person was to get back to her roots, to rediscover Mexico with new eyes and an open heart full of sensitivity and awareness. I'd never really gotten along with my older sister in the first place, so she now seemed to me even more despicable, she and my parents sharing an incomprehensible love of Mexico, of their roots and ancestry. Often I saw them huddled at the kitchen table discussing what the Mexican Revolution had accomplished, whether there were any positive aspects of the Porfiriato era, poring over a point in some boring textbook Carolina had bought at the college bookstore. Blah, blah, blah. Nincompoops, the three of them. They belonged to another world, an unreal, romanticized world, while I belonged to the real world, to the world of San Diego, California, in the present. Spare me the *¡Viva México!* exhortations and hoots. My reality included Denise, Kenny, Lydia, Farrell's Ice Cream Parlor, Southwest Junior High, and British literature. We four were inseparable and spent most of our time at the Chula Vista Shopping Center. Denise and Kenny were the only whites in our neighborhood—"*gringuitos*" my father called them, although it bothered me that he should refer to them that way. Maybe it wasn't a bad word or anything, but it sounded as if he were making fun of my friends just because they were blond and blue-eyed. We were Americans, too, I protested. We were light-skinned and blue-eyed, too.

There are whites and then there are whites, Carolina had pronounced solemnly. She didn't approve of my friendship with Denise and Kenny, said that such close and frequent associations with those "Anglos" were, at the very least, going to have people calling me a "coconut"—brown on the outside, white on the inside. (But we're not brown on the outside either, I argued. We're talking about state of mind, she countered. We are brown on the outside in a *figurative* way. Was Carolina preparing herself to become a lawyer?) At the very worst (and here she always paused three seconds for dramatic effect), hanging around these gringos was going to make me too Americanized, assimilating into the mainstream at the cost of losing respect and love for our rich and beautiful heritage. Yes, I knew those big words, too, and I would have answered back with my own academic explanation, but since I hated the Wicked Witch of the Southwest, I usually simply raspberried her and walked away.

"It says here that 'wind-sculpted sand dunes, volcanic craters, and unusual lava deposits characterize Pinacate.'" Carolina was reading from her travel guide to Mexico.

"Sí, mi'ja," Papá said, "our Pinacate Desert National Park is very impressive, *eso sí*."

Our Pinacate Desert National Park, I thought, wanting to puke from so much sentimentality. Papá and Carolina were tight, daddy's girl wrapped in a halo of Mexican pride and righteousness. Somewhere along the history of our family, I had taken a backseat. Just looking at us now said it all: Carolina sitting up front between Mamá and Papá, both occasionally looking over at something she was pointing to on the map of Mexico, while I was banished to the backseat with Ana María and two pesky younger sisters. It was humiliating and gave me more reason to cringe and withdraw into my real world.

"Where do you want to spend this night, Hermosillo or Guaymas?" Carolina asked, already scanning the motel section for Hermosillo in her handy travel guide.

Beyond our car, outside in the middle of the desert, the black asphalt road shimmered in waves of heat. Our annual two-days-one-night trip into central Mexico was forever boring and seemingly interminable, and it was a good thing I had brought along enough reading material: Shakespeare, Chaucer, English and American modern short stories. I was preparing myself for an academic career in British literature, planning on participating in the education abroad program in England where I would probably live indefinitely. (I could already imagine my high school counselor saying, "Oh my, you read the complete works of Shakespeare by the age of thirteen? A precocious child, indeed!")

Santa Ana, Hermosillo, Guaymas, Ciudad Obregón, Los Mochis—I read out loud to Luz and Monica from the map the main cities we would be passing in Mexico's northwest. But then I had a better idea. "Hey," I whispered to my two little sisters, "let's take turns twirling our middle finger three times in the air and then closing our eyes and pointing somewhere on the map, calling out the town nearest our finger."

"What for?" Luz asked.

"Well, whoever calls out the funniest-sounding name wins."

"What do we win?" Monica asked.

"What do you win?" I thought about this a moment. Then in a low whisper, I said, "You win the wonderful wrath of Carolina Sahagún, Righteous Queen of the Chicanos."

Luz and Monica giggled, glancing over at our parents and Carolina in the front seat.

Opedope, Meresichi, Banamichi, Aconchi, Baviacora, Vicam, Bacum—the small dots on the map were a way from the main highway, not really part of our route, somewhere off the beaten track, but what fun we had trying to pronounce these silly-sounding words, what laughter, and of course, the special bonus of Carolina glaring at us every so often from her privileged spot in the front seat.

Mocorito, Mochicahui, Pericos, Culiacancito, Topolobampo. The words began to rhyme, and long after Luz and Monica dozed off, one head drooped to the side against the car door, another against a shoulder, I continued reading the names of the towns. Twilight found me slightly swaying with the hum of the car, the rhythm of the names, and because my eyes were tired and sleepy from reading the small print on the map, the foreign names—Huatabampo, Agiabampo, Pitiquito, Oquitoa, Bonancita—seemed to skip and twirl, chant and sing, abandoning their proper spot on the map as we neared the city of Hermosillo for our first night's stop in Mexico.

Usually our summer vacations were spent entirely in El Grullo, but this summer one of our destinations would be Manzanillo, where my widowed tía Conchita and her two sons were starting up a restaurant, and so they were having an inauguration party. The whole clan was going to be there: uncles, aunts, cousins, godparents, *compadres*, and *comadres*.

"Our bloodline *en vivo*, don't you understand?" Carolina had explained as she packed her favorite party dresses back in San Diego, and I had watched her, feeling a mixture of disgust and disdain. My college-educated Chicana sister out to impress the "familia."

You could tell by the change in landscape that we had long ago left the dry, hot desert and were now entering a warm, rainy tropical terrain. We were nearing Mazatlán, which, according to the map, was a little bit below the Tropic of Cancer on the Pacific coast. This made me perk up a bit: the car journey was getting very tiresome, and so the prospect of soon reaching our destinations—even if they were only El Grullo and Manzanillo—was inviting. Just to be out of this stuffy old car, beyond hearing range of Carolina and her lectures.

The plan was to arrive early in El Grullo to pick up the aunts and then be off for the three-hour trip to Manzanillo and the *gran fiesta de inauguración.*

Guadalajara 228 km. Reading the highway signs, I found myself getting excited, and I hated to realize it, so I tried to will myself to stop. I pretended not to notice the lush, verdant highlands of Nayarit, the bulging, billowy clouds floating below us.

"Look at that," Monica whispered. "It looks like we're in heaven, way above the clouds."

"Do you think we'll see God?" Little Luz asked, her nose pressed against the car window, hoping to get a better view.

"No," Monica said with utmost authority. "He's too busy to be standing around waving to all of us. But if you look carefully down at the clouds, you might see an angel standing guard, making sure we don't fall off the cliff and land on top of one of them."

There was a hush in the station wagon as we all stared intently out the window, and I had the eerie feeling that everyone—including me—believed Monica. We slowly spiraled up the green, mossy mountain, the surrounding fog enveloping us, making it difficult to see out. Our blue station wagon seemed to be slowly entering a misty fairyland, nearing the castle at the top, and all eyes were carefully watching the narrow road ahead, making sure we didn't fall of the cliff and land on a billowy white angel.

The thunderstorms caught us by surprise. Up to then we had been doing fine in the muffled rainy mist of Nayarit, but once we reached Guadalajara and made our way southwest toward El Grullo, heaven seemed to have opened its door with teasing gusto, as if God and his angels were having a hose fight. My sisters loved it, and they squealed with excitement and fear every time they heard the now-familiar sound of rumbling. Thunder and lightning storms were not very common in San Diego, one or two a year at the most, so my sisters were having a great time getting scared. Now and then they would roll down the window to better hear the thunder. About the third time they did this I realized that my copy of *The Canterbury Tales* was wet from the rain coming through the window.

"Shit, now look what you've done," I hissed at my two pesky sisters, picking up the book and drying its cover with my blouse. The *Tales* looked a little wilted and rather humble for a classic, but my sisters were too engrossed in the magic of their lightning and thunderstorm to give my book a thought or me an apology.

❀ ❀ ❀

"María del Socorro Parra de García is your aunt. She's a first cousin to your father's father. She will be there but with only seven of her children since the four others—who are they, let's see: there was Sylvia, Tomasito, Pepe, and Carmen—yes, that's right, well, they all live up in San Francisco, have become real gringos, I've been told, so they aren't going to be here." Were they not going to be here because they lived in San Francisco or because they were "real gringos," I wondered. Tía Rebeca was talking nonstop, trying to help my mother catch up on the latest Who's Who and Who's Not at the inauguration party. Tía Rebeca seemed to feel it was of utmost importance that we have a crash course in our family's genealogy. "So you don't stick your foot in it and ask the wrong questions to the right people, if you know what I mean."

And so she proceeded to tell us which cousins to stay away from: the Parra family was absolutely crazy—all of them—but very talented. You could tell them a mile away because they had the pearly white skin and blue eyes. They were all weird and unpredictable, too much European blood in them, not enough Indian blood, that's one reason (coming from Tía Rebeca with her own pearly white skin and green eyes, this seemed odd for her to say, as if she hadn't noticed that she could easily be clumped with those weird relatives). The other reason they're crazy, she continued, is because they intermarry.

"Cousins with cousins—first cousins, second cousins. I suppose they think that by marrying each other their skin will get whiter and whiter with each generation, their eyes so blue they could soon claim to be descendants of German royalty. What a shame, those lovely blue eyes gone to waste on such crazy people," Tía Rebeca said, shaking her head in sincere disappointment, as if she'd given this quite a bit of thought. "They're all from Guadalajara, big city slickers, a little on the *fuy-fuy* side, sort of stuck-up, you know."

The three-hour drive to Manzanillo was going to be torture, I could already tell: Ana María, Tía Celeste, Carolina, and I in back with each of us taking turns having Monica sit on our laps. Now that our aunts were on board with us en route to Manzanillo, Tía Rebeca was sitting up front next to my father and mother (with Luz on her lap), and Carolina had been temporarily dethroned and demoted—ha, ha!—to the backseat with us.

The road from El Grullo to the Pacific coast curved and spiraled, ascending, descending, and ascending again, so that when Carolina said, "Stop the car. I'm going to be sick," no one was surprised. As Carolina staggered out of the car as fast as she could, followed by Mamá to help her, we all lazily climbed out too for a little stretch of the legs.

The heat was truly unreal, and the humidity clung to me with a perverse urgency. I felt it embrace me in suffocating waves as I got out of the car.

In an effort to stay cool and to ignore Tía's cram course on la familia I had been reading the past hour. I was one of those lucky people who could be reading and riding on a roller coaster after a big meal and not get sick, so when I looked around me, at the mountain we were on, at the steep cliff below, I felt a surprising dizziness, and at the same time an involuntary thrill and shiver crept up my back, along my legs and arms, hardening the nipples of my small breasts.

Miles upon miles of thick green trees and plants. Ferns on top of ferns on top of trees on top of ivy-covered hills in an almost obscene entanglement of vegetation. Mangos, bananas, mameyes, chirimoyas, *nances*, and *tamarindos*—everything grew wild and voluptuously here. Trees I had never before seen in San Diego loomed before me in a taunting way, as if to invite me to see more.

When I stepped to the edge of the steep cliff and looked down at the lush greenery, I felt a delicious light-headedness permeate my whole thirteen-year-old body.

"It's the Parra blood in you, Carolina, that's why you have a weak stomach," Tía Rebeca said as we resumed our course to Manzanillo. "Too bad you didn't inherit the Ramos blood—good, healthy Indian blood, that's for sure. Dark, dark skin, as dark as any Aztec god, for sure the descendants of some powerful handsome tribe of Nahuas. And those eyes, what eyes. Every single Ramos man has those black, black eyes that penetrate right through you. They know what you're thinking. Watch out for them; they're nobody's fool. Ever see a picture of Emiliano Zapata, that famous one where he's sitting next to Pancho Villa in the presidential palace after they overtake the capital?"

"Tía, it's the presidential chair, but it's not in the presidential palace," Carolina corrected her, having recovered quickly enough from her nausea so as not to miss a chance to show off her knowledge of Mexican history. "The picture was taken in the Chapultepec Castle."

"Well, whatever," Tía Rebeca said. "Remember the way Emiliano looks into the camera, like a shy calf with thick eyebrows? That's the look of the Ramos family, known throughout El Grullo and La Huerta for their rugged handsomeness. Now there's a family nobody would call fuy-fuy. Bien machos every one of them, and I won't tell you what other reputations they have, not with the young ones listening. Pero con cuidado. Watch out for those men . . ."

"Rebeca, please," Mamá said.

I had long since abandoned Chaucer's *Tales*, resigned to my own kind of pilgrimage and weird characters, and sat staring out the window, the hot tropical air blowing in my face, up my nostrils, down into my lungs, sticky, warm, lethargic heat. My head was plunging into the moist thicket surrounding me, and I was surrendering to the swelter.

"Although in recent years Manzanillo has been trying to become a major resort in competition with Puerto Vallarta and Acapulco, this coastal town is first and foremost a large commercial seaport, with its paradoxical mixture of tropical beauty and gray industrial factories." Carolina was reading again from her travel guide.

I could practically taste the tangy sea air as our station wagon made its way along the coast heading into Manzanillo, and with Monica fast asleep and limp on my lap, the air felt extra heavy.

"Ay, por el amor de Dios," said Tía Rebeca, "look who's over there, standing in front of that restaurant waving to us. It's Conchita."

The car came to a slow stop on the bumpy shoulder of the road, and before I knew what was happening, everyone was piling out of the station wagon, hugging, kissing, and squeezing and crying and hugging again. Soon we were whisked into Tía María de la Concepción Ramos vuida de Zuñiga's—Tía Conchita for short—cool, dark house-made-into-a-restaurant and promptly handed cold bottles of *sidra*, a kind of apple cider soda. The festivities had begun.

Purple and gold streamers graced the high ceilings of the corridors while tables were set throughout the building, each round table draped with a yellow tablecloth and plastic flowers in a vase as the centerpiece. The restaurant sign, with purple Gothic lettering and gold background, hung at the entrance: Fonda Manzanillo. English Spoken Here.

I shuffled about, feeling alone and listening to the crowd that was gathering at the other end of the corridor, near the long entryway. The actual celebration wouldn't begin until after dark, after the daily storm, Tía Rebeca had told us in the car. Then the air would cool down and everyone would be ready to drink and dance the night away.

From where I stood I could see Carolina in the midst of the crowd, so into her Mexican heritage, her cherished, newly discovered familia introducing themselves, Mamá and Papá at her side. It was plain to see that the Manzanillo branch of the family had the scoop on us and surely knew that the lovely Carolina, daughter of Lorenzo Sahagún and Dolores Ramos de Sahagún, was attending college in Los Estados Unidos and, as if that were not enough, she had not turned her back, thanks be to God, on her people as so many educated Mexican Americans did. No, Carolina was instead *proud*—yes, yes, it's true—proud to say her parents were Mexican.

"And you must be Yolanda the poet," a guy's voice behind me said, "or is it Yolanda the antisocial one?"

I turned slowly, for though the voice had startled me, the heat had an even greater power over my body. All the energy and activity about me seemed to come in slow motion. When I finally faced the rude voice, I saw before me Emiliano Zapata reincarnated.

"You can't blame them for being proud of her," he continued, nodding and following my gaze over to where the crowd stood, surrounding my parents and Carolina. It was as if he had been listening in on my thoughts, reading my mind at that very moment.

I stared at him without saying anything. He was older than my thirteen years, around sixteen or seventeen, I guessed.

"Forgive me my horrible manners," he said. "I am Claudio Ramos *a sus órdenes.*" At my service? Was this guy for real, I wondered, as I shook hands with him.

And how did he know my name?

"Conchita is my mother, so that makes you and me relatives. But there will be time soon enough to get to know each other," he said, smiling, his black eyes twinkling a little. Was he teasing me? Mocking me in some way? I wasn't sure.

There was a loud rumbling in the distance. Looking up at the sky from the courtyard, this Emiliano Zapata reincarnated, this alleged cousin of mine, said, "It'll soon rain and I need to do some things before the water comes. God granting and you granting, I will have the pleasure of getting to know you better at the fiesta. If I'm truly lucky, I'll have the honor of the first dance with you. *Con permiso,*" he said, leaving as quickly as he had appeared.

Soon, I too was whisked into the hubbub of handshakes and *abrazos* with people I had never before met, long-lost cousins and aunts and uncles offering me *antojitos*, replenishing my bottle of soda, already planning a series of activities and things to see during our stay in Manzanillo.

From where I stood in the middle of the courtyard, I had a view of the back of the house, of the corral. I could see him as he gathered the chickens into the coop, filling their feeders. He had taken his shirt off, and I noticed how smooth and brown his back looked, the way he gracefully maneuvered the stubborn pigs into their pen. The sky had now darkened.

What happens during the rainy season in the tropics is this: the morning and early afternoon are seething hot; the oppressive humid heat surrounds and enfolds you, permeating your every pore, every muscle, and every bone. You are suffocating and your whole body is numb with exhaustion and just to think clearly—to remember where you are, who you are, and what small, easy tasks you can perform today—takes all your energy, unnerving you and making you want to melt into oblivion. It is in this state, then, that the afternoon passes into siesta hour and as you finish eating in quiet, sluggish slow motion, the beginning faraway rumblings of thunder can be heard. Within an hour, the skies blacken with thunderclouds, the air stirs for the first time all day, and soon you can even feel a tickling breeze. And when you can no longer hold on, when the thunderclouds looming above have teased and flirted with your stupor, then the fabulous, dramatic release of gushing rain and crackling, ripping thunder is powerful and sweet and you embrace it with helpless gratitude.

"Isn't he sexy?" Carolina said, unpacking her dresses and selecting the one she would wear for tonight's party.

"Who?" I asked.

"Oh, don't think I didn't notice you two talking over there all alone. I mean, how can you not notice the gorgeous *papacito*? What were you two talking about, anyway?" she asked me.

"God, Carolina, don't gross me out. He's your cousin, for Christ's sake," I said. "Tía Rebeca wasn't kidding—you are a Parra with all that intermarriage stuff on your mind."

"So what? We'll keep it in the family. Besides, he's a third cousin; that's far enough away to let us get close," she said, laughing. She dabbed some perfume on her neck and then between her breasts, winking at me, and then she went downstairs, ready for the gran fiesta de inaguración.

I sat there on the bed, not knowing what to do, whether to get dressed for the damned party or just stay hidden in this bedroom, finish reading Chaucer's *Tales*. I could hear the mariachi tuning up in the long, echoing corridors downstairs in the restaurant.

Looking around the room, I noticed that Carolina had already made herself at home: suitcase opened on the bed, clothes spilling out, dresses, shoes, makeup bag, a hairdryer, even a textbook of Mexican history. She thought of everything, this darling sister of mine.

I picked up the book and flipped through its pages, now and then stopping to look at the black and white photographs. At the chapter entitled "The Mexican Revolution," I slowed down and carefully leafed through the book, pausing to look at each photo—grainy, sepia-toned, faded. *Rebels with Cannon, 1911. Villa's Troops, 1914. Pancho Villa and Wife, Luz Corral.* Then the picture I had been looking for without realizing it: Emiliano Zapata and Pancho Villa posing at Chapultepec Castle.

Tía Rebeca was right; he did resemble a shy calf looking warily into the camera. And while Pancho Villa was laughing with the crowd of men surrounding him, looking to his right at the moment the picture was taken, Emiliano stared solemnly into the camera, at me.

So I stared back at him, and soon he was taking me by the hand down a long, dusty road. It must have been the Sonora desert, the black asphalt hot and shimmering.

We stopped and sat under a saguaro, and when I offered him strawberry ice cream from Farrell's, he laughed and brushed it away. It disappeared. In its place he held a mango, smooth oval-shaped fruit from the tropics. I looked at him in surprise, about to ask him how he'd done that, but he put his finger to my lips to quiet me. With a small knife, he sliced the sides of the mango in many sections, the thick peel opening and cascading like a graceful, ballooning skirt around the fleshy fruit. He took a juicy bite and then offered it to me.

And somewhere in the distance, in that summer of my thirteenth year in Manzanillo, Mexico, land of my mother and father, I could hear the mariachi playing—violins, guitars, trumpets—in dramatic harmony.

✿ ✿ ✿

My love affair with Mexico: my ambivalent, passionate love-hate relationship with my parents' *tierra*. At times this affair played out like a romance novel; at times it played out like a Gothic mystery. Mexico equals Mamá; Mexico equals Papá. And so, good Doctor Freud, where was my place in this equation?

Eighteen

Our father beat us to the punch, called all of us children together, said he had something important to tell us. So on a Sunday evening, exactly one week after our sibling conference, we gathered in the Sahagún dining room, my brothers and sisters and their spouses, in this little house on Conifer Street where I'd lived my whole life. Ana María, Luz, Monica, and I had prepared dinner along with Carolina who, from her condominium, organized the potluck. "We might as well make a little dinner party out of this," she explained. "It'll make our family meeting seem less confrontational." Carolina seized any Sahagún family situation to practice her therapy techniques.

Carolina and Tom arrived early to help set up borrowed six-foot-long tables, the living room now converted into a dining room with tables lined up next to each other, draped with white tablecloths, now looking like one long table—long enough to seat us five sisters, brother-in-law Tom, Armando and Sonia, Tony and Marisa, and Octavio and Chuy—enough seating space for all twelve members of the family plus our father.

"Feels like Thanksgiving," Luz said. She set the plates and flatware. Monica was in charge of glasses. They both seemed happy for the first time in a long time—as if this family gathering were just like old times.

"Do you think Papá will start singing the 'Corrido del Caballo Blanco'?" Monica asked me as I folded the paper napkins and placed one next to each plate. "You know, because he thinks it's a Thanksgiving dinner?"

"Well, not if you don't bring it up," I said. Monica loved to *darle cuerda*, winding Papá up with talk of horses, and next thing you knew, Thanksgiving or no Thanksgiving, Papá was belting out his melodramatic rendition of the white horse making its way from Jalisco all the way up the coast to el norte—much like his trek with our mother to the north. "Just don't get him started, Monica," I warned her. "We have important matters to discuss."

I surveyed the sight before me: a long table set for thirteen. Thanksgiving was not what came to mind. For some reason, I had an uneasy feeling about this family meeting. I was thinking more along the lines of The Last Supper.

Armando and Sonia arrived with a large salad bowl of nopalitos—diced cactus mixed with cilantro, onions, tomatoes, *un poco de chilito*, and lemon juice. Sonia's specialty. Then Octavio and Chuy, driving over together, entered with dessert. Seeing Octavio and Chuy together, I thought of that song, "He Ain't Heavy, He's My Brother." I knew we were all grateful to Octavio. It was as if Octavio had passed up the chance of getting married, of seriously committing to a relationship with a woman because his mission was to take care of Chuy, trying to help our brother erase the Vietnam memories—to shoo the ghosts away—as best he could. I often wondered if Chuy saw himself as a different person than the one he was in 1969 when all hell let loose in our personal lives and in our country. Chuy, our family's sacrificial lamb, now back in the family fold, all of us brothers and sisters hoping that he was healing, healing with doses of love, loyalty, and lithium.

As I watched Chuy and Octavio hug each of us sisters hello, now the two brothers en route to the kitchen for a beer, I thought that in some small or large way all of us brothers and sisters had been each other's keeper: Our little Luz, a family loyalist through and through, had eighteen-year-old Monica to confide in; and Monica, in turn, listened respectfully, her cowboy hat and boots making her look like some wise old cowgirl; la Ms. Freudiana, Carolina, turned out to have wizardry abilities with finances and was quickly climbing the socioeconomic ladder with Tom. Carolina had become—whether she liked it or not—the matriarch of the Sahagún family. Ana María was in the throes of wedding preparations for her marriage to Roger, and her present vocabulary consisted of words like tulle, *azahares*, bridal dresses, and flower arrangements. Then Tony showed up with his wife Marisa, who was wearing her favorite color: light lavender blouse and dressy dark lavender slacks. We teased her, saying, "Here comes the Lavender Girl." Marisa, the girl next door, now our sister.

We were there then, all twelve of us, waiting for Papá to arrive. He'd been living at the Del Sol senior citizen apartment complex for about six months now. And as I looked around, I wondered if my brothers and sisters were feeling as anxious as I was. Our father had something important to talk with us about. What? I glanced at the Sacred Heart of Jesus picture above the mantlepiece, wondering—even though I knew Lydia would scold me for finding symbolism in every moment of my life—whether Jesus Christ's twelve disciples felt anxious on that Thursday night.

I heard his truck drive up to the front of the house. The sound of the car door slamming shut. While everyone else was talking, laughing, pointing to some silly commercial on the TV, I followed, in my mind, our father's progress toward the house, now making his way up the three steps to the front porch. As was his custom, he rang the doorbell and opened the door at the same time, now entering. Papá was dressed in a suit—a worn blue suit that in its prime was sharp looking and distinguished. His tie was navy blue with a sprinkling of barely discernible fleurs-de-lis in red. At the tip of his tie was a stain that looked like the outline of a country on a cursory map—perhaps South America. And although his suit was weary and frayed, Papá was not. He stood at the doorway, hesitant, this small-boned man, thin as a bird—maybe a sparrow, or a *golondrina*. Maybe a messenger pigeon, a harbinger of bad news, I thought. But I couldn't help admitting that he did look young for his sixty-five years. Young and handsome and happy. His hair was thinning, but it was still there with just a bit of white. He had a few wrinkles on his face, but his blue eyes were lively and—I could tell because I knew this man well—still full of plans and dreams and schemes. His long, slender nose, so unlike my mother's and my pudgy one, made him look dignified and important—more important than I'd ever before noticed. But the suit. Why a suit?

We each took turns hugging Papá—even me. I was trying hard to contain myself though I could feel the anger rising. What possible explanation could he have that would prove him innocent, that wouldn't make him look like a foolish old man with a too-young trophy girlfriend?

We made our way to the kitchen table where the dishes of food had been set, buffet style. For dessert there would be flan, pineapple upside-down cake, and chocolate chip cookies. We sisters took turns heating the tortillas on the stove burners, quickly transferring them to a dish-towel to keep them warm. As we sat at the grand table, we passed the towel-wrapped warm tortillas around. And that made me think of Holy Communion, the tortillas our Communion wafer.

"For a hungry stomach there is no . . ." Papá pronounced from his repertoire of *dichos*, sayings we had heard over and over for as long as I could remember. He was sitting at the head of the table, six children to his right, six children to his left. And if once I was patient with his never-ending, Polonius-like dichos, now I had no patience for this man. Why should I? Mamá was no longer alive to get the brunt of his wrath when we children misbehaved. So why should I sit there listening respectfully to this fool when all I could see was this old man with that young señorita, his arm around her in a *not* fatherly way. She looked sexy and poor, and he looked, well, he looked like the King of the Jungle. So why should I laugh at his worn jokes, sayings that were clichéd and pontifical?

Carolina's *pipián* was the best I'd ever tasted (I had to admit). She had outdone herself once again. I glanced her way as she and Ana María discussed the colors for the wedding and flowers that would match whichever color Ana decided on. Then I quickly scanned each of my brothers and sisters. Papá was cajoling and flirting with Marisa, whom he called "*la flor de lavanda.*" Yes, she did look like a lavender flower. Sonia was intently explaining to Luz and Monica her trick for getting the slimy *baba* off the cactus, while Octavio was thinking of going over to Sammy's to play some pool later on. Did you guys want to come, he asked our brothers. It occurred to me that they must have all been think-ing the same thing I was thinking: something was up with our father. Unlike me, though, they had decided to proceed in a normal way, wait until Papá was ready to speak.

"So what is this important thing you have to tell us?" I said once everyone had sat down to eat.

My brothers and sisters turned to look at me as if I'd just said something hideously disrespectful—something like "fuck this shit, I want to know what's on your mind right now, Papá." They looked at me as if it'd just dawned on them that I might be the traitor among them. (Or maybe they didn't really look at me this way, but I just imagined they did, thanks to vestiges of a well-bred Catholic guilt, a guilt much like the crusty barnacles that cling stubbornly to a pier's pillars.)

Unlike me, my brothers and sisters were probably still respectful of our father.

My father looked at me—sadly? Mysteriously? I couldn't quite figure out his look.

"It can wait until later," he said simply, his eyes firmly on me.

He knew that I knew. That was it. Well, then fine, we'd play this little game his way. I could bide my time.

It was during dessert, once the coffee and the sugar and the can of condensed milk were set in front of him that Papá tapped his coffee cup with a spoon.

"Atención, hijos," he said. "I've assembled you all here to talk over some new developments." He reached into his suit pocket and pulled out a business envelope. "This came in the mail last week . . ." He took the letter out of the envelope and passed it over to Armando. "*Tú que hablas más inglés,*" he said as he handed the letter to our oldest sibling. Another tired expression, his way of getting us kids to do anything he needed done, his way of beginning a statement that ended in an order: You, who speak more English, go help your mother bring down the clothes from the line; you, who speak more English, empty the trash can; you, who speak more English, help your sister pick up the dirty dishes. Now, because he spoke more English—whatever that meant in our father's foolish mind—Armando was silently reading the letter to himself. After a few minutes, he looked up at all of us.

"It's from the state of California," Armando announced. "The Department of Transportation. They're widening the freeway and need to buy this property in order to widen it."

Everyone started talking at once: Where? When? How much? What would they do to the house? Where would we go? Would it be enough money to buy a new home? Little Luz started crying, "But where will we go?"

Obviously they weren't going to throw you onto the street, Armando reassured Luz, reassured all of us. It was a good sum of money, he said.

"There'll be enough money to buy something else, right Papá?" he said.

Papá looked at each of us, at our shocked and worried expressions. He didn't say anything. Monica wondered if we could buy a house with enough property to keep a pony. Luz was the sentimental one, wishing we didn't have to leave, could live in this home forever.

Our mother died in this house, in the only house I have known in these twenty years of my life, I thought to myself. Would her spirit follow us to our new home, protect and guide us? Or would it remain in this house, on this piece of land?

It was then that I glanced at Chuy, who had been quietly listening to the commotion. He was eating his piece of pineapple upside-down cake with a glass of milk, and in truth he was the only one who didn't seem upside-down at the moment. He was quiet and pensive as he glanced, every so often, at our father. Nobody else seemed to notice that Papá had not said a word since Armando's announcement. Nobody except for Chuy and me. I put down my fork and folded my hands on the table, realizing in that moment when Chuy glanced at Papá that there was more. The bomb had not yet dropped. That was just the prologue.

"Hijos," he began. "I have something important to say." He cleared his throat, this wiry, sprightly little man with shocking light blue eyes who was my father. Yes, I would grant my brothers that much: Papá wasn't all that bad looking for a sixty-five-year-old man.

He cleared his throat again nervously. And I knew for sure that whatever he was about to say would change the path of my life. I just knew it.

"I've received this letter from the state, and they want to buy our house and property because they are widening the freeway." Yes, we knew this. Armando had just told us, didn't he remember, tú que hablas más inglés, remember? Okay, we get money for our property, buy another house, and life goes on.

At first no one said anything, as if we were trying to figure out what this really meant. Then Carolina, ever pragmatic and sensible, asked, "When is this going to happen, and where are you and the girls going to live?"

"Well, you see, this is the thing," he said, raising his cup and taking a sip of the coffee. The cup was shaking slightly, unsteady in his hand. He quickly set it on its saucer with a rattle.

"As you know, I have these senior citizen apartments that I manage, but children are not allowed to live there. Nobody under fifty-five, you understand."

"Yeah, we know that," said Ana María. "So you'll buy another house where the girls can live."

"Well, you see," our father said, "that's the thing. I don't think I want—I don't think I'm going to buy another house."

There was silence, all of us brothers and sisters quickly registering this in our minds, quickly assessing the import of what he'd just said.

"What do you mean, Papá?" Carolina asked in a low, calm voice.

"Mi'jos," he said, now looking over at his sons for—what? Help? Support? Encouragement? Who knew. "I could use the money. Now that I'm an apartment manager, and have a place to live, I don't want to be tied down with a house. Las niñas," he said, now looking at Luz and Monica, "can live with Carolina and Tom, and Ana María and Yoli can find a nice little apartment to live in." He was staring at the TV, which wasn't on. "Of course, I'll help with the rent and all," he said.

And I wondered if my father had ever noticed how thin Luz had become, how rarely Monica smiled. Had he forgotten that Ana María was planning to get married soon?

"What do you mean you need money?" Armando quietly spoke up. "Are you in debt or something? We can help you."

He shook his head. No, it wasn't that. His eyes were still planted on the dark TV, as if he were expecting it to go on any minute now and some lively, fun show would entertain us all.

It was just that he needed to start a new life.

Our mother's death and all.

A new life.

His voice trailed off.

We were speechless.

This constituted the ultimate traitorous act, I thought. A coup d'état. Abandonment of the worst kind. The act of a self-centered man who was riding high with his young trophy señorita girlfriend, who wanted to flaunt whatever money he had coming from the state. He was a young man again, I thought to myself, this money from the state about to give him power and freedom to buy sex from a young but poor señorita.

He got up from his seat at the head of the table and made his way to the front door. Papá looked like a scraggly old man now, his shoulders hunched, the frayed blue suit way too large for him, making him look like a homeless vagrant walking away from a public that wondered why. His withered blue eyes looked at each of his children, hoping for understanding. This father of ours who protected us from evil boyfriends, who inculcated in us the importance of prayer and God and Holy Days of Obligation, kneeling next to Mamá, barking orders for us to cross our arms and stop fidgeting while praying the rosary. Now his tired blue eyes implored us to understand him, to understand that he was not the same father as before—as before our mother died, as before Dolores Ramos left him to be, alone, the patriarch of his nine children. Left him to give orders that even he, our father, knew we would no longer take from him. His whole being fading, fading from our lives. His defeated stoop, his weary eyes begging us to understand his bid for one last chance at life.

He reached for the door handle. "Hijos," he said, glancing at the black TV console one last time, at the green velvet armchair, at anything other than us, his nine children. "Perdónenme," he said, his apology an explanation, his entreaties a plea that we allow him a second chance at another kind of life that did not include us.

We watched in silence as he opened the door and walked out, softly closing the front door of 2215 Conifer Street, a home he built for us with his determination to give us a better life. As he closed the door to his past as the patriarch of these nine children, it was as if a shadow has suddenly darkened the house; as if our father were already a fading picture of his former self; as if he had known all along that with Dolores's death his influence in our lives would slowly diminish and finally disappear, his spirit and presence perhaps less formidable than Mamá's spirit—his importance in our lives dependent on our mother being alive and at his side.

We brothers and sisters were too stunned to say anything. Our initial intention of bringing up the subject of his hot little señorita girlfriend flew out the window, lost in the rushing ocean wave sound of the freeway nearby, a freeway soon to bulldoze our shoe-cottage, a freeway about to reroute our destinies.

"Boy, this is a good one," Ana María finally said. "He sure knows how to get our attention."

But this is what I'd wanted, wasn't it? To sever all ties with this man? Little by little our connection to one another fading and finally ending? Yes, yes, I knew he was my father. What a thing to say, no? Well, no, it wasn't a terrible thing to say. Let him marry his hot little señorita, let her take him to the cleaners, wringing him of money—more money than he'd ever before had! Who was this man I called Papá, this man who abandoned his young daughters, who rushed off as if pursued by the devil—ha!—little knowing that he himself was the devil?

A part of me wanted to go running after my father and tell him to wait, wasn't he going to protect us from evil men who might want to take advantage of his daughters? Didn't he realize there were still corrupt forces out there, that we needed his protection?

But another part of me said great, fine, go. Who needs you, anyway? Yes, leave us. What do I care?

"This is all that he's capable of, you know."

We all turned to look at Chuy, who kept his eyes on the just-closed front door, his hands folded on the table, straight soldierlike posture. Chuy, our Vietnam veteran brother who had been to hell and back, who rarely spoke, most of the time looking confused at what we were saying, or simply staring out the window at another reality.

"This is as much as he can give, don't you see?" He said this quietly, matter-of-factly, now looking at each of us, one at a time, as if entreating us to understand what he was saying.

We stared at him as we silently took in this bit of valuable information—information we never would have thought of in a million years, information we must sort out individually. And because each person naturally processed things differently (I was beginning to realize that we responded and reacted to and remembered our shared past in our own ways), we would be left to think about this action and churn it in our minds as we felt shocked, outraged, angry, confused, hurt, depressed, sad, accepting, understanding—or all of the above.

We slowly got up from our places and cleared the table.

Nineteen

Lydia tried to be positive about the dramatic turn of events in the Sahagún household. "My God, Yoli," she said as she, Luz, and I were packing things, "this is a godsend." Lydia said all of this in a too-perky sort of way. I appreciated her trying to cheer us up. We were in the kitchen, and Lydia was working on bringing down the stuff in one set of cupboards; I was working on the pots and pans in the oven; and Luz had the pantry shelf. We'd earlier called out to Monica in the back room, but she had her radio on full blast and I decided to let her be. She hadn't seemed to want to talk about this, wanted to be left alone.

Lydia claimed that now that the state of California was buying our house and we were forced to find somewhere else to live, it had saved her life. She convinced her parents to let her move in with Ana María and me. We could've gone to live with Carolina and Tom, or any one of my brothers and their wives—they all offered at least a thousand times. But Ana María, who postponed her marriage to Roger, felt like we could handle living on our own. We were confident we could take care of each other. During the school week Luz and Monica would live with Carolina, but on weekends they could come and hang out with Ana, Lydia, and me at our apartment. An informal child custody arrangement, you could say.

"Freedom and liberty are calling us, girls," Lydia said as she finished packing the last glass from the cupboard, carefully wrapping it in old newspaper and placing it in the box. Her extraordinary efforts to cheer us up left me weary.

"Let's take a break," I said, "have some lunch."

I went outside to the back room to get Monica, to ask her if she wanted to join us. The door was slightly open, the radio on full blast, so I walked in. The room was dark, the curtains drawn, though it was midday. It took me a few seconds to adjust my eyes to the shadows. And when I did get a better picture of the room, I saw that Monica was asleep on one of the beds, curled up in a tight fetal position, her knees so close to her chest that I wondered how she could be comfortable. She breathed deeply, rhythmically, as if in a profound slumber. And she must have been because the music was blasting and it didn't wake her. I sat on the edge of the other bed, watching my cowgirl sister, not sure if I should wake her or not, she seemed to be in such a grateful sleep. I looked around what had been the guys' room. The trophy case was gone, and the room no longer had the look or the smell of a "guys' room," a room I used to clean—at least for a little while— when I was fourteen and loved snooping about. Now the room was mostly bare, only a chest of drawers, the desk, and the beds. I glanced at the tin wastebasket, the painting of a mallard in midflight decorating the exterior, and I noticed that the can was full to the brim. I stepped closer and looked inside. Monica's cowboy boots were at the top, and when I removed them I saw that the rest of the trash can was filled with her formidable collection of miniature horses: a spotted black and white pinto she named Frijoles; the golden palomino with cream-colored mane and tail she called Sol; her white Arabian, Mora; the stocky Clydesdale named Cerveza; a Shetland pony she named Flicka in honor of our old dog; and her favorite Appaloosa, which she named Raindrop because of the spots on its loins. Some of these horses I'd passed on to her when I was over my horse-crazy stage—though I never gave them names as Monica did—but most of them she collected herself over the years, easily fifteen or so exquisitely detailed and lifelike plastic horses. Her pride and joy stuffed in the trash can ready to be thrown out.

There was an extra blanket folded at the foot of her bed, and I quietly unfolded it and covered her with it. She stirred, tossing her head slightly as if she were flicking a fly, but she didn't wake. Then I walked out of the room, with only the blast of her raucous music in my wake.

But this is what I had wanted, wasn't it? I kept telling myself this over and over in a kind of mantra. No more strict, ridiculous orders. No more hanging up on guys who called us. No longer need I be a witness to his erratic behavior full of wrath and fury. No more melodrama from the likes of our father. But still. And it was this hesitation of being free of my father that I didn't understand.

❄ ❄ ❄

In the fall of 1967, when I was twelve years old and Abuelito Ramón was dying of cancer, Mamá quickly made travel plans to go to El Grullo to spend the last days of her father's life with him. During that time, Papá worked as a maintenance manager at a trailer park in La Mesa, about twenty miles northeast of our Palm City home. I've always looked back at that period of our lives as the Golden Age of the Sahagúns. Since he was the maintenance manager, our father lived in a small, one-bedroom trailer there on the premises. On weekends, we five daughters and Mamá, with eighteen-year-old Carolina driving, would pile into the station wagon to visit Papá, or else he dropped by the house to check in on all of us. The Golden Age of the Sahagúns because he was not living with us full-time, and so we had our space away from him as he had his space from us. Mamá was easygoing, loving, levelheaded, and, during that brief time, our only full-time parent. The Golden Age of the Sahagúns because when we visited him at his La Mesa trailer park, we spent most of the time in the park's pool or taking walks in the nearby woods. We'd spend Sunday there, enough time to say hello to Papá and then by evening be off, feeling relieved and safe, knowing that we were returning to a home protected by Mamá's gentle but firm hand as the head of the Sahagún household.

But Mamá's plans to go to El Grullo on a minute's notice presented a problem: who was going to take care of us five daughters? The idea of letting eighteen-year-old sister Carolina take care of us all was out of the question. My brothers worked full-time, so no, they couldn't either. After some discussion, Papá and Mamá settled on asking a dear old friend of the family, a spinster whom they had known since childhood, to come and stay with us for the two to three weeks it was anticipated that Mamá would be out of town. Thus it was that dear old Agueda came to stay with us. "Dear old Agueda" because she really was a dear to put up with my younger sisters' antics and mine as we three youngsters argued and quibbled with extra gusto and mischief, with the single intention of making Agueda's life miserable as she unsuccessfully and despairingly tried to keep us from hitting each other, from harming each other as we swore to do any minute. What a delight to watch her beg us to behave, all the while we sisters knowing that this ugly, Frankenstein-looking old lady would never tattle on us, would keep our mischief to herself. We knew from the moment she walked into our house and our parents introduced her to us that she was terrified of our father. Afraid to look him in the eyes, bowed her head as if in prayer when he talked (not that I could blame the poor old lady: our father's loud, commanding, nervous voice was enough to make any human or beast cower and run off to a safe corner, although when I thought of poor old Agueda, the fact that she was real religious and never married made me think she probably was afraid of all men, pobre viejita). So we knew instinctively, as only young children know with their brilliantly intuitive radar, that this old lady—our temporary guardian—was going to let us walk all over her, and, dear old father-frightened lady that she was, she would never think of complaining to Papá about our interminable, perpetual fighting. Luz, Monica, and I had dominion of the house, screaming at each other, arguing with such an authentic-seeming sibling rivalry intensity as to easily have earned us three young Sahagún sisters a Special Recognition Academy Award.

Papá checked in by phone every day, making sure we were all behaving and being respectful of Agueda. In her timid, trembling voice—so out of proportion to her tall, husky build—she reassured Papá that we were *unas hijas maravillosas*.

Really?! What a dear, all right, not to blow our cover.

So on a Friday night during Agueda's stay with us, Carolina got ready to go to Mar Vista High's Sadie Hawkins dance. We four sisters watched as she fixed herself up. Luz and Monica sat on the top bed, their legs dangling, while Ana tried on lipstick, practicing the proper way to evenly smudge her lips. I sat on the single bed watching as well, anxious for *my* day to come to get all dolled up for a high school dance.

"When Papá calls," Carolina instructed, "just tell him I went over to Esther's to study." The same explanation was given to Agueda.

At 7:30, a friend of hers honked the horn and Carolina happily bounded out the door.

By 7:45, the phone was ringing. It was Papá. Carolina is where? What's Esther's number? He demanded.

As soon as we hung up, we dialed Esther's number to let her know she was supposed to be an alibi. Damn it, the phone was busy. At 7:48, we tried her number again.

Yes, he just called, Esther's mother said. She told him Carolina wasn't there, that maybe she was at the school dance. That's where Esther was. Should she not have said that? Esther's mom asked us, now worried.

Damn.

By 8:15, Papá's small pickup truck was screeching to a halt in the driveway, a door now slamming. "Where is she?" he demanded of Agueda. He was standing in the middle of the small living room, arms akimbo as the four of us sisters came out of the bedroom. Agueda looked like she was ready to cry.

"She went to Mar Vista High's dance," Ana María spoke, her voice sounding defiant and terrified at the same time.

"Who gave her permission?" he shouted. "Who?! Did you, Agueda?" We all turned to look at Agueda, who shook her head timidly, her small eyes bugging out in despair and confusion.

Then she said, "Well, the girls told me . . ."

"*Olvídalo*," he shouted. "Just forget it. I'm going to go get her, and you," he pointed to the four of us younger daughters, "get on your knees and pray the rosary right now." Then turning to look at Agueda, "You, too," he commanded. And then he was out the door, slamming it shut extra hard.

We sisters knelt in the living room before the Sacred Heart of Jesus and prayed the rosary, led by Agueda who was quietly weeping and interjecting a "Dios mío, dale paciencia" between Hail Marys.

I was tempted to scoot over to where Agueda was kneeling and put my arm around the frightened old lady and say, "Patience? Papá? Save your prayers, Señorita Agueda. Patience and good sense are not in Papá's vocabulary."

But the truth was I was just as terrified as Agueda—we all were, I could tell from my sisters' scared looks—and every so often we glanced at the front door, as if waiting for the tornado to rip it open any minute.

By the time we came to the last mystery of the rosary, we heard the pickup at the front of the house, doors slamming shut. In they came, Papá and Carolina, who was puffy-eyed and miserable as she cried and blew her nose.

"Get whatever you need for the weekend," he ordered her. And then he turned to Ana María. "And you too, so hurry it up."

"But why me?" Ana María began. Already her eyes were filling with tears of angry resignation.

"I don't want to hear another word from any of you," he said, his voice hoarse with rage.

As the girls miserably walked to the bedroom to pack some overnight stuff, Papá turned to Agueda and said, "Well, you obviously can't take care of these girls, so I'm taking them with me." The three of us younger sisters quickly got up from the couch and scurried into the bedroom as Papá continued to scold Agueda.

In the bedroom, the girls were packing pajamas and stuff in a grocery bag, crying as Carolina told us what happened. She'd been in the middle of a slow dance with Carlos—just a childhood friend from the neighborhood, nothing heavy, so she wasn't in some hot, delicious embrace with him or anything like that. Papá marched right up onto the dance floor and pulled Carolina away from Carlos and said, "Chamaca ingrata, how dare you sneak off to a party?" He had his hand tightly around her arm.

"Papá," Carolina had said, "you're hurting me. Let go . . ."

He loosened his grip on her, looking momentarily startled out of his rage. But then he promptly led her off the dance floor, grasping her upper arm as if he were taking her into custody.

One of the chaperone teachers, Mr. McGinnis, came forward.

"Hello," he said. "Is there a problem?"

"No," Papá said, "there is no problem now. This is my daughter and I'm taking her home where she belongs. She sneaked over here without my permission."

"Papá," Carolina said, now breaking her stoic silence. "I'm eighteen years old and if I want . . ."

"Cállate," he cut her off. "How dare you talk that way to me . . ."

"Sir, if your daughter's eighteen," Mr. McGinnis said, "she has the right . . ."

"Who are you to tell me what rights my daughter has, eh?" he shouted at Mr. McGinnis.

By this time, lots of heads were turning their way, wanting to know what all the commotion was over by the entrance to the gymnasium.

Carolina just wanted to get the hell out of there before the scene got even bigger.

"Vámonos, Papá," Carolina said, resigned to the inevitable, and turning to the biology teacher, said, "thank you, Mr. McGinnis." Then she walked out to the parking lot with Papá.

The only thing he said on the way home was a terse "Get whatever you need for the weekend because you and Ana María are coming with me to the trailer."

So here they were packing some deodorant, underwear, a change of clothes. Luz, Monica, and I looked on with miserable horror knowing full well they were packing for a grim stay at the Lorenzo Sahagún Penitentiary.

And then, just like that, they were gone, Papá barking one last order at Agueda to keep her vigilant eye on us *at all times.*

No doubt Papá would be keeping a vigilant eye on his two older daughters.

After they left, Agueda suggested we do another round of rosary praying. My God, I thought to myself, how many Hail Marys and Our Fathers would it take to have a little miracle happen in the Sahagún household? Patience and good sense? Papá? Forget it.

Fearing for my sisters' lives, afraid that whatever happened this weekend might traumatize them for life, I knelt down and prayed the rosary along with my little sisters and Agueda. Papá's temper and erratic behavior were famous in the neighborhood. It was no secret to anyone— not to busybody Socorrito next door; not to Don Epifranio, our revered viejito, sage old man that he was; not to the old German spies who lived in an immaculate duplex at the entrance to the street; not to Mr. Lawka, the Swiss watch repairman. No, our father's anger and rage were legendary on Conifer Street, and though neighbors didn't directly comment to us about it, we Sahagúns were certain they commented on it among themselves, a new opportunity for gossip. It gave me little relief to know that my family provided ample gossip for the neighbors. I forced myself to believe that every family—no matter how normal they might look on the outside—had stuff inside that was just as bad as ours.

That was what I kept telling myself as Luz, Monica, and I worried like hell for my sisters. In solidarity, we prayed and even stopped our pretend fighting with each other. Suddenly, mortifying Agueda was no longer fun. We knew she was just as sick over this as we were. We were prohibited from calling the girls at Papá's trailer in La Mesa, and so the four of us waited, quiet and full of dread, for their safe return home. He simply announced in one of his phone calls that he would be returning with the girls on Sunday evening since they had school the next day. Fortunately for all of us, Mamá was expected back on Wednesday.

Sunday came, and we waited expectantly for them, and felt both relief and dread when we saw Papá's red pickup pull up to the front of the house. We watched from the window as Carolina and Ana María got out, along with Papá. Tear-stained faces, angry words, slamming of doors, silent and bitter stoicism, my sisters' blue eyes red with nonstop crying all weekend—this was what we expected was coming.

The first thing we noticed when Carolina and Ana María got out of the truck was that they were wearing cute pairs of slacks and blouses we had never seen before. New clothes. Then we noticed the girls chatting with each other and with Papá as the three of them went to the back of the pickup, now pulling out bags—The Broadway, JCPenney department store logos on the shopping bags. Our mouths were wide open, astounded, as we watched the three of them make their way up to the front porch and door. Papá was saying something, and the girls started laughing.

"Agueda," little Luz called out to our distraught and nervous babysitter hiding out in the kitchen. "*Ven, rápido,*" she said. "There's been a miracle!"

Then they were in the house, and Papá was giving Agueda some instructions while we younger sisters automatically followed our older sisters into the bedroom. But just as we got there, Carolina and Ana María abruptly stopped as if they'd just remembered something, and went back out to the living room, walked over to Papá, and gave him a kiss. "Gracias, Papá," they both said.

He smiled and winked at them.

So this was the deal: while we three younger sisters were sick with worry that whole hot weekend, knowing Carolina and Ana were being driven off to a maximum security prison, they—these wretched, innocent "prisoners"—had the time of their lives!

The first thing Papá did Saturday morning, after waking the girls to the delicious smells of bacon, eggs, and pancakes—yes, *panqueques,* too!—was take them to the shopping center nearby and pretty much let them buy whatever they wanted, reminding them that they were going to need bathing suits for swimming in the pool. The Broadway, JCPenney—nice department stores.

Ana and Carolina were excited, sometimes talking at the same time as they described the fun weekend they had at Papá's. First the shopping: a cute floral print blouse, a couple of pairs of pants, and a sweater each, some new lipstick and perfume, even. The bathing suits were these little umpire-style blouses that were detachable and—bingo!—you had a bikini. Papá didn't even check to see what they had bought, did not give his stamp of approval or disapproval. Then off to the pool they went and such perfect hot weather, too! (Yeah, maybe for you two "prisoners," I thought, but not for us who worried to death over you.) While lounging at the pool all afternoon, they met some other trailer park visitors, including three gorgeous brothers who asked for their telephone number although they were from out of town; still, it was nice that they wanted, really wanted, their phone number, which they didn't give them because they had a strict father. After this wonderful, glorious afternoon of feeling like young ladies of luxury at the side of the pool, Papá took them out to dinner at this fancy seafood restaurant nearby, Carolina and Ana María wearing their new slacks and cute blouses, taking along their new light cardigans, one a sunflower yellow, the other a periwinkle blue that Ana claimed made her eyes look luminous and dreamy.

Sunday's breakfast was even more scrumptious, the girls lazily waking up with happy new sunburns that made them ache and feel warm and lazy—sunburns they would be showing off in school the whole next week. That morning the small trailer was filled with the smell of chilaquiles, warmed flour tortillas and Papá's famous rice pudding with extra raisins and sticks of cinnamon the way he knew Ana María liked. The girls had slept in Papá's double bed while Papá had slept on the couch. And since it promised to be another warm day, well, what's a princess to do, they said to us, laughing and giggling as they wallowed in happiness, but go out and spend another torturous day at the side of the pool. This was one of their most memorable weekends ever, the poor "prisoners."

Monica, Luz, and I listened with a mixture of envy, relief, and most of all, wonder.

"But he was so mad on Friday," I said.

"Well, you know Papá," Carolina said as she hung her new blouse. "One minute he's mad, the next he's not. It's just the way he is."

And I knew what she meant: his erratic, inconsistent behavior, this dramatic moody pendulum that was Papá. Yes, I supposed, that was just the way he was.

But now when I thought about that time, I wondered why my sisters weren't more guarded or uneasy about Papá's radical mood switches. Were we children so resilient as to automatically block out the bad stuff when good stuff happened? Or was it just an intuitive understanding and acceptance—get out of his way when he's on the warpath, be grateful and unquestioning when he was not—that that was "just the way he is"?

Twenty

My four sisters and I gathered in the living room of the house at 2215 Conifer Street, the house that in a few months' time would be demolished by the state of California. We had stacks of boxes against the wall, stuff we were giving away, another tall pile with stuff we were taking to our apartment, bed linens and kitchen things. In many ways, the disbursing of these items reminded me of the Sunday rides to the swap meet, a chance to buy perfectly useable, practical—and inexpensive— items for the home, or the chance to sell something ourselves, like the litter of puppies Flicka always seemed to have. The house already felt vacant, a slight echo bouncing off the unadorned walls where once an assortment of family photos, the Sacred Heart of Jesus, and Our Lady of Guadalupe hung with dignity and with a grand sense of proprietorship. Little by little, we'd been packing stuff and sending it on its way—be it to our apartment, to our cousins in Colonia Libertad, to an orphanage in Tijuana, or to the dump. Our father, brothers, and sisters-in-law had bowed out of wanting any of these things, felt comfortable letting us sisters be the conservators of the Sahagún family heirlooms. And there were some: a collection of tablecloths cross-stitched by my mother as a young woman; the seemingly ancient sewing machine of solid mahogany and intricately scrolled metal work, "SINGER" in gold lettering.

Then there were Mamá's more personal things. It was nearing a year since she'd died, yet in that time none of us had ventured into her closet or thought to clear her dresser, having instead left our mother's possessions intact, as they'd always been, her toiletries sitting on the white crocheted doilies: the pink and white jar of cold cream, its label depicting blonde, brunette, and redhead Barbie-looking women as if to impress on the consumer that this cold cream was for all types of women; loose face powder in a peach-colored cylindrical box decorated with white powder puffs looking like wispy dandelions; a Mother's Day brush, comb, and mirror gift set with decorative gilded handles; the tattered old beige, vinyl-covered jewelry box filled with odds and ends—broken watches, an old silver coin, a pair of earrings in the shape of gold primroses, a 1969 postcard from Philadelphia sent to Chuy from a girl named Tania—trinkets with history or significance that we might or might not remember. In her closet hung brown and white sweaters, a black wool coat, a small collection of dresses sewn by her; on the floor underneath the dresses sat three pairs of low-heeled shoes in brown, beige, and black, with two dressy pairs of patent leather high heels and a pair of worn, pale blue slippers to match her robe. These few pairs of shoes were lined up neatly in a row, as if waiting for Mamá to appear and slip her feet into them. Her belongings had remained intact all those months because, well, because maybe we wanted to believe our mother was on an extended trip—not dead at all—just visiting her sisters in El Grullo.

Slowly, we brought her clothes out into the living room, draped them, hangers and all, over the back of the sofa while empty boxes in the middle of the room waited to be filled. Before we gave away whatever it was we were going to give away, we'd agreed to go through her possessions and keep what we wanted. Luz and I sat on the orange vinyl love seat, while Carolina and Ana María pulled up a couple of kitchen chairs near the sofa that had our mother's clothes draped over it. Monica sat a way from us on a kitchen chair next to the sewing machine, wearing her frayed pair of detested sneakers. She absentmindedly opened and closed the long, narrow middle drawer where my mother kept the stitch-ripper, a few straight pins, some extra bobbins, a chunky fabric-marking pencil. We all watched, as if mesmerized, as she tilted the drawer open and closed, open and closed. None of us had the courage to get up and look at the dresses and choose.

Then Carolina coaxed us on, telling us how psychologically important it was, in order to bring a healthy closure to our mother's death, to take something of her things with us to our new home. We all turned to look at her as if she were our PE coach now informing us that we must climb that fifteen-foot wall of slate in less than five minutes' time if we were to pass the class; we looked at her as if she were asking the impossible of four young women with broken legs and arms.

So Carolina began by asking us if it'd be all right if she took Mamá's beige brocade suit that was made expressly for Carolina's wedding.

We nodded, looking at the clothing draped over the sofa, moments in our mother's life revealed and remembered in a beige brocade suit; a sky blue jacquard dress; a light green summer short-sleeved dress dotted with yellow primroses and four yellow silver-dollar-size buttons on the bodice; the white velvet wedding dress, now yellowed and pockmarked with tiny drill-like bug holes; a brown cashmerelike car coat she herself made. Then we slowly, painfully made our choices.

There were other household items of sentimental value: Ana María asked for the silver tea set given to our parents for their twenty-fifth wedding anniversary; Luz was thrilled to have the black and white "Five Sisters" portrait in which she, at the innocent age of eleven months, sat on Carolina's lap, quietly and earnestly peeing, the urine seeping through the cloth diaper and drenching Carolina's lap as Carolina obediently sat motionless while the photographer went about his business of perfecting their pose; Monica asked for our parents' 1940 wedding picture, a full-length portrait of a handsome but serious couple. Our mother was draped in a white velvet gown, which elegantly hugged her petite frame while she held a cascading bouquet of lilies; our father was dressed in a black suit, a cluster of waxed azahares as his boutonniere, and both of them, most probably afraid and nervous about what awaited them, looked earnestly into the camera.

"Where's Mamá's rosary?" Luz asked, rummaging through the jewelry box.

"Which one?" Carolina said. "She had a bunch of them."

"The one made of rose petals," Luz said.

Nobody said anything, each one probably trying to remember where she had last seen it.

"I'd like to have the 1967 studio photo, if that's okay with you guys," I said, dismissing Luz's question as I reached for the handsome portrait of all eleven of us taken in Tijuana a year before Chuy was drafted to Vietnam.

We all stared at the eight-by-ten photo a moment as if each of us were wishing back that time in our lives.

"Let's take a break," Carolina said.

Monica and Ana María headed for the kitchen, Luz to the bathroom, while Carolina, the reluctant new matriarch of our family, slipped outside, standing just beyond the front screen door, crying quietly. But we all left the living room together. We couldn't bear to be alone in the room surrounded by the objects that represented our family life, that represented Mamá and Papá, these items thick with meaning and messages, objects completely imbued with a history that promised never to leave us—memories that promised to follow or haunt us for the rest of our lives.

I made my way to the back door out into the orchard. The little round mounds of dirt encircling the tree trunks were dry and hard. None of us had bothered to water the trees. What for? What month was it now, anyway? What week? What day? I had lost track of time, of the seasons, of all the things that were important to me. It didn't matter that the trees were parched and hungry for water. We'd be vacating the premises soon, and then it was all going to be bulldozed anyway. Then I noticed a pomegranate, just one left, which had fallen into its dry harbor. I picked it up. It was an old, overripe one, the skin at once leathery and soft. I held it in my hand tightly, squeezing it with all my might. The skin ripped, and I applied more pressure to it, the juice of the ruby kernels squirting on my arm, sprinkling my blue T-shirt. Some more pressure now that I'd gotten it going. Soon my hand was stained red like it was bleeding, but I refused to cry, and I refused to let go of the pomegranate. Just wished this was real blood and I was dying. Then the phrases came to me, "poor banished children of Eve," something about the "valley of tears," and before I could catch myself—for I'd had it with my parents' Catholicism and Hail Marys and Our Fathers—I was reciting something on automatic pilot. Stop it! Stop it this instant! I commanded my lips to stop moving, to stop saying what they were saying, much like when we recited the Pledge of Allegiance at that Daughters of the American Revolution tea party and Mamá very naturally recited with us—but recited a Hail Mary—oh, yes, much like that natural instinct to adapt, and especially then, when anger and grief swept me into automatic pilot, and I was reluctantly carried away by my instinct to survive, to seek help murmuring the "Hail Holy Queen, Mother of Mercy, our life, our sweetness, our hope, to thee do we cry, poor banished children of Eve, to thee do we send up our sighs, mourning and weeping in this valley of tears, turn then, most gracious advocate of mercy, thine eyes of mercy toward us and after this our exalted showing to thee—O Clement! O Loving! O Sweet Virgin Mary! Pray for us, O Holy Mother of God, that we may be worthy of the promises of Christ," letting the dramatic prayer and self-pity wash over me in an attempt to cleanse myself, or maybe exorcise myself.

I examined the wet palm of my hand, the newly stained red creases intersecting like confused, bloody rivers of a map. Then I wiped my crimson hand and arm on my jeans, wiped the juice off as best I could, and went back in.

Once in the living room, I selected the yellowed velvet wedding dress. I held it up against me, placing its shoulders to my shoulders as if I were checking to see if it might fit, the way we take dresses off the racks and, still on their hangers, place them against our bodies to see if they might just be the very thing we'd been looking for. The dress no longer had its long train as in the wedding photo (my ingenious, practical mother had cut that extra fabric and made a little white velvet suit for her firstborn toddler). It was now just barely down to the floor. "The reason I want this dress," I said to my sisters as I ran my hands over the coarse, rotting velvet, "is to remind me of the horrible marriage my parents had, so I don't have one like theirs."

Carolina and Ana María looked at me, startled. Had I just cursed myself? I imagined Carolina would file this comment in her mind, later try to analyze what was going on with me, perhaps pull out one of her psychology textbooks and do some reviewing in an attempt to rid me of these self-destructive, negative thoughts. Monica glanced at me briefly, hadn't said a word from the start, then looked back down as she wrapped thread tightly around her index finger, tight enough that when she finally released the thread you could see the redness and swelling, the thread markings looking like an odd, spiraled scar.

So it was thirteen-year-old Luz who asked me what I meant by that.

Luz, forever loyal and sentimental about the family, as if she had the responsibility of being the *luz*—the light—at the end of the Sahagún tunnel. And she probably was: It was she who loved to follow our mother around the house like a happy puppy; it was she who, when our mother died, accompanied our father on as many errands as she possibly could. So it was Luz who asked me what I meant by that.

I looked over at Carolina, who was busy folding a large tablecloth into a neat square. She quickly glanced at me, discreetly shook her head no.

But nothing was lost on Luz, who caught this unspoken communication between Carolina and me. "Just because I'm only thirteen," she said, "doesn't mean I don't know things." And there was hurt in her voice—but also disapproval, as if she were reminding me that they were, after all was said and done, our parents, and because of this we owed them our loyalty. Or maybe that's what my guilty conscience thought she was saying.

What I meant, I now said to Luz, was that every marriage has its ups and downs, pockmarks like the ones on this dress. "Don't mind me, Luz," I said. "You know how I am, la Miss Simbólica."

Luz looked relieved.

❀ ❀ ❀

In the years that followed this one, probably for the rest of my life, I would have these same kinds of dreams. They would accompany me to all my future destinations. The House Dreams, I called them: I'm running out the raggedy screen door, into the front yard and grass. Sweet peas are intertwined in the white fence and pink plastic flamingos are dipping their black beaks into the cement birdbath. I sit down on the grass and play with my baby dolls. In other dreams, I'm not playing. I'm walking through the little house, looking for something, feeling troubled and confused. I walk through the living room, searching, see the orange vinyl love seat, the fake fireplace, the cracked glass coffee table, the black and white TV console. Nothing matches—odds and ends, orphaned furniture taken from this or that house, about to be demolished. A love-hate relationship with my house? How could it be otherwise? It was so small and humble. No, go ahead and say it, Yolanda: it was a rickety poor shoe of a house. We five sisters shared one bedroom, four brothers shared another. One of us sisters always had to sleep on the hide-a-bed couch in the living room. To get to the only bathroom we had, you had to pass through the girls' room—our room constantly serving as a hallway full of busy bathroom traffic. Field mice from the canyon across the street scurried about inside the walls of the house, and during rainy winter days, pots and buckets were set on the kitchen floor, the living room, two more buckets in the girls' room, to catch the raindrops. Luz would say it sounded like music—a symphony of raindrops, she'd say.

Okay, I'd grant her that much.

Yes, yes, I knew there was another side to this, the story of the white cottage surrounded by gladioli, rosebushes, pastel-colored sweet peas in April. Flowers and plants and more junglelike plants—a hide-and-seeker's true delight. Across the street on the empty lot, the bushy, lacy California pepper tree, the mysterious canyon, the tall, sentrylike eucalyptus trees. And in the spring, the whole of the canyon covered with sour grass so tart it made our mouths and faces contort and pucker for a moment as we chewed on the green stalk. How many times did we play hide-and-seek under a full moon?

This Conifer Street house, then, would be my point of departure and my destination. The question—what is the measure of a house and home?—would follow me to all future abodes, and every house compared to the house I'd lived in the first twenty years of my life. Not the physical structure—no, that would be too easy, too quick to dismiss this home—but the spirit of my future houses, each one with its own ghosts and history. That was what I'd compare to the house on 2215 Conifer Street.

I stood in the middle of the street in front of our vacant house along with Monica, Luz, and Ana María. We were waiting for the rest of our brothers and sisters to arrive, for today was demolition day, and we wanted to be here—as we were with Mamá when she died in her bedroom—to say good-bye to our little house.

The house looked hollow and abandoned. Lonely. And suddenly I was reminded of the metal dollhouses we played with as children: lovely, tidy abodes, the interiors with their painted light fixtures, curtains, carpets, and pictures; walls in lime green and pastel pink; the requisite, stately fireplace with white molding; the red-tiled kitchen and white and green checked bathroom floor. How I loved to peek out the windows from the open side of the house, to look at the world from the inside out! And when it was time to stop playing, to peek one last time from the outside in. And just as I would walk away from my dollhouse, as I was being called to dinner or to sleep, I would give a final, loving good-night glance at my house.

It was April 1976, and I noticed the bushy tangle of sweet peas that we did not bother to tie up that year. What for? It was all going to be destroyed anyway. Our neighbor Socorrito had called Carolina a week ago, asking her if she and the rest of the neighbors could pick some flowers and take them home. Of course, what an honor! I was grateful that the neighbors had helped themselves to our flowers, to the roses, the elegant calla lilies. So you see, remnants of 2215 Conifer Street would be present in an assortment of lovingly arranged vases on our neighbors' coffee tables and kitchen counters, on top of TV consoles and bookshelves. The likes of Socorrito and Don Epifranio, the recluse Swiss watch repairman John Lawka, even the no-nonsense German spies at the other end of the street, would honor us by carrying home with them a bit of the Sahagún Estate. And though April was usually my favorite month—my birthday month—this year it was a cruel month. I would remember it as the April of Our House's Demise.

Then the rest of them arrived, and we stood in the middle of the street in front of the house, early that spring morning as the two bulldozers roared their way down the street toward us, toward our little house. The sounds of the bulldozers woke the whole neighborhood, and soon Socorrito was rushing out to meet up with us in her fluffy blue mules and frayed blue robe, which she held tightly around herself in that crisp, cool spring morning. Don Epifranio tottered over as quickly as he could with his cane in tow; why, even the German spies came out, their faces looking less stern, almost soft and compassionate. They nodded their good morning to us and then turned their gaze in the direction of the bulldozers. We all watched as the monster machines made their way to our property.

I was surprised to see Socorrito crying openly, heartfully. "Thank God your mother is not here to witness this." She blew her nose with a loud honk. Then, "Where's your father?"

"He couldn't make it," I simply said in response to her question.

The truth was we had decided not to include him in this. When we called the transportation department to ask them for the date of demolition, we agreed that this was something we wanted to share among just us brothers and sisters. Having the neighbors here was a pleasant surprise. And yes, Socorrito was right: thank God Mamá was not here to witness this. She had been dead for a year and a half. What would have become of our lives and destinies had she been alive to guide us? What would become of our lives and destinies now that she was not here to guide us?

Then, just like that, the bulldozers charged forward like two hungry monsters, steel dragons devouring our little house, collapsing the walls the way you collapse that big cardboard box that holds your new refrigerator. That was it then, a cardboard house neatly collapsing, first one wall then another.

"We still have the memories to hold on to," Carolina said.

Yes, we did, didn't we? It was her idea for us to meet for this goodbye—"for closure," she'd said. But her words did little to comfort me. And I noticed she was crying, too. Our big brother Armando put his arm around our baby sister Luz who was sobbing in gulps, who seemed to be doing the most crying even though she'd lived in that house the least amount of time. It was she who had the sentimental foresight to take down the numbers—two 2s, a 1, and a 5—just before the crew got here, and she tightly clutched these four black metal numerals, tiny rusty nails dangling from their holes. What was she thinking? What were all my brothers and sisters thinking as they witnessed our home being folded into neat little piles of nothing, of dust and ashes? Being folded into its demise.

Part Three

Vine a Comala porque me dijeron

que acá vivía mi padre, un tal Pedro Páramo.

Mi madre me lo dijo. Y yo le prometí que

vendría a verlo en cuanto ella muriera.

Le apreté sus manos en señal de que lo haría, pues

ella estaba por morirse y yo en un plan

de prometerlo todo.

I came to Comala because they said that

my father lived over here, a Pedro Páramo.

My mother told me. And I promised her that

I would come as soon as she died.

I squeezed her hands as a signal that I would do it,

well, she was about to die and I was set

to promise anything.

—From *Pedro Páramo* by Juan Rulfo

Twenty-one

Even then I knew we needed direction—we all knew this, my sisters and I. A destination, a mission, something that llueva o truene would set us on a definite course. Would lead us forward.

Ana decided on pink in a silklike polyester fabric for the brides-maids. We all were happy to agree to anything just as long as she went through with this wedding she'd been putting off. The style was simple: a sleeveless empire gown with a matching long-sleeved jacket, elegant but not overdone—the motto for her June wedding.

First it was my mother's death, then my father moving out, and then our moving out of the house, the wanting to take care of us three younger sisters. Roger was ever patient and understanding of her hesi-tation, but enough was enough, we sisters finally said. Lydia, Ana, and I had been living in a two-bedroom apartment in Chula Vista these few months with weekend visits from Luz and Monica who lived with Carolina and Tom. Yes, enough was enough because we knew Ana wanted to get married but felt guilty about this decision, as if to get mar-ried were to abandon us three younger sisters. So all five of us and Lydia piled into the car one day for what we told Ana María was a Sunday cruise to Coronado, and we drove her straight to the fabric shops in San Ysidro and insisted—as we held her in loving hostage—she make a selection right then and there on a pattern and fabric. Father Stadler at St. Charles Church had managed to reserve a Saturday in June for us to get Ana and Roger married off.

With five sisters and a plethora of girlfriends to help with arrange-ments—the sewing of the bridesmaids dresses, floral arrangements, tuxedo rentals, decoration setup of St. Charles's parish hall for the recep-tion—we managed, in record time, to be ready-set-go for Ana María's wedding day. The food was being catered by one of the local Mexican restaurants—Cuca's Café—in Imperial Beach.

Monica wondered, as we sisters and Lydia were getting dressed in the master bedroom in Carolina and Tom's condominium (Tom had been sent on a third errand—film for the camera—and so only feminine voices could be heard in the small house), whether the café would bring along the two-headed red car that stood in front of the restaurant with "Cuca's Café" painted in elegant script on the side for all the traffic on Palm Avenue to see. "Two-headed" we called it because the funky jalopy was joined together by two front parts at both ends.

"You can never tell if you're coming or going in that car," Monica said. "I think it would make a great wedding centerpiece. Very symbolic, you know." She grinned at her reflection in the mirror as she carefully rubbed the facial mask on her face, careful to keep large flesh-colored areas around the eyes. She was in her jumbo curlers and bathrobe like the rest of us.

We laughed.

"Watch out, Monica," Lydia said. "You're starting to sound like Yoli. Toda simbólica."

Ha, ha, so funny, I said, now tossing a pink Kleenex flower—decorations for the cars—at Lydia.

Monica had come back to life—we all had—in the excitement of wedding plans. This celebration was as much for us, in a therapeutic way, as it was for Ana and Roger, and Carolina must have known that we needed a celebratory distraction. It was she who had the idea that we pile into the car and force Ana to make decisions on her wedding. A distraction, yes, but did Carolina ever consider the fact that this celebration would include our father? I wasn't sure how the rest of my siblings felt about him—I'd kept my feelings to myself—but I'd rather not have anything to do with him.

I was thinking about this when we got the call from Armando.

"Are you kidding?" I heard Carolina ask, distraught. She and I were in the kitchen where she'd picked up the phone on the wall. The rest of the girls were either in the bedroom or in one of the two bathrooms. "He wore a tux to *my* wedding," she said, now walking the length of the telephone cord, reaching for a kitchen chair. I quickly went over to help her since the cord had gone as far as it could and she just barely reached the chair. I pulled it up close to her and she sat down. I stood next to her, listening to her side of the conversation.

Then, "Jesus, what am I going to tell Ana?" A pause. "Yeah, okay. How about if I talk to him . . ."

Another pause as Armando explained something to her.

From the look on her face I knew immediately who they were talking about. No, not Chuy, or Roger, or any one of my brothers. No, of course not. Leave it to *him*, el señor Lorenzo Sahagún, to be up to some sort of obstinate shenanigans.

"Okay," Carolina said into the phone. "I'll tell her. Bye." And she hung up.

She looked at me. "Papá refuses to wear the tuxedo," she says. "He told Armando that tuxedos are too formal and pretentious, and he is a humble man and proud of it. He will wear his charro suit."

"His charro suit!?"

His charro suit was at least forty years old, the suit he used to wear every Thanksgiving as he was doling out the turkey and singing his dramatic rendition of the "Corrido del Caballo Blanco," forcing all of us in attendance to join him and the white horse on their musical trek up north beginning in Guadalajara onward to Tijuana and Ensenada.

His charro suit, for God's sake.

Since we sisters moved out of the house on Conifer Street, since its demolition, our father called now and then to say hello to me and Ana María, although Carolina claimed he called her house every day to talk with Luz and Monica, took them out to dinner often. Carolina said he was trying very hard to stay connected, and she was proud of his efforts.

Well, goody-goody-gumdrop for him.

Tom returned with the film and soon everyone was in the kitchen grabbing a cookie, a glass of juice. Yes, eat something, Carolina warned; it was going to be a warm day and we wouldn't be eating for another four hours or so, what with the ceremony and picture taking before we even got to the parish hall.

Ana María, with her long, curly black hair and deep blue eyes, was still in her bathrobe and, like the rest of us, in her facial mask. She smiled calmly. It's okay, she said. Let him wear whatever he wants. He was entitled. Besides, she wasn't going to let that ruin her day, she said philosophically, as if she'd given this a lot of thought over the last few weeks. If Papá, in his usual inimitable style, made a scene, did something foolish, tried to ruin her moment of being Queen for a Day, she would not let him. Even in her old pink bathrobe and green facial mask, Ana María looked radiant and calm and in charge of herself.

"Well, at least he's agreed to walk you down the aisle to the altar *y entregarte*," Miss Optimist Luz said.

Nobody bothered to remind her that he walked Carolina to the altar IN A TUXEDO, and not in some funky old charro suit.

But what I really didn't get was Ana María's calm acceptance of this situation. Yes, Ana María, who not too long ago was begging our mother to divorce our father. I didn't get it, and yet I didn't want to be a spoiler and go up to her and suggest she throw a fit, maybe uninvite him to the wedding. I'd noticed a change in Ana María's attitude toward our father since we moved out of the house and into our own apartment. As if she'd come to some sort of peace with him, as if maybe now that she was on her own, or now that our mother was no longer alive to be the brunt of his wrath, she could let go of her anger toward him. Funny, wasn't it? My anger had just climbed up a hundred notches. Try explaining that.

I felt like a lone soldier fighting against—what? Patriarchal injustices? Machismo? Fighting for the liberation of the oppressed daughters of the world? And, as always, there were the thoughts, nagging and guilty: What would my mother say? How would my mother want me to behave toward my father? Be accepting and forgiving, or wage an all-out war against him? But I knew what she'd say, didn't I? "He's your father, Yolanda," I could hear her soft but firm voice saying. "Be understanding of him." But she was wrong to say that. Wrong, wrong, wrong. Because this was my war now—my revolution, Mamá. All mine.

It was time to get dressed for the ceremony, to leave for St. Charles Church to get Ana María married off. But first Lydia called us all into the living room where she had turned on the stereo and set an album on the turntable, raising the volume just as the Fifth Dimension began to sing "Wedding Bell Blues." She handed each of us sisters a brush or a comb to serve as microphones, then grabbed her camera as we belted out the words. And while Lydia was taking pictures, Tom, dressed in his tuxedo, was our sole audience, sitting attentively on the couch, laughing and shaking his head as he watched his wife and four crazy sisters-in-law in their bathrobes and pink jumbo curlers and fluorescent green facial masks standing in a line facing him, dancing and entreating him with outstretched arms to marry them because "kisses and love won't carry me 'til you marry me, Bill."

St. Charles Church was in Imperial Beach, and now that we no longer lived in Palm City the distance to this parish was a few miles farther for us than, say, Our Lady of Guadalupe in Otay or St. Rose of Lima in Chula Vista. But we felt a loyalty to our childhood parish, and Father Stadler had been kind enough to squeeze this wedding in on short notice. Even though St. Charles was the parish of our childhood, a new structure had since been built, the original small church serving as the parish hall. The new church was large and modern, minimalist in comparison to most traditional Catholic churches that I knew with their large party of saints and virgin statues in every nook and cranny. St. Charles Church had kept its saints and virgins to a minimum: a small side altar for the Virgin of Guadalupe and another for old Charlie himself.

We piled out of the cars and headed for the bride's room in the church. I looked up at the sky and noticed that the June Gloom—a thick marine layer that sat over San Diego a few weeks every June—was lifting and dissipating as patches of blue appeared. We were a flurry of pink and white, Ana's veil dancing in the breeze, all of us being careful not to walk too fast in our rose-colored satin high heels.

Our brothers were already there, waiting at the entrance, each one in a tuxedo looking handsome and distinguished; Roger was inside somewhere talking with Father Stadler, so we bridesmaids quickly whisked Ana María into the side room before anyone—especially Roger—had a chance to see the lovely bride before the ceremony. I scanned the church, the pews, but I didn't spot my father anywhere.

We girls were in the bride's room for a last-chance check in the mirror for smeared lipstick, hair smooth and shiny and just right, making sure Ana's headpiece was not lopsided, the veil extended and slightly fluffed up (I was surprised at how Lydia, a bridesmaid herself, took over here, making sure each of us looked just right—no loose threads, no bra straps showing—as if she were the wedding director). Monica, just back from the bathroom, reported that the German spies were sitting near the front next to John Lawka, the watch repairman.

"You invited the German spies?" I said to Ana. Even though they'd been our neighbors for as long as I could remember, I'd never considered them friends exactly. And John Lawka, too? Well, he I could understand. We'd taken many a broken watch to his shop for repair. A quiet, small fellow, he'd wave to us in the school bus when we passed him as he walked to his shop. But the German spies?

Ana María smiled, as if she might at any minute prop her elbow on the table, chin on hand, and wax philosophical. But she didn't. Instead, she looked at me in the mirror and tilted her head to one side, then the other, as if she were doing neck exercises, her hands clasped demurely in front of her, standing regally, like the queen she was that day. She was stunning. "I was feeling a little nostalgic when I sent the invitations," she explained.

"El Chango is sitting with this real pretty girl—a mystery woman," Monica said. She estimated about a hundred people in the church so far, more coming in. Old Tía Pachita from Tecate looked ancient in her pure white hair and powdery white face. No, she didn't look like she'd seen a ghost, said Monica, she *was* the ghost. And Luz and Monica giggled, Monica pleased with her own clever comments, Luz ready and willing to laugh at most anything. We were all a little giddy.

"Oh, and the tías from El Grullo are here," she announced, a little out of breath from excitement and nonstop talk.

Their delayed flight made us all worry last night that our favorite tías—my mother's younger sisters—would not make it in to Tijuana on time. But they had, thank God for that.

"And your father?" I said to my sister.

"Who?"

"You know, el señor Lorenzo Sahagún," I said. "Is he here?"

"C'mon everybody," Lydia interrupted, "Father Stadler wants us lined up now."

So here was the lineup: Little Luz with brother Octavio; Monica and Lydia escorted by two of Roger's friends; my brother Chuy and I; Tony and Marisa; Armando and Sonia; and Carolina and Tom—in other words, a whole bunch of us whose names and faces even our cousins and aunts and uncles couldn't always keep straight. Suffice it to say the whole Sahagún clan.

Then I saw him, way at the end of the line, talking with Ana María, who smiled as if she were in some sort of trance—as if, no matter what foolishness he was probably saying, she would be gracious and attentive.

It was hard to tell what he looked more like: the court jester, a rodeo ringmaster, or a withered old bullfighter who refused to get out of the bull ring even though his time was long over. His charro suit was so old and weathered it looked more like a dark blue gray than the original black wool. The silver buttons running along the sides of his pant legs looked tarnished and tired. His short bolero-style jacket was too short at the sleeves, but—I'd give him credit for this much—he had ironed his white shirt.

Elegant but not overdone—Ana María's wedding motto—and add to this one frayed *brincacharcos*, high-water charro suit, which looked about a hundred years old. After all, he was a humble man and proud of it.

For God's sake.

Now he was shaking hands with some guests who were entering. He said something to them and they laughed delightedly. His eyes sparkled; his smile was grand and generous as befitted the father of the bride. He pointed to his outfit, explaining something to them (really he was nothing more than the wedding buffoon, and I couldn't for the life of me understand how he didn't realize this, how he didn't take a good look at himself in the mirror and see himself for the fool that he was). I was relieved to see that he had the good sense not to have brought his señorita lady friend.

"Did you already say hello to him, Yoli?" Chuy said quietly, looking at me with his deep blue eyes, not exactly scolding but not exactly just curious to know the answer. We were lining up at the entrance to the church, and he was my escort.

I quickly looked away, as if I'd just been caught looking at something prohibited.

"Huh?" I said, avoiding Chuy's eyes, keeping my gaze fixed on my cousins Tina and Manuel as they tiptoed in and past the lineup.

"Yoli, he's our father," Chuy said.

At first I didn't say anything, busied myself rearranging the ribbon on my bouquet since one side was way longer than the other and so the ribbon looked lopsided. What I really wanted to say was that Lorenzo Sahagún was *his* father, not mine, but even in the depths of my anger I didn't want to startle or hurt Chuy. I didn't want him to think I was some sort of bitter, angry daughter. It bugged me, though, this loyalty that my siblings—especially my brothers—seemed to have for our father. And now to have Chuy making me feel bad about ignoring *our* father— especially coming from Chuy, who I'd thought understood me better than any of my brothers, but I guess that was a long time ago. Was I the only one who saw through this buffoon? Was I the only one who remembered what a wild, erratic and unpredictable father he'd always been? Didn't anyone remember what he just did—selling the house and then leaving us daughters to fend for ourselves? I refused to believe I was the only one thinking, Why couldn't it have been *him* instead of her?

"Yes, he is our father, isn't he?" I finally said.

The organ music began—the wedding party's cue to get going—and Lydia's authoritative voice called out in a loud whisper, "Shh, everybody be quiet," so I was spared any more talk about that man.

The altar at St. Charles Catholic Church was dressed in pink roses, thanks to Lydia, who coordinated the trip to the Tijuana florist to pick up all the flowers and bouquets and boutonnieres. There were two huge bouquets in tall wicker baskets looking like long-legged pink peacocks at each side of the altar, another shorter one at the foot of the altar table itself; the ends of each pew had white satin bows; the bridesmaids' bouquets were pink rosebuds and carnations with sprays of baby's breath, and the bride had three—yes, three!—bouquets: one to toss to a lucky bachelorette; one for the Virgin of Guadalupe; and a third bouquet of large white lilies for my mother.

As the dramatic wedding march started up with much pomp, we bridesmaids and ushers now standing at the front of the altar turned, along with the guests, to watch as Ana María and our father slowly made their way to the front. She held her bouquet of roses and the bouquet of white lilies. Once at the altar, my father lifted her veil to kiss her on the forehead in a dramatic, fatherly way and then brought down the veil to cover her face again (my goodness, what the good doctor Freud would have to say about this veiling and unveiling of the bride—first the father, then the husband!), and then he stepped aside to his pew as Ana María set the bouquet of lilies next to him, where our mother would have sat. Afterward, when the wedding was over and the newlyweds set off on their road trip honeymoon to San Francisco, we siblings would take the bouquet of lilies to the cemetery for our mother.

Carolina was right: we all should've had something to eat beforehand. It was a warm June Saturday afternoon and what with the competing smells of flowers and perfumes and aftershave lotions, the packed church felt stuffy as seven bridesmaids and seven ushers stood at attention to the side of the bride and groom. The church was full, and I was looking forward to the reception when I'd get a chance to visit with old friends, long-lost relatives. There was bound to be great gossip to catch up on. Why did the Mass have to be so interminably long? My stomach was beginning to growl.

Finally Father Stadler pronounced them man and wife—hallelujah!— and they were turning to face the guests, the organ starting up with a dramatic flourish when suddenly we noticed Ana María glance over her shoulder at us sisters; she looked panicked, or stricken. Pale. Then she whispered something to Roger, who had reached over to kiss her, and she fainted right there, just like that, in his arms, like some sort of soap opera actress. Soon guests were rushing forward, Father Stadler offering to lend a hand, but Roger had everything under control as he swooped her into his arms, the satin train of her gown cascading and trailing behind as he whisked his lovely, fainted bride out into the fresh air.

Everyone tumbled out behind them in a panic, scared. There was a concerned hum of voices, talking, and conjectures. My uncle Abelardo, the owner of the chain of "Licores AS" in Tijuana, was in the lead as he quickly rushed to his brand-new silver Coup DeVille, opened the trunk, and retrieved a bottle of tequila. He rushed to Ana María as Roger continued holding the fainted damsel-bride in his arms, both of them looking like fairy-tale prince and princess in the throes of danger and evil. (I didn't mean to make light of the situation, but we were a family of fainters, and Ana María hadn't had anything to eat beforehand, even though Carolina warned all of us to eat something. And if you are going to faint, as was almost a sure thing in our family, you couldn't have asked for a more dramatic, wonderfully timed moment to do so!)

One swig of the tequila and Ana was back to life again. Like some wilting flower in need of water—¡tequila!—and boom, she sprung back to life in no time at all.

A great way to start the reception. The conjectures, shall we call them, were seriously funny. No doubt busybody Socorrito and her entourage of viejitas (gossipy old biddies) were certain that Ana María was pregnant, which explained the rushed wedding. Rushed wedding?! We'd been trying to get her married off to Roger for close to two years now. Viejas *chismosas*. Other theories were that she had a terminal illness and that was why the rushed marriage—a bride on her deathbed—or else this fainting spell would signal a terminal illness and next week the doctor was going to tell her, this radiant, ephemeral bride, that she had one month left to live. It was easy for me to joke about it, knowing what I knew, that Ana María had outlived these conjectures. I'll confess that, at the time of her wedding and her fainting, even knowing that we were a family of fainters, I was a little apprehensive. I'd watched my share of good Mexican soap operas along with my mother and sisters, and, well, you never knew for sure. Busybody

Socorrito wasn't the only one entitled to conjure dramatic and tragic love scenarios in her mind.

❁ ❁ ❁

"So what kind of men do you think we're going to wind up marrying?" Lydia asked me as we watched Ana and Roger dance together in the middle of the parish hall, the gray vinyl tile polished and gleaming for the occasion. They were dancing to Chicago's "Color My World." We sat at the long wedding party table, and I wasn't sure if Lydia was really wanting an answer or if this was one of her rhetorical musings.

"I mean, is there any way to know?" she continued. "Like is there a pattern—say, you date big, burly macho Chicanos, or you have a propensity for dorky-looking men, or redheads, or gringos; maybe you're partial to Filipinos . . ."

I didn't answer her.

"How do we know who our match is, really?" Now she was looking at me and not at the guests, so I knew she really wanted to get into this conversation. "Yoli, who is my match? Who's your match?"

Now it was our father's turn to dance with the bride while Roger's mother danced with Roger.

"Or is that it?" she said, gesturing with her chin to the couples on the floor. "Do we end up marrying men like our fathers, and do men end up marrying women like their mothers?"

I didn't say anything.

"Will we just be a new—maybe improved—version of our parents' marriage?"

"Goddammit, Lydia," I said, now getting up, "can't you just leave it alone? What do you want to do, *hecharnos la sal*—hex both of us?" I scooted my chair back to give me and my long gown a chance to get out. "No, I take that back," I said, "since you have a pretty neat father. Don't hex *me* with that kind of talk, okay?" And I walked away from the table.

Somehow he had managed to steal the show. Don't ask me how. The guests seemed delighted with Lorenzo Sahagún, who had made his grand entrance as befitted a "humble and proud man." Dancing with Ana María, this skinny bird of a man shone and played up to the occasion with much bowing and hand kissing for the ladies—charmer that he was!—and robust, affectionate hugs for the men. Ana María and Roger, gracious prince and princess, seemed happy to have His Royal Humble Majesty Lorenzo Sahagún taking the show. In truth, Ana and Roger looked a little weary, ready to hit the road on their own.

Then the dollar dance, and our father was the first in line for a dance with his daughter. He had a bill in his hand, and Luz, in charge of this task, gave him a pin. Now he walked—no, strutted!—over to his daughter and pinned a bill to her dress.

A hundred-dollar bill, for God's sake.

By the time the dollar dance was over, Roger had green bills covering his tuxedo jacket and Ana had green bills on her dress and veil, the bills dangling like frilly green piñata tissue paper.

Later, when I saw the bridal bouquet flying our way, right to Lydia and me, I ducked and stepped aside. Lydia could have it.

Then it was time for the garter toss, and I was shocked to see my brothers urging my father to go up with the rest of the bachelors. He laughed, shook his head (finally, some humility!), and gestured for them to go up instead. I quickly looked over at my tías from El Grullo to see what their reaction was to all of this. Their faces were expressionless—small smiles, a rehearsed, on-automatic-pilot graciousness that I had come to recognize whenever they were in my father's presence. They were proud and classy, and, after all, he was our father and Dolores was no longer with us, so why start up with old resentments and disappointments, they must have been thinking.

But now a few other men, including old Don Epifranio, were encouraging my father to go up for the garter toss. And just as one guy—was that El Chango?—playfully pulled on his arm as if to help him up off the chair, just as it seemed my father was getting up, our eyes met, my father's and mine, for just an instant, but long enough for both of us to have felt the shame in that moment. He immediately sat back down, his smile dwindling, suddenly looking weary and self-conscious as he shook his head at the young bachelors, imploring them to leave him be; he'd already had his turn. He waved them away with an awkward flourish.

Don Epifranio, our revered viejito from Conifer Street, caught the garter and wrapped it around his cane. I was certain it was understood that this was intentional, the young bachelors backing away so that Don Epifranio could catch it and then be the subject of sexy jokes among the men the rest of the evening. And I knew that if my father had gone up there, he would have been the one allowed to catch the garter, and he would have been the star of sexy jokes—and with our mother less than two years dead. Had he really considered going up to try his luck at catching the garter? Me marry a man like my father? Heaven forbid.

Twenty-two

The visit from our tías from El Grullo—really, it should be in caps: Our Tías From El Grullo, because that was how we referred to them so as not to get them confused with all the other hundreds of aunts we had—was brief. My father came from a family of eleven siblings, and those were just the ones we knew about, you know, his full brothers and sisters. But these Tías From El Grullo were, after all, not just our aunts. They were the only two sisters of our mother, and to have them here near us was, well, almost like having our mother near us. They were in town just long enough to attend the wedding, because my Tía Celeste had to return to her fabric shop.

We gathered at Carolina's home for dinner with our tías before their departure the next day. It was only us sisters, minus Ana María, away on her honeymoon, and our two aunts. Talk turned first to Saturday's wedding. Monica was certain that Don Epifranio had a crush on Socorrito. He kept tapping her knee with his cane as they sat together with a few other viejitos. And did we notice El Chango's mystery lady? She sure was pretty: silky black hair down to her waist, petite, and did we notice how she kept smiling at El Chango, at everything he said? No, we said to Monica, we didn't notice. We weren't *fijonas* like you—were you getting ready to be the Socorrito of the next generation? "Ha, ha, very funny," she said, sticking her tongue out at me as Carolina passed us small dessert plates with chocolate cake. She was using her fine china—Noritake china from a White Front special they'd had just before her wedding. She couldn't resist the special, as our Ms. Freudiana was also a wizard at budgeting. We sisters teased her about this often—the Coupon Queen, the Mistress of Bluelight Specials—but she was having the last laugh as she and Tom climbed the socioeconomic ladder. Wow, we all said when we first sat down at her dining table to eat, we each get a whole paper napkin and not the usual cut-in-half napkin. We're splurging, eh Carolina? Is this in honor of our tías' visit? Oooh-weee! Ahuwa!

Hee-haw, brayed Monica.

Our aunts laughed at our silliness, and as my sisters talked about this or that guest, the funky dancing on the dance floor, how even Chuy got up and danced a few with our sisters-in-law, I noticed no one had yet mentioned our father and his ridiculous getup.

Luz's "Who do you think will get married next?" and my "Didn't our father look stupid?" came out simultaneously, our sentences stumbling and bumping into each other. We looked at each other and then at the rest of the women, who couldn't understand either question as they collided and toppled over one another. Only Luz and I knew what we were trying to say—and maybe Ms. Psychologist Carolina, who had a way of analyzing between the lines no matter how tangled they were. She had a way of diverting the potential collision, and so she ignored our questions and now turned to look at our aunts.

"Tías," she said, her hands folded on the table, "please tell us the story of our parents' wedding day."

Everyone looked at Tía Rebeca since she was the chattier one of the two, the storyteller in a family of quiet, reserved, and exquisitely private sisters.

From our point of view, as you know, she said, there was not much to tell since we didn't go to the wedding, remember? She'd heard from Don Tomás that it was a quiet, brief ceremony. From the photos, one could guess that Dolores looked like every bride looks: stunning and regal and singular. It seemed to Tía Rebeca that weddings were about the bride, really, that it was her day and her day only. Yes, Dolores must have been radiant. What Tía Rebeca remembered, and Celeste could attest to this moment too, was when Dolores packed her things to leave and start her married life.

"We were so hurt—felt our beloved and adored sister was abandoning us. Felt that Lorenzo Sahagún was snatching away our own tender princess."

Go ahead, say it, I thought to myself, that Lorenzo Sahagún was *undeserving* of Dolores Ramos. But they didn't say it.

So instead of handing Dolores the luggage, they tossed the suitcases on the floor at her feet in a rough and disrespectful manner. They were jealous sisters, you see, she explained, smiling sadly, regretfully (perhaps now thinking that their actions might have hecharle la sal in some way, tainted her day and her destiny). And I wanted to scream, to beg them not to be so kind. Go ahead and tell us what you really thought, how undeserving this conceited, vain, charmer of a man was. How you two couldn't understand—with all the formidable beaus she had eager for her hand in marriage—how she could have chosen this wild-eyed nomad dreamer. How could her clear green eyes not see into her future, the future of a nomadic family—yes, yes, just like the Ballad of the White Horse, all right—and foresee her slow but sure descent into poverty, first one child in El Grullo, then up the country to Ensenada, another in Rosarito, then another in Tijuana, on to Tecate, and a hop and skip to San Diego where the remaining four daughters were born. Dolores Ramos proudly refused to accept any money from her own family, she now a part of this nomadic family, dropping a baby in this town and that, as if they were Hansel and Gretel dropping bread crumbs to mark their trail north, and yet not going home like Hansel and Gretel. Go ahead and say it, tías.

But that was the end of Tía Rebeca's story. Abrupt, short, and respectful. And still I had enough venom stored up in me to last me a lifetime. I couldn't help it. I wanted to know the story, to understand why she had chosen him. What spell had been cast on her, what curse? How could this intelligent woman have chosen so poorly?

"And the ghosts," said Monica, "tell us about the ghosts. What have they been up to lately?"

They were so cavalier and light about the ghosts, my sisters were. It bugged me. How could they listen to the latest ghost shenanigans and not lose any sleep over it?

Tía Rebeca laughed, and Tía Celeste shook her head at us. If they told us more ghost stories, they were afraid we wouldn't come visit. They didn't want to scare us away, they said.

"You won't scare us away," reassured Monica. "The only one who you'll scare away is Yoli, but don't worry," she said, now looking at me, "we'll make sure you have a hefty dose of sleeping pills next time you're in El Grullo."

Ha, ha, very funny.

"What do you think the ghosts want? Why do they haunt the house?" Luz wanted to know. We had moved into the living room. Carolina's antique French Provincial furniture was at once cozy and appropriate for ghost tales. Since it was another June Gloom day and even cold by San Diego standards, Tom had lit the fireplace before discreetly exiting and allowing us our women's time together.

"They're tormented," I said. The fireplace crackled, there was a pop, and we quickly looked that way, intently watching the fire.

Then everyone turned to look at me. My cue to continue.

"They want to tell us their stories," I said quietly, remembering my mother's explanation at the DAR tea party, "but we can't hear them."

"What do you mean?" Luz asked.

Tía Celeste and Tía Rebeca nodded their agreement. Yes, they are tormented, without a doubt.

But how could we listen to their stories if they're ghosts? Luz insisted. She wanted to get to the bottom of this, as if she were prepared to console the ghosts. Are they friendly ghosts, mean ghosts? Please, tías, tell us more.

It usually began with the smells. Our tías might be in the living room, sometimes the door to the corridors closed. They'd be watching TV and suddenly the thick, sickly sweet smell of cheap perfume would permeate the room—just a minute or so—followed by cigar smoke, heavy and pungent. And just as the women were getting up to open the door, air out the room, the smell of sewage, a rotting stench appeared. Yes, other times it was the shadow. Tía Rebeca was at the kitchen sink, the westward-moving sun behind her, so the bright sun illuminated her back and the wall in front of her. "Ah, Celeste, don't forget to stop off . . ." she began to say as she noticed the shadow on the wall as Celeste crossed behind Rebeca, momentarily blocking the sunlight. She turned from the sink to make sure Celeste had heard her, but no, there was no one there. She stepped out of the kitchen, called to Celeste. No one. Celeste, as it turned out, had not left her fabric shop since that morning, was there now as Rebeca called out to her in the courtyard. At another moment, the door—only one of the double doors leading to the dining area—would begin to rattle as if someone were trying to get in and the door was locked. An insistent, angry rattling of the door. The door was not locked. Perhaps the most annoying, and here even my aunts admitted *que les daba escalofríos*—that it gave them goose bumps—was when the phantoms touched them. Just recently, when Tía Celeste woke up in the morning earlier than usual, she sat up in bed, looking out at the barely delineated furniture in the fading dark. As she was thinking about getting up, maybe getting a head start on the laundry, someone—or something—gently but firmly pushed her upper body down, back on the bed. She called out to Rebeca on the twin bed next to her, but Rebeca was in a profound sleep, and Celeste, lying there on the bed, afraid to move or breathe, was too terrified to raise her voice to anything more than a whisper.

The El Grullo ghost stories. The priests were periodically summoned to bless the house, its corridors, the courtyard, each room. The floors drizzled with holy water, the air filled with Catholic incantations, with the Our Fathers and Hail Marys of my heritage. She imagined, Tía Rebeca said, laughing, that the ghosts must look on at all this fanfare in their honor and think that we humans on this side of life were funny and superstitious. And if the holy water didn't do the trick, then my aunt Rebeca resorted to one last thing. She hadn't been much bothered by the ghosts; at least they'd stopped touching her, playing with her hair while she was watching TV, since the time she got so angry at them—something was pulling her hair—that she stomped her foot and cried, "Hijos de la chingada, ya déjenme en paz." And would you believe it? They left her in peace.

Still the phantoms had dominion of the home and continued to remind our aunts every so often of their presence, and my tías, pragmatic and clear of conscience, had made their peace with what they had no control over. The tormented phantoms might or might not one day yet reveal their stories at a point when we could understand and interpret them.

Enough ghost stories for now, they said.

Our leave-taking was always sad and fraught with the urge to hold on to our aunts as if we were trying to hold on to Mamá. I knew this to be so for me, and I imagined it must be so for my sisters.

Twenty-three

Lydia and I decided to ride our bikes over to the Imperial Beach pier, have a picnic, and perfect our tans. Our last summer foray as undergraduates, I reminded her. In a few weeks, we would be heading back to our senior year in college—she to San Diego State and I to UCSD. The beach was about an eight-mile ride each way from our apartment in Chula Vista, but we knew Palm City and Imperial Beach well enough to figure out shortcuts here and there. But it didn't really matter how long the route was. Lydia was so excited about having lost weight because of our bicycle rides that she was now becoming quite a cycling enthusiast. Nowadays, she was even out of her denim overalls and *brazenly*, I remarked to her, sporting blue Bermuda shorts and a white tank top.

It was 1976 and we were feeling on top of the world, riding on our bikes down Third Avenue, then South Main Street, picking up speed by the time we reached Hollister Street, past my old Conifer Street and then a straight jaunt on Imperial Beach Boulevard toward the pier. The soft August breeze was in our faces, the summer day still ahead of us, both of us smelling of coconut tanning lotion, wearing sun visors and sunglasses, each of us carrying a backpack stuffed with the necessary beach paraphernalia: beach towel, transistor radio, package of Red Vines, peanut butter and jelly sandwich, can of soda, and a paperback. We had become serious beachgoers this summer, and to look at us now, nothing —absolutely nothing—could stop us, headed as we were to the beach, to our Bachelor of Arts degrees, to graduate school, to life.

We headed for our favorite spot south of the pier and a way from the lifeguard station. Since neither Lydia nor I knew how to swim, we didn't have to be near the station, which was dense with beachgoers anyway, mostly swimmers who were required to stay within certain lifeguard station confines. We might not even bother getting into the water up to our knees today, for all we wanted was peace and quiet mixed with a rejuvenating sea breeze in our quest for the perfect bronze skin.

We parked our bikes near some large rocks, rummaged in our backpacks for our long, colorful beach towels, and set them down on the warm sand. We propped the transistor radio on a smaller, smooth rock, Lydia now turning on the radio, adjusting the knob to our favorite station of oldies and rock music. We both sat up in identical positions, our arms hugging our knees close to our chests. Our bathing suits were underneath our shorts and shirts, which we hadn't yet taken off. The Beach Boys were singing "California Girls" and I wondered, listening to the song, if Lydia was thinking the same thing I was as we quietly watched the water, a few surfers dotting the horizon.

"Lydia," I said, my eyes on one of the surfers paddling farther out to larger waves, "why is it we don't know how to swim? I mean, we're California girls, aren't we? So why haven't we ever learned to swim?"

Lydia shrugged. A big seagull swooped down into the water, probably spotting something yummy to eat.

"Well, the way I look at it," she said, "if it requires putting on a bathing suit, getting naked to any degree, forget it. Not with the body I was born with."

"But why didn't our parents insist we learn how to swim?" I asked. "You know, for safety purposes. We've been Southern California girls all our lives, live a few minutes away from the beach—it's embarrassing, don't you think? Why aren't we like Gidget? What kind of Southern California girls are we if we can't swim?" Now I was looking at Lydia, who simply nodded in agreement. "I mean, I bet if we took a poll of all the Chicanas—college-educated ones, at that—I bet you could count on one hand those who know how to swim."

She looked at me, thoughtful, as if maybe I was on to something interesting. "Why don't you make it a MEChA project?" she said. "Find out which Chicanas *and* Chicanos—because I bet you there's quite a few guys, too—don't know how to swim, then sign them up for swimming lessons."

"Very funny, Lydia," I said, now getting my novel and tube of suntanning lotion out of the backpack.

"But I'm serious," she said. "Really. Instead of you MEChistas ranting and raving about cultural nationalism versus Marxist Leninism, and just bullshitting during your weekly Congreso meetings, why don't you do something really useful and productive like you and your comrades learning how to swim. Seriously."

Lydia loved to tease me about being involved in the Chicano movement—my MEChistas, she called them. Carolina, on the other hand, well, she felt smugly vindicated, having tolerated jabs from me years ago, calling her Miss Righteous Chicana. Now look who was talking!

"Hmmm," I said, now slipping my shorts off, then my T-shirt. My one-piece bathing suit was a modest, simple black, not exactly something the Beach Boys would sing about. "I suppose Carolina would say that it would do wonders for our self-esteem . . ."

"Yeah, there you go," said Lydia. "Call it empowering." She now took off her Bermuda shorts and tank top, dressed only in a navy blue one-piece suit.

Then it occurred to me that my brothers—all four of them—knew how to swim. How could that be? But once I got to thinking about it, I recalled that each brother did a job stint at Brown's Market, and every year the Brown family put on a big pool party at their home for the employees, Mr. Brown and his sons teaching whoever didn't know how to swim. And it seemed my brothers hung out at the Browns' pool all summer long. In the meantime, we sisters took our turns doing job stints at the Kastlungers' home, our Saturday morning housecleaning job. There was no pool or yearly employee party there, but Mrs. Kastlunger did teach me how to knit some clever checkered booties.

Then I wondered about my mother: had she known how to swim? I couldn't recall ever seeing her in a pool or the ocean, nor in a bathing suit, for that matter. Was it a modesty thing, I now asked Lydia. Was it just not culturally relevant?

"Look," said Lydia, now yawning, ready for her beach nap, "don't get all *sociológica* on me. Just think of it this way: some people just never learn how to swim—for whatever reason."

We rubbed gobs of suntanning lotion over our entire seminaked bodies, smelling like a coconut grove. Then, as had become our ritual, we baked in the sun twenty minutes face up, then twenty minutes on our backs, and over again—like rotisserie chickens—for most of the afternoon, taking breaks to sit up and eat our sandwiches and Red Vines.

"Yoli, what about graduate school?" Lydia said, her tone of voice too serious. "You're going to apply to UCLA, aren't you?"

"No," I said.

"Why not?"

"I need to stay here in San Diego." I looked at the water, avoiding Lydia's eyes.

"Don't start in with that shit, Yoli," she said. "I mean it. You've been wanting to go to UCLA since you were a babe in diapers."

I gave her an oh-brother look.

"Weren't there some hotshot professors you wanted to study under? You always talked about leaving San Diego for the big city—off into the deep blue yonder, you used to say. Don't you remember?" Lydia sounded exasperated, sounded like she'd been storing this up for just the right moment to bring it up and give me a piece of her mind on the subject.

"Did you say 'deep blue yonder' or 'wonder'?" I asked, noticing a pesky seagull slyly making its way over to us as if our sole reason for lying on the beach were to feed it. "Or maybe you said 'wander'?"

"Yonder, wonder, wander," Lydia said with an impatient shrug, refusing to be sidetracked by my question. "I don't care what you call it, Yoli. You gotta go; it's as simple as that."

I didn't say anything, concentrating as I was on the annoying seagull. "Shoo, go away, Jonathan," I said, now waving my arms, hoping the damn bird would get the hint and leave. "Scramboola, get out of here . . ."

"Yes," Lydia said, looking at me with eyes that could kill. "My point exactly."

"I don't want to talk about it, Lydia."

I didn't want to talk about this with her—or with anyone, for that matter. I wanted to be left alone about it. What did Lydia know of ghosts and shattered families? How could she possibly understand that I couldn't leave, couldn't abandon my little sisters? The unity of the family depended on us sticking together. Moving to LA wouldn't help.

"What about you, Lydia?" I asked, wanting to change the focus of conversation. "Are you still bent on going for your teaching credential at State? And aren't you going to need me as your roommate?"

"Don't start in with that," Lydia said. She sounded angry and ready to pounce on me. "Yoli, you better not be using me as an excuse for staying in San Diego. Don't you dare," she said with enough vehemence that I knew she probably would do something drastic if I *did* dare her.

Neither of us said anything for a long time. We resumed our activity of lying on our stomachs, reading our paperbacks. My guess was that Lydia had decided she'd presented the case in as clear a manner as possible. For now, she was going to leave it alone.

The ocean breeze, the oldies coming from the transistor radio, the rhythmic sound of waves crashing, this bright blue August summer day—I was gratefully lulled into a gentle nap.

"Uh, hi, excuse me," said the sound of a guy's voice. Lydia looked up first, since she'd been reading. I sleepily opened my eyes and slowly turned toward the sound of the voice behind me. The sun was behind them, so they were backlit.

Two guys were standing at the foot of our beach towels, good-looking guys from what I could see; one was blonde, the other dark, Chicano maybe. "We were wondering if you could tell us what time it is. We forgot our watches . . ."

Lydia laughed. "Boy, you guys, that's a good one." But she said it in a kind way, delighted by their flirtation. She invited them to sit on the sand near us, held out the package of Red Vines as an offering.

We talked with them for about an hour, nice guys, just graduated from State, were living in Imperial Beach for the summer with their families before taking off for grad school up north. I was attracted to the dark one and Lydia seemed starstruck with the *güero*.

Finally, it was time for us to leave and they asked for our number, wanted to get together before the summer was over, if that was fine with us. Yes, that was fine with us. We waved good-bye as they made their way back to their beach towels near the lifeguard station and the swimming area.

Lydia teased me the entire bike ride home, saying that she could tell that Fernando guy was totally smitten by me.

"Oh, stop it, Lydia," I said, laughing. "You and that Steve guy looked like you were on another planet all your own." The cool August evening air was refreshing. I stood up a moment on the midway point of the aligned pedals, now coasting downhill, letting the breeze ruffle through my T-shirt and shorts.

"Maybe we *were* on another planet," Lydia said, dramatically mysterious. "But it's also true, you know, that you have *pegue* with guys. Such good luck!" she said, not yet wanting to let go of the subject she'd just started.

Not long ago, when Carolina inquired—as elder-sisters-turned-matriarchs are apt to do—about the latest in my love life, she mentioned that our mother had been known to be quite a *noviera* herself in her young days, never without a beau just around the corner, a suitor waiting for a fleeting glimpse of her as she made her way with mother and sisters to church for nine o'clock Mass, watched by a desperate lover vying for a glimpse of her near the *farmacia*, the poor lovesick young man not realizing that a block away, at Mueblería Zepeda, there was yet another handsome young man standing under the awning of the large furniture store, vigilant to her passing by on her way to the Catedral del Sagrado Corazón. This much our aunts had shared with us. When I pictured this image of my mother, it made me pause and think: Be careful about being a noviera, Yoli—a collector of boyfriends—like your mother. Look what she wished for; look what she got. Careful, Yoli, what you wish for.

Yes, I had boyfriends, guys I went out with, but my newfound politics were my real passion. Joining MEChA, the Chicano student political group on campus, was a natural, inevitable path for me (at least this is what I thought every time I remembered how much I teased Carolina about her proud Mexican Chicanismo). Could Miss Righteous Chicana have been right, after all? I gracefully ate my words as I made my way to the campus student center for the weekly Congreso meetings. I passed an elderly Anglo lady. (I was conscious of that now, you know: Anglo-Saxon, Chicano, Asian, black—now everyone I looked at was automatically and subconsciously pegged into one of these categories. You were either with us or you were against us, was my mantra of the moment.) She was a small woman in a tailored light blue suit and comfortable but dressy black pumps. She was probably grandmother to one of the students, or a rich local benefactor of the university, maybe the wife of one of our Nobel laureate professors. She reminded me of the rich La Jolla grannies I'd met at that Daughters of the American Revolution tea party my mother and I attended over three years ago. Our eyes met briefly and she smiled at me with a slight nod, and suddenly I felt self-conscious and ashamed of myself, as if my mother were walking next to me and giving me her look, the look that said, "I know what you're thinking, and it's disrespectful to pigeonhole every person who crosses your path. Don't be foolishly righteous in your politics. Don't be full of arrogance and contempt, Yolanda," which made me remember my mother's comment on our way home from the tea party that day: that I had everything to do with the American Revolution. What had she meant by that? What was my "revolution"? What was it I was fighting for?

What I found in MEChA was a much-needed family of friends on campus who reminded me of home and Palm City—Concha, Rosario, Cristina, Enrique, Raúl, José Luis, Chito, Poli—friends who contributed to my ever-growing vocabulary, a litany of words that constituted a new kind of prayer for me, words such as "cultural nationalism," "Marxist Leninism," "oppression," "exploitation," and "dialectical materialism," blended with the literary and philosophical movements: naturalism and formalism versus the favored structuralism and realism, a form that "mediates between concrete and general, essence and existence, type and individual." Craving answers to my own raison d'être, I gobbled these words and concepts and philosophies with the ravenous hunger of a vulnerable and naive apprentice. I was hungry for direction and enlightenment in my young university student mind, for a kind of Joycean epiphany, so I read on: "A 'realist' work is rich in a complex, comprehensive set of relations between man, nature and history . . ." I ran my yellow highlighter across these lines.

"Hey you, stop it!" I said, giggling, trying to push Raúl away as he nibbled at my ear. "Can't you see I'm trying to study?" and I hunched my shoulders and shuddered, ticklish and sensitive to the touch of his tongue. Because it was impossible to study with him around, I closed my textbook and studied him, another kind of concrete and general, the essence and the existence. I studied the type of guy he was—sexy, Chicano, horny as all hell, and the individual—Raúl, the oldest of eight kids, president of MEChA, with curly black hair and a mustache, a pre-med student from east LA with the more immediate goal of getting me to have sex with him.

And it wasn't that I was purposely trying to torture these men with some sort of feminine, hard-to-get wiles. No, that wasn't why I hadn't gone all the way. Not at all. It was more complicated than that. And for a moment, as I thought about why at the ripe age of twenty-two I hadn't yet had sex, I had to erase from my mind the words and concepts that had as of late been a part of my world. I had to force myself not to think about things like the subjugation of women by society's imposed, oppressive sexual rules and social mores, women who historically were only chattel, men's property. I had to ignore for a moment, as I thought about why I hadn't yet had sex, that women were just now, in this century, allowed to vote, to have a say in the world around them. To have a voice. Then the Pill came along, that tiny little tablet that opened a whole world of freedom and choice for women—choices about sex. Finally a tablet that allowed us to decide for ourselves, gave us the opportunity to actually enjoy sex without the fear of getting pregnant. I sighed as I gently, expertly, once again removed Raúl's roaming hands from my zipper. I was not on the Pill.

Okay, so what was going on with me, Lydia always asked. She could not for the life of her understand how these men kept coming after me, held on for as long as I let them, even though we didn't go all the way. Even Lydia had already had sex. Some guy from her statistics class at State over a year ago. Some brute of a man, I suspected, because Lydia, once the deed was done, reported that it was not all it was cracked up to be, which led me to believe the selfish bastard hadn't considered her needs and satisfaction, not even for a moment, as he most probably plunged into her. No, not even a moment's hesitation to think of what *she* might find arousing and delicious. That must've been the case, and as I pried a little further into our conversation—"For Christ's sake, Lydia," I said, "if we can't share our most intimate moments after all these years of knowing each other and being best friends . . ."—she confirmed what I'd suspected since the moment she announced in a hurried, trying-to-be-nonchalant-but-not-succeeding tone of voice, that she'd gone all the way and believe you me, she said, I wasn't missing out on much.

"Really," she said, a little uncomfortable, maybe sad and regretful. "It's no big deal."

Maybe that was it, Lydia said. Maybe it was the fact that I hadn't yet gone all the way, the fact that I was a virgin that so drove these guys wild, coming back to me, calling me all the time, hoping I'd make a boyfriend-girlfriend commitment. They were intelligent, kind, respectful guys, and I enjoyed dating them, one at a time for a few months each. But after my high school stint with Ernesto followed by the hopeful fantasy love affair I'd been anticipating with Johnny Angel that never happened, I played it safe and dated. That was all.

Raúl was whispering something to me that caught my attention. The foxy and sexy MEChA president was very experienced with girls. Something from Dylan Thomas, one of Shakespeare's sonnets, or maybe e. e. cummings. (Get it? He said e. e. *cummings*.) Raúl was not as clever as he thought, but he was good-looking and bright and had graduated magna cum laude this past June, scored very high on the MCAT, and had been accepted to a number of medical schools including Harvard and Stanford. Not bad for a kid from east LA who was the first college graduate ever in his family. And I loved his corny sense of humor.

Though I was very attracted to this man, it was the poetry-reading thing that he'd just whispered in my ear that finally did me in. After coming, he explained, you have such an adrenaline rush that you're full of energy. And Shakespeare's sonnets, a segment of Gibran's *The Prophet* was just the thing, man, both of you taking turns reading from the book, or if you wanted to parallel your orgasmic experience, both of you reading the same poem out loud to each other *at the same time.* We were at his apartment in Pacific Beach on Lamont Street, also known as apartment row because there were tons of apartment buildings, one right after the other, capitalist pig landowners happily accommodating hungry and desperate college students from UCSD and State. He had the *Abraxas* album on and "Samba Pa Ti" was playing, sexy and pleading strings of guitar coming through the speakers, like sexy and pleading Raúl. Somehow we'd landed in his bedroom on the queen-size waterbed that was slushy and uncomfortable. Ship ahoy! it seemed to be saying, and I giggled at my thought.

And I wanted to surrender to him, of course I did, but still there was the good angel and the bad angel, there was the Sacred Heart of Jesus looming over me, Jesus's bleeding heart seeping through my mind, filling any empty crevices of my conscience with a guilt as solid as a tooth filling—all because of this sexual act, this, what promised to be delicious lovemaking I had been wanting for oh so long. And the fact was, I did love Raúl, loved him for his patience all these eight months we'd been dating, loved him for letting the foreplay serve as the play itself, but dammit, I was just as hungry as he for more, and how long could a girl hold out on a guy before she realized she was holding out on herself too, and that was oh so unfair, after all she had to do to struggle just to be a good girl, wondering what all the hullabaloo was about when it came to doing it, and hearing that it was so good, so why not let myself enjoy it, my God, this was so good, and yet the angel of darkness and the angel of light were just to my right or maybe to my left, sloshing on the waterbed next to me, Raúl's condom now expertly slipped into place, both angels arguing with each other, competing for my attention, but I was too damn gone and in a whole other world of moans and heaves, and "oh baby, yes" that kept coming from above me, and me reminding myself to tell Lydia this, that this was how it should be, that the guy should be concerned about *you* coming, too, and not just looking out for his own sexual pleasure, but then Raúl was heaving real loud and I was thinking it was a good thing he put that silk tie around the knob of of the front door to alert his roommate, should he return any minute, that he had girl company in his bedroom so keep quiet and don't barge into my room, and me wondering what exactly that silk tie really meant to these two guy roommates, what kind of code it kept hidden in its silky design, whether it was some kind of score-keeping or victory banner, and hanging from the doorknob, the tie itself phallic, and yes, just when the good and the bad angel had quieted down, their arguments just a small, faraway last ditch, an urgent whisper, Raúl was moaning loudly, on a path of no return and coming inside me way before kingdom and I had come.

"Oftentimes in denying yourself pleasure," Gibran wrote, "you do but store the desire in the recesses of your being. Who knows but that which seems omitted today, waits for tomorrow? Even your body knows its heritage and its rightful need and will not be deceived." I closed the book a moment, now glancing at Raúl who was snoring, even and steadily, once he came. Just like that, rolled over on his side of this stupid, slushy bed, immediately going off into a deep sleep, leaving me to entertain myself with the stack of books on the night table that I had set there just before we hopped into bed. No, forget the poetry readings after making love. I was there with that tiny, dim night-light on, and Gibran and I were the only ones awake to read. In truth, I was alone. And just for a moment, right before he gave me a big kiss and said I had absolutely drained him of all his energy, just before he said that, I was going to remind him of the postcoital activities, you know, the readings out loud together, maybe something about love or pleasure from Gibran, a romantic sonnet from the Portuguese, hey, even a goofy, topsy-turvy poem from e. e. cummings. Whatever suited his fancy. But the immediate snoring stopped me in my tracks. And when he rolled over away from me on his side of that asinine bed, I turned on the skinny lamp next to me and glanced at the stack of books, knowing what I knew already with my first lovemaking session over with, that the postcoital activities of my future might—if I wasn't more proactive—comprise pretty much this pattern: a fantastic lay for the man, followed by a kiss of gratitude, an "I love you," and then the immediate snoring. I didn't even bother to whine and accuse him of false advertising, because I knew what he'd say, how he'd explain it, bright guy that he was. He'd say that I was such a fantastic lover that I'd drained him of his energy—something that'd never before happened with any of his past lovers. Damn, I was so good. And I knew I was good, so the hell with it, I thought, as I wondered what I was going to say to Lydia after all about this sex stuff.

And my mother came to mind. Of course. What must've it been like for her, her first time, no doubt, with my father? Had she cringed and gasped in pain? Had she thought, "My God, I should've joined the convent"? Had she just closed her eyes and resigned herself, her teeth clenched in pain, to her wifely duties? Was there even the slightest possibility—the hope—that it had been pleasurable for her?

A few last lines from Gibran: "And now you ask in your heart, 'How shall we distinguish that which is good in pleasure from that which is not good?'" Etcetera, etcetera, and then the punch line: "And to both, bee and flower, the giving and the receiving of pleasure is a need and an ecstasy."

I tossed the slim book on the floor, turned off the light, and went to sleep.

Twenty-four

The questions, then: Did we date men like our fathers? Did we end up marrying our fathers? Did all roads leading to love and marriage end with fatherlike men? Could this all be reduced to a Freudian interpretation, the Electra complex—nothing more, nothing less? No, I told myself, no.

"I'm a revolutionary woman," I proclaimed to my audience of three, though no one asked, and I could tell from the looks on their faces that they wondered where this random proclamation had come from. "I'm a progressive and sociopolitically conscious Chicana, and perhaps my revolutionary objective is just that: to ensure that I *don't* marry someone like my father, to ensure that I don't have the kind of marriage my mother had."

"What the heck are you talking about?" Monica asked me, shaking me out of my smug self-revelation. "What's wrong with marrying someone like our father?"

Lydia gave me a look.

Okay, okay. Me and my big mouth.

We were sitting at the green Formica kitchen table at our apartment—Lydia and I along with my little sisters Luz and Monica (though they were not so little anymore, already taller than I was), eating tuna sandwiches. It was a Saturday, so Luz and Monica were hanging out with us.

"Oh, never mind," I said.

"No, no, no," said Monica. "You can't take it back, Yoli." Was she twenty years old or fifty?

"What's your problem with Papá?" She asked.

Everyone was looking at me as if this were the defining moment, the answer they'd been waiting for all these years.

I shrugged and shook my head, took another bite of my sandwich.

"Papá takes Luz and me out to dinner every week," she continued.

"He says you rarely call him. He wants to invite you too, but you never return his calls."

"Why, Yoli?" Luz said with disappointment or sadness.

How old were they? Didn't they know I was the older, wiser sister here?

And I could've reminded them about his erratic outbursts, you know, his crazy temperament. And what kind of father abandoned his kids like that? But I didn't, don't ask me why. For some reason I felt that my explanation would've been too disrespectful or disloyal, and besides, my little sisters would never in a hundred years understand.

"What movie do you guys want to see?" I said, reaching for the newspaper.

The three of them were smart enough to back off and let it go.

❀ ❀ ❀

"Thank you for not bringing up the Raúl sex thing in front of my sisters," I said to Lydia once we were alone.

Lydia shook her head with disapproval. "Your sisters should know what's coming up. One of these days, probably sooner than later," Lydia said with that annoying miss-know-it-all voice, "they're going to be devirginized, too. You're way too protective of them, Yoli."

Ever since she'd been dating that Steve guy we met at the beach, Lydia'd been acting all mature—way too grown-up for her own good. But I had to hand it to both of them: they seemed to be madly in love with each other.

"So you're a revolutionary woman, eh?" Lydia said.

I didn't bother to answer, refusing to be sucked into another wearisome discourse with her.

"So where do your gentleman callers stand with you and your revolution?" Lydia asked, more a rhetorical question than anything else. She glanced my way one last time before heading to the living room.

Raúl—*el doctorcito*, as Lydia referred to him—was at Harvard Medical School now. Yes, Lydia was right: at least with Raúl, sex was not what it was cut out to be. And somehow, once the deed was done, the magic went out of my relationship with him. I backed away real quick, claimed I had so much studying to do, term papers, a James Joyce seminar given by visiting professor Terry Eagleton from Cambridge, England. And we were required to read Joyce's first three books—yes, could you believe it?—even the 783-page *Ulysses*, as if we didn't have enough reading materials in our other classes for this ten-week quarter system. Yes, I care for you too, but this is my senior year and I want to make sure that I graduate with honors. Of course I'm going to read all 783 pages. That's what an honor student does. You understand, don't you, Raúl, you yourself a magna cum laude graduate? Phone calls from Boston to San Diego are expensive. Just write.

I wanted to keep it simple and uncomplicated. There were more pressing matters at hand, namely the care of my little sisters. I needed to be near them, to guide them. I already talked with Carolina about having them move in with Lydia and me. She was considering it. Yes, simple and uncomplicated because I wasn't sure about this love and relationship thing anymore. I was afraid that in a weak moment, when my revolutionary guard and political consciousness were distracted, I might fall in love with a man like my father.

❀ ❀ ❀

My law student friend Fernando was a fun-loving, articulate Chicano, grew his own top-quality pot, and said he planned to work for the DA, wanted to be a criminal prosecutor. Was there some irony in this, I wondered, whenever I dropped by the house he was renting in Golden Hills, the lush crop of cannabis gracing the edges of his backyard? He always offered me a joint, gracious host that he was, and I always refused; there were enough insane people in my family. He loved horticulture and was considering dabbling in some serious marijuana farming, buying himself a big piece of fertile land out in the sticks, Jamul or Alpine maybe, once he'd made some money as "the best fucking"—his words, not mine—criminal prosecutor in San Diego. He was dead serious about his career goals, and I found something endearing about this, his seriousness, his inability to see anything ironic about his harvesting habits and his grooming himself to be a criminal prosecutor. This, and the fact that we got into some lively intellectual and political discourses on my man of the year, President Jimmy Carter, made for fun dates. But that was all. After our dates we parted with a kiss on the cheek, a hug, and an understanding that we would always only be good friends. The same held true for the doctorcito at Harvard Medical School. My intuition said they were not my match—whatever that might mean—in the world of relationships and love.

❋ ❋ ❋

A few weeks later, already into fall midterms, Lydia tossed a folder on the table. "Here," she said. "An application form for UCLA graduate school, Miss Revolucionaria."

"I'm not going."

"Yoli, please," she said. "Just apply. It doesn't mean you have to go."

Okay, I'd apply, but I was pretty set on not going. How could I explain to Lydia that I needed to stay put here in San Diego where my family was? Keep the Sahagúns together. And there's the other stuff—my home on Conifer Street, my mother, my childhood memories. I felt safe with these ghosts.

So Lydia had taken to calling me la Miss Revolucionaria. That was fine; I didn't mind. In truth, I did have a new kind of bible, the one we'd been studying in our private group of—what? Top secret comrades? Our underground workshop? No, "underground" sounded too dramatic. After all, we were very much aboveground as we assembled in my comrade's sixth-floor apartment. Whatever you wanted to call it, it was a group of my university friends and me, about eight of us getting together once a week in the evening to discuss the week's readings. We were on the *The Woman Question*—selections from the writings of Karl Marx, Friedrich Engels, V. I. Lenin, and yes, okay, laugh all you wanted, Joseph Stalin, too. Our group concentrated on Marx and Lenin as our primary guides. This little red book—yes, it really was red!—was first published in 1951, but the copy I had was a 1975 printing. But 1951?! Why hadn't someone passed this on to my mother and her women friends? They could've sneaked a read in the late, wee hours of the night when the children and the hubby were fast asleep. They could've perused the chapters, each with its intriguing heading—"The Enslavement of Women," "The Exploitation of Women," "The Bourgeois Family," "Women in the Struggle for Socialism," "Socialism and the Emancipation of Women"—quietly plotting a revolt.

I loved these new friends of mine, friends born into the working class, friends whose fathers were construction workers, janitors, and gardeners, same as my father. We had two in the group who were not born into the blue-collar segment of society, who'd come from fancy neighborhoods in west LA and the Bay Area, but we invited them, accepted them. Poor things, it was enough that they had to deal with their bourgeois guilt. And the funny thing was that in this Marxist workshop, at least, we true proletarians felt like royalty among our guilt-ridden—yes, yes, feel guilty, you privileged children!—bourgeois comrades.

I wondered if this was what my mother meant when she said I had everything to do with the American Revolution.

We were in the middle of discussing the role of women in the struggle for freedom, an excerpt from Lenin's work, when somebody piped in with the suggestion that we have a birthday party for me, and that we should invite some of our professor friends, you know, the progressive ones. Invite Professor Eagleton too, someone said.

Everybody turned to look at me (I was the one taking the visiting professor's class). I knew they were dying to have a party—for whatever reason—just so they'd have an excuse to invite the renowned Marxist literary critic.

"Yoli," someone asked, "do you think he'd come?"

Did I think he'd come? For Pete's sake, I wanted to shout, to scold these idealistic infidels, would Lenin buzz on over to the party? Would Marx drop by for a beer? I suddenly felt shy and scared at the prospect of inviting Professor Eagleton to a humble party of well-meaning Marxist understudies.

"Well, he did announce the first day of class that he doesn't have a car and would anyone have the time to show him around town . . ." I offered, naively hopeful.

My month-early birthday party took place at the apartment of one of my fellow comrades. (Which comrade's apartment, you want to know? Didn't matter. This insistence on names, on the individual was so—yes, you guessed it!—so bourgeois and capitalistic. We were all no-name comrades for the time being, okay?) It seemed every Chicano from UCSD and San Diego State was in attendance. The apartment was packed with well-wishers—many of them strangers to me. And among them was my guest, dressed in a brown tweed jacket (so British) and Levi's (so California). Professor Eagleton danced with me to the tunes of Earth, Wind and Fire, and no, he was not the best dancer, but he was a great sport. His lit pipe seemed to allow him a certain balance. I mean, at least we knew he was coordinated enough to dance and smoke a pipe at the same time. I liked this guy, liked him a lot. I was tempted to call across to him amid the loud music and ask him what he meant when he wrote that great writers managed to transpose into art the world vision of the class to which they belonged and to do this in a "peculiarly unified and translucent way." I really wanted to know this. Yes, how did these great writers do it? But "Shining Star" was playing and boy, oh boy, did I have the perfect rhythm for that song!

Later, when I drove him back to his lodgings on Prospect Place in La Jolla, I was too shy to say anything more than a "thank you so much for coming to the party." He smiled his easy, boyish smile at me, his pipe now in his jacket pocket. Just before he got out of the car, he leaned over and kissed me on the cheek and said he'd had a jolly good time.

I watched as he made his way up the steps to his building, grateful as I was for his cameo appearance in my life. "I hope, gentle professor," I whispered with starstruck fervor, "that someday I can be your kind of great writer and write in a peculiarly unified and translucent way."

Twenty-five

Here's what I remembered the most about my childhood visits to Mexico: my father's complete, dramatic personality change. In San Diego, he was always scheming to start a business in Rosarito or Tecate, border towns near San Diego, and there was in his schemes, I sensed even as a child, a certain desperation, a ravenous need to prove himself. But to whom? His wife? His children? His siblings? Himself? There was in him a need to be thought of as a businessman and not just a gardener, though he was a wonderful gardener, sought after and highly respected by the rich people who lived in La Jolla and Rancho Santa Fe estates. My father was an exquisite gardener—one of the best in San Diego, I was sure—and I never understood his vehement efforts to start a *carnitas* restaurant in Rosarito or a Mexican folk art shop in Tijuana. These schemes and dreams left him frustrated. (Yes, his rich big brother who owned the chain of liquor stores in Tijuana lent him the money, accompanied, I have no doubt—because my uncle Abelardo was a successful businessman—by a sermon on how to be a good businessman; and yes, his short-lived carnitas restaurant floundered and went under.) Papá was not an astute businessman, and even Mamá, as she loyally spent the weekends making huge pots of beans and rice in the hot little makeshift kitchen of his makeshift, side-of-the-road restaurant, beans and rice to accompany his tacos de carnitas, knew what his problem was: he was too generous and foolish with his money.

I peered out the airplane window, the flight en route to Guadalajara. Below me was the Sea of Cortez and to my right the long brown finger of the Baja California peninsula. It was spring break and I was going to spend Holy Week with my tías in El Grullo.

But in Mexico, once we drove across the *línea*, Papá was a relaxed and fun dad.

"So how many *conquistas* did you girls make this summer?" he'd ask us five daughters as we piled into the station wagon for our ride back up the coast to San Diego at the end of our summer stay in El Grullo.

Conquests? Can you believe he asked that? This from a father who didn't allow us to receive phone calls from guys? Now he was asking us about our "conquests" with a lively, light sort of *alcahueta*, matchmaker enthusiasm.

As if returning to the old country with his billfold of *dólares* now changed into even more plentiful pesos made him the cock of the roost. Or was he at ease because he was in his hometown among his people, not having to struggle with his broken English, which must have left him feeling dumb or frustrated? And no, Papá was not dumb in the least. Intelligent, yes, but complicated and too explosive to allow him to use his intelligence in any productive way.

We learned very quickly in life, as was natural for children of volatile parents, to interpret his moods and either hide from him as we saw his car drive up the street, or welcome him. We had nicknames for him: In Mexico, he was el Doctor Jekyll—fun, gracious, easygoing, charming; in the United States he was el Señor Hyde—tense, grouchy, moody, impossible. (Once in adolescent anger at him, I swore to myself that someday I would write a novel about the Strange Case of el Señor Lorenzo Sahagún.) Suffice it to say he was the psychologically complex San Diego resident gardener of nine children and a wife.

True, there were some business ventures here in San Diego as well: he started out small, raising worms for fishing bait; then the chickens for their eggs, followed by the pheasants for their meat; my God, even a small herd of goats for the milk (which I was weaned on and, my father claimed, made me the most pacific and noble child)—farm animals that illegally inhabited our within-city-limits backyard at one time or another.

What saved us from total ruin and impoverishment were Mamá's miracles of biblical proportions with money. If the Maccabees could somehow make a day's supply of oil last eight days, well, there you have it, so could Mamá! The interesting point in all of this was that Mamá should have had this skill at all, which we children were immensely grateful for, I was sure, given that she came from an upper-middle-class family where these hidden talents of hers—a penny saved is a penny earned—never needed to be used.

The pilot announced that we were beginning to descend into the Guadalajara airport.

This was something new for me, going to El Grullo during Easter Week—*para las Pascuas*. What did it mean? Why was I here? What business, really, did I have in my parents' old country? What business did I have celebrating the *pascua florida* with my tías in El Grullo?

I knew that Lydia would scold me at this point, impatient with my habit of looking for symbolism in my everyday life. So why was I going to visit my mother's sisters during this celebration of the resurrection of Christ? Wasn't I being a hypocrite, having quietly denounced and divorced myself from my Catholic upbringing? Or was I looking for a kind of "resurrection" or epiphany of my own? Was it time for me to talk to the ghosts?

The captain announced that we would be landing in a few minutes, so we should have our seatbelts on. And why did I do this every time I came to Mexico, these futile attempts at psychoanalyzing my father? Why did I still resent him so much?

A resurrection? An epiphany? How about a simple answer to the puzzle of this incongruous couple I called Mamá and Papá? Or maybe I just needed to get away from Raúl, who had asked me to marry him, wanted me to catch up with him in Boston now that he was finishing his first year of medical school. No and no and no—a hundred times no, but Raúl was persistent. He didn't know what no meant, and I wasn't sure I wanted to know what yes meant.

Salvador, my aunts' private driver, was waiting for me at the airport. My aunts insisted on this arrangement. No, don't take the bus. It had become too complicated, and there had been a spate of bus hijackings and robberies. For a moment I wondered whether my aunts didn't want me to take the bus because they were afraid I might strike up a conversation with an El Grullense who knew too much about my mother and father. Perhaps they were afraid of potential messengers of truth like that lady Abundia Páramo from my last bus ride over there.

At the airport near the luggage terminals, a crowd of people stood at the metal barricades that separated the incoming travelers from the waiting friends and family, and I spotted Salvador waving to me and grinning—as if I were his own daughter—as he waited along with rest. Salvador had been with the family for some thirty or forty years—all my life, anyway. He drove my aunts to Guadalajara when Tía Celeste went in to purchase supplies—bolts of fabric, wooden spools of thread, plastic and metal bobbins—for her fabric shop. Or for holidays on the coast, Salvador drove them to Barra de Navidad or Melaque, a few weekend drives to Manzanillo to see their cousin Conchita, have lunch at her thriving restaurant. He was errand boy, butler, and handyman all in one. Yes, in some ways, Salvador was indeed my tías' savior. He was somewhere in his sixties, a small man with balding light brown hair, soft hazel eyes. He had a wife and six children, and they lived in what I assumed was a modest home somewhere near the foot of the hill that led to *la capilla a* Nuestra Señora de Guadalupe en el Cerro de la Cruz, the town's hilltop chapel. And I wondered, with the zeal of my new philosophy and progressive politics, whether he had been exploited all these years. How was I to bring up this delicate matter without denouncing or seeming to criticize my aunts, but at the same time getting to the bottom of this servant-master relationship?

We headed for the van, and he put my one small suitcase in the back. Was this all, he asked with a smile, more to tease me than anything else since he knew by now that yes, this was all, my efforts to travel light, not carry more baggage—symbolic, don't forget!—than I had to. It was always a mistake, too, since I'd forget to pack this or that which I'd come to find indispensable, and so I'd be off to La Compañía, El Grullo's version of Kmart, and all because I didn't want to pack one more tote bag.

He opened the door to the van, while at the same time bowing to me and with a big grin, stepping aside for "la Señorita Yolanda" to climb in.

A couple of hours into the journey, after inquiring about his family and news from the valley, I initiated the delicate conversation I felt I must have with Salvador: How long have you been working for the family, I asked him, trying to sound nonchalant but already working on a protest and argument with my aunts on this subject of exploitation and servant-master relationships.

There was a big semi in front of us on the narrow road, and Salvador didn't answer right away, concentrating as he was on passing the truck when the coast was clear. And just when I thought maybe he hadn't heard my question, after I'd politely waited until he'd passed the semi, he said, "For as long as God has allowed me," not turning to look at me, but looking intently at the road ahead of us.

So I tried again. "How did you meet the Ramos family?" I asked.

He turned and looked at me as if he could see through my question, as if he understood my intentions. His smile—knowing? Ironic? Reproving?—told me that he knew what I was getting at: how long had he been in the servitude of my family. (Or maybe I was just feeling a little guilty about prying into his life and the relationship between him and my mother's family.)

"You are asking the wrong question, Yoli," he said quietly, now skillfully passing another truck. I was struck—maybe even a little shocked— that he just called me "Yoli" and not the usual "Señorita Yolanda" of all my life. It was as if he had set aside his servant's mask in order to speak with me as an equal, as if what he was about to say required this unmasking. Required an unprecedented honesty.

"What you should ask," he said, not for a moment taking his eyes off the road, "is how long have I loved your mother. Then this will answer all your other questions."

"What?" There was a whistling from the half-opened window and so I rolled the window up until the whistling stopped and I could better hear Salvador. "I'm sorry, I didn't hear you very well."

He was grinning at me, a full-blown amused grin. And he honked a friendly honk-honk at nobody in particular. "You are her very image, Yolanda," he said. "To see you is to see Dolores all over again, may she rest in peace."

He had loved her since the moment he set eyes on her as she walked to Mass with her sisters and mother. He was seventeen, she was fifteen, and there was an immense economic chasm that would separate them forever. No matter, there were other ways he could stay in the world of Señorita Dolores Ramos. He asked her father—my grandfather Ramón—for a job as a ranch hand, an errand boy, anything. "I remember he looked at me carefully, as if trying to size me up. He was just about to mount his mule, make his way back home when I went up to him and asked him for a job. He knew little about me other than that I was a strong, strapping young man eager to work for him."

My grandfather didn't say no or shoo him away. He simply told Salvador he would think about it, and with his big white hat on, he swung his leg over his faithful mule and made his way to his formidable home on Avenida Netzahualcoyotl.

"I suppose he made inquiries, found that I came from a religious, respectful, humble family of twelve. Soon I was working for him, accompanying him to the ranch, or running errands for him in town. With time, I became, if you don't mind my taking the liberty of saying so, a part of the family. That was enough for me, my way of loving your mother without her knowing, this serving her family as a way of keeping close to her."

"Did she ever know?" I asked, feeling dizzy and confused. Sad, tremendously sad—but for whom? For Salvador or for me?

"'Did she know,' you ask," he said, and he looked at me in a conspiratorial way, as if he sensed my question was—must be!—rhetorical. "Does the moon know it is the lovers' lantern? Does the sun know it is the blanket of the poor?" He laughed, self-conscious, embarrassed. "Forgive me, little Yoli, I can't help but be poetic when I talk of your mother."

"But," I said, "so many years . . ."

"I am not a servant to your family," he reassured me. "No," he chuckled, proud of himself, it seemed, as he glanced at me and said with appropriate drama and poetry and lovely conviction, "I am a servant to love."

I wasn't sure whether to roll down the window—it was suddenly so warm in the van—or just let myself melt into oblivion. I was dizzy beyond understanding.

"I never had aspirations of winning her love. There was an army of men—distinguished suitors—who had that privilege. For me, it was enough to be near her, serve her and her family in whatever humble way I could. I was always discreet in my feelings. It wasn't until she was courted by Lorenzo Sahagún that I regretted not having been bold; I regretted not having proclaimed my love for her . . ."

"What do you mean?" I asked, now feeling like I couldn't breathe very well. Sensing I was getting information I had been wanting forever and ever.

"We're here now, at the bridge near El Grullo," he said. "And it is just as well, my little Yoli, for this is all you need to know. Perhaps it was his blue eyes—who could compete with such blue eyes? He knew how to talk; he was poetic, I've heard tell. He had a way with women. He was, well, he is your father, Yoli, and perhaps this roundabout way of talking to you is my way of letting you know—because I know about you radical, *comunista* college kids—that you need not worry or be critical of my relationship with your family. They have been very generous to me, have paid for private schooling with the nuns for all of my children—the best education money can buy. I lead a comfortable life with my wife and children. I was servant to no one but love, and I am now servant only to the memory of your mother. That is all you need to know, Señorita Yolanda."

And I wondered, for more than just a moment, what my life would have been like if Salvador had been my father, who I would've been. And I realized—sadly, frustratingly—that there were more stories here than I could fit into my small suitcase.

❀ ❀ ❀

We had the Stations of the Cross, Mass, rosaries, and weeklong preparations for the resurrection of Christ. On Holy Thursday we dressed in our best clothes, *catrines*, all of us, in honor of the institution of the sacrament of Communion. This year, la Señorita María del Rosario Ramos was in town and had invited my tías and me over for dinner. She lived at the corner of Avenida Netzahualcoyotl, in a formidable home comparable to my aunts' (remember, this was a neighborhood of formidable homes of the respected founders of El Grullo). Señorita Rosario was known to the townspeople as the *"heredera de la Hacienda de Cajellones"*—that is to say, as an only child, she was the sole inheritor of a great fortune. She was mistress of herself, a generous benefactress to the town of El Grullo and respected by all. Unlike my aunts who were reserved and very private, Señorita Chayito was chatty and vivacious and completely involved in El Grullo life and its inhabitants. She organized a soup kitchen for the poor elderly, welcoming close to a hundred into her large grassy yard where tables were set up to feed the indigent every Wednesday.

But for now, for that Holy Thursday, she insisted amid my aunts' protests—no, no, Chayito, you are much too busy to bother with one more event—that they come, along with Dolores's daughter (me!), for dinner. She promised to make it simple.

I didn't know Señorita Chayito that well, although she was my mother's cousin. She traveled back and forth from her hacienda and properties throughout Jalisco and seemed not to stay too long in one place, but I could tell by my aunts' preparations—lovely, floral dresses, just a bit of rouge, a little lipstick, a dab of perfume, nail polish—that this invitation from Chayito to have Holy Thursday dinner in her home was quite a treat.

She herself greeted us at the door, joked with Tía Celeste about not being able to buy wedding dress fabric from her for, alas, it seemed her destiny was like Tía Celeste's: not to marry. Now she hugged Tía Rebeca, whom she entreated with playful charm to tell us one of her famous, engrossing stories at the hour of dessert—her story, of course, being the real dessert. Only if the dessert you are serving us to eat is worth my weight in words, retorted Tía Rebeca affectionately. And then she turned to me, and I noticed a briefly startled look. It passed quickly, long enough for perhaps only me to have noticed. She blinked and then hugged me.

"Little Dolores," she whispered.

She ushered us down the long corridor and into her formal living room for appetizers and a glass of wine or *ponche*, a drink made of rum and fruit. She had invited a few more people—Father Cobián of the Sacred Heart of Jesus, and twin brother and sister Guillermo and Guillermina, the owners of the Compañía, the one and only huge department store in the whole region. They were already in the living room, standing at the grand piano listening to Señorita Guillermina who was playing a somber, religious-sounding song.

As we entered the living room and before Doña Chayito could say anything, Father Cobián, respected old priest that he was, beat her, proclaiming loudly, as if he were one of those stately butlers at a grand ball who announce the arrival of new guests, "The Ramos sisters have arrived!" and then, giving me a firm stare, said, "Yolanda Sahagún! Por Dios, niña, you are the very image of your mother." He said this loudly enough, in case everyone else in the room was hard of hearing like he was.

The other guests nodded in agreement.

"Yes, indeed, you are, but are you like her in personality?" Father Cobián asked. "For it is one thing to look like her physically, quite another to have the same *carácter* . . ." and there was in his voice the same stern voice of the priests I had known all my life, priests to whom I'd confessed my menial sins. The "but are you like her in carácter" sounded like a stern say-three-Hail-Marys-and-two-Our-Fathers voice. Or maybe I was just feeling, as I stood there before this religious man, a little guilty about my self-imposed excommunication from Catholicism.

"What a question," chimed in Guillermina. "Nobody can be like Dolores. They broke the mold when she—"

"Every one of them," Tía Rebeca interrupted, now standing next to me with her arm around me. Her voice was clear and proud. "Every one of Dolores's daughters has a part of Dolores in her. That is her legacy, perhaps. To imbue each daughter—" and here Tía Rebeca's voice trembled, faltered.

"Dolores was unique," Father Cobián insisted, interrupting her. "Let us say that she was like the mysteries of a rosary. And her children, perhaps," he said, looking at me with a suspicious eye—he must've known what was going on in my heart!—"are each a bead of this rosary . . ."

"Ahh," said Guillermina and Guillermo, as if their status as twins included simultaneous identical talk. "So true, so true."

"Although I must admit," Father Cobián said, "when I first saw you I thought I was seeing Dolores's ghost."

The others nodded.

"Speaking of ghosts," said Chayito, now turning to my aunts, "how are things at your house?"

"It is wonderful to have Yoli with us," said Tía Celeste. "And the ghosts left us years ago. They no longer bother us."

The other guests looked at me, understanding what Tía Celeste was getting at.

"Yes," Tía Rebeca said as reinforcement. "There are no more ghosts."

I was quiet in all of this. Somehow I felt that this was how it must be: that I should be quiet and listen, and that if I listened long enough—to conversations here in El Grullo, to the hollow footsteps in the corridors, to the wailings of phantoms, to the rustling of the tree leaves in the middle of the night—I would know my mother and know myself.

Before long we made our way across the large courtyard where a tamarind tree took dominion of the center, its long, strong branches and leaves extending the whole of the courtyard, creating an elegant, filigreed canopy of shade for warm, subtropical days. I was in awe of the tree, its lower branches dropping just above our heads while the top branches reached beyond the second floor to the heavens. There was no doubt that this tamarind tree was the true master of the home, its dark trunk imposing and protective at the same time. I had a silly, inexplicable urge to climb up it and sit perched on its farthest-reaching branch and see all of El Grullo and Jalisco and Nayarit and Sinaloa and Sonora, on and on across the border to San Diego. To see the world with new eyes.

"This tree is my pride and joy," Chayito said, now pausing a moment next to me while the rest of the guests continued across the courtyard into the formal dining room. "And I can tell from the way you are look-ing at it—the same expression as your mother's—that you too see its possibilities, its magic."

"My mother—?"

"Yes, your mother loved this tree, too," Doña Chayito said. "The few times we played at my house instead of hers, she asked if we could climb the tree. She asked this every time, and well, nobody could say no to Dolores. You see, we other kids sensed it even then, that she was special, maybe an angel sent from heaven, a blessing. 'Can we climb the tree today, Chayito?' she would ask me in her soft, polite voice. But I could also hear the barely contained excitement in her voice, her wish to climb the tree, sit on the highest limb and read—"

"Read?" I looked at Chayito as if maybe I'd misunderstood.

"Yes," she laughed. "We used to sit perched on a strong limb, sitting elegantly, our backs against the trunk, our legs extended in front of us as if the branch were a divan. We would read quietly an hour, maybe two, until we were called down for refreshments."

"My mother climbing a tree?" I asked. I couldn't imagine it. It was tomboyish, and she was such a prim and proper sort of person.

"Ah, how little you know your mother, niña. She was a daydreamer, a most formidable daydreamer. And the tree—this one, or her ceiba tree—was her favorite daydreaming spot." She laughed. "Come, let's eat. There will be time later for more reminiscing."

Chayito sat at one end of the table, as befitted the matriarch of this home, of this town. Father Cobián sat at the other, while I was next to my aunts, across from Guillermo and Guillermina. Father Cobián was talking about this Saturday's Mass and something about the burning of Judases, but I only half listened, distracted as I was, looking around me at the large dining room, the intricately designed, pedimented doorways that looked like passages to ancient monasteries and secret-filled convents. On the wall, above the ornately carved wooden buffet table, hung a long, large replica of Da Vinci's *The Last Supper*. Staring at the painting, I was reminded of my own family's "last supper," of my father's decision to be on his own, of the turn of events in the Sahagún household—of what might've been had my mother not died. And I couldn't help myself, for now I felt an overwhelming despair mixed with rage. I held back the tears with a vicious, private defiance.

I was suddenly brought back to the present conversation by

something Father Cobián was explaining, precisely something about the painting I had been absentmindedly staring at.

" . . . the sacrament of Communion comes from that day, when Jesus Christ was celebrating the Jewish Passover holiday," he finished by way of explanation to someone's question.

Holy Thursday dinner: the traditional *tortitas* of shrimp with *nopales*. On my first bite I choked with its spiciness, coughing, turning red, eyes watering. Everyone at the table laughed affectionately, teasing me because I had no *aguante* for spicy food. "You are a gringa through and through," Doña Chayito laughed as I nodded, quickly reaching for my glass and gulping down more water.

As we said our fond good-byes to Guillermo and Guillermina, to Father Cobián and Doña Chayito, making our way down the cobblestone street to our home, I was quiet and pensive, wondering what this all meant. I remembered a quote I'd once read and memorized: "I have but one lamp by which my feet are guided and that is the lamp of experience. I have no way of knowing of the future but by the past . . ." I was fifteen or sixteen when I came across the quote and I memorized it because, well, because it seemed true. So what was my experience? What had I learned? What in this past would I take to my future?

"You're too quiet," Tía Rebeca said, putting her arm around me just as we arrived at the house.

I smiled but said nothing, and she didn't probe. They knew me well, these sisters of my mother—well enough to understand that I was grieving even now.

We stood before the huge pockmarked front door, waiting as Tía Celeste opened her clutch purse and got out the key—an old-fashioned key the size of the purse, a good ten inches long. It was a relic as old as the home. A key that had opened and closed this door many, many times in the last seventy years. Oh, if only I could open this door, or the next, or the next, make a deal with Monty Hall, agree to be a devout, holy Catholic if only my mother were behind one of the doors, coming out to greet me.

As we entered the vestibule, I heard it, a distinct giggling, some whispering somewhere beyond the lighted hallway, maybe in the dark courtyard. I quickly looked at Tía Rebeca, but she had bent down to examine a fern in one of the planters. Tía Celeste was putting the key back in her purse and seemed not to have heard either. And I couldn't speak, terror momentarily leaving me gasping for air.

More whispers and giggles. I was now certain it was coming from the dark courtyard.

"Do you hear them?" I could barely get out.

My tías stopped, raised their heads to listen.

"It's the wind, *hija*," Tía Rebeca said. "It's only the wind."

"No, no it isn't," I said, still frozen in the same spot at the entrance to the house. Unable to move, to breathe. "No, it's them, the ghosts of El Grullo. I heard them."

Tía Celeste looked at me, startled. "Por Dios, niña, look at you! Rebeca," she called out to her sister, "quick, bring the smelling salts. This child is going to die of fright."

I take them with me—all the way to Palm City, to my home—ánimas from the time of the revolution. We're at the pepper tree, my favorite one across the street from my home on Conifer Street. Some of them have guns strapped to their torsos, belted in an X while others are dressed in peasant clothes, swaths of white fabric, simple tunics, wide-brimmed sombreros for the searing summer heat—all of them, about twenty ghosts, stand guard at the trunk of the tree. I hear giggling and quickly look up, beyond the branch where I'm sitting. Mamá's laughing, sitting on the highest branch, her legs dangling. And when I take a closer look I notice my father sitting next to her. A seagull's perched nearby. "Jonathan," she says, giggling. "Yes, I like that, Yolanda. That's very cute." Was she mocking me? "Oh, Mr. Livingston," she calls out to the seagull, "will you please take my daughter of the American Revolution with you? Let her fly high beyond this tree, this city, this country—high, high, high. Let her see the world with new eyes." She turns to look at my father with a love I can't bear seeing. He smiles at her comment. "My, what a poet you've become, Dolores!" he says with obvious pride. And I'm sobbing and shaking my head, furious at them. Yes, she's mocking me, I know she is. "I hate you, Mamá," I call out to her, but she doesn't seem to hear, to notice I'm there. Louder now, I say, "I hate you for leaving us to deal with this man on our own, do you hear me? I hate you! And I hate you too, God, for taking her away from me. Who is left to take care of us, goddamit, to keep the Sahagún family together?"

In the background I heard my tías talking to each other, whispering. "Estás bien, niña," Tía Rebeca said as she placed a cool, damp towel on my forehead. I opened my eyes wide enough to notice it was day, the sun coming in through the small window. I was lying on my bed, unsure of how long I'd been dreaming. "You'll be okay now," she said, gently brushing my hair away from my face with her hand. So soothing. "We had Dr. Ramírez inject you with a sedative. You've been asleep all night and morning."

"Fue un pequeño susto," Tía Celeste said. "A little fright, my child, that's all."

Still weak with fear or anger or I don't know what, I managed a slight nod of agreement, reassuring my worried aunts that yes, they were right, it was just a little fright, that's all. I closed my eyes and slept.

❀ ❀ ❀

On Easter Saturday—el Sábado de Gloria—my aunts and I made our way in the evening up the steps to Our Lady of Guadalupe for Mass. In row after row of pews, I saw the hypnotic flutter of handheld fans—lace-decorated fans, bamboo fans, fans with seashells on the handles, fans made of thin cardboard with floral designs. Enough fans fluttering to make the gold church seem filled with butterflies ready to take flight. I was lethargic and dreamy from the evening's heat and happily spellbound by the flutter. I sat or stood or kneeled. I did this for my aunts, out of respect and love for them; no need to alarm and shock them, or hurt them with talk of the opiate of the masses and other such diatribes. And I was keenly aware of the church's smells, musty and humid like the smell of wet stone, the smell of perfumes and lotions and incense. Smells familiar to me, smells of my youth and my visits to Mexico, smells that I now scrutinized with a purposeful and cold impartiality, with an intellectual and scientific eye meant only to take note of their existence and then be done with them. What was the priest saying in his sermon? How did he beseech us? No matter. It was a seemingly interminable, boring sermon that resounded and echoed in the tall stone church, sounds that bounced against the pillars, against the gold encrusted altar, echoes perhaps only the statues of saints and the Virgin Mary herself could understand as they sat perched in niches along the length of the church, the Virgin and saints looking like loyal and lofty sentries.

In truth, I had no business with them anymore.

Once Mass was over, the women—my aunts included—expertly, with a quick, dainty snap, closed their fans. We were making our way out of the church, which was thick with congregants, and heading across the street to the plaza when we crossed paths with the woman I met a few years ago on the bus. She'd been looking our way, as if to get our attention, as if she'd been waiting for us to catch up with her. Abundia Páramo.

My aunts noticed her too, and when we caught up to her, we all greeted each other.

"This is Yolanda," Tía Celeste began.

"Yes, I know who she is," Abundia said, looking at me as if she and I shared a secret. "Who wouldn't know who she is, eh? The very image of Dolores." Then turning to my aunts and before they could get in a word, she said, "That's the reason I was waiting for you. I had a dream about Dolores yesterday, can you believe it? First I have a dream and then the next day I see her daughter—what a coincidence, yes?"

My aunts nodded, giving Abundia their full attention.

"What did you dream?" Tía Celeste said.

"Well, you see," she said, relishing the attention, "that's the strange part about it. Dolores, may she rest in peace, was anxious and very *preocupada*—not at all resting in peace. In my dream she was pacing the floor of her house—this one here in El Grullo—and she was saying something about Joseph the Prophet, saying that what saved his life was his ability to interpret his dreams. 'Why doesn't she understand this? Why doesn't she listen and interpret?' That's what she kept saying, but I don't know who she was referring to."

I was feeling faint. This heat was so damn suffocating!

"Such a mystery these dreams are," she said, looking at me.

My tías turned to me, looking alarmed. "Let's get you a raspado," Tía Celeste said, forcing herself to smile, trying to sound nonchalant, unconcerned. "A strawberry snow cone is just the thing to refresh you."

When we turned to say our good-byes to Abundia Páramo, she was nowhere to be found, had simply disappeared.

"Quickly," said Tía Rebeca, always the leader of the three, and not one to dillydally or stand around trying to analyze other people's dreams. "A crowd is already gathering and we need to find a good spot." And she said this in a tone I had come to understand: it meant no more talk of dreams and ghosts.

We headed across the street along with the zealous crowd, and while Tía Celeste and I made our way to the center of the plaza where a stage had been erected for the burning of Judas, Tía Rebeca was paying for a strawberry raspado at one of the carts. In the middle of the stage, the man-sized, grotesque papier-mâché piñata hung from a noose in a makeshift, pretend gallows. This grimacing, devil-looking Judas was decked out with fireworks, and the crowd, which was pushing its way dangerously close to the figure, seemed anxious to jeer and taunt Judas.

My aunts and I were in the hub of the excitement, standing far enough from where Judas hung so as not to be dangerously close to the fireworks, but close enough to have a good look when the firecrackers began to go off. There was a bloodthirsty zeal and energy in the crowd, it seemed to me, and I was reminded of biblical and literary scenes of stonings by the townspeople, a kind of primitive harvest ritual or a springtime cleansing and resurrection with its customary sacrificial victim. Burning heretics at the stake—in this case, Judas of Iscariot.

When the mayor and other *políticos* arrived and stood near the gallows, marking the beginning of the zealously awaited moment, the jeers and boos and the shrill whistles began, the noise growing like a wave, gaining monstrous momentum, growing louder and louder, a sound soon ear-shattering and impossible. The fireworks went off in ugly, thunderous explosions, piercing and ripping the sky apart. I was both repulsed and fascinated. The fireworks sounded like gunfire from the firing squad, and within seconds Judas's body had been ripped open, bits and pieces of cardboard flying in the smoky air as it burned in shreds. The crowd applauded and hurrahed the spectacle; there was laugher and good-natured whooping as ashes drifted down on us like snow, like black, ominous Lenten confetti.

A street vendor skillfully made his way through the crowd, selling smaller doll-size Judases grouped together on a tall pole, dangling Judases in the form of skeletons, political figures, charros, and dandies—perhaps there was one of me in the bunch—and I didn't know why, but suddenly I felt immensely sad and heavy, weighted down. And yes, I felt sorry for him, for this Judas figure that had been hanged and burned at the stake.

Twenty-six

"God, Yoli," Lydia said as she took my one small suitcase from me, "you look like shit."

"Yes, thank you. It's good to see you too," I said.

"Are you okay?" she asked. "Did something happen?"

"No, nothing happened," I said. "Just couldn't sleep well, as usual."

Lydia looked at me.

"Are you still having bad dreams?" she asked.

"Yeah," I said, wanting to be done with the whole conversation. "Bad dreams."

We walked out of the Tijuana airport toward the parked car. I had told Lydia that I would grab a cab and she could just meet me at the border instead of coming into Tijuana and having to deal with the long lines back. She wouldn't hear of it, insisting, when I called her from my aunts' house to tell her that I was coming home two days early—on Easter Sunday—that she would be at the airport to pick me up. She cheerfully hung up before I could continue my protest.

We got to her car and she tossed my suitcase in the backseat. "This suitcase doesn't look big enough for even my makeup," Lydia said. "Boy, you sure do believe in traveling light, don't you?"

I left a lot of stuff at my aunts' home, in what used to be my mother's armoire: a dress, some slacks, a couple of blouses, a pair of shoes—my way, perhaps, of reassuring my aunts that I would return. My aunts seemed disappointed, even alarmed, when I told them I was leaving on Easter after all. I quickly explained to them that I'd just realized I had a term paper due on Wednesday, which I hadn't even begun. They seemed relieved to know that was the reason. Since my fainting spell on Holy Thursday, they'd been protective of me, not leaving me alone lest I faint again. Nothing more was said about the incident, and I for one wanted to obliterate the whole weird thing from my mind. Stupid dreams, melodramatic hallucinations. A good little fright, that was all.

As we made our way to the Mexico-U.S. border, I closed my eyes and rested my head against the seat's back. Lydia raised the volume on the "oldies but goodies" station and hummed to herself. We understood each other well and respected each other's privacy or need to just close our eyes and tune out everything.

I timed my flight just right, in the middle of the day, so that I would miss the Easter festivities with my aunts. I insisted on catching an early morning bus ride back to Guadalajara, insisted that Salvador not be called upon to drive me for what would amount to a six-hour round-trip drive for him on Easter Sunday. The early morning bus departure made it convenient for me to miss Easter Sunday Mass with my aunts. And now it was late afternoon, with a minimum two-hour wait at the border. By the time Lydia and I made it across to Chula Vista, the Sahagún family reunion would be over, everyone headed home, and Easter Sunday done with. Perfect timing, Yoli.

Once at our apartment, I noticed Lydia had straightened up the place, magazines in a neat stack on the glass coffee table, the burgundy Indian print curtains tied back with a wide sash ribbon. I was flattered to see she had tidied up the place in my honor. She was like that, Lydia was. Acted sarcastic and impatient with me one moment, and the next a surrogate mother, reminding me to take a sweater with me when I left for school. And then it hit me, what was different about Lydia: she wasn't wearing her usual denim overalls and feminine blouse. Instead, she wore nicely tailored slacks and a simple shirt. She'd lost a lot of weight because of our bike rides to the beach and she looked, I don't know, she looked different in a way I couldn't quite put my finger on— not just the weight, but something in her face, a happiness, a secretive look about her that was not there when I left for El Grullo a week ago. Something was up.

"Are you hungry?" she asked. "I bought sandwich stuff—turkey, tomatoes, avocados . . ."

"No," I said, now sitting at the green Formica kitchen table that I'd inherited by default. None of my older siblings needed any more furniture, and so I kept whatever I would need for my apartment: the orange vinyl love seat; the kitchen table; the slightly cracked glass coffee table; the green velvet fireside chair (though we never had a real fireplace, just the fake facade below the framed Sacred Heart). This chair with its thick scrolled arms and cushiony wings was my favorite piece of furniture. And I couldn't help it: I looked around me at this furniture and tried to understand what it meant in the bigger scheme of my life, what it would come to mean. For now, I found an unabashed comfort in possessing it, and Lydia—ahhh, Lydia, my most wonderful friend and roommate—said she didn't mind the furniture. "Hey, it's free, isn't it?" she reasoned, though we had already made three trips to our favorite store that specialized in imports from India and China, lots of bamboo furniture and cotton Indian prints in rich colors, cushiony beanbags for chairs—beautiful things that might have been just the ticket for a really cool bachelorette pad. Not that we could've afforded the furniture anyway, but hey, we two were experts at dreaming and planning.

So we were sitting at the kitchen table when she told me.

"Steve and I got married in Vegas this week," she said quietly.

"You what?" I asked.

"Yup," she said.

I was looking at the Emma Goldman poster across from me. Underneath her picture—a solid, peasant-looking Russian woman with a plain, haughty, and intelligent demeanor, rimless glasses, her hair pulled back in a severe, don't-fuck-with-me bun—was her quote: "Women need not always open their wombs and close their mouths."

"Are you pregnant?" I asked.

"No, but thanks for the vote of confidence," she said.

"I didn't mean it that way," I said, "but then what's the rush?"

"Well, actually we were worried for a while there. That's when we had The Talk. We thought I was pregnant and so we started talking about what we would do, and next thing you know he's proposing. I started my period the next day. We were both relieved and then he said, 'Let's do it. Let's get married anyway. Now.' So we drove to Vegas."

"Wow, Lydia. Gee," I said, stunned.

"Look," she said, now looking directly at me in a motherly, no-nonsense way, as if she were about to say something very important and wanted her child's complete attention. "There's two reasons why I did it now: number one, because I love Steve very much. Ever since we met him and his friend at the beach last summer, I just felt it. Knew he was It."

"Yes," I said. "You did look pretty starstruck. You sure were pedaling fast on the way home, left me way behind a couple of times. I remember."

We laughed.

"But there's another reason why I thought this was as good a time as ever. I noticed you were—what's the word I'm looking for, um—*subdued*, that's the word. Yes, you seemed a little subdued about being accepted to UCLA's graduate program," she said. "It's time to move on, Yoli."

Suddenly the tears were coming out of my eyes, though I was trying to force them back.

"You've got to go, Yoli," she said, coming over to put her arm around me. "You've been dying to move on to bigger and better things, to that big ol' world out yonder waiting for you. So don't be a pinche cabrona and chicken out on me now."

I laughed. She hadn't cussed like that since we were teenagers, when we thought we were cool and sassy and on top of the world, and the neatest thing in the world was to call each other "pinche cabrona" or "pendeja." But I knew what she meant. She knew me well, this mother-sister-friend did. When I got the acceptance letter from UCLA earlier that month I was euphoric, excited as all hell. Yes, on to bigger and (I hoped) better. And then I thought about what I was leaving behind, and suddenly my euphoria flattened out, made a quick dash for the door.

I wanted to change the subject.

"And what about your parents, Lydia?" I asked. "My God, what did they say about your eloping?"

"Ay, my parents," she said, now kicking off her shoes and walking into the living room. She sat on the old brown couch, her legs tucked snugly up. "Well, my mom must be going through some changes herself," Lydia said. "She was pretty cool with it. When Steve and I showed up for

Sunday dinner a week after our elopement, we just told them. There at the dinner table. At first my mom stared at us as if we'd just announced that we were part of an undercover Marxist guerrilla group, but then she got all teary-eyed and said, 'Congratulations.' Came up to hug us. You know my dad just follows her lead, so they both hugged us. Then my mom sat down, in a back-to-business kind of way, and said, 'Okay, we need to talk to the priest and set a date.' She counted with her fingers, a finger held up for each task we need to attend to. It helps that they love Steve, too."

Steve. Who would've thought, though I did have my suspicions after the initial meeting, when Lydia and I were at the beach and he and his friend approached us. He went up north to graduate school for a year, but they wrote to each other almost daily, saw each other about once a month—he coming down to visit Lydia and his parents, or she going up for a romantic weekend to his apartment. And then he landed a job as a high school math teacher here in town.

I was happy for Lydia. She'd gained a husband, and I'd gained a friend-in-law.

"By the way," Lydia said, "Raúl has been calling you all week. Long-distance calls from Boston. After about the fourth call, I got the feeling he didn't believe me when I told him you were in Mexico. *Pobrecito*, he really has it bad for you, Yoli. Give the doctorcito a chance, why don't you?"

I didn't bother to answer. What was there to say that Lydia didn't already know? Raúl chose Harvard Medical School and I chose to move on. I hadn't counted on his wanting me to marry him and go to Boston with him.

"Oh," she added, "Chuy called a few days ago, told me to tell you he wanted to talk to you when you got back."

❖ ❖ ❖

The Imperial Beach trailer park where my brother Chuy lived was just a few miles from my apartment in Chula Vista. I drove up to his cemented rectangle of a driveway, space number forty-three, and knocked on the door of his small trailer. There was a canvas overhang that served as a front patio with a lush collection of creeping Charlies and pothos hanging in pots lining the whole perimeter of his patio. He had the rusted patio table and three chairs that used to be ours in Palm City. I knocked on the door, having called earlier to make sure this was an okay time to come see him.

Because the thing was this: it was the luck of the draw whether Chuy was lucid enough to talk in a logical way. But even when it wasn't a real good day for Chuy, say he'd been busy nailing shut the kitchen cupboard doors so that when the big earthquake came he'd be prepared and jars and cans of food wouldn't come spilling out, there was still some coherence to his behavior. When I was fourteen and Chuy came back from Vietnam, I was certain that he had experienced a horrific reality that forced him to see life with different eyes. He was a person whose reality had been disturbed enough, shaken too hard, so hard that it shattered— like when a long-treasured snow globe with a perfect scene of a small town fell and broke, and you knew with a grim certainty that you would never hold that same scene in your hand, never again imagine yourself a part of it. Shattered and destroyed. So now you looked at snow globes with nervousness, fear, anxiety—maybe paranoia. You looked at them from a distance, afraid that if you imagined yourself a part of that scene once again, it would only shatter once again. You held yourself apart and watched it with new eyes, a more guarded perspective—perhaps the wiser for what you knew, perhaps not.

He opened the door and came out.

"Hi, Yoli," he said. "It's good to see you." He gave me a quick, self-conscious hug, and then we took a seat on the rusty patio chairs.

Chuy was not comfortable having people inside his house, in his only bit of quiet. He was wearing a pair of jeans, a dark blue T-shirt, his hair looked freshly combed, still damp. He held a pack of cigarettes, set a clear glass ashtray on the table, the metal table clanking as he did so. His hands trembled as usual when he was in need of a cigarette or had just taken his meds.

"What's up, Chuy?" I asked quietly.

"Have you talked to our dad?" he asked, and I couldn't help feeling that I was being admonished.

I shook my head, hoping to flick away conversation of our father.

"He was fired from his job at the apartments," Chuy said. "He had a young girlfriend coming over all the time . . ."

"Probably that hot señorita I saw him with that one time . . ." I said as if I knew all along that it would come to this, that it would be our father's undoing.

"What happened," Chuy said, ignoring my comment, "is that some of the widows in the complex complained, accused him of letting a young *piruja* live on the premises with him . . ."

"Boy, they can say that again," I said.

"Our father said he didn't give a damn what they said," Chuy told me. "Our father called the old widows a *bola de viejas chismosas* because they couldn't get any with their wrinkly old droopy *chichis*." Chuy smiled when he said this.

"Papá said that?" I said, trying not to smile.

That was the last straw. The group of widows demanded to talk with the owner of the senior citizen apartments: it was either he or they. So he was out of a comfortable job, most probably out of money, now working and living at the Sweetwater Riding Stables.

"What about the money from the state, for the house?" I asked.

"I don't know," Chuy said, "but it looks like he might've spent most of it."

"Yeah," I said. "And it doesn't take a lot of brains to figure out who helped him spend it."

"Go talk to him, Yoli. Convince him to find himself a decent little apartment or trailer to live in," he said, looking at his lit cigarette. "We've all tried. We told him we'd help him with money and all. Carolina even invited him to move in with her and Tom, but he says he's just fine where he's at now."

"So you see? He's just fine. What's there to ask?" I said, now gathering my car keys and getting up. "And why me? Why ask me, Chuy? You, probably more than anyone, know I don't want to have anything—"

"Because you've always been his consentida," he said quietly, interrupting me. "The apple of his eye, Yoli, that's why."

"No," I said. "No."

I stood up from the table, keys in hand. "That was a long time ago, Chuy. I'm not his little performing monkey-child anymore."

"Please, Yoli," he said one last time, quietly, urgently. "He listens to you." And it was as if my brother were trying to piece back together, with whatever resources he had left, the Sahagún snow globe.

I left Chuy's trailer, driving west to the Imperial Beach pier. After our father walked out on us at The Last Supper, walked out on his responsibilities as a father, I severed my ties with him. Let him have his pirujas, sluts who would clean him out of house and money—a house and money that our mother had worked so hard to keep intact. I wanted nothing more to do with him. At Ana María's wedding, I made a concerted effort to keep my distance from him. So I had to think about Chuy's request that I visit our father.

I parked the car and got out, now walking the length of the pier.

Since moving into an apartment with Lydia, I pretty much had been my own woman, taking no more parental or older sibling orders. Sure as hell not from my father. So why did Chuy ask *me* to go see our father? If Carolina, our resident psychologist, couldn't convince him, what made Chuy think I could? Besides, my brothers and sisters were more accepting and forgiving of him. So good, fine for them, let them feel bad if he was living in some junky old stable-hand shack. That's what he gets, really. And besides, I'm not so forgiving, okay?

And why did Chuy have to bring that stuff up—apple of my father's eye, su consentida. Crap like that, all in the past now. Over and done with. *Finito.*

There were a lot of surfers out that day, even though the surf wasn't big. It was a warm day and this had everyone out on the beach or in the water. I watched as one surfer lay belly down on his board and hand paddled toward the water, toward the big wave that might or might not come. Terrified of water and unable to swim, I couldn't understand how these surfers went searching for the big wave, knowing that the inevitable would happen: they'd sooner or later fall off the board and crash into the water. Now I squinted, searching for the surfer who just a minute ago was paddling vigorously toward the deep blue. Where'd he go? I couldn't see him. My God, what if he drowned? I held my breath. Didn't they worry about that, drowning, being pulled away into the deep ocean never to be seen again? Why did these surfers take such risks? A humongous monster wave roared forward, a big snarl of a smile as it enveloped the little piece of human standing on a bit of plank, and then in one clean swoop, with one quick curl of the lips, swallowed the dark human speck. What risks people took! Preposterous. Perverse. Ah, there was the surfer. I saw him sitting on his board, waiting for just the right wave at the right time.

And yet it was hard for me to say no to Chuy, not to do as he asked. He was my favorite brother in a group of wonderful, all-favorite brothers. Chuy was a good son, after all, and I—well, I was an angry daughter.

Twenty-seven

From my apartment in Chula Vista, the Sweetwater Riding Stables were just a few miles north off 805. In many ways it seemed appropriate that my father should, at some point in his older years, end up living with horses. He was raised on a ranch with horses and chickens, pigs and such, and I remembered once having an argument with him—how old was I? Fourteen? Fifteen?—and retorting that he got along better with animals than with people, which caused him to smile, delighted for some reason by my comment. He countered with, "At least they don't talk back to their elders." Fuming, I stomped out of the room to the sound of his laughter. That—my ability to talk back to him cleverly—and my youthful love of horses seemed to have endeared me to my father forever. My horse-craze stage was brief but intense. I pored over horse magazines, read *Black Beauty* at least ten times and *My Friend Flicka* another twenty. Papá seemed to relish my passion, buying me every little horse trinket he could get his hands on—a plastic pinto, the beautiful palomino (Barbie's favorite), the quarter horse, a small tin box decorated with a picture of a young boy and his pony, the inside holding horse-shaped candies—stopping short of buying me a real horse, which we could not afford. Later, when Monica in turn fell in love with all things having to do with horses, Papá didn't seem to have the same enthusiasm, even though Monica's interest had long outlasted mine. No, it was as if my father had plucked me arbitrarily to be his chosen cowgirl.

I turned off at the Sweetwater Road off-ramp and made my way up the path to the riding stables. And even though the stables were practically right next to the busy freeway, once you'd driven down the winding graveled dirt path, caught sight of the horses in the pasture or in corrals, you felt as if you were in another world, rural and bucolic. I drove up to a cluster of buildings as my father had instructed me to do when I called, the call most certainly catching him by surprise.

"Sí, sí, of course, come by whenever you like, Yoli," he had said. And I detected in his voice a gratitude that embarrassed me for him and shamed me.

He was waiting for me in front of one of the dilapidated buildings, waving to me like some excited schoolboy waving hello to a classmate he hadn't seen all summer.

I parked the car and got out. He was wearing a baggy old pair of slacks and a short-sleeved shirt, clean but worn and wrinkled, as if he'd just taken them out of a drawer overflowing with wrinkly clothes and quickly put them on in honor of my visit. He greeted me with a hug, which I allowed. Yet there was nothing he could do or say, I had determined, that would make me feel any differently about him. Hugs or no hugs.

"Welcome, welcome," he said to me as if he were the master of the premises and not the stable hand. "Let me show you around." And he gave me a tour of the place, beginning with his lodgings—a ramshackle room with twin beds, one for him and one for the other worker. Each had a dresser, and on top of my father's there was a crowded cluster of family photos—including a five-by-seven wedding portrait of him and Mamá. Did this mean his hot little señorita had vanished now that Papá's cushy job as apartment manager had vanished? Did I really care?

Next he led me to the office where he introduced me to the owners, a big burly man and a petite woman, her brown hair in a no-nonsense ponytail, sitting at identical desks.

"Mr. and Mrs. Gilbert," he began. "This is one of my five daughters, Yolanda—and she's the ugliest." He had a satisfied, proud grin on his face.

I cringed, embarrassed that he should still introduce us this way. I couldn't believe he was still up to his old tricks, his clichéd expressions, embarrassing and just plain self-aggrandizing. So typical of him. I wondered why I'd bothered to come.

He showed me the stables and the grounds, leading me over to see his favorite horse. The Sweetwater Riding Stables served as both a place to rent space for your horse and a place to rent a horse for an afternoon of horseback riding. Papá's favorite was a rental horse.

"Here she is," he said. "Hermosa, I call her." She was a handsome quarter horse with a golden coat. I moved closer and petted her long, sleek neck.

"Yes," I said with respect. "She is a beauty."

"I'll get her saddled up and we'll go for a ride. I'll ride Blackie over there," he said as he walked away to get the riding gear.

"No," I called out. "No, I don't want to ride, Papá."

"What?" he said, calling back over his shoulder as he continued to walk. "You come to visit your viejito at the best riding stables in town and not ride a horse? Nonsense. Hermosa is the most *mansita* mare you could possibly ride. She has style and she's a real lady . . ." His voice trailed off as he entered the shed where the riding equipment was kept.

My God, I couldn't believe him. How stubborn, how belligerent he was! If he thought he was going to hold me hostage, well, he had another think coming. "Mansita," he said, as he probably said of all horses. Tame and docile. Ha! What did he know about tame and docile?

I was twelve years old when we had the famous—or infamous—argument about horses. I was madly in love with horses and even a little arrogant in my knowledge of all things having to do with them. Papá and I were sitting at the kitchen table. He'd just returned from working late, and my mother was heating up his dinner. I was excited to tell him what I'd learned from an article I'd just read. As he sipped his café con leche, more evaporated milk than coffee, I explained to him that there was a difference between a wild, untamed horse and a horse that was crazy or loco—as they were called. He listened quietly as I told him that wild, untamed horses could be tamed, but that loco horses could never be tamed; they were simply indomitable, had something in their blood that had them crazy and so could never be tamed.

"Qué tonterías," he said. "Where did you read such foolishness? Of course you can tame a horse. Any horse is tamable. That's ridiculous, Yolanda."

"No it isn't," I countered. "It makes perfect sense to me that there can be crazy horses that you can never tame."

"It's only a crazy horse until it's tamed," he said.

"But that's what I'm saying," I said, my voice rising. "You can't tame these kinds of horses."

"Well maybe you can't," he said, laughing and sipping the last of his coffee, "but I can."

"No, you can't. No one can. That's why they're called crazy horses. It's different than a wild horse."

"That's ridiculous and untrue, Yolanda." Papá's voice was steady and amused.

"No, it isn't ridiculous." My voice was quivering.

"Yes, it is, Yolanda. All horses can be tamed. I don't know where you get this silly information . . ."

"It's true, it's true," I said, and the flood of tears came pouring out, and I hated myself for not standing my ground in a dignified manner, for not being able to hold this discussion without reducing myself to a puddle of tears. "It *is* true, it *is* true."

"No it isn't," he said, openly delighted to see me angry to the point of hot tears.

Mamá had been washing the dishes during our feisty discourse. She came to the table to pick up my plate of cookie crumbs and, as she did so, she mumbled so only I could hear. To me, her twelve-year-old daughter, not to her husband, she mumbled a plea, "No le des cuerda"—don't wind him up—let it be. Enough, already. To me, her twelve-year-old daughter, and not to her grown-up husband!

But I would not let it be. There *was* a difference between a wild horse and a crazy horse. Where at first my father was amused by my insistence, now he seemed weary and ready to end the argument—as soon as he could have the last word.

"So tell me, Yolanda," he said, trying to hide his smile, now pushing his coffee cup aside to let me know he was finished, "if there is a difference between a wild but tameable horse and a crazy and untameable horse, which kind are you?" His grand finale, guaranteed to shut me up there on the spot or see me charging out of the room in a seething huff.

But Papá had underestimated my wrath.

"I am the horse you don't want me to be—the horse that you can never, ever tame. And you, Papá, you're nothing more than a stupid, stubborn gelding."

A slap in the face that was! And then I stormed out, seething, furious, and—having had the last word—feeling victorious.

Now I thought about this and knew that had any one of my brothers or sisters said this to our father—calling him a castrated horse, of all things!—he probably would've had his belt off in a split second. What disrespect! But instead of hearing the clinking of the belt buckle, I heard his delighted laughter as I stormed out. So there you had it: I was his chosen cowgirl.

He returned with the riding gear.

"Papá," I explained, "I just came by to say hello. That's all. I really have to go now."

"Nonsense, " he said. "How can you not want to ride Hermosa? How can you resist this beauty of an animal?" And it was as if Papá were seeing me as the twelve-year-old daughter of yesteryear, the one who loved animals and begged for riding lessons for her birthday. It was as if he refused to see me for what I was now, a twenty-two-year-old in charge of her life, independent and impatient with fools like him. I didn't at all want to go on this horse ride. I was a long way away from when I romanticized these beasts, imagined myself galloping over rugged terrain, my long hair flowing behind me, my lover on his black stallion galloping next to me. Yes, I was twelve when I loved horses, already into puberty, which explained the romantic part of this vision. The truth be known, now that I was no longer twelve years old, the large animals with their muscular flanks terrified me.

He heaved the saddle over and onto the tall horse's back.

"We'll go for just a little ride. There's a pretty riding trail beyond Sweetwater Road," he said, smiling, adjusting Hermosa's bridle.

Then he turned toward the corral and whistled, calling out to someone. Immediately a brown mutt of a dog came running over as if it had been hiding behind the shed, waiting for its cue.

"I call her Flicka," he explained to me. "Like our old dog. And she's just as loyal."

Yes, she was loyal. On three occasions we drove our old dog Flicka, after so many litters of puppies, to Tecate to live on a friend's ranch. Tecate, Mexico, was about sixty miles away. And within a week she would be back—tired, hungry, and thirsty—barking at our front door.

Flicka—like Lassie—had found her way home.

My father helped me up, hoisting me gently.

"There, you got it. Hold the reins like this," he said, showing me how to hold them just right. "Let her know you're the one leading, not her."

I nodded, trying hard not to show my fear.

Once I got over the initial terror of being on such a tall, strong beast, I did kind of like the steady, rhythmic clop of the horses as we made our way down a rugged bridle path. The thing was, for some stupid reason—what did it matter what he thought?—I didn't want my father to know I was scared of horses.

"During the Cristero Wars," Papá suddenly said, "when your uncles and I were up here working, the thing I missed the most was my family, my home, the life I was used to."

I looked at him, wondering where this was leading. Why was he bringing this up at all?

"Los Estados Unidos was very different from my Mexico lindo," he said, chuckling.

I nodded, listening closely. Suspicious.

"But the best part of leaving home was the coming back, Yoli," he said, now looking at me like he was trying to relay some message between the lines.

"I learned to appreciate my home more," he said, "to understand it better. Come, let's go through this path. I want to show you something."

I followed behind my father, and every so often he pointed to a squirrel or a jackrabbit, but he didn't say anything—as if what he had to say had now been said. A diamondback rattlesnake silently slithered out of our path into the brush. Hermosa was indeed mansita, not missing a confident step even when we passed the snake.

The quiet of the woods relaxed me, made me a little daydreamy. The late summer sun was warm and comforting. Lazy slow-motion day, with only the sound of clippity clops and crunching twigs.

And there were the good memories: My father working on the house's plumbing, calling out to whichever daughter was around, showing us how to unclog a drain "so that when you get married," he'd say, as he called for us to turn on the hose, "you can teach your husband how to unclog a drain." And we sisters in turn might roll our eyes up to the heavens, each of us thinking, "Oh, brother, how will we ever get married, having such a strict father as this!" Or assembling all of us at the kitchen table for the monthly lessons of multiplication tables—*dos por cuartro son . . . cinco por ocho son*—so that we wouldn't be burros in the classroom.

The breeze stirred every so often. I leaned forward in my saddle to pet Hermosa's neck, running my hand slowly down the length of her sleek, golden coat. Maybe that was why I was so awful with numbers, I thought, smiling to myself. A subconscious rebellion to Papá's math lessons. Yikes, I was starting to sound like Carolina!

From the corner of my eye, I glanced at my father who seemed smaller and thinner than normal. Boney and fragile. Even meek. He was looking straight ahead, serious and engrossed, as if the burden of finding a clearing for our successful journey were upon him. Could he be repentant? Was he sorry for having bowed out of his fatherly duties? How long back into the past do we count, and for which sins was he repentant?

And maybe that was it after all: I would never come to understand my father fully, or I would come to understand him bit by bit, memory remnant by memory remnant until I could sew together a quilt of good memories large enough to soothe and warm my soul. Large enough to learn to forgive. Oh, for Pete's sake, Yolanda, stop it already! See? Even I could get impatient with my symbolizing.

But for now there was the matter of my father and what the hell he was trying to prove by living in these humble, substandard conditions.

"Papá," I said, finally broaching the subject. "Where are all your things, clothes and furniture and stuff? How long do you plan to stay here?"

"My clothes are in the dresser. I've put my other things in storage.

As you get older," he said, leaning forward and patting Blackie's neck, "you realize how little you really need."

When he moved out of the house, back when he'd gotten the job as apartment manager, he'd taken very little with him: his clothing, a few family photographs, the small wooden telephone table. His apartment was furnished, he explained when Ana María told him to take whatever he needed.

He needed very little, he said.

"How long do you plan to stay here?" I asked. I felt a sudden cool breeze on this August afternoon, noticed it was getting late.

"As long as they'll have me," he said.

"But Papá, this is no place to live out your life as a senior . . ."

"This is fine for me. I'm happy here," he said. "And you, what about you, Yoli? Do you need help moving to Los Angeles?"

"What?"

"Chuy told me you were accepted to UCLA."

"He did?"

"Yes," my father said, "he fills me in on your life."

"Well, I've been very busy—"

"Yoli," he said, "it's okay. I understand. I can't expect all my children to forgive me."

A red-tailed hawk suddenly swooped down a few feet from us, as if it were so busy eyeing a tasty field mouse that it hadn't noticed us.

And I hated myself for stammering a stupid, insincere excuse so as not to hurt his feelings. "I've been very busy." Ha! Why didn't I just tell him off and be done with the whole charade?

And just as I was about to open my mouth and speak, say something raw and honest, he suddenly raised his finger to his lips for silence. He pulled in the reins to stop his horse, and I did likewise.

"Look over there," he whispered, pointing to a clearing in the chaparral.

There were four of them, about fifty feet away from us, slightly hidden by the tall shrubs: two adult deer and two baby deer. Or perhaps we were the ones hidden from them. They didn't seem startled or scared;

they didn't even look up. This surprised me since we were so near. Surely they could smell our scent, couldn't they? I held my breath, and it seemed so did the horses and the dog and my father. It was all I could do to keep from crying because this was the thing I didn't want to admit, the part I'd tossed to the back of my mind as I watched this skinny old man who was my father, petite and still limber, earlier saddle the horse, punching her belly so she sucked it in at just the moment my father tightened the girth to make sure it didn't slide off while I was riding the horse. This was the thing I'd tried these past months, now that I was living on my own, to ignore or refuse to believe. The thing that caused me to turn away from him now, pretend I didn't notice how delighted he was to have come upon his secret—this graceful family of deer—and share it with me. The thing was this: I loved the old fool.

Twenty-eight

Our Tías From El Grullo were visiting for the summer, staying at Carolina and Tom's house, and we five Sahagún sisters—Las Hermanas de Palm City?—had planned a little surprise for our tías Rebeca and Celeste. All we told them was that we would be taking them for a ride, the plan being for all of us to meet at Carolina's house.

We five sisters and our Tías were waiting out front on the driveway. Carolina was pretending to look in her purse for her car keys while the rest of us pretended to be deciding who was going to drive, which cars to take. We told our aunts to dress casually in slacks, same as us. While the rest of us were wearing sandals with our pants, I was happy to notice that Monica had on a pair of new cowboy boots, black and pointy-toed and very Monica. She noticed that I was looking at them. "Hee-haw," she said so only I could hear. She had a great big grin.

It was near the end of summer, September already, a warm and delicious late afternoon. The sky was blue with a few straggly clouds looking like my hair in the morning. We planned our little surprise for this night in particular—September fifth, our mother's birthday—and it was as if God were on our side all along, really the coincidence seemed almost too good to be true, but I would take any hokey and corny coincidence in my life to draw parallels and juxtapositions; I took it, gratefully, as a way of finding signs and meaning in my life. So there you had it: a full harvest moon on our mother's birthday.

Although the afternoon promised to be balmy and tepid into the evening, each of us took along sweaters, draped over our arms. I noticed our tías wore their light pastel-colored cardigans loosely over their shoulders, like ladylike capes, and so I did the same, extending my sweater in front of me, the backside facing me, then with a delicate swish bringing it up and over my head onto my shoulders. Now Ana, Monica, and Luz were doing the same. Why, even Carolina, who always advocated for independence and individuality and the importance of not following along with the crowd, daintily swished her sweater up and over, onto her shoulders.

We were ready to take flight, it seemed.

Imagine the surprised look on my aunts' faces when a sleek, white stretch limousine drove up to the front where we were waiting. What? What's this, my aunts said as the limousine stopped in front of us. Carolina's neighbors were coming to their front doors, taking a look, one burly man crossing the street for a closer look. The handsome chauffeur in his tuxedo uniform got out and came across to the passenger's side, greeted us with an elegant "good evening, ladies" as he opened the side door with his white-gloved hands. He bowed with a flourish as we led our open-mouthed tías to the limousine. Just as we were about to enter the limousine, we sisters followed Carolina's lead and waved to the neighbors with a generous smile, our glamorous sunglasses making us look like movie stars, before ducking and entering the car.

We couldn't stop giggling and oohing and ahhing at all the fancy things in the elegantly upholstered, cushiony interior. This was Luz's idea, the limousine ride, and she was grinning and beaming with pride. We had a basket full of dainty cucumber sandwiches, fruit, cheese, and pastries and, of course, an assortment of teas. High tea at the beach, but first a ride through San Diego. My tías shook their heads in wonder and amusement at us, and we were happy to see that they were delighted with our little surprise. Sitting in the extravagant vehicle, giggling and laughing, we wondered if the chauffeur understood Spanish and knew that we were talking about him—and that we unanimously agreed he was a gorgeous mango.

And the ghosts? Someone asked. What had they been up to lately? Any shadowy sightings? Exotic smells, odd noises, rearranged furniture? My tías laughed, shook their heads, told us that all had been quiet, no more ghosts. But my sisters didn't believe them, were certain that they were saying this because if they told us the truth—yes, the phantoms have been up to their usual *travesuras*, mischief galore—then we might not want to visit them, so afraid of the ghosts we'd be.

"No more ghosts," our aunts reassured us, glancing quickly at me, then away.

Look, look, to the east, pointed my little sister Luz who was not so little anymore—she herself a lovely damita now. And we all turned to look. We were driving on the Silver Strand, a narrow stretch of land that separated the ocean to our west and the San Diego Bay to the east. Yes, there it was, the huge moon coming up from behind the dark blue foothills of east county, the bright moon—*el farol de los enamorados*, the lovers' lantern—daring us to mistake it for the Union 76 station disk. No, we knew the real thing when we saw it. Majestic, imposing, a mother moon preparing to light our way at harvest time. We glanced at each other, silent and smiling, as if we were holding our breaths, as if we knew, even as we were living it, that this was a moment being sketched in our memories, a moment that we must try to pass on to our children and their children. Yes, a moment for us and our progeny to see beauty and understand it. For now as a young woman I saw what I could not see just a few years earlier in the thick of grief and anger: I understood it was not that my aunts didn't want to answer my questions about my mother. No, it wasn't that. It was that I wasn't yet ready to hear the answers, to understand the stories that were there in the house, in the furniture, walls, corridors—tales more palpable, perhaps more real, than the Boston ferns spilling out of planters along the hallways, stories ingrained in the dark, heavy furniture that bore witness for years and years to the human tragedy and comedy played out before it, ancient furniture silent and stoic like musty, loyal sentries. No, I was not yet ready to clearly understand the answers to my questions. Or maybe the true answer was that I would have to return again and again to El Grullo, to the country of my ancestors, and learn that there were really no answers to my questions, simply methods of hearing the despairing whispers of the phantoms, a way to quiet and comfort us penitents. I would learn that there were simply stages of understanding, and from this understanding comes the ultimate gift of forgiveness. Understanding my parents' marriage. Understanding my own life in relation to theirs. Understanding that some things will never change: a family that loves each other; brothers and sisters who will carry on as a family, no matter where we go off to. Yes, 2215 Conifer Street in Palm City would always be with us.

We crossed the San Diego–Coronado Bay Bridge, making our way into downtown San Diego, which in the lazy, soft twilight, had a sprinkling of lights on its skyscrapers, buildings of all glass or brick, stucco or stone. Look over there, I said, pointing to the old El Cortez Hotel where I attended my senior prom, the historical landmark now abandoned and waiting to be rediscovered. My San Diego, yes. And I felt the urge to become the tourist guide, to point out every single detail to my aunts. I was eager to show them my favorite spots—Cabrillo Bridge on highway 163 surrounded by Balboa Park and the largest, and surely the most beautiful, zoo in the world. I was that proud of my San Diego, this border town where my parents had the great foresight to settle and raise us. And it wasn't just Balboa Park with its coral, eucalyptus, and California pepper trees that did it to me. It was that this—Conifer Street, Palm City, San Diego, California, the United States via Avenida Netzahualcoyotl, El Grullo, Jalisco, Mexico—was who I was.

Now the chauffeur headed to La Jolla Cove, a cozy stretch of beach with a grassy area perfect for our sisters-and-aunts tea party. Slowly, luxuriously, we got out of the limousine, the chauffeur lugging our picnic supplies from the trunk to the grass: twin bedspreads with a design of bulging maroon and purple roses on their thorny stems—old, frayed bunk bedspreads on which to stretch out; low-lying aluminum beach chairs; a porcelain tea set for eight that Ana María had bought. "You'll need this in grad school," she said when she'd presented me with the wrapped box. "It'll keep you civilized amid the madness of all-night studying in the big city." Luz and Monica were setting the picnic table, and our tías, shaking their heads in wonder at all the lovely hustle and bustle about them, stood patiently waiting, as instructed, for my going-away tea party to begin. And while every one of us was organizing the beach stuff, Carolina looked at us, her arms akimbo, until finally she exaggeratedly cleared her throat to get our attention. She had set a cardboard box in front of her, the print on the box announcing there was a nineteen-inch TV inside.

Again she cleared her throat and called out, "May I have your attention, please."

We all turned toward her, noticing the box.

"Are we going to watch TV on the beach, Carolina?" Luz said, laughing.

She waited—like a patient mother hen with her unruly chicks—until we had all quieted down. "I have a little surprise for all of you," she said as she opened the flaps, reaching into the box, bringing out five pointy straw hats stacked one on top of the other with the word "Manzanillo" embroidered on the front of each. They looked browner than when we first wore them, but make no mistake, we all remembered them well, and my aunts remembered too: 1968, the summer Conchita had the inauguration party for her new restaurant. Yes, that was the summer. Hotter than usual, my mother and father and us five sisters and my two aunts squished in the station wagon, our trek from El Grullo to Manzanillo. What a trip, we said, now laughing. Where did you dig these up, someone asked. I didn't even know we still had them. Wasn't *that* a trip to end all trips! If only we'd had this lovely limousine to drive down in—with the lovely papacito chauffeur, piped in Ana María. Well, then, that would've been a trip. Can you imagine, swooshing down the Pan-American Highway in a limousine? Yes, but we'd still have to put up with Carolina's lectures on Mexican history. Her showing off, said another sister. But at least we didn't have to contend with Tony's farts—*fuchi*!

Carolina insisted we all wear our pointy Manzanillo hats, and so that our tías didn't feel left out among their fashionable nieces sporting debonair hats, she dipped into the box once again and presented them with a hat each, not pointy like ours, but still in keeping with the straw hat motif. Embroidered on the brims were the words "San Diego."

Here we were—my four sisters and I along with my mother's sisters—celebrating each other with dainty cucumber sandwiches and tea. And I sensed, as we stood in a conspiratorial circle of close-knit women, that our aunts must be looking at each of us—Carolina, Ana María, Monica, Luz, and me—and seeing a part of their sister Dolores in each of us. They must have known that we were the daughters of our mother.

The waves crashing against the rocks sounded soothing and familiar, sounded like freeway cars whooshing by.

Then it came to me like a whisper: We're in the beach village of Barra de Navidad the summer of '68. I'm thirteen and, along with my sisters, Tía Celeste and Tía Rebeca, Mamá and Papá, piling out of the station wagon for a picnic at the beach. The weather is balmy and soft, the ocean's breeze salty enough to taste. There are thunderclouds in the distance promising to charge over for the punctual late afternoon thunderstorm, but for now the sky is clear and blue and kind. It's a remote area of the beach, a deserted cove, and we are the only ones here. Our private little paradise, I think as I pull off my shorts and blouse, which have been covering my orange one-piece bathing suit. Our Eden. Soon all of us sisters have peeled our clothes off and are heading toward the water in our matching orange bathing suits, all five of us wearing pointy straw sun hats with the word "Manzanillo" sewn on, straw hats reminiscent of Indo-Chinese peasants working the rice paddies, straw hats bought at the market in Manzanillo just as we were heading out, back up to El Grullo and then to our home in San Diego. But for now we are here in Mexico, on a secluded, quiet beach in the state of Jalisco, five sisters who love each other very much, who love Mamá and Papá, and their four brothers too. Five sisters marching off to wet our knees in the warm water. And while Mamá is setting up the beach towels, the bags of food, and drinks on the sand, Papá discreetly goes behind a tree to change into his bathing trunks.

Monica, Luz, and I stand in knee-deep water, our limit since we don't know how to swim. Luz and Monica are splashing each other, and so I move away from them, out of splashing distance. Carolina and Ana María, along with Tías Celeste and Rebeca, have decided to go hunting for seashells, hopeful that they might find an ancient archeological relic, Carolina, all the while—I'm sure—inserting Mexican history tidbits into their conversation. No way was I going to join them for her pedantic prattle. So I'm standing alone, the infinite, deep blue yonder in front of me, land and civilization behind me.

Then he comes out from behind the tree and heads for the water. I stare at him, my mouth open, gaping. I can't remember ever seeing Papá in bathing trunks, ever seeing him that naked. My God, what skinny toothpick white legs he has! I look around, spot my sisters a way from me, wondering if they've noticed my father too. But no, I seem to be the only one of us who notices him, and it shocks me to see so much of Papá's person, his physiognomy, his *nakedness*, for God's sake. I then turn to look at Mamá up on the sandy beach. She is setting up the food, rummaging through the cooler, now and then looking distractedly out at the ocean, but not at anyone or anything in particular.

Now Papá gingerly makes his way to the lukewarm water, lifting each leg in an exaggerated marching step, his naked white beanpole legs immersed, now his waist. He has his arms crossed near his armpits like he's shivering or something, but that can't be because the water is tepid. He seems a little self-conscious, looking around so as to make sure no one notices him as he slowly makes his way into deeper water. Does he know how to swim? He slowly, almost reluctantly uncrosses his arms and touches the water, splashing it with his hands. Then he stops, the water near his chest, and looks about him as if he is surprised to find himself way out there in the middle of the great blue yonder. He looks off to his left where his older daughters and sisters-in-law are heading farther away, orange dots in the far distance; then he turns to his right where Monica and Luz are still engaging in an all-out water splashing war. I'm the one closest to him in distance, but in knee-deep water. And just at the moment he turns and spots me nearby, sees me watching him, our eyes meeting for an instant, a big, giant monster wave out of nowhere comes and hungrily curls around him, and he tumbles and goes under, and I alone witness this moment. My two little sisters are laughing at each other, splashing water and calling out names, "You idiot, stop it!" So I alone witness and stare, wondering with horror and fear—or hope—if the wave might sweep him away. And it is as if the wave has engulfed me too: I hold my breath. For this is the defining moment, the moment I've been waiting for all my life. I must have sensed it then at the age of thirteen, know it for certain now at the age of twenty-two. Because really it is all up to me, whether I want my father dead—violently pulled under into the deep recesses of the sea, never to return, to simply and brutally, once and for all, disappear from our lives. No more terrifying temper, no more erratic, foolish, incomprehensible behavior threatening the unity of our family. And now, perhaps, at last, an answer to my question, the question that, were I to find an answer, would lighten the load, one bag at a time, off my shoulders, off my heart, the question I have been asking myself since I realized there was man and there was woman, there was Mamá and there was Papá, and there was an immense system of complex woven threads adorning this simple biological fact. The question—did they love each other, really love each other?—looming over me all these years. So I hold my breath, the conflicting fear and hope filling my lungs.

Then he reappears, pushed up from under by some unknown force, first his tousled wet head of hair, and then he's rubbing his eyes with one hand, holding on to his drooping swim trunks with the other. He looks stunned and unbalanced as he awkwardly stumbles forward, coughing and choking on the salty ocean water. I know that feeling of having downed too much water in one gulp, the sensation that you can neither swallow nor regurgitate it, and the momentary panic this creates, feeling like you're somewhere between life and death. Still coughing, he heads toward the beach, the sand—toward Mamá and terra firma. I follow close behind.

And this is the part I'd forgotten, the part I now remember: Mamá is standing up, as if she has been waiting for him, and she is laughing and laughing, her head bent back in the grandest of laughter—joyous, unreserved, unabashed laughter, happy tears now in her lovely green eyes. Her summer dress, dotted with yellow primroses and four yellow buttons on the bodice, is flapping in the gentle wind, she looking like the lighthouse, the buoy, the lifesaver that she has always been. Her green floral dress is signaling and reassuring distressed sailors in the midst of sea storms.

Now he's standing before her, safe but dripping wet, a sheepish grin on his face, a little out of breath. He didn't know what to do first, he says to her, gasping for breath between words, smiling self-consciously—rub his eyes or grab hold of his falling trunks. Now he is doubled over, laughing with her. And there we are, Mamá, Papá, and I, standing in clean soft sand, in the middle of a lush, green banana and palm tree grove on a remote beach in the seaside village of Barra de Navidad, in the state of Jalisco, Mexico, land of my father and mother—and perhaps my land too, after all.

Then he wraps his wet, skinny arms around Mamá's petite body, the ocean breeze softly ruffling her short curly hair, one wispy errant curl dancing near her temple, and he gives her a wet kiss on the lips, right here, just like that, in front of me, something I've never seen in my life: a kiss between Mamá and Papá. And she is grinning at him, and I can tell they've forgotten for a moment that I'm here because now Dolores Ramos is reaching over and kissing him back, kissing Lorenzo Sahagún's salty, wet face, in all his skinny nakedness. Yes, just like that.

Acknowledgments

I am grateful to Rudolfo and Patricia Anaya for the use of their peaceful writers' retreat in the Jemez Mountains of New Mexico. "La Casita" is where this story first began to bloom.

I salute my editors Beth Hadas, Valerie Larkin, and the entire University of New Mexico Press staff.

Mucho cariño to Gayla Thompson-Big Eagle, Laurie Sanders-Cannon, Sylvia Mendoza, Sheila Bhalla, Delores Nims, Yolanda Guerrero, Eve Lill, Francisco X. Stork, Chuck Charter, Tim Pagaard, David Detwiler, Jackie Hider, Alicia Muñoz, Gerri Brooks, Gloria Ensey, Leonita Cole, Pei Hua Chou, Patti Kingston, Locke Epsten, Pat and Ted Wehking, Lucinda Rubio-Barrick and Larry Barrick, Marta Sánchez and Paul Espinosa, Joanne and Pat Setzer, Nancy and Brian Jennings, and Naomi and Kevin McLean—for kindness, laughter, and good counsel.

To my lovely Loire Valley Book Club cohorts: Trudy Snell, Ginger Cunningham, Pam Montanille, Linda Mimms, Amy Patashnik, Theresa Boyle, Clarice Hester, Geri Gabriel, Suzi French, Debbie Nichols, Shuri Gray, and Lynne Raudaskoski.

To Judy Epstein for teaching me how to open the door.

To my readers and fellow writers, Julie Cárdenas and Kari Wergeland, for their generous editorial eyes.

To Rava Villon, who understands what I need to do in my writing long before I do.

To my Bob Zamba, along with Kenny, Liz, Kim, Chad, Dusty, Rob, and Julie—all have been an important part of my family these past ten years. To Cathy Anthony Tkach, who has saved my life more times than she will ever know.

To my seventeen nieces and nephews, who claim to have survived one more Santana Christmas and still don't mind coming back for more.

To my brothers- and sisters-in-law: Patty, Lucy, Alma Alicia, Henry, Richard, Victor, and Héctor—their patience and sense of humor still intact.

To my beloved brothers and sisters: Victor, Oscar, Jorge, Sergio, Gloria, Delia, Irma, and Beatriz—who provide endless hero material for past, present, and future stories.

To the memory of my brother Sergio Luis—always nearby, waving as he zooms past on his motorcycle.

Tías Lupe, Baudelia, Cecilia y Teresa—*con el aprecio y cariño de siempre.*

My love to my daughter, Deborah Victoria, who graciously weighs in with a keen eye for voice and word choice; and my son, Isaac Manuel, a ready coach with a "toughen up, Mom" philosophy—both keep me honest and young.

And finally, to the memory of my mother and father, whose dream and a prayer legacy, as Jorge so aptly described it, includes nine children who love and respect each other beyond our parents' greatest hopes. Gracias, Mamá y Papá.

❀ ❀ ❀